YEAGER'S CHOICE

AN ABEL YEAGER THRILLER

SCOTT BELL

Yeager's Choice
Red Adept Publishing, LLC
104 Bugenfield Court
Garner, NC 27529
https://RedAdeptPublishing.com/

Cover Art by Streetlight Graphics[1]

This is a work of fiction. Names, characters, places, and incidents either are the product of the author's imagination or are used fictitiously, and any resemblance to locales, events, business establishments, or actual persons—living or dead—is entirely coincidental.

---

1. http://StreetlightGraphics.com

To the woman who keeps my beast from breaking out of the
cellar and damaging the crockery: my wife, Margaret.

CHAPTER ONE

Abel Yeager approached the problem as if it were a range exercise. Distance: eight meters. Elevation: two meters. Wind: negligible. Hitting the target depended upon skill, determination, and experience, offset by the fickle trajectory of a two-dollar spinner bait lure at the end of a twelve-pound test line cast by an old Zebco rod and reel.

Target: A narrow gap between the sprawling, lure-hungry branches of an ancient live oak and the calm muddy-green surface of his stock pond. Six lures dangled from the tree already, like a fisherman's Christmas ornaments, hanging by monofilament threads. The tree mocked Yeager. It waved its branches as if to say, "Bring it, puny human."

"Don't tempt me," Yeager muttered. "I have a chainsaw."

In the murky shade of this ornery spread of future firewood lurked a canny school of large-mouth bass of the species *Texius Maximus Linus-Breakerus*. These monstrous lunkers would rip the rod from a fisherman's hands, climb out of the water, and beat him with it, then go back under and flip a fin on the way down. If Yeager managed to horse one up onto the bank, the result would be a legendary fishing story and a trophy mounted over the fireplace.

The first obstacle was the damn tree. He had to cast low enough to miss the grasping branches, yet high enough not to drop short of the shaded bit of pond.

Yeager thumbed the trigger on his old Zebco and side-armed the cast.

Plonk!

The lure hit the water about two inches off his aimpoint, which was good enough for fishing and fireworks. He allowed the lure to settle for a moment then started working it back. Tug, crank, tug, crank, all the way across the pond. Nothing hit it. The bass ignored his shiny new spinner, and it popped free of the water near his feet.

Yeager eyeballed the throw and cast again, avoiding the lure-eating tree once more. Lather, rinse, repeat, curse. The art of fishing, right there in a nutshell.

Central Texas in early June and the temperature at five thirty in the afternoon was warm with a side helping of muggy. Spring storms had filled the pond to the brim, and water lapped at the top of the embankment upon which Yeager stood. The sun hung a couple of hours above the western horizon, and the big oak threw shade over Yeager's position, which slid the temperature toward approaching comfortable and turned his thoughts away from chainsaws and firewood.

The boy, David, and his dog sat cross-legged by the water's edge. David's nimble fingers worked a knot in a new leader. Born David Buchanan, the kid now went by David Yeager. The adoption paperwork had gone through and made Abel a daddy twice over in under a year, once with newborn John Riley and then with twelve-year-old David. The boy had shot up like a bottle rocket since Christmas, outgrowing two sizes of jeans in a few months. Dark-haired, studious, and as intense as a pinpoint of magnified sunlight, the boy could outsmart a Harvard professor with enough brains left over to do the *NY Times* crossword.

Yeager chuckled to himself. *He can damn sure outsmart me.* Then Victor's voice spoke in his head, and he laughed again: *That ain't no high bar. A damned fish can outsmart you, ese.*

"Even when he ain't around, he's still zinging me."

David looked up at him, eyebrows raised. Beside him, as if mirroring his question, Rascal popped his head up and perked his ears in Yeager's direction.

"Just talking to myself," Yeager said. "Bad habit I picked up from driving a truck."

The boy nodded. "Do you think it's safe to go back inside yet? I've had about all the fishing I want to do."

"Yeah, me too." Yeager glanced in the direction of their home, as if he could determine his wife's temper by reading the sky. "I don't see no mushroom clouds, so maybe we're good."

"Abel? Can I ask you something?" David had always called him Abel, although there were times the boy called him Dad without realizing. Abel's insides melted to goo when that happened, though he kept a straight face as befitting a he-man role model.

"Always. Bring it on."

"Why is Mom so... angry all the time? Or not all the time, I guess. But it's like she's..."

"Ready to explode without warning?"

"Yeah. Exactly."

Yeager reeled in a twist of weeds and busied his hands working the gunk loose from the treble-hook spinner as he thought how best to respond. He worked hard at keeping David's trust, and one of his self-imposed rules was he wouldn't lie to the boy. He might not tell the kid everything, as some details of a rough life weren't fit to be shared with a young'un, but Yeager never purposely misled him.

"You know your mom went through a lot a while back, out in Hawaii. And before that, y'all had that thing with the wannabe hit man from Mexico. The year before that, she had a spot of trouble"—now, there was an evasion—"from them people when we first met. That's a lot of... bad stuff... for anybody to handle. I know people spent their whole lives in the Marines and hadn't seen as much violence as your mom has. You with me so far?"

David nodded.

Yeager sat down beside him then tucked the hook into the rod's second eyelet and gave the crank a turn to tighten it. Rascal came over to inspect the job, and Yeager nudged the fool dog's nose away from the hook. "You ever hear the term post-traumatic stress disorder? PTSD? Yeah? Good."

Yeager smiled at the way David said yes. He figured David would look it up on the internet and be able to write a ten-page paper on the subject before Yeager had his teeth brushed for bed. "It affects different people different ways. Some get depressed. Some get a twitch, or they can't sleep at night. And some get moody. They lash out at people. That's what's happening to your mom. Her brain is trying to work through all the horrible things that happened to her, and it's jacking up her emotions. How's that for layman's terms?"

"Does it ever get better?"

"Sure, it does." Yeager squeezed the boy's shoulder then gave it a pat. "Your mom's no dummy. She knows what's going on, and she's seeing some doctors and whatnot"—Yeager held back saying the word *psychiatrist*—"and I expect time and love will help her to the right place. Although... To be honest, I've read some things saying it don't ever completely go away."

David frowned. "What about you? You've seen a ton of bad things."

"That's true. And done a few as well."

"But you don't have PTSD."

"Sure I do," Yeager said. "Sure I do. I just... have learned how to hide it a little better than most. Meeting you and your mom helped me a lot. I was pretty down on life before that happened. You could say you guys are the exact medicine I needed."

"Then why aren't we the right medicine for Mom?"

Uh-oh. Dug yourself a hole now, Yeager. "Well, like I said. Everybody's different. Not the same medication works for every brain.

Your mom's real smart, and she's sensitive, to boot. Me, well, my brain is just not as developed as a normal human, so I don't need as much to stay in balance. A fellow once told me I could compartmentalize real well. Tuck things in boxes and stash 'em away where I can't see them anymore."

David appeared unconvinced. Rascal barked and raced away. David's eyes shifted past Yeager and widened at what he saw. "Uncle Victor!"

Victor Ruiz stood atop the embankment, fending off a fifty-pound fur missile. The evening sun threw his shadow out well past his five-foot-five body. Victor wrestled the dog away from his lick fest and said, "What's this? The redneck version of *Old Man and the Sea*? Or *Moby Duck Pond*?"

Yeager dusted off his pants and dragged the shorter man into a back-slapping half-hug. "Just explaining to David here how teeny Mexicans make the best fish bait."

"Yeah, I see how well you fish, *cabrón*." Victor hitched his chin at the lures dangling from the tree. "You never could cast for shit."

Yeager turned to David. "Don't repeat any words coming out of Por Que's mouth, in either Spanish or English."

"Oh, like I haven't heard those words a million times at school." David rolled his eyes. He climbed up and man-hugged Victor in an awkward imitation of his adopted father. Yeager smiled to see it. Rascal bounced in circles around the pair, barking.

"Dang, *ese*," Por Que said. "You almost tall as me!"

"A tomato plant's almost as tall as you," Yeager chipped in.

"Huh. That's racist, dude."

"Tomatoes are a race?"

"No, but short people are, and we'll bite your ankles, you don't watch it."

"Did you get the chopper fixed?" David chirped. "Can I go for a ride?"

"Sadly, no." Victor shook his head. "The motor is fried. Gonna take a miracle to bring the Huey back to life."

"Go on to the house, boy," Yeager said. "See if it's safe for us to come back inside."

David set off for the house, with Rascal bounding circles around him.

Victor side-eyed him. "Sending the boy off to run point?"

"Charlie's been in a temper all day, which was why we went fishing to start with. You showing up..." Yeager waggled a hand. "Could go either way."

An unannounced visit from Victor could mean a lot of things... some not good. The last time he'd appeared without warning, he'd dragged Yeager off to Mexico, where they'd both damn near died. Charlie's mood was finicky enough without dumping pure nitro into her combustion chamber. Yeager found himself dragging his feet. It didn't take long for Victor to confirm his fears.

"I found Cujo," Victor said. "And you ain't gonna like it a damn bit."

Yeager breathed out hard through his nostrils and pitched his voice low. "I haven't told Charlie about this thing with Cujo, okay? About you going to check out the rumor. She was torn up about him getting killed down there. Thinks it was her fault, because she's the one teed him up to go. I didn't want to get her hopes up. She's... dealing with a lot. Surgery on her hand. The baby." Yeager shrugged. "And the thing in Hawaii really messed her up."

"Man, I saw the size of that dude. The one broke her hand? That'd mess me up too."

"Amen."

Victor frowned at the house. "And Charlie ain't gonna like this thing with Cujo even more than you ain't gonna like it. Maybe we should go get a beer somewhere."

Yeah. Like in China. Yeager took a deep breath. He stopped and put a hand on Victor's shoulder, looking him in the eye. "What we're gonna do—I want to hear the story first. Once I know how bad the situation is, then I'll figure out a way to break it to Charlie. Not a word to her about Cujo. Clear?"

"Crystal."

"Okay, then." Yeager patted Victor's shoulder twice, for emphasis. Or for courage. "Let's go face the music."

C harlie held her teething baby, John Riley Yeager, on her hip, propped up by her left hand. When she forgot and tried to use her right hand for anything, fiery bolts of pain shot up her arm. The cast helped her remember, but at times, John tried some death-defying stunt that required an instant, reflexive reaction. Now that he was walking, the toddler seemed determined to kill himself and could find trouble faster than a squirrel could climb a tree, giving Charlie ample opportunities to test her reaction speed.

Faint rattles emanated from the garage, where David had disappeared with the fishing tackle. Charlie ignored those sounds as she stood in the kitchen, watching her husband and his bestie have some serious, eye-to-eye conversation before coming into the house. She had a pretty good suspicion the talk was about her. It played in her head like *Watch out for the wife—she's riding an angry red cotton saddle these days. Oh, homie, dude, sucks to be you.*

Her hackles were already raised, and then Victor had appeared with his toothy smile. She'd no sooner told him Abel was at the pond than he darted past her, avoiding eye contact, and zoomed out the back door like his ass was on fire. Another notch twisted into the wiry tension in her neck. And now here they were, as thick as thieves, sneaking glances at the house like two schoolboys telling dirty jokes.

Charlie's estrogen radar warned her they were hatching a plan to do something she wouldn't like.

John gnawed a teething biscuit, mouth open wide. Brownish drool sagged from his bottom lip. With her hand in a cast, Charlie pinched the spit-up towel off her shoulder with her exposed fingertips and swiped at the gunk, managing to smear it across his cheek. The baby wobbled his face away, making a fussy noise.

"Shh-shh," she cooed. "Look, Daddy's coming. You want to go drool cookie goo on Daddy? Sure you do. Have a nice spit-up down his neck, too, while you're at it."

Charlie switched on a bright smile as the men came through the back door into the kitchen. Her Stepford Wife mask, brittle and false, covered her face. "Hey, guys. How was the fishing?"

"Not so good," Abel said. "On the other hand, I didn't lose no lures."

A twitch ran up her spine at her husband's redneck grammar. It was the kind of thing that never used to bother her, but now, it drove pins under her nails when the moodiness was on her. Victor could switch his Chicano gang-banger dialect on or off, depending on the company, and Abel could speak properly if forced... though he seemed to be acting an ignoramus on purpose lately. Like he was deliberately provoking her.

"That's nice." Charlie shifted John higher on her hip and turned to Victor. "So, Por Que... did you find Cujo?"

Victor blinked, and his jaw fell open.

"How did you know?" The look of shock on Abel's face was priceless. He rounded on Victor, who responded with a huge Charlie Chaplin shrug.

"Wasn't me, dude. I swear."

"Alexandra told me," she said. "Now, are you going to fill me in, or does the *little lady* have to beat it out of you with a rolling pin?"

Abel scrubbed his face with both hands, as if rubbing away the egg on his face. "Well. Looks like I stepped in it again, pardner." To Charlie, he said, "Victor here was just about to fill me in on his story. Why don't we grab a beer and all sit down to hear it at once?"

"Great idea," Charlie said in her sparkly, falsely happy voice. "Take your son and hose him down. See if he'll take some juice. I'll run to the ladies', and then we can gather 'round for story time!"

CHAPTER TWO

"Okay," Victor said when they were gathered at the kitchen table.

Charlie preferred the kitchen table to the one in the formal dining room, which they only used on Christmas and Easter. This table was built from rough-finished oak and resembled something a farm wife would load down with biscuits and bacon and grits, with a blue enamel coffee pot. A family table, where they could share stories, build memories, and break bread.

Victor and Yeager cradled longnecks, and Charlie held a glass of chardonnay. One of the perks of no longer having to nurse was the freedom to drink booze again. David had disappeared into his room, no doubt to avoid her moodiness. A knot tightened in her chest.

Victor cleared his throat and started over. "Okay, so. This government Q-tip called me when we were all still in Hawaii, cool? Tol' me this story about Cujo—only he called him Quattle-something... ahh... Quattlebaum. Milton Quattlebaum. Told me he was in the prison there in Hermosillo, right? No charges yet, but still... you know. In prison." Victor sighed at the injustice of it all. "Anyway, it took some time, you know, getting out of Hawaii after all that mess. Then Alex, she be like"—in falsetto—"Oh, we have to plan the wedding, send out the invitations, I have to tell mi mama y mi papa..." Victor threw up his hands. "It's like I was trapped! In wedding hell. With Bridezilla."

Charlie had the urge to snap at him, to say, "What do you know about being trapped? Try being a prisoner in a jungle hut, waiting for rape and torture." She pushed it down. She recognized the anger was a result of post-traumatic stress, and it hadn't taken a shrink—*excuse me, therapist*—to help her see it. Often, Charlie felt like a second person lived inside her skin—her original self and this new creature she'd become. The original Charlotte became a backseat passenger when the mutant grabbed the wheel, and it happened with an alarming frequency. She'd been an emotional wreck for six weeks. Snappish. Irritable. Moody.

Let's face it. I've been a stark, raving bitch.

And just like that, the depression sank through her. She could feel her mood plummeting, like her soul was sinking through her chair. Charlie turned her attention to John playing in his bassinet and gurgling at his toys. If a snake crawled into his pen right now, Charlie wasn't sure she had the energy to go over and pull him out of danger. The thought scared her... in a remote, academic kind of way.

"So I escape from the Demon Bride," Victor continued, "and flew commercial into Hermosillo. And here's what happened..."

He arrived in Hermosillo well after seven in the evening, having flown in on a Dare You to Crash commuter flight from Mexico City to Hermosillo International. As bad as the flight was, Victor had confessed to himself his immense relief at escaping the frozen politeness of his prospective in-laws' house. One more hairy-eyed, fake-smiled "So, Victor, what do you do for a living?" from one of Alexandra's many brothers might have resulted in a broken nose and a broken engagement.

The prison presumably holding Milton "Cujo" Quattlebaum, *Centro Federal de Readaptación Social número 11,* would almost certainly not be accepting visitors at this time of night. Truthfully, he wasn't sure when they *would* be accepting visitors—something to check out when he could use the hotel's internet connection.

"And speaking of hotels," Victor muttered through a yawn, "I need one."

After a stop at the rental counter, he drove to a US-branded hotel chain and checked into a room with a king bed. He changed into shorts and a T-shirt, found the hotel's gym, and used the elliptical. He followed that with a few sets of curls, flies, push-ups, and crunches. By the time he'd showered and changed clothes, he'd shaken off travel-induced zombie-ism.

The closest decent restaurant, according to the desk clerk, turned out to be a quarter mile away, on the other side of the four-lane divided Colosio Boulevard. Victor decided to hike it, which turned out to be good because he scarfed about three thousand calories of *diezmillo, chorizo, tocino, y cebolla blanca, bañada en salsa de tomatillo y queso gratinado*, along with two... well, two and a half... *cervezas*, with flan and coffee for dessert. He needed the walk afterward. The four-lane road was well lit by overhead sodium-vapor lights and the headlights of passing cars. Light filled the street so well, in fact, that by the time Victor made it back to the lobby of the Holiday Inn, he had no trouble spotting the tail.

Victor rolled out of the hotel parking lot at six minutes after nine in the morning for the thirty-kilometer drive to the prison. The sun flared off his rearview mirror, forcing him to squint to pick out the surveillance team in their blue late-model Charger. *There you are, pendejos.* Six cars back. Two guys in the front seat of what had to be a plain-wrapped cop car. No way to tell if it was the same pair who'd tailed him on foot last night. Those two had never gotten close enough to make out details, and these were merely two silhouettes behind a windshield.

"What are you after?" he asked the car in his mirror. A nervous prickle broke out on his neck. The carnage at the mission in San Felipe would be an obvious answer. Did the Federales know what had happened there? That would be bad. He and his *campaneros* hadn't made their identities a big secret at Rascón, so anybody in the village might have dropped a name to the authorities. But crap, the "victims" were a bunch of stinking drug bunnies. *Who gives a shit about drug bunnies?*

Or is it about Monterrey? He and Yeager—and Cujo too—had left a lot of bodies belonging to the Sinaloa cartel people behind at the hacienda in Monterrey. Had the cartel tagged him for that little romp in the desert? They had their hooks into every law enforcement agency in Mexico. It wouldn't be a stretch to imagine the cops behind him were in the drug lord's pocket.

Victor shook off the worries and concentrated on his driving, following Sonora State Highway 100 past the airport and toward the arid western plain, which dropped toward the Bay of California in ninety or so kilometers. An occasional glance in the mirror confirmed his shadow remained fixed behind him. They had closed up to a couple of car lengths and seemed content to stay there, as plain as a tick on a hound dog's ear.

A utilitarian sign sticking up from the weeds by the highway announced the cut-off to the prison before Victor expected it. He stood on the brakes at the last second and whipped the rental car to the right. Dust and gravel sprayed up from the shoulder of the road as he waggled the Ford back onto the asphalt.

He laughed when he noticed his tail had overshot the turn. Their blue Charger nosed down in a hard stop, just beyond the cutoff. "Heh. See how you like them apples."

Victor followed the two-lane road for a bit then parked the rental in the large lot outside the prison gates. He followed a crowd of about forty people as they bunched up in front of the chain-link entrance and shuffled forward with the herd. The intake process was simple enough. An indifferent secretary snapped his picture, scribbled his information on a slip of paper, and handed him a number tag. The metal detector was broken, so a bored guard waved a handheld wand in his general direction and followed it up with an approximation of a pat-down. Victor reckoned he could've carried in anything from a penknife to a rocket launcher. The last guard in line checked his number chit, added it to a clipboard he carried, then gestured to a door at the back.

Victor stepped out into a courtyard. The inside of CEFERESO *número* 11 resembled a ghetto playground in an American inner city more than a prison. Visitors and inmates congregated around picnic tables, unwrapping homemade food and baskets of treats. A group of guys kicked around a yellowed football on an open field to his left. In isolated pairs, couples embraced, smooched, and groped. Some held hands and hurried to a row of doors set into a low building on the right. Conjugal quarters, Victor presumed. No one wore prison clothes, so it was impossible to tell who were inmates and who were visitors. The acrid smell of both tobacco and pot smoke laced the air.

A group of lean young wolves hung around the entrance, waiting for visitors to appear.

"Who do you want?" one of them asked. Victor told him, and the prisoner held out a hand. "Five dollars."

"One."

"Four."

"Here." Victor pulled three ones from his wallet. "Let's cut to the chase."

The skinny man grinned and loped away. Victor found an unoccupied table and sat down to wait.

It didn't take long. Cujo appeared much the same as he always had: a scraggly Tommy Chong beard and wild hair, average build, though thinner now, with deeper hollows around his eyes. A vivid red scar snaked across his forehead like a jagged lightning bolt.

"Hey, lookit you," Victor crowed. "Harry-fucking-Potter, dude!"

They slapped backs, and Victor felt the sharp points of the smaller man's spine through his thin T-shirt. They took seats at the picnic table. "You getting enough to eat, homeboy?"

"Yeah, but I was in the hospital for a while, man." Cujo winced. "And the food here sucks. Man, it's good to see you."

"Yeager said he went to look at you when you crashed, but you was dead. Then Verdugo's boys got the drop on him, and he had to leave you. You gotta know, Yeager would've never left you out there if he had a way not to."

"I should've been dead." Cujo tapped his forehead with a knuckle. "Steel plate. The Army doctors stuck it in my head in Germany, remember? Saved my life."

"So how're they treating you, Iron Man? You need anything? Besides a nail file in a cake?"

Cujo grinned his goofy, shy grin then ducked his head. "Really pretty good. Nobody's bothered me at all. Nice cell, by myself. Has a minifridge and clean sheets and whatnot." Cujo shrugged. "If it wasn't for the bars..."

Victor's eyes narrowed. "A minifridge? No shit. And all the gangs and druggies have left you alone?"

"Not a scratch on me since I got here."

"Amazing."

"I know, right?" Cujo said, oblivious to Victor's flat tone. "I think this place is run more by the prisoners than the guards, though. I've seen some shit, man..." Cujo snickered. "There's this one guy that runs the block. He's got a TV, a little kitchen, man, and even some cold beer. Dude, it's fricking incredible. And the guards are, like, 'Yeah, whatever.'"

The conversation shifted to Cujo telling him about how he'd made it from a mountain to prison, but Victor listened with half an ear. A nagging grain of sand remained stuck in Victor's mental gears, refusing to smooth out. *Okay, call it a pebble. Why in the hell would a gringo American get the white-gloves treatment in a Mexican prison? And especially somebody who bombed the shit out of the cartel people? They had to be pissed as hell, right? Damn.*

Cujo should have been beaten, shanked, shot trying to escape, and thrown down a well by now.

"Hokay," Victor said at last. "We need to get you fixed up with some primo legal counsel, correcto?"

"Yeah, man. I haven't even been charged yet. I don't know what the fuck's happening out there. I can't get anybody to tell me what's going on." Cujo's face worked, and he couldn't speak. The pilot swallowed and looked away. "Man, you don't know how good it is to see a friendly face."

"Don't worry, bro. I got you now." Victor patted Cujo's forearm and stood. "You hang tight, okay? Let Por Que handle things on the outside. You just stay frosty in here and don't bend over in the shower."

Cujo tried on a fake-surprise expression. "Shower? What shower?"

Victor handed in his chit and had his ID checked against the information recorded by the bored secretary when he entered. The exiting process, though antiquated and simple, insured the average prisoner didn't wander out with the visitors, though Victor suspected the right application of financial leverage could make it happen. *A thought for later, maybe.*

He waited while another secretary consulted a written ledger, running her finger down a list of names with myopic intensity. She took so long, Victor started to wonder if they'd screwed up and "lost" his records. His face tickled when a bead of sweat curled along his brow and wandered down his cheekbone. He gritted his teeth, resisting the temptation to mop his forehead.

The tension didn't leave his belly until the final guard waved him toward the exit. All along, he'd half suspected a team of officers would draw down on him, wrestle him to the ground, and pitch him back into the general population, never to be seen again. Instead, the level of indifference with which he was treated was almost insulting.

"I should file a complaint," he said under his breath.

Victor's tail picked up right where they'd left off, falling a half dozen car lengths behind and sticking there all the way back to the Holiday Inn. Victor kept an uneasy eye on the rearview mirror, wondering when exactly this particular shoe would drop. The *federales* didn't follow a man this blatantly unless they wanted to make a statement. But what were they trying to say? *We know who you are, and we're coming for you?* Or were they trying to goad him into doing something stupid out of nervousness?

Or what if they aren't police? What if they're cartel? Victor snorted. *Shit. Not likely.* Drug smugglers didn't follow people around—they just walked up and shot them to pieces or grabbed them off the street and chopped their heads off. The chapter on subtlety was not a particularly large part of the drug-bunny playbook.

Victor lost sight of the trail car as he peeled off into the Holiday Inn parking lot, locked up, and crossed the hot pavement to the main entry. The air conditioning huffed from the automatic doors, promising a chilly relief from the midday sun burning in a cloudless sky. Victor's running shoes squeaked on the tile, and the desk clerk tossed out a cheery "Hola, señor!"

Victor waved, turned down the corridor to the elevators, and missed a step. Two tough-looking hombres in black suits, black ties, and white shirts waited by the elevator.

Victor hesitated then shrugged mentally. *Might as well get this over with.* He crossed to the panel and punched the Up button under the watchful eye of the two stooges in spit-shined shoes.

"You know what you look like?" he asked the twin pairs of mirrored sunglasses. Like with most people, they were taller than he was. Victor had to look up to see their faces. "You the Chicano Division of the Men in Black? Agents Pendejo and Puta?"

No response.

"You wanna see if I'm an alien?"

Not even a glimmer of acknowledgment. He might as well have been talking to cardboard cutouts.

"Do Texicans count as aliens here? 'Cause, you know..." Victor made a crazy-as-fuck face and waggled his fingers near his ears. "We be, like, from Planet Nutjob, you know?"

The elevator dinged, and still no response.

"Tough crowd." Victor shrugged and stepped into the empty car. He was not surprised when the Men in Black followed him aboard. As they rode in silence, Victor was hyperaware of his two towering shadows behind him. Could he take them both before one pulled a weapon and shot him?

He sighed. *Only in the movies.*

On the third floor, he led Agents Pendejo and Puta to his room, where he was surprised to see them take up station on either side of his door, like sentries.

"You sure you don't want to come in?" Victor dug out his key-card and slipped it into the lock. "I got bottled water. Some snacks. No?"

The cloud of tobacco smoke punched Victor in the face when he opened the door to his nonsmoking room. A man wearing a black suit of his own lounged in the easy chair by the window. He dumped his cigarette into a water glass. Judging by the number of butts and the fog in the room, he had been there for at least half an hour. Thin as a greyhound, with an Errol Flynn mustache and thick black hair, the man projected the air of one comfortable with the exercise of ultimate power. The hollow shadows under his eyes added to his Godfather impression.

"Señor Ruiz?" the man asked in English. "I am Captain Oswaldo Arriga Mendoza, of the 3rd Brigade, 6th Battalion, Cuerpo de Fuerzas Especiales. You are familiar with the CFE?"

Victor kept his face neutral. "And what does a Mexican Special Forces captain want with me?"

"I have a proposition." Mendoza smiled and tapped another cigarette from his pack of Marlboro Reds. "I understand the idiom in English is 'I have a deal you cannot refuse.'"

CHAPTER THREE

"Victor Eduardo Lorca Ruiz," Mendoza announced. He gestured for Victor to take a seat in the room's other chair. "I see your parents chose to follow the Anglo custom of father's name last. US citizen. Entered the country through Mexico City in May, traveling from Hawaii, according to passport control. A unique experience for you, going through passport control, yes?"

Victor kept his face politely blank and said nothing.

Mendoza sucked on his cigarette and spoke through the exhale. "Decorated US Army helicopter pilot—"

"Marine. US Marine."

"Of course. My apologies. And now soldier of fortune? Smuggler? Mercenary? Which job description would you say fits you best?"

Victor shrugged. "Casual man-about-town. Dashing caballero. More of a tourist than anything else."

"With more tourists like you, Mexico will need bigger graveyards." Mendoza's cigarette butt died with a brief hiss when he dropped it into the water glass. The special forces captain appeared calm and in charge, though wrapped so tightly, if he farted, it would squeal. "So tell me—is your friend Yeager with you this time?"

"Who?" *Keep still. No twitches. Look this asshole right in the brown pucker and say nothing.*

"The CFE is deeply involved in the fight against the cartels," Mendoza continued. "We become very interested when battles between the various factions result in many casualties. And when a vicious killing machine like Grupo Verdugo is effectively destroyed, we become very interested in who destroyed it. Many witnesses are interviewed. Survivors questioned. The perpetrators of these massacres never get away without a trace. And surprise! We find one of these mercenaries in a crashed plane near the scene of the battle, near a tiny little village called Rascón. So we suggest to some of our friends inside the prison that they should watch over this gringo. See he comes to no harm. Enjoys some extra amenities. Then we sit back and watch, and—surprise, again—that survivor contacts Victor Ruiz, who matches the description of a man the people of Rascón called 'a tiny Hercules.'" Mendoza toyed with his pack of Marlboros, popping some loose and tamping them back down. "Another name uncovered in that investigation was that of a man named Yeager, who drove a truckload of supplies to the mission in Rascón before the fighting broke out. We found this very, very interesting because... Do you want to know why?"

Victor shrugged again and tried to look bored—instead of curling up into a ball and crying for his mama. On Victor's list of Things Not to Do, coming to the attention of the Mexican authorities rated close to shaving his ass with a cheese grater.

"It was interesting," Mendoza said, "because we recovered a burned truck from the scene of another cartel massacre. This one near Monterrey. This truck was owned by a man named Yeager, who reported his vehicle stolen in the United States. Survivors of that attack reported two men, one a medium-tall gringo and the other a short, pumped-up Latino, fighting the cartel people."

"Mm." *Shit-shit-shit.* Coming back to Mexico had been a mistake, Alexandra or no Alexandra. After getting out of the hospital, he had returned to the US to tidy up some business, and that was where he should have stayed. But no. He had come back to chase after Alexandra like a teenager with a crush on the high school beauty queen. He'd underestimated the amount of official interest the Mexican government would take in a bunch of dead drug bunnies, and now it looked like he was about to get locked up for following his heart instead of his head.

"An aircraft was involved there, as well," Mendoza continued. "It flew in and carried off these two men after they inflicted numerous casualties on members of the Sinaloa cartel."

"Coupla badass dudes, I'd say." Victor shook his head. "Wouldn't want to fuck with those hombres. Especially the tiny Hercules."

"Allow me to describe some of the evidence our forensic people have collected from both sites. Fingerprints. DNA. Eyewitness statements. CCTV video recordings..." Mendoza raised a finger at each point, starting with his thumb. He held the pinkie down for a long beat, then added, "And many of our close friends in law enforcement agencies of the United States have been very happy to provide numerous documents pertaining to the aircraft operated by Señor Quattlebaum and Victor Eduardo Lorca Ruiz." The captain closed his hand into a fist. He smiled. "I have you by the balls, Ruiz."

"Give 'em a scratch, would you? They starting to itch."

"Okay, time out." Yeager dribbled the last dregs of beer onto his tongue and set the bottle down. He fought the urge to go to the fridge for another. After coming back from Hawaii, he had been hitting the booze pretty hard—his own reaction to the stress of combat and Charlie's continuing misery. He had failed to protect her, and as a result, she had been taken captive, psychologically tortured, physically assaulted, and escaped only through the sacrifice of some brave men. The guilt gnawed at him, and he sought the pain-killing effect of alcohol to dull its sharp teeth. Instead of heading for the fridge, he focused on his friend. "What's Mendoza's game?"

"I'm coming to that." Victor drained his own beer, got up, and retrieved two more from the refrigerator without asking. Yeager examined the beads of condensation forming on the brown glass and thought about putting it back into the fridge. He could sense Charlie's disapproval radiating from her like an overheated engine block. Yeager deliberately avoided looking at his wife when he popped the top. Charlie sniffed but held her tongue.

His drinking had become another sore subject on the class schedule at the Yeager School of Many Failures.

At least David has the sense to stay in his room. I should probably join him.

"What's your read on this guy? Mendoza?" Yeager asked.

"A snake," Victor said without hesitation. "But an uptight, shrink-wrapped snake with a capital *S*, hermano. God has personally whispered in this dude's ear and shown him his way is the Way."

Yeager heard the capitals in Victor's words. "Not to be trusted then."

"Roger that."

"Okay." Yeager unscrewed the cap on his beer and swigged a solid hit. "What happened then?"

"**A**m I under arrest or what?" Victor asked the Special Forces captain. "If so, let's get the foreplay over with, huh?"

Mendoza left off fooling with his cigarette pack and pulled out a smartphone the size of a dinner tray. He keyed the screen and turned it so Victor could see a grainy picture. The photo had been snapped with a long lens and a shaky hand in an outdoor setting, like a patio. The features could have been any Latin male between the ages of forty and sixty, with medium-length hair and a full mustache, wearing a white short-sleeve shirt and no tie.

Victor leaned back after peering at the screen. "Friend of yours?"

"Herman Gustaffson." Mendoza tucked his phone away. "El Es-corpión."

"The Scorpion, huh? Ooh. Spooky. I think I just wet myself a lit-tle."

"Gustaffson is a freelance power broker. He has no allegiance to any cartel and has worked for all of them. Destroyed some and elevated others. Killed dictators and reformers—or had them killed, to be more precise."

Victor got up and fiddled with the thermostat on the hotel room wall. The window unit fan kicked on high, stirring the smoke of Mendoza's cigarette habit. The hazy cloud was beginning to make his eyes burn and the back of his throat itch. He resumed his seat and raised his eyebrows at Mendoza in a "who gives a damn" look.

Mendoza smirked. "Gustaffson is a plague on this planet. He is a spider in his web, accountable to none, fearful of none, and utterly ruthless. He lives in a compound in the mountains of Guatemala, protected by his own army, as well as many generals of the Guatemalan army, bought and paid for with blood money."

"So you can't get to him."

"I can't get to him." Mendoza held up a finger. "Officially."

Ah-fucking-hah. Victor leaned over, elbows on knees, and rubbed his eyes. "Look, bro, I'm a chopper driver. I fly de planes. You want somebody to go kill him for you, you should dial 1-800-SNIPER-4-HIRE. That's not me. So lay out what you want, so I can get some lunch, maybe take a siesta."

"We want Gustaffson dead." Mendoza sighed smoke through his nostrils. "And before you ask—no, I can't go through official channels. My leadership is rotten with informants, all on Gustaffson's payroll or the payroll of someone El Escorpión controls. The instant I go to my superiors with an op plan, he'll know. He'll vanish. Like smoke." Mendoza waved the hand holding his burning cigarette and added with a grim smile, "Or, more likely, I and my family will die in horrific ways."

"If cigarettes don't kill you first, jefe." Victor glanced at the plastic bucket on the bureau, half full of semi-melted ice. *What if I pour it over this guy the next time he lights up?*

The captain dumped his cigarette and consulted his watch. "A bullet will catch me long before cancer. The life expectancy of someone in my profession, who fights the cartels and monsters like Gustaffson, refusing to be on their payroll... that time is measured in months, not years."

"Are you saying you're the last honest man in Mexico? Gonna bring down the cartels by yourself?"

"Not at all. Money has corrupted many, and fear has compromised many more. And the appetite for drugs has created a hydra that will never die. Gustaffson is but one head of the beast. But a very, very unique head. Very specialized. In a position to change the balance of power among nations. Dead or imprisoned, he will be hard to replace." Mendoza shrugged. "I'm not naïve. Someone will fill the void. But it will take time, and perhaps the next Gustaffson will not be as effective."

"And if I somehow pull this off? Kill Mr. MacGuffin? Then what?"

"You and Señor Quattlebaum are free to go back to the United States. And stay there." The thin man paused for a moment, pinning Victor with his liquid, dark eyes. His brooding look turned hard. "If I were to find you back in Mexico..."

"You look like a Mexican vampire when you do that, you know?"

Mendoza said nothing, and Victor dropped his eyes to study the carpet. The walls of the budget motel room seemed tighter, closer, and heavy with the reek of burned tobacco—and the smell of a rotten deal.

Alexandra.

They hadn't talked about it, but Victor suspected she wanted to continue her work here, in her home country—not traipse off with him to exile in Texas. *How am I supposed to break this news to her? And how strong is Mendoza's case, really?*

The Mexican army carried the brunt of the fight against the drug lords, but the battle was one-sided, with the cartels having more money, better guns, and stronger motivation. A day's profit for the drug bunnies could buy a few generals, a half-dozen colonels, and enough majors to stuff a Winnebago. The military and government could be easily compromised at any level, meaning Mendoza's claim of being unable to mount an effective clandestine mission sounded like it held a grain of truth. Why would a man like Mendoza turn to an off-book solution to a vexing problem like Gustaffson? What was in it for him? Would Cujo's life be forfeit if he said no? Or would both their lives be measured in days if he said yes?

I need time to think. Victor squinted up at Mendoza. "You expect me to do this all on my own, huh?"

"No, of course not. We will provide logistic help, weapons, supplies."

"And troops?"

Mendoza's lips thinned in a wolfish smile. "You and Señor Yeager are quite capable of handling that end of the... arrangement. Or your friend is as good as dead."

A chill washed over him, as though Mendoza had beaten him to the punch and poured the bucket of half-melted ice over *his* head. "Wait, what?"

"You have seventy-two hours to find your friend, Abel Yeager, and bring him back here. The man with whom you destroyed the Sinaloa ranch in Monterrey and ripped Grupo Verdugo to shreds in the Sierra Madres is quite the effective soldier. Both of you together should be sufficient at... solving the Gustaffson situation."

"Then I went back to the prison and gave Cujo the news," Victor said. "He took it well. Said to forget about him and let it go, that we didn't owe him nothing. I told him to hang tight, that I'd come see you and work out a plan."

The momentary silence in the kitchen was interrupted by the refrigerator's ice maker chunking over. The rattle seemed very loud in the sudden stillness. Yeager studied the remaining inch of beer in the bottle cupped in his hands. Victor leaned back in his chair, one leg thrown out as though he planned to bolt for the door any second. *And Charlie...*

Yeager snuck a glance up from under his brows. His wife's pale, freckled complexion had drained to resemble a blood-dotted sheet of white. She held herself rigid in the chair, her fingers turning her wine glass in little half-circles, as if she were tuning a radio. The pause after Victor finished his story felt to Yeager like the moment between a soldier's foot depressing the trigger on a landmine and the instant of the explosion. He wanted to run for cover, but he knew there was no point.

"Are you saying," Charlie started in a whisper, "that you and Abel have to kill a man in Guatemala before this Mendoza character will release Cujo from jail? And this man you have to kill is some kind of government-owning villain who lives in a castle on a mountain?" Her voice had started to rise, not as much in volume as in ferocity. "And this is what the Mexican government wants? Have they condoned this... this... *suicide mission*? Are you fucking kidding me?"

Por Que winced. "Yeah, not so much... *condone*, I would say."

"You have to mount some military operation," Charlie continued as if she hadn't heard Victor's response. "Some *clandestine* military operation, in a foreign country? Without backup, without sanction, without... without anything? And that's the price we have to pay for Cujo's release? I have to risk losing my husband for this? I have to lose the father of my child for this… for this pig Mendoza! So he can play Godfather!"

"Charlie—" Yeager reached for his wife's hand.

She recoiled and bolted upright. "No! Don't you 'Charlie' me!"

Bright-red spots blotched Charlie's neck and cheeks. With a lefty sidearm fastball, she threw her wineglass at the sink. It exploded and rained glass shards over the countertop and tile floor. "Don't you dare think for one instant that you're going to Guatemala and getting killed over some macho, idiotic, never-leave-a-man-behind Marine Corps *horseshit!*"

Charlie stormed from the room with her hands over her face.

Yeager blew out his cheeks. "Yeah. That actually went better than I expected."

CHAPTER FOUR

The meeting had been arranged via a delicate balance of diplomacy, paranoia, and prickly obsession regarding relative status of the two principals. One simply did not call up Herman Gustaffson and arrange a tête-à-tête at a Marriott. Likewise, Youssef al-Masrahi did not venture from the warrens of his modest Rawalpindi neighborhood, cross the ocean, and take an in-person meeting without investing in security protocols worthy of a summit between the presidents of the United States and Russia.

The two principals met in a conference room reserved under the guise of a business retreat hosted by one of Gustaffson's shell companies. The hotel was in Guatemala City, requiring al-Masrahi to travel into Gustaffson's backyard, as befitted his position as a potential client seeking services. Gustaffson arrived first, as befitting the host of the meeting.

The conference room had been swept by technicians of both sides and was located in an interior space, well away from laser-based listening devices. Coffee, water, and other refreshments waited on a sideboard. A long oval table took up the center of the room, surrounded by plush leather chairs. Gustaffson chose a seat at the middle of a long side, rather than take one at either end, as if meeting with an equal. He saw no reason to wrong-foot the first meeting with a potential client and felt it better to appear neutral rather than try to establish dominance. Gustaffson gestured to his money man, Milosh Jovanovic, to take a seat next to him.

There would be no guards or other observers present.

While Gustaffson waited for his guest, he mused at how well the man had managed to conceal his true level of importance. Western intelligence agencies thought al-Masrahi to be a peripheral player in the scrum of loosely affiliated terrorist cells known generally as Al Qaeda. The boot heel of Western armies had smashed Al Qaeda, yet, like a nest of cockroaches, it had splintered and decentralized. The organization had effectively franchised to affiliates in Africa, notably Syria and Somalia, and the Arab peninsula, with a core group of leaders remaining active in Pakistan. Led by Ayman al-Zawahiri, the organization remained a significant threat to the West, even with the Islamic State of Iraq and the Levant, aka ISIL or ISIS, taking center stage. As such things were measured in modern armies, al-Masrahi would be considered at least a general on al-Zawahiri's staff, an S-4, charged with logistics and supply. If freedom fighters in Syria needed guns, al-Masrahi procured them and facilitated shipping. If a martyr was needed in Paris to blow up a café, al-Masrahi arranged transportation to get him from the slums of Tikrit to the Champs Élysées.

At the stroke of three o'clock, exactly on time, the door opened, and al-Masrahi was ushered in, followed by a younger man. Both wore Western suits with simple black-and-white checked keffiyehs tied around their heads, and both sported matching bramble-patch beards, one white and billowy, the other black and coarse. Gustaffson had been told to expect the younger man, and his contacts had vouched for the security aspects related to the extra person, just as the other side had vetted Jovanovic.

"Welcome, my friends!" Gustaffson and Jovanovic rose to greet their guests. Gustaffson spoke in English, the only language they had in common. "Please, come in. And who is this fine young man?"

Al-Masrahi introduced the youth as Qusay, with no information volunteered beyond that. Given that he tended to hover near the old man, who tottered a bit and seemed thin enough to blow away in a strong wind, Gustaffson suspected Qusay was there as a medical attendant as much as an attaché.

An hour of small talk followed—everything from the weather to vicissitudes of travel in this modern age. Gustaffson forbore mentioning that al-Masrahi and his ilk were largely responsible for much of the discomfort of air travel, their historical pastime being hijacking and blowing up commercial aircraft. He was the host; it was his job to be gracious, so he held his tongue.

At a lull in the conversation, tea and coffee having been served and consumed, Gustaffson sensed that al-Masrahi was ready to talk business.

"You have traveled a long way," Gustaffson said, "under difficult circumstances. Though I am very glad for your company and welcome your visit, may I ask, what brings you to undertake such hardship?"

"We have some... washing machines... we need delivered to their final destination in the United States. We understand you specialize in negotiating customs for such merchandise."

"Surely we do," Gustaffson said. "How many machines?"

"Twelve," the Arab replied.

Of course, Gustaffson was under no illusion that al-Masrahi engaged in the commercial trade of appliances. He was here because one of Gustaffson's organizations specialized in the traffic of human cargo from debarkation points in Latin America to their final destinations in the United States, and in all ways bypassing the now-toothless interdiction efforts undertaken by the US military, drug enforcement, and border patrol agents. The old buzzard wanted to move twelve of his jihadi martyrs across the borders of the Great Satan without the risk of passport controls. The use of student visas, work visas, and other legal means to embed agents into the US required preparation, groundwork, and, most importantly, time to accomplish. Since al-Masrahi needed a more expeditious route, it meant these twelve were slated for a time-critical mission and needed to get across the border quickly and without papers. Al-Masrahi was in a hurry, and that made him a fat calf ready for slaughter.

Gustaffson would have helped al-Masrahi for free if it meant stabbing the United States in its soft underbelly, but decades of negotiations had stifled his impulse for generosity. One did not become a billionaire by giving away freebies. Whether the "washing machines" intended to shoot up a mall in Minnesota or reduce Los Angeles to glowing embers didn't matter to him. Any kind of pain and suffering imposed upon the United States met with Gustaffson's approval.

He almost licked his chops. *Getting paid to kick Uncle Sam in the balls. Nothing could be finer.*

"I will handle your merchandise personally," he assured al-Masrahi. "Your washing machines will be treated as treasure, with nothing left to chance."

"Killing is easy," Macerio Borges said to his apprentice, Dominic Martinez. "Any thug can kill. A grandmama can kill. A child, even." The man in the kitchen chair whimpered, and Macerio tut-tutted him back to silence. "The soldier kills in war, the street criminal kills for drugs. A wife kills a husband because he beats her one too many times, eh?"

Martinez offered a half-smile, obviously not sure enough of himself to be at ease. The younger man stood attentively, like a student during a lecture by his professor. He betrayed his nerves by his excessive swallowing and restless eyes, which refused to settle for more than an instant on the man in the chair.

"You are too young to remember the civil war, but no doubt you know of the Kaibiles?" Borges asked. "The Special Forces soldiers? Butchers. They killed hundreds, maybe thousands of civilians.

No finesse, just bang-bang-bang"—Borges mimed firing a machine gun—"and shoot everything that moves, down to the chickens."

A digital clock on the microwave oven read 3:32 a.m. The small night-light glowed from underneath the microwave, its light pooling on the kitchen counter. That, plus the kitchen's window panels, painted luminous silver by the outdoor security light, provided enough light for their dark-adapted vision. Fat tears glistened on the cheeks of the man in the chair. He sat in his underwear, his round white belly pressed against the table. On the placemat in front of him, as though being offered for a late-night snack, rested a sheet of paper, a pen, a bottle of vodka, and a white prescription bottle.

"But," Borges said, raising a nitrile-gloved finger. "To assassinate the carefully chosen target. To remove from the body human a single soul, using such precision as a surgeon when excising a lump of cancerous tissue, or like a gardener who prunes the bad branches so the tree may grow stronger... Well, that is as much art as it is science." To the man in the chair, he said, "Now, Mr. Arbogast, please finish the note as we instructed. And have another drink. It will help."

"Waa... why... are you doing this?" Arbogast's voice squeaked like a rusty hinge. He was an American who spoke only English, whereas Borges had been speaking in Spanish to his apprentice. He had been getting appreciably agitated as Borges lectured his student on the art of death. The man's chins wobbled as he spoke. "What have I done?"

Borges schooled his face and answered the way a professor would if a student asked a particularly obtuse question. In English, he said, "You know why."

"Please." Arbogast fixed his eyes on Borges. "Please. I'll keep quiet. I'll... I'll tell them I can't testify..." He twisted in the chair and reached for Borges as if to implore him with a touch of his pudgy hands. "I'll—"

"Don't beg," Borges snapped then stepped back with a grimace of distaste. "It is unmanly and dishonorable. Now, please hurry along.

Your wife and children are sleeping upstairs, and we would hate to wake them. *You* would hate to wake them. Do not make me ask this again."

Arbogast sagged like a sack of wet sand. He reached for the pen with a shaky hand, passing right over the medicine bottle. Wetness glistened on his chubby cheeks, and he passed gas with a sound like a balloon deflating. "This isn't right," he whined.

"Where was I?" Borges asked Dominic in Spanish.

"As much art as science." Ever vigilant, Dominic held the brilliantly sharp knife that was Plan B, should Arbogast be capable of more resistance than Borges suspected.

"Ah, yes. The science of assassination is like a doctor learning how to stitch a wound. It is necessary to learn, but it does not make one a good surgeon. An average assassin can learn to shoot, even shoot very well. A good marksman can hit his target at a thousand meters or more. But that is not art. That is mechanics. Wind velocity, ballistics. To facilitate a death so that a competent coroner will rule it a suicide is where the craft becomes challenging. And"—he waved a hand to indicate the scene in front of them—"to engineer it so the target actually does the deed himself: writes the note, uses a prescription filled in his name. He swallows the pills with his own hand. All the forensics will tell one story and leave no hint of foul play. And there is honor in it. We have given this man a choice, yes? Kill himself or see his wife and daughters violated and slaughtered. Now, this man may decide to attack us..." Borges shrugged. "In which case I expect you to handle it with your trusty blade. We will stage the crime as a burglary, which is not optimal, but salvageable. Watch closely! It will be the final moment, when he picks up the pill bottle. That will be the tipping point. You will see it in his eyes."

Dominic's head bobbed in nervous acknowledgment. He swallowed, flexing his grip on the knife. The boy showed promise. Educated. Intelligent. Nothing like the last two thugs El Patron had sad-dled him with. Dominic had handled the removal of Arbogast from his bedroom with a delicate touch then brought the fat man to the kitchen without violence, thus preserving the scene and leaving no traces. Dominic had already proved he could kill, a test administered before being selected as Borges's protégé. An entrance exam, so to speak. But as Borges had just explained, any halfwit could kill. The question was, could he kill like Borges? Could he kill with style?

"Come, Mr. Arbogast. It is time." Borges spoke with a firm kindness. The voice of a teacher telling his class the test was over and they must put down their pencils. "Remember what will happen if you fail to comply. You have my word: your wife and daughters will be safe if you act with honor. Have courage now. You will go to sleep and pass peacefully, or you will die horribly, in pain, and so will your family."

In the end, Arbogast swallowed the pills. Much to Borges's satisfaction, the fat man chose honor over self-preservation. He and Dominic departed the home, locking the door behind them.

The evening had not gone well.

When dinnertime rolled around, Yeager called out to Charlie through their closed bedroom door to say that he and Victor were taking the boys out for food and ask if she wanted anything. No answer.

When he came back and mentioned he had a to-go order if she wanted it, the silent treatment continued. At one point, he thought he heard crying on the other side of the door. His hand hovered over the knob for a long, indecisive moment before he chickened out and walked away.

Charlie had appeared at John's bedtime and taken the boy to his room. David had locked himself away with his computer soon after, no doubt calculating ways to alter the space-time continuum, plan a mission to Venus, or whatever that boy did for fun. Yeager knew better than to ask. No need to appear more stupid than he felt.

Yeager had gotten Victor settled in the guest room. By mutual consent, they had tabled the discussion of Cujo's situation and instead spoken of other things. Or tried to. The elephant in the room kept stomping around, making both of them uncomfortable. Charlie put the baby to bed and left them to it without a word. She practically crackled with radioactivity during her brief appearances, forcing too-brittle smiles and wordless shrugs when he tried to engage her in conversation. Yeager half-expected to find the bedroom door locked. It was a relief when the door opened at his touch.

Charlie was in the shower when Yeager brushed his teeth, stripped to his boxers, and climbed into bed. Early in the evening, he had stopped his beer intake at three and switched to black coffee. As a consequence, he was wired so tightly, he practically vibrated. Sleep would be a long time coming.

He sat up in bed, double pillows behind his back, and tried focusing on the pages of a book. The words failed to take root the instant after he read them. Something about a Texas Ranger getting caught in bed with a dead woman, a candidate for US Senate. *Bleh.*

The sound of Charlie puttering in the bathroom kept intruding on the story. The baby monitor burbled a moment with normal night sounds from John's room. The sound of his son's breathing calmed Yeager's spirit.

When his wife switched off the bathroom light and stepped into the bedroom, Yeager nearly dropped his book. Charlie wore a T-shirt and obviously nothing else—obvious because the T-shirt was oh-wow-sizes too short. Yeager's nostrils flared as Charlie crossed to the bedroom door and twisted the lock with a click. She glided across the room, lifting the hem of the shirt over her hips and holding it there. She paused at the foot of the bed. Yeager's heart lurched at the smoldering look in her eyes—it was something he hadn't seen in quite a while.

"Why don't you put the book down?" she murmured.

The paperback hit the floor with a thump.

Charlie prowled up the bed like a tiger scenting prey. She mounted Yeager's midsection and leaned into him, and when he reached for her, Charlie pinned his wrists to the headboard. Her warm lips pressed against his, soft and wet. She kissed him as if she wanted to eat him, sucking his tongue and nipping at his lips. Her breath escaped into his lungs, and she drank his breath in return. Charlie roamed his body with her mouth, kissing his neck, collarbone, and ear. Her tongue probed every sensitive spot he owned, and by the time her lips encircled one of his nipples and worked it wetly with her tongue, Yeager's blood drummed. His breathing came hard and fast.

She smelled of apple blossoms.

Red hair trailed over his belly as Charlie worked her way down. Nimble fingers hooked his shorts and peeled them off. Her hot breath teased his erection. Yeager groaned when warm wetness engulfed him. Charlie knew every trick to Yeager's body, and she drove him mercilessly, working him with her mouth wantonly, hungrily. Yeager's vision grayed out. His thighs tightened, and his toes curled.

Charlie paused then stopped. She pulled up and straddled him. Holding his eyes with hers in a look of such love, it nearly broke his heart, Charlie slid down over him, impaling herself inch by torturous inch. Only then did she peel the T-shirt over her head. Even after breastfeeding her second child, Charlie's breasts were a marvel to Yeager. Firm and compact, tipped with pink nipples and dotted with freckles. She brought his hands up to cover them and began undulating her hips in a slow and sultry dance. Her eyes squeezed shut, and she siphoned a breath between clenched teeth. Charlie shuddered and tensed, tensed and shuddered.

Yeager's hands dropped to her hips, and Charlie's motion became frenetic. Urgent. Compelling. Her eyes begged him. Her breath rasped out, harsh and ragged.

She hissed the first words she'd spoken since destroying her wine glass. "Come on, baby," she urged. "Come on. Give it to me."

Yeager needed no encouragement. He bit his lip. His hands dug into her hips. He grunted and bucked, and his mind blanked out in furious release. He squeezed his eyes shut and gasped, over and over.

Too soon, it was over. Charlie collapsed atop him. Both of them slick with sweat. Breathing hard. Together. A minute. An hour. Yeager didn't know how much later, Charlie raised herself and looked him in the eye. She remained silent. Unreadable.

Yeager finally asked the question that had been troubling him since she locked the door. "Not that I'm complaining, but... that was not what I was expecting tonight."

"It's simple," Charlie stated in a flat voice. She rolled off the bed and gathered her T-shirt into a ball. Stood and looked down on him with an emotionless expression. "That was a reminder of what you'll be leaving behind if you run off to Mexico with Victor."

"Say what?"

"You have a choice, Abel." Charlie padded naked toward the bathroom. "Leave if you want. Go chase off after this Gustaffson character, locked, cocked, and ready to rock. Just don't expect me and the kids to be here when you return. *If* you return." She paused at the doorway and turned to face him. "Trouble follows you, Abel Yeager. It finds you and rains all over you. Anybody close to you gets drenched... and I'm tired of getting wet."

The bathroom door closed behind her with a click.

CHAPTER FIVE

Blanca Trevejo clamped her hand onto her right knee as a reminder to not let her leg start bouncing. It was her nervous tell. The training officers at Camp Peary had dinged her for it time and again. *Freeze that leg, Trevejo! You look like goddamn Thumper!* And just like that, she had a nickname. Thumper. She hated it, so of course, it had stuck throughout training and was well on its way to following her for the remainder of her career in the Central Intelligence Agency.

In the sweltering heat of a Guatemala evening, Blanca's hyperactive leg was the least of her concerns, but the only one she could control. She sat at a table on a patio attached to the side of a *tienda*—a small convenience store—a bottle of Pepsi gone too warm to drink in front of her. Sweat stuck the lightweight cotton Tehuacan blouse to her back, and more dribbled down her ribcage. At a table in the far corner, a pair of workmen ate *pupusas* and drank Gallo beer with industrious efficiency. They glanced her way now and again, nothing that triggered her early warning system. In a country where the murder rate among women was so high, they had practically coined the term *feminicide* as a result, Blanca had her vigilance dialed up to paranoid levels. However, these two seemed nothing more than a pair of working stiffs checking out the single girl sitting alone at a nearby table.

About the size of a tennis court, the patio contained three metal tables, each with an oddball assortment of chairs. A spreading ceiba tree in the back-rear corner provided shade from the setting sun. A cinderblock wall separated the space from the street. Laid on their sides, the blocks created a latticework of rectangular holes, allowing visibility into and out of the patio. Blanca scanned the passing traffic for her contact. She cataloged pedestrians and passing cars, just like her training officers demanded. *Don't look at the clothes. Look at the noses, the ears, the way people walk. Those things are hard to disguise. Check out the cars for anybody circling the block.*

Exactly what she planned to do if she had been compromised remained to be seen. Escape would be difficult. The only exit was back through the store, though Blanca supposed she could climb the wall in a pinch. It was a terrible location. She would need to plan better for future meetings.

Relax. Get into character. You have a nice new friend you met at church—a sweet and naïve girl who happens to work for the incoming administration. Blanca grimaced to herself. *A sweet and naïve girl you plan to entrap into betraying her country.*

A three-wheeled taxi puttered by, puffing blue smoke and mariachi music into the patio. Locally known as a *tuk-tuk*, the red-and-decal painted cabs were as obnoxious as they were ubiquitous, and—like yellow cabs in New York City—they made counter-surveillance a pain in the ass. How was she supposed to spot a tail when all the cars looked the same?

"Hola!" said a bright voice from the open door of the *tienda*. Blanca looked up as Marisol Pareda breezed across the patio, an orange soda in one hand. She wore a pale-green knee-length skirt and a white blouse. The workmen followed the young woman with appraising eyes. One said something low and quiet, with a sly grin, and his companion snickered with the back of his hand pressed to his lips.

Blanca was as lean as a distance runner and pretty enough. She often drew more male attention than a boat show, but compared to Marisol, she was a tramp steamer with a leaky bottom. The Guatemalan girl had a beauty contestant figure and exotic Mayan-

Asian ancestry that should have placed her in a slinky dress on the cover of *Vogue*.

"I'm sorry I'm late," Marisol lamented. "It's crazy busy with my boss and Señor Modena preparing for the big day."

"That must be exciting!" Blanca leaned in tight, eyes wide. Just one of the girls, nothing deeper on her mind than the latest gossip. "Will you move into the palace with the big man?"

Marisol shrugged, trying to pull off nonchalance, then lost it with a giggle. "Maybe. Who knows? A girl can dream, right?"

Marisol Pareda worked as a personal secretary to Alfonso Bustamante, the president-elect's righthand man. Everyone expected Bustamante to be given one of the top jobs in the new government—the head of a ministry at least, perhaps even that of the Ministry of the Interior.

Marisol's excitement was understandable. Though she hinted that part of her duties for Bustamante included more than typing and filing, he was older and married. The incoming president of Guatemala was young, handsome, and single. Marisol obviously hoped she would catch the eye of the man many described as the Guatemalan version of JFK.

A bit of a crusader, Guillermo Modena portrayed the image of a lone wolf, standing tall and firm against the injustice of the United States. He had been elected after the last president had signed the hugely unpopular agreement with the US to stop immigrants from other countries as they fled from points south. The agreement forced those refugees and hopeful migrants to remain in Guatemala instead of continuing their journey to the US's southern border. As far as the majority of citizens were concerned, Guatemala had enough poverty and misery on its own without more refugees adding to their problems. Modena promised to rescind that agreement and go toe-to-toe with big, bad Uncle Sam del Norte. Further, he planned to reinstate the charter of the United Nations–backed anti-corruption commission known as CICIG, the International Commission against Impunity in Guatemala. Revoked by a previous administration, this body identified and presented for prosecution cases of corruption in the Guatemalan government. Modena's stance against the US and corruption met with a lot of popular approval from the average citizen, enabling Modena to claim a mandate to govern.

With Modena's election having caught Uncle Sam a bit by surprise, the pressure was on for the intelligence community to develop a source—any source—inside the new administration. Marisol Pareda, whether she would remain as "sex-a-tary" to Bustamante or be drawn into the orbit of the young president, would be in position to provide valuable insight into the plans of the Guatemalan government. In spy jargon, she would be considered a medium-to-high-value source, depending upon how long she retained access. For a very junior officer on her first assignment for the Clandestine Services Division of the Central Intelligence Agency, recruiting Marisol would be a coup.

Blanca slipped into her cover as Juanita Alvares, a secretary working for a coffee export company, and allowed the conversation to flow. She dropped in pertinent questions when the opportunity arose, all geared toward determining Marisol's access to sensitive information. What she heard pleased her.

"The boss," Marisol said, referring to President-elect Modena, "is taking a trip. Very hush-hush. No one is supposed to know, but Alfonso said they are visiting a very bad man. Someone who can do much for them or wreck everything." Marisol lowered her voice, sharing her secret with delicious glee. "He told me this man was El Escorpión, and they would have to make nice with him. Maybe even invite him to the ball."

Blanca allowed her jaw to drop. "The inaugural ball?"

"Sí!"

The two workmen left. A woman shepherded three kids with ice cream sticks outside. The store owner turned on a yellow outdoor light as darkness gathered. The air on the patio grew heavy with the scent of ripe fruit, unwashed bodies, and open trash cans, all mixed with ever-present car exhaust. Marisol practically gushed with chatter. Señor Bustamante's secretary seemed to enjoy having an audience willing to soak up her lurid tales of office gossip, and Blanca was more than happy to let her ramble.

At a lull in Marisol's monologue, Blanca leaned in and asked, "Did you get it?"

"Get what?" Marisol tried looking coy.

"You know..." Blanca glanced around. "You were going to bring me something from the Big Guacamole..."

The Guatemalan version of the White House, the Palacio Nacional de la Cultura, was also known as the Big Guacamole for its distinctive green-tinted limestone exterior. After church the previous Sunday, "Juanita" had expressed a fascination with all things having to do with the palace and wondered aloud if Marisol could maybe bring her a souvenir. "Something real, not some cheap knock-off crap from the gift shop."

Marisol smirked and dug into her handbag. She produced from its depths a small bread plate made of delicate china, trimmed in gold and embossed with the presidential seal. "From the private dining room of El Presidente. We were on a tour of the building—'measuring the drapes' is what Alfie called it." Marisol shrugged and flashed an impish grin. "It was just sitting there, in a stack with a bunch of others on a sideboard."

Outwardly, Blanca projected shock and delight. "Oh, Marisol, you must be careful! You could lose your job for something like this." Inside, Blanca was turning handsprings. A few more little "gifts" like this, and she would own the woman. She ruthlessly crushed the twinge of conscience that poked its head up. She handled the plate by the edges, mindful to not smudge Marisol's fingerprints.

They hugged and kissed cheeks on parting. Blanca promised to see Marisol at church on Sunday, where they would take communion together. Blanca planned to skip confession, though. *Forgive me, Father, for I have entrapped a young woman to commit treason against her country…*

No. Some things were best kept secret, even from God.

President-elect Guillermo Modena powered the black Mercedes sedan down the rutted asphalt excuse for a road as fast as he dared. From the corner of his eye, he noticed Alfonso clenching his hands in his lap, checking himself from reaching for the dash. Guillermo kept his smile to himself and pressed the accelerator. The big car leapt forward. For a fearless leader of men, Alfonso Bustamante was an old woman when it came to riding in a car driven by his best friend, the next president of Guatemala.

They had traveled many hours from the capital for this meeting with one of Guatemala's most infamous oligarchs. The Mexican border was not much farther north from their destination. Modena felt sure the distance was another lesson in power from the billionaire to the politician. *See, I can make you come to me when I whistle. No matter how far.*

Only he and Alfonso rode in the car. They had slipped away from their normal entourage of security men, aides, and flunkies, using a combination of subterfuge and shouting. Arranging for a car without a driver or security was no easy feat for the president-elect of a nation with the highest murder rate in the Western Hemisphere.

"I have Little Maria," Alfonso proclaimed, displaying the ancient .32 caliber breakover revolver he had carried for decades. "We will be safe!"

"Safe!" Modena had scoffed. "When did you last change the bullets? In the seventies?"

"Eh. Trivial, trivial." Alfonso had tucked Little Maria back in his coat pocket and pointedly looked away.

A few years ago, Modena would never have imagined the colossal three-ring circus his life had become. Little did he dream, as a boy growing up in a pisspot of a village, that he would one day drive a Mercedes, let alone have to fight off his army of supporters and bodyguards for the privilege of driving it himself. The head of his security detail had been nearly apoplectic, red-faced and threatened to quit several times. Modena had shouted him down.

The secrecy was necessary. For this meeting, Modena wanted no witnesses. Except of course for Alfonso Bustamante, his friend from the same little pisspot village in the highlands, the chubby boy with whom Modena had picked coffee beans, smoked pilfered cigarettes, and peeked through the curtains of Graciela Batzibal's bedroom every Saturday night, when she would bathe standing next to a bucket of soapy water, dripping suds and sponging herself all over. An older girl of sixteen, Graciela had been the subject of many late-night conversations between he and Alfonso, mainly along the lines of who would be the first to kiss her, who would marry her, and what mysteries were concealed between those lush, wet thighs.

Bustamante had stuck with him throughout their time in their one-room school, always competing for the highest scores. Racing him to be the first with the correct answer. Matching him move for move over the chess board they had made from a cardboard box and a handful of wooden counters, upon which were drawn pictures of the pieces.

In the end, the village had raised the money to send both of them to college, with the proviso that Modena and Bustamante would come back after graduation and pay back in sweat equity the investment in their education. And they had done so. That pisspot village was a pisspot no longer. It was now one of the central hubs for the collection and processing of coffee in the highlands of Guatemala. Farming, feed stores, livestock, banking—all had come to the village because of their efforts.

And from there, it was a natural leap to enter politics...

"And now," Modena muttered, "this piece of shit."

"This piece of shit is a kingmaker," Bustamante said, as if reading his mind. Twenty years of office work and politicking had not been kind to Alfonso Bustamante's body. Fast food, late nights, and alcohol had turned the chubby boy into a paunchy, round-faced man with borderline diabetes, high blood pressure, and chronic indigestion. Modena's long-time friend stifled a belch with the back of his hand and added, "Or a king*breaker*."

Modena pulled a face.

"Do not think for a minute," Bustamante said, "that you would have even been on the ballot without his fingertip on the scales. And do not think for a minute that you will remain president without his permission."

"And now we run to him," Modena said with an audible sneer in his voice. "Like a pair of faithful hounds who come to their master's whistle. In a few weeks, we will have the army to command. What's to say we don't move against our *benefactor*"—Modena laced the word with venom—"with a tank division and some artillery?"

Bustamante deflated with a long-suffering sigh. "And are you sure, *mi compadre*, that the generals to whom you give such an order will obey it? Or are they already in the pocket of Herman Gustaffson—aayyy!"

Bustamante grabbed the dash as Modena rounded a bend at sixty kilometers per hour and found his lane occupied by a man pedaling a bicycle cart piled high with melons. Modena twitched the wheel and swerved around the cart, so close he could almost taste the melons. In his rearview mirror, the man raised a fist and shouted things Modena couldn't hear.

"This is not how it should be," Modena said, still on the topic of their kowtowing to a criminal oligarch. "This country is riddled with *corruption*. It's *intolerable*. It is our *duty*—"

"Please don't get started on another speech." Bustamante pinched the bridge of his nose and squinted his eyes closed. "You build up a head of steam and won't shut up for an hour. I am getting a headache already."

Modena huffed and swallowed the fire burning in his belly. He followed the written directions he had been given and turned off the main road onto a beautifully paved concrete driveway, stopping at a set of massive iron gates mounted in a brick-and-mortar wall. A guard post, complete with a tactically garbed sentry behind glass so thick that it appeared green, anchored the left side of the entrance. Modena brought the car alongside the guard shack.

"State your name," the guard said. His tinny and robotic words issued from a microphone mounted on the side of the shack.

Modena felt like he was ordering fast food from a gringo chain restaurant and had a sudden urge to ask for fries and a shake.

A second sentry appeared on the far side of the gates. This one held a military-style rifle casually pointed through the bars at the windshield of the Mercedes. Modena's momentary impulse toward flippancy evaporated.

After Modena and Bustamante had been cleared, the gate guard pushed a button, and the gate retracted along a track to one side. Modena drove past the guard with the rifle, feeling the man's eyes on his neck as the Mercedes cruised onto the property.

Property was a misnomer. *Botanical garden* was more like it. The driveway cut through the heart of a tropical forest. A variety of multicolored birds flitted among the trees like bright dashes of paint against the green canopy. In a clearing trimmed with masses of flowering bushes so thick they created an ad hoc corral, a dozen alpacas grazed on thick, manicured grass.

"I wonder if a jaguar would eat us if we left the car," Bustamante said.

"He would eat you first, my friend."

"Not so. They go for the lame before the fat."

Modena had torn a few important tendons playing football for a semi-pro team in college. The doctor who'd performed the surgery had apparently learned his trade at a butcher's shop, for the knee had never healed right. Modena walked with a limp to this day, and his attempts at running made him look like a spastic baboon. It only ached on rainy days, and it rained a lot in Guatemala.

"Mary, Mother of God." Bustamante's jaw dropped. "What kind of cubist architectural hell is this?"

The house was not what Modena expected. He had pictured Herman Gustaffson, the criminal overlord who ate fried *narcotraficantes* for breakfast and roasted prime ministers for dinner, would live in a classic Spanish-style mansion with whitewashed walls and a red tile roof. Instead, the home was a Frank Lloyd Wright knockoff, all cubes and angles, clean lines and huge, expansive windows.

"All that glass," Modena said. "I hope it's bulletproof."

Bustamante smirked. "You start another speech, I hope *we're* bulletproof."

CHAPTER SIX

Yeager ate a cold breakfast while standing at the sink. The gray light of an overcast dawn seeped through the windows, providing enough light to navigate the furniture, but leaving much of the kitchen dark. And silent.

The baby and David were still asleep. The dog, Rascal, lay draped over the older boy's bed like a black-and-tan foot warmer. When Yeager peeked in, the dog had raised his head, yawned, and flopped back down. Charlie, if she was awake, had not made an appearance yet. Yeager's gut clenched at the thought of facing her, given the way she had thrown down the gauntlet last night.

For the first time in three years, Yeager thought seriously about living the rest of his life without Charlotte Yeager in it. She had sounded pretty adamant about what he could expect if he raced off on a gunslinging mission to Guatemala. Her stance had surprised him. Charlie had always been so torn up about Cujo dying after she had asked him to fly down to Mexico to find Yeager and bring him back. Cujo had flown down all right and found Yeager. The pilot had then saved their bacon by flying close air support in his illegally modified twin-engine jet. The hell he had unleashed on the small army of Grupo Verdugo soldiers had ripped the guts out of the attackers and bought time for Yeager and the boys to get the orphans away from the battle. Then Cujo had flown his plane into dense trees on the side of a mountain and, when Yeager had gone to check on him, appeared in every way as dead as roadkill.

But now they knew differently. Somehow, Cujo had lived through the crash and ended up in a Mexican prison. Yeager had expected Charlie to be happy with the news, and maybe she would have been, had it been a simple matter of hiring a lawyer and getting him sprung from jail. This thing with Mendoza, though... that painted the barn a bad shade of shit. And now, if Yeager went and did what it seemed he had to do to get Cujo out of prison, he risked losing his wife.

Yeager rinsed out his cereal bowl, dropped both the bowl and spoon in the dishwasher, and dried his hands. Propping himself against the counter, he studied the field behind his house through the window over the sink. Their homestead wasn't big by Texas standards. Ten acres, mostly of trees and rocks. A four-bedroom farmhouse with a wraparound porch. A barn. Stock pond. Maybe not a lot for some folks, but Yeager loved it. Not nearly as much as he loved Charlie, David, and John Riley. He even loved the damn dog, though the critter was as dumb as a broken hammer.

The fear that he'd buried for so long, that his marriage to Charlie wasn't really meant to be, came roaring back to sink its claws deep into his heart. Since the very beginning, he had wondered what she saw in him, a truck-driving redneck more accustomed to plastic forks than silverware. A Marine staff sergeant. Literate enough to read shampoo bottle instructions, maybe, on a good day. She came from money, though. Her parents lived in a multimillion-dollar home in Highland Park, an enclave of the very rich tucked just north of downtown Dallas. The first time he and Charlie had gone to visit, her mother had given him a look suggesting he should come in through the back door. Charlie had been a successful businesswoman. She could pick up the phone and get a meeting with the governor. She understood who was on which side of the battles in the Middle East.

Hell, she even reads books without pictures.

And she was right. *What have I ever brought her but trouble?*

Yeager took a look around the kitchen. Neat. Clean. Modern appliances with more buttons than a nuclear submarine. Pots and pans to rival a Food Network show. The rest of the house was the same, like something pictured in *Southern Living* magazine. More house than he ever deserved and bought with Charlie's money. He had brought very little to the marriage beyond a broad back, a pair of willing hands, and the smell of gunpowder. If he dropped out of her life, would Charlie be better off? Or worse? He had a sinking feeling he knew the answer.

What about David? And John Riley? Yeager clamped his jaw so tight, his teeth hurt. He would miss those kids. David's biological father hadn't been much of a presence in the boy's life and had turned out to be a crook. Yeager had worked hard to gain David's trust. Leaving him felt like the worst kind of betrayal. And abandoning the baby? John Riley Yeager was his only natural-born son. Charlie was a beautiful, healthy woman. She wouldn't stay single forever. Sooner or later, she would marry again, and his kid would have somebody else for a daddy. Maybe even somebody else's name.

Yeager's fists clenched. His vision swam. He wanted to punch something, but everything in his vicinity would break his hand or wreck a piece of his life. He swallowed the knot in his throat and clamped down hard on the anger, which felt like squeezing steam back into a boiler.

His go bag was packed, sitting by his feet. All he had to do was pick it up, walk out the door, fire up his piece-of-crap truck, and drive into town with Victor. They would head down to Mexico, meet this Mendoza character, then... what would happen would happen. Assuming he lived through it, Charlie might or might not take him back, though now that he thought about it, he wasn't sure coming back was a good idea. In the short time since he had come into her life, she had been assaulted, beaten, kidnapped twice, and forced to kill more than one asshole in order to stay alive. Maybe he really was a bad luck charm for her.

Yeager stared at the bag for a long time.

Charlie padded into the kitchen in her robe, hair mussed. She stopped when she saw the bag on the floor. Her eyes rose to meet his, and Yeager was struck by the dark circles that dimmed their vibrant blue. They were silent for a long moment.

"I have to," Yeager said.

"I know." Charlie turned and walked away.

It would be fatal for her asset, Marisol, if a hostile agent followed Blanca directly from their meeting back to the US embassy. And practicing solid tradecraft, regardless of the situation or perceived danger, always struck Blanca as a good rule to follow. Consequently, after she left her meeting with Marisol, the first leg of Blanca's surveillance detection route involved catching a random bus outside the tienda. The initial direction didn't matter, and the very randomness of the selection added to the difficulty of a surveillance team pre-positioning assets in anticipation of her route.

The urban planners had divided Guatemala City into twenty-two zones, numbered one through twenty-five. For reasons she didn't understand, there were no Zones 20, 22, or 23. Blanca had heard that saying someone went to Zone 20 in Guatemala City was a euphemistic way of saying they died. The meeting with Marisol had taken place in Zone 2, due north of the downtown historic district, and the embassy was located in Zone 10, almost due south from the same point. As her luck would have it, her random bus turned onto CA9 and followed it around to the *west* of downtown, into Zone 3, one of the most crime-ridden parts of the city.

Blanca found an open seat near the middle of the bus and settled in with her handbag on her lap. She toyed with the flap on her purse, tempted to pull out her phone and begin a search on "El Escorpión." But she forced the urge back down. Paying attention to her SDR was more important than digging into the "very bad man" who could tug the chain of the president-elect at his whim. The possible connection needed exploration, no doubt, as any contact with criminal elements was a point of vulnerability and potential compromise for the administration. But now was not the time.

An hour after dusk, the vehicle and pedestrian traffic had thinned, and Blanca strained her eyes, trying to see through the grimy black window to identify any following cars, which was difficult since she could only make out blurry shapes.

The vehicle had no AC. It was the kind of bus Blanca had ridden in high school to track meets. Sliding windows provided the only ventilation. In Guatemala City, that ventilation came heavily scented with diesel fumes, car exhaust, and corn tortillas frying on griddles. Crawling along its route at the pace of a Valium-addled turtle, the bus jerked and jolted, sloshing Blanca's insides. For the sake of her stomach and her patience, she collected her small shoulder-strap handbag and hopped off at the next stop.

The sign on the corner gave her location as 14 Calle at Avenida Elena. Not the worst part of Zone 3, though worst was relative, given that the best parts of Zone 3 made Skid Row in LA look like a summer camp at Disney World. Avenida Elena, or CA9, ran roughly north to south. She would need to take it or a parallel street for several miles to reach a cross street that would take her to Zone 10 and the embassy. Ahead of her lay some of the most poverty-stricken, crime-ridden territory in the Western Hemisphere. The infamous Guatemala City *basurero*, garbage dump, blighted an entire corner of Zone 3, where CA9 bent westward. For dozens of blocks around the *basurero,* the tenements housed a subset of the population whose only livelihood came from picking through the dump for salvageable items. The smell was... intense. On days like this, Blanca hated her job.

Against orders, Blanca carried a Fairbairn Sykes dagger in a sheath attached horizontally to the back of her belt. No gun. Hunter Davidson, the station chief for Guatemala, didn't believe CIA officers should carry guns and refused to issue her one. If she was caught with a firearm, he reasoned, or heaven forbid, shot a citizen, it would damage the reputation of the CIA and harm relationships with the host government. Blanca had listened to this little speech with her "are you fucking stupid?" expression calmly concealed behind a mask of professional attention.

She had since been tempted to use her false papers and apply for a permit to possess a firearm, which was legal in Guatemala. Or to buy one off the street. She had chickened out on both actions. At the moment, standing on a night-shrouded avenue in Zone 3, she regretted that.

"I get through tonight," she said under her breath, "I'm buying a gun. Fuck Davidson."

Blanca lingered at the intersection, checking the pedestrians by leaning against a brick wall and pretending to scroll through her phone. After ten minutes of no repeaters and no suspicious idlers, she took off at a fast walk, cutting down 14 Calle instead of remaining on the better-lighted Avenida Elena. She reasoned that any tails would stand out in a more sparsely populated area.

Two blocks along 14 Calle convinced Blanca that she had made a very serious error in judgment.

Guillermo Modena and Alfonso Bustamante were led through Gustaffson's mansion and introduced to their host in a room almost big enough to stage a tennis match. Modena's first impressions of the decor in El Escorpión's lair was one of monochrome sterility. The white walls were accented with recessed lighting and chrome fixtures. Carrara marble floors lent a subtle, gray-veined contrast. Sculptures in bold colors—red coral, obsidian, and jade—occupied end tables and shelves made of glass. A wall of clear glass overlooked a verdant green vista of forested cliffs. As Modena approached, he realized the room was poised over a chasm, and going out the window would mean dropping hundreds of feet before hitting the ground.

"Please, gentlemen," Herman Gustaffson said after greetings and handshakes. "Have a seat. Make yourself comfortable."

Modena sank into a creamy leather sofa, butter soft and as white as a pillow. Bustamante took a matching chair to his left, and Gustaffson resumed the seat he had occupied when he came in. His back was to the window, framing the criminal overlord against a backdrop of rugged cliffs. Four other men were in the room: the butler who had let them in, a thin man with the pinched look of someone holding in a ferret between his ass cheeks, and two more stone-eyed guards in tactical gear and carrying black machine guns.

"May I offer you a drink?" their host inquired. "Coffee? Something stronger, perhaps?"

"Coffee would be nice," Modena said in the same instant that Bustamante declined any refreshment.

"Right away, sir," the butler said before Gustaffson had even completed his gesture of dismissal.

"So, Mr. President," Gustaffson said. "How was your journey? Not too taxing, I hope. We are a long way from Guatemala City, I know, but I find this retreat to be my most secure location."

As he engaged El Escorpión in small talk, Modena sized up the notorious puppet master. Like many men who wielded terrible power from the shadows, Gustaffson looked like no one special. In a different setting, he could have been a hotel manager or the dean of a college. He carried age well, appearing somewhere past fifty, with an aristocratic bearing and the eyes of a shrewd poker player. A fringe of white hair circled his bald head and continued down his jawline to form a neatly trimmed beard. Slightly built, but with a powerful personal presence, Herman Gustaffson made Modena feel as though he had been called into the principal's office for an unspecified infraction with unknown consequences.

Long after the dregs of Modena's coffee had grown cold and Bustamante had begun to fidget as if he needed to urinate—which he probably did, as his old friend had a bladder the size of a thimble—Gustaffson steered the conversation to business.

"I thank you for accepting my invitation to visit," Gustaffson said, "but I'm sure you are a very busy man and would no doubt like to talk about more productive things than the price of coffee."

The two silent guards had remained watchful. The thin, dyspeptic man with the pinched look had been introduced as Milosh Jovanovic, and if Modena understood the subtext correctly, he was Gustaffson's financial adviser. The pale Eastern European would be in charge of moving the money from where it was to where it needed to be, overseeing the minutiae of cash-laundering schemes so complex, fraud examiners would have kittens trying to follow the trail. So far, Jovanovic had added very little to the conversation.

"Not at all," said the politician in Modena. "We are grateful for your hospitality and support, Don Herman." *As if we had a choice to be otherwise,* seethed the rebel inside Modena's soul.

Bustamante cleared his throat, as if he'd heard the rebel voice and was sending a warning.

Gustaffson inclined his head in acknowledgment of Modena's gratitude. "One of the reasons I supported your candidacy, Guillermo, is you have taken a very strong stance in opposition of the United States and the foolish agreements curtailing the migration of... dispossessed... citizens to their country."

"Yes, this is true," was all Modena allowed himself to say. "With the change in administration, these agreements have become nearly moot." His gift for oration had gotten him into trouble with slick politicians and oily businessmen in the past. As a consequence, he was learning to hold his tongue until the other party had laid out their cards.

"Which could change with the next election or the one after that," Gustaffson said. "I have long been a facilitator of migrants seeking a better life. Helping the poor and indigent to realize their dreams is a personal passion of mine and truly a good work in the eyes of God."

Modena clamped down a derisive laugh before it escaped. He nodded as if he believed Gustaffson to be a true benefactor, an altruistic philanthropist with a heart of gold. In reality, his organization ran a network of agents and coordinators in the underworld of human trafficking. More than simple coyotes, Gustaffson's people promised streets of gold to peasants from as far south as Columbia, Ecuador, and Venezuela, and offered them guides, instructions, and transportation for their journey north. For a price. El Escorpión's ticket to ride was expensive, and the results were not guaranteed. Still, his pipeline remained filled with a flood of gullible and hopeful bumpkins.

Modena himself had no illusions about the need to keep that pipeline open. Money sent back from immigrants who landed jobs in the United States made up a large segment of the Guatemalan economy. Without it, his country's GDP would plummet. Guatemala needed to export her poor and siphon their meager paychecks for cash to prop up her economy.

And not only Guatemala benefited. Modena had read classified reports of interests both internal and external to the United States who, for political or economic reasons, wished the stream of immigrants to remain open. The desire for cheap labor was insatiable, such that big business had no interest in closing down the border. On the other side, the desire for a voting block that could be guaranteed to keep the US liberal party in power guaranteed the gates to the promised land would remain open as long as the liberals could hold it so.

Of peasants seeking to leave, Latin America had an endless supply. Crushing poverty enforced by the ruling class who controlled all the wealth while peasants starved, coupled with the everlasting brush wars caused by the lust for power, ensured an unending supply of the dispossessed and desperate. Supply, high. Demand, high. Price, high. Simple economics.

Modena saw the refugees as nothing more than a nuisance straining his country's economy and ballooning the infestation of criminals in their ghettos. Solving his country's income disparity—Guatemala had one of the greatest GDP indexes in Latin America, and one of the greatest gaps between the rich and poor—would only become more difficult with an ever-expanding refugee population. Returning some modicum of that wealth to the people would mean going to war with entrenched powers like Gustaffson. It was a war Modena was very sure he would not win. Not from the outside.

He needed Gustaffson. For now.

"I am glad that we share a common vision," Modena said.

His attention was arrested by an original oil painting by Néstor Martín Fernández de la Torre. One of the artist's *Poema de la Tierra* series, it featured a nude man and woman entwined on a background of verdant greenery. For Modena, it always brought to mind thoughts of Adam and Eve in the Garden of Eden, eating from the apple of sexual knowledge. At the moment, he saw the painting without noticing the imagery, his brain working on choosing his words carefully. "How do you believe we should work together to ensure the future of Guatemala remains bright?"

Gustaffson smiled like a lizard. "I'm glad you asked."

Khayyat Halabi walked on a cushion of air. Quiet pride infused his soul and lifted him from the mundane surface of dusty streets in the plains city of Khost, in eastern Afghanistan. Fertile farmland stretched out in all directions from the capital city of the Khost Province, located a few kilometers from the border with Pakistan. Such borders meant little to Halabi, who was Pashtun and considered himself more aligned with his tribe than with any nation-state. Khost had, thanks be to God, returned to Taliban control after the armies of Satan had been driven from the land. He felt weightless, though his feet scuffed up clouds of dust from the pavement as he passed through a neighborhood of residential homes mixed with small shops and broken up by sections of open field.

His destination lay ahead—a two-story home with dingy white walls, blocky and rectangular, and heavy carpets hung in the glassless windows. His heart lifted further at the sight.

He had been chosen.

Halabi had labored long for the defeat of the Americans. In this very city, he had played a small role in al-Zawahiri's running of the double agent, al-Balawi, who had martyred himself and taken seven CIA agents and a Jordanian to their deaths. Many other battles had been fought since that fateful day in December, 2009.

Halabi was older. Wiser. Tougher. And now it was his turn.

He entered the home without knocking. The two mujahideen at the first-floor windows had seen him coming and nodded as he passed into the dim front room. Seating rugs and cushions lay around a short table. A tea set with a steaming pot and plates of cakes occupied most of the table.

Halabi ignored the tea and cakes. Too many butterflies flew in his stomach to tolerate anything else. He stalked through the house to a back bedroom. Just inside the doorway stood a longtime friend of his, Asha Gazali.

"You have made ready, I see," Halabi said with satisfaction.

"As you requested." Asha, whose face was covered with a mask that revealed only his eyes, measured him with a narrowed gaze. "You have news?"

Halabi allowed his pride to show. "I have been chosen."

"God is great!"

"Yes, praise be to God." Halabi waved a hand. "All that remains is this task."

The task he indicated knelt before him. Two missionaries of the Christian infidels, who had proclaimed to the world that they would travel the lands of Islam and bring understanding by extending their open palms to peace-loving Muslims, thereby bridging the gap between their two religions, had been taken into custody by the local Taliban leadership and handed over to Halabi's men. God, the missionaries had said prior to their departure from Kabul, would protect them from harm, as would the basic goodness inherent in the followers of Allah.

Now the stench of body odor and human waste soaked the small windowless room where the missionaries knelt before the tripod-mounted video camera. The flag of the Taliban hung on the wall behind them. The pair slumped, hair and faces ragged with sweat, and sat on their heels with their own bodily fluids staining their pants. The blond female had been raped repeatedly. She shivered constantly, like a small dog. The dark-haired male wept, dripping tears to splash the dusty floor at his knees.

"Turn on the camera," Halabi told Asha. "I would make this quick as I have much to do before I depart."

Halabi removed the straight-bladed knife from the sheath at his waist. The blade was a souvenir from a captured Spetznaz officer who had died in the siege of Khost during the Russian invasion of Afghanistan in the 80s. It had been passed down to Halabi from his father, and Halabi had kept it razor sharp ever since.

By the will of Allah, these two throats would not be the last to taste the steel of his Russian knife, though with his upcoming mission, he could well see having to leave the blade behind for future generations to make use of. Where he was going, a knife would not be needed.

Halabi pulled up his neckerchief to hide his features and stepped up behind the male missionary. He spoke long into the camera lens, delivering his message of Allah's will. The words came by rote, but he delivered them with special passion, for this time, he spoke with the knowledge that he would be taking the fight into the guts of the decadent West. When he finished, he punctuated his words with action.

First the man. Then the woman. As always, he found the temperature of fresh arterial blood to be surprisingly warm.

CHAPTER SEVEN

Two blocks down 14 Calle and all the small hairs on Blanca Trevejo's neck were dancing boogie nights. Flat-fronted two-story buildings hulked along both sides of the road. The structures alternated between derelict and marginally habitable, some with broken pits for windows, others with concertina wire circling the top. Every one was painted a different color of despair. Rare lights pushed at the darkness, braving the shadows in forlorn puddles of yellow. Latino rap thumped from open windows, and the smell of urine floated up from the gutter.

Men, as feral as wild cats, watched from doorways or clumped together near parked cars, in knots of suspicious tension. An old lady in a headscarf pulled a squeaky cart loaded with bags of trash along the sidewalk parallel to Blanca's position, keeping her head down and churning forward as if on the way to her certain death. Blanca passed two guys sitting on the hood of a Dodge, sharing a joint. Their eyes tracked her like radar.

This is bad. I need an exit plan.

Blanca spotted a gap between the buildings. The alley led due south, which was the direction she wanted to go. She flicked a glance back as she made the turn. No tails, but the two smokers watched her with wolfish looks. One wore a red-striped Where's Waldo shirt, and the other a short-sleeved cowboy plaid. Blanca rounded the corner and lost sight of them.

She stifled a groan. The alley was darker than the street. Light came from a rare high window, spilling out along with the smell of frying peppers and the ubiquitous corn tortillas. Small animals—cats, not rats, she hoped—scuttled away at her approach, rustling the trash piles nesting against walls. Blanca picked up her pace. A footstep scuffed behind her, though when she looked over her shoulder, there was no one visible. The voice of a TV announcer rapid firing a Spanish-language newscast echoed from a nearby apartment. A woman shrieked at someone to come to dinner. Blanca shivered and hurried on.

To hell with this. Not a surveillance team on the planet would dare to follow me down this rathole. First left turn I find, I'm getting back to Avenida Elena and calling—

The slap of running feet was her only warning. Blanca half-turned. A weight slammed into her and tackled her to the ground. Her head bounced on the pavement, and light flashed behind her eyes. Her small purse went flying. The rough concrete sandpapered her shoulder and hip. The weight atop her reeked of pot and sweat, and he panted in her ear like a dog. Before Blanca's mind had grasped the obvious, her attacker grabbed a fistful of her hair and bounced her head off the ground. Once. Twice.

"Don't kill her." The voice echoed in triplicate inside her ringing skull. "Not yet."

"Just getting her attention," said the man holding her down.

They were speaking Spanish.

All of Blanca's motor control had deserted her. She was aware of all her parts, but creating coherent movement was well beyond her capacity. Blinding pain pulsed in her skull.

Hands. There were hands all over her. Twisting her onto her back. Her pretty Tehuacan blouse gaped open, torn at the collar. Air cooled the sweat on her ribs. Hands tugged at her belt.

Move! The thought drilled through the fog in her brain, like a headlight from a far-off locomotive, promising... something. *Move! Or take a trip to Zone 20. Another statistic.*

Blanca fought for focus. Shook her head to burn through the cobwebs. The pain helped, oddly enough. As loud as a trumpet blowing in her ear, as bright as a sun, the pain raked her attention back from wherever it had wandered.

Two of them—one straddling her legs, working at her waist, and the one in the Where's Waldo shirt. Her belt flopped open, and he worked at the button on her jeans. The one in the patterned shirt stood behind him, a dark shape outlined by thin light.

The button of her jeans came free. Waldo jerked, and her hips bucked up. She used the movement to snake a hand behind her back. She had all the dexterity of a zombie. Grabbing the hilt of her dagger felt like using tongs to pick up pearls. Waldo ripped her jeans over her hips, rolling her panties into a twisted wad. Blanca's grip on the dagger slipped. She convulsed her fist around the hilt, and the knife slid out of the sheath as Waldo raked her jeans down around her knees. She held it awkwardly, the cold steel against her bare buttock. Linear thought derailed, a train wreck of jumbled images and impulses. One memory skittered to the surface. *Point, not edge*, her instructors had insisted. *Wide slashes are easy to block. Straight jabs, not so much.*

Waldo seemed fixated on her exposed pubic hair, having paused his insistent tugging at her jeans to admire the view. His leering grin revealed glistening yellow teeth. Blanca had moved somewhere beyond terror, as if this were all happening to someone else. Her lungs worked in a stuttering pant, unable to draw a full breath. Her vision echoed, images superimposing.

An atavistic impulse, less than a clear thought, came to her: *Now!*

Blanca lunged. The blade found Waldo's throat. There was some resistance, like punching a straw into a juice box.

"Grrk!" Waldo's eyes bulged.

A weird giggle bubbled up in Blanca's chest, triggered by the comic look of surprise on Waldo's face. He clawed at his neck.

"What's wrong?" asked the man in the patterned shirt. He stood above and behind Waldo, his view blocked by his friend's body, and concealed by the darkness. "Hurry up! I want my turn."

Waldo thrashed, and Blanca's blood-slicked grip slipped. The blade was stuck deep. It refused to come loose. She dug a palm into Waldo's chin and shoved him back, wiggling the Fairbairn's ridged hilt, tearing the cut wider. Blood flushed over her when the knife popped free. Air whistled through the gaping hole in Waldo's throat. Warm liquid sprayed her face, splashed over her chest.

"What the fuck?" Pattern Shirt leaned over and pulled his friend's shoulder back. Waldo rolled over, and a fountain of arterial blood sprayed Pattern Shirt in the face. "Mother of God!"

Blanca slashed, and the man leaped away, clutching a deep gash on his forearm. He disappeared with the sound of running footsteps.

The night crept back in, leaving Blanca with the wet gasps of the dying Waldo. Then the gasps ended in a rattle, and nothing remained but her thundering heart and ragged breathing. Somewhere, a dog barked. A television played a sitcom, its banal laugh track rising and falling.

Still partially nude, Blanca curled into a ball and lay in the stinking alley, weeping.

The meeting had run long. Night cloaked the view from Gustaffson's window wall, and all Modena saw was a reflection of the scene inside, reminding him of the famous painting of people seen through a diner's glass window. This room, though, was hazy with cigar smoke and littered with empty glasses, plates of crumbs, and balled-up napkins.

A lot of small things had been decided. A deal here. A deal there. Nothing that committed an outright criminal act, though several would raise the eyebrow of an ethics professor. Bustamante called it the art of compromise, rationalizing that they were necessary to build a better Guatemala. Give a little to get a little. Modena considered it bartering away pieces of his soul.

They had danced around for hours, he and Gustaffson, waltzing around the landmines of their future relationship. Earlier, in the car, Bustamante had stated the problem crudely...

"Gustaffson put the money on the dresser," his friend had said. "He got you elected. Now he will want to fuck you in every hole. Our goal is to get out with only having to give him a hand job."

The time for dancing had passed. Bustamante sensed it, for he sat up in his chair, scrubbed his face with both hands, and came on point like a dog hearing a noise outside the door. He passed a subtle message with a microscopic nod in Modena's direction.

"We want the CICIG to return," Modena stated, referring to the UN organization charged with battling the criminal syndicates that truly ruled Guatemala. The International Commission Against Impunity in Guatemala had made great progress in returning the rule of law to his country before powerful interests—those specifically targeted by CICIG—had seen to its demise.

"You understand that is not good for me." El Escorpión had loosened his tie and relaxed into his chair. He held a smoldering cigar over an ashtray on the chair arm. A diluted glass of mescal and ice rested on the other arm. "Reconstituting CICIG would... inconvenience... a number of my clients."

"We understand," Bustamante said. "This is a huge favor we are asking."

To lump Gustaffson in with cartels like the Zetas or CJNG, who operated with impunity and often with the cooperation of the Guatemalan armed forces, would be a mistake. Gustaffson used his spiderweb of connections to facilitate drug running, human trafficking, and protection from prosecution for those he called "clients."

The transportation of drugs and humans through Guatemala was big business, and the leaders of that business held the people hostage to their schemes. Modena despised all organizations of power, with the cartels ranking high on that list. Making deals with a man who whored for them felt like trying to wipe shit off his shoe—no matter how many times he rubbed at it, the stink of feces remained.

"And we have not come empty-handed, to ask for a favor," Modena said, choking down his self-loathing. "We have become privy to intelligence briefings from some very confidential sources. Sources of which even you may not be aware." Modena schooled his face to sell the lie. His source had nothing to do with the Guatemalan intelligence community and everything to do with Bustamante's family relationships. "There is an active plot to assassinate you, coming from a direction you may not expect."

Gustaffson's eyebrows climbed his forehead. Modena kept the smile from his face. It was rare to surprise a rat like Herman Gustaffson, and Modena was convinced the man was caught off guard.

"Well, this is news," Gustaffson said. "If this intelligence has merit, then perhaps our gratitude might extend to aiding you in your worthy quest for justice."

Modena enjoyed a momentary victory dance in his heart. "Indeed. I am working the details even now"—which translated to: you're getting a down payment now and nothing more until we reach an agreement—"but apparently a Mexican Special Forces captain has contracted with some off-book soldiers of the United States armed forces to have you killed..."

"And do we know who these, ah, off-book soldiers are?"

"Yes. They are named Abel Yeager and Victor Ruiz."

Blanca jerked awake in the middle of a very bad dream. She lay in a knot of twisted, damp sheets, her pillow soaked with sweat. Sunlight streamed in the window of the CIA safe house in Zone 5's Colonia Saravia neighborhood.

Today marked the second morning since the... incident... in Zone 3. Thirty-six hours ago, she had killed a man. Her memory of the time immediately after she sliced Waldo's throat remained spotty. She recalled pulling herself together. Rinsing off the blood with a garden hose from a spigot protruding into the alley. Holding her blouse closed throughout the *tuk-tuk* ride across the city. Somehow, she'd had the presence of mind to divert from her original destination at the embassy and head for the safe house instead.

Wish I'd thought of that to begin with.

Blanca had sent her boss an "all is well" message soon after arriving at the apartment then showered until the water ran cold before falling into bed. All of yesterday and last night, Blanca had wrestled with how to report what had happened.

She had killed a man—in self-defense, of course. Then she'd failed to report it to the authorities. *How would that play in a Guatemalan courtroom? "CIA officer kills a man to avoid rape."*

Neither her station chief nor the ambassador would be thrilled to see that headline. And the looks she would get from the rest of the embassy staffers? All those Tommy Hilfiger millennials with their Ivy League diplomas and their woke bullshit—they were pampered brats who'd never pulled the silver spoon from their asses. *Oh, look at the Latina, so helpless. Can't even walk outside without nearly getting raped. Poor girl. Too bad, so sad.* Blanca shuddered. She hated pity.

Blanca groaned and levered herself out of bed. All her aches and pains had settled in for the duration, and what had been an annoyance earlier had turned into a full-blown aggravation. She had a lump on her forehead and road rash on her back and shoulder. Various bruises bloomed in places she didn't recall getting hit. Her hair and the right clothes could conceal all of it, though. Every minute that passed made reporting the assault more problematic, and by remaining silent, she was tacitly deciding to not tell anyone. It meant relying on the incompetence—or indifference—of the Guatemalan police. In a city with a murder rate higher than Chicago's and a police force riddled with corruption, that seemed a safe bet. Her only weak link was the taxi driver. She had a vague memory of hailing the taxi somewhere on Avenida Elena and rattling out some incoherent story of her boyfriend beating her up. Would he hear about the dead man knifed in a nearby alley? Would he make the connection between the killing and the blood-smeared woman he'd picked up? Could the cops track her down based on where the taxi had dropped her, several blocks away from the safe house, and where she had ended up? Both of her attackers had the graffiti of gang ink on their arms, marking them as low-level bangers. With over one hundred murders per week in Guatemala, Blanca liked her chances of the police lacking the resources to find the killer of one junior member of that demographic.

Of course, if they did, then it was the end of her career... and potentially the end of her freedom. The safe thing to do would be to report the incident to Hunter Davidson, her station chief, and beg for mercy. She would no doubt be on the next plane to Washington, facing either reassignment or termination of employment.

"Screw that," she said to her reflection in the bathroom mirror. "Suck it up and drive on."

Blanca turned on the hot water for her sixth shower since the attack. The safe house was stocked with enough clothes to get her back to her embassy apartment. First, she would destroy her bloody clothes and dump the Fairbairn down a sewer drain. Then she would conduct a full SDR back to the embassy, write up the contact report on Marisol, and get her ass busy researching this Scorpion dude.

Waldo was going to get boxed up in a tight little space and tucked away somewhere deep in the back of her mind, never to be thought of again. *Served the bastard right. His bad luck, picking a CIA officer as his victim. Justice served.*

Blanca stepped into the shower and scrubbed her skin until it burned.

CHAPTER EIGHT

The heavy, organic tang of freshly spilled blood permeated the family's living room. The wife and three small children of the state prosecutor for Chiapas had been attended to, and only the prosecutor himself remained. Catatonic, blood-splattered, but physically unharmed, the once forceful and confident man had been reduced to a shell, living in his own personal horror movie repeated on an endless loop.

Macerio Borges pinched his lips in displeasure. He turned his attention to his disciple, Dominic, who blinked like a signal lamp shutter and appeared ready to lose his breakfast. "At times, a message is required, and the surgeon must give way to the butcher."

The three tattooed animals, contracted through his employer's associates with Mara Salvatrucha, panted from their exertions. Naked and slathered with gore, the MS-13 killers bore very little resemblance to something produced by a loving mother of human origin. Their actions of the past hour had removed any doubt from Borges's mind regarding their humanity. Though he had ordered the work to be done, Borges took no pleasure in the way these cartoon-covered savages inflicted maximum pain and degradation on their victims.

"There is no honor in this," Borges said to Dominic. He spoke in French as a precaution. The chances one of these genital sores knew another language approached infinitesimal, and giving offense to these savages might cause them to forget who held their leash. Killing one of them would be bad for relations with his employer's purported allies. "Which is why we contract these jobs to those who have no honor."

Dominic swallowed and sipped small breaths through his lips.

Borges nodded to the leader of the three. "Finish it."

The bald thug grinned. With disgust, Borges noted the man's penis remained turgid, despite his recent... exertions. Borges clamped down on his expression and schooled his face to passive indifference. He stepped back out of the spray zone as the MS-13s went to work with their machetes. Dominic left the room.

Borges forgave the younger man his squeamishness. It was one thing to kill and feel nothing. Wanton animal savagery, on the other hand, took some getting used to.

Abel Yeager and Victor Ruiz occupied a table in the restaurant attached to the Sanborns de los Azulejos in Mexico City. Victor had complained about the choice being too touristy, saying he could find a dozen better places to eat in the city.

"It's busy," Yeager said. "Crowded and anonymous. Lots of exits."

"You think we gonna have to run for it?"

"Think about it. Could be this guy, Mendoza, all he wants is to get us both back to Mexico to arrest us for that San Felipe thing. He tempts us with this bullshit mission to Guatemala, supposed to save Cujo, and nets both of us at once. Avoids any extradition paperwork."

Victor waggled his head as if tossing the idea around. "Hmpfh. Devious and paranoid. That's what I like about you, Holmes."

"Although if this Mendoza is really a captain in the Mexican Special Forces, he'll have the place surrounded with a hundred troops. Running means we just die tired."

"And it's your positive outlook on life that really sets you apart. So what's the play?"

"We tell this guy to blow it out his ass. Play it from there."

"Hardball, huh?"

"Let's see what he does when we tell him to go get fucked."

They had arrived early and snagged a table with a view of the entrance. Light poured into the restaurant's atrium from decorative glass panes set high on the walls, near the ceiling. Tall, Colonial-style columns surrounded the dining area and supported a second-floor mezzanine. The floor was a mosaic of square tiles, which gave the restaurant its name, *de los azulejos* meaning "of the tiles." Yeager picked his way through a plate of *arrachera*—marinated and grilled flank steak—with Tex-Mex refried beans, and Victor was all in on a breaded steak that Yeager would have called "chicken fried" had they been north of the border, but here was known as *milanesa*. Ten minutes before noon, and the place was filling up with tourists and a few locals, creating a racket that made conversation difficult.

"You're awful damn moody, Sunshine," Victor said after a long silence. "More than usual, I mean."

"You ever play golf?" Yeager said without looking up.

"Golf? What?"

"It's a game played with sticks and balls. Low score wins. Everybody keeps a scorecard in their pocket, and they write down how many tries it took to pot the ball."

"Yeah, okay," Victor said. "I may have heard of it."

"What if..." Yeager paused to rub his temples, ordering his thoughts by pushing them together. "What if your mistakes and... bad deeds are like strokes in golf. You have a mark on your scorecard for every... like commandment, or whatever, that you break. Then at the end, when you're at the entrance to the pearly gates, old Saint Pete takes up your scorecard and sees whether or not you're under par. Too high a score, you lose."

"And what's par for this course?"

"Hell if I know. I just feel like I'm pretty far over it. Like I already lost, no matter what I do."

Victor motioned with his fork. "There he is."

Yeager tracked Oswaldo Mendoza as the Mexican captain wove through the tables, carrying a leather briefcase. The man certainly moved like a soldier—watchful and controlled, as if he expected a grenade to fall at his feet at any moment, giving him a split second to react. Mendoza's eyes had a haunted, hunted look. The look of a man who had seen much and expected more horror to come. Yeager knew the look well, having seen it in the mirror when he shaved.

Mendoza pulled out a chair at their table without waiting for an invitation and carried it around to a point between Yeager and Victor, situating it so his back was not toward the door. His expression gave a serious "fuck you" to any possible question of the awkward seating arrangement. The man reeked of burned cigarettes.

"You must be Señor Yeager," Mendoza said. He didn't extend a hand, and Yeager didn't bother.

Yeager swished a bit of steak around in some red sauce with his fork and popped it in his mouth without answering.

Mendoza smirked. "Has your friend told you what is required?"

Yeager chewed and swallowed. "My friend," he said at last, "is a mite gullible. Almost childlike in his trust of strange men bearing gifts. I try and try to warn him, but he just keeps falling for the craziest stories."

"Stranger danger." Victor tapped the side of his nose. "I remember now."

"He heard some fairy tale," Yeager continued, "about how if we go squash some scorpion down in Guatemala, that somehow a feller goes by the name of Quattlebaum gets a free pass out of a Mexican prison. No judicial proceedings, no charges, no nothing..."

Mendoza's condescending expression remained fixed. "I believe you say, 'No harm, no foul.'"

"I believe I say bullshit." Yeager tossed his fork down. "What kind of *Mission Impossible* wet dream are you livin' in? You think Tiny Tim here and me are gonna hare off to the boonies and take out some criminal warlord like one of them video games my oldest boy plays. That we're gonna"—Yeager tiptoed his fingers across the table—"stealth insert into this mountain fortress and Chuck Norris all his henchmen and render this motherfucker to room temperature like SEAL Team Six did to Bin Laden?"

"Tiny Tim?" Victor asked with a wounded look. "Man. That's hurtful."

The waiter stopped by, but Mendoza waved him away. Too late, Victor raised his empty soda glass in vain appeal to the waiter's vanishing back.

"A mission like that," Yeager continued, "takes intel, logistics, local support, air assets, weapons, and… and shit that I ain't even thought of. And then, and only then, you're saying our prize for this colossal clusterfuck-in-the-making is that our pal gets to walk? Shee-it." Yeager leaned back and hooked an arm over the back of his chair. "I'd rather take my chances on a courtroom. Hire Cujo a Mexican Johnny Cochran and see what happens."

"And if I were to remove my protection from Mr. Quattlebaum?" Mendoza asked with a cocked eyebrow. "Mexican prisons can be a dangerous place."

Yeager eased forward, filling the space between him and Mendoza with malice so thick, the special forces captain visibly tensed. "I believe I can find you and drop your ass a whole lot easier than I can do it to this El Escorpión."

Mendoza's sigh sounded like one of a man to whom nothing ever came easy. "I thought you might say that." The thin captain scraped back from the table and stood. He made as if to leave, though Yeager suspected there was more to come. And there was. Mendoza braced his palms on the table and fixed Yeager with a dead stare. "Do you know a man called Macerio Borges?"

Yeager shrugged, waiting for the shoe to drop.

"Señor Borges is Gustaffson's top sicario. He looks like a school-teacher but has killed more people than the flu. His killings include judges, politicians, witnesses, and really anyone who is... unfriendly... to the Scorpion or his clients. In special cases, this includes the loved ones of those who have threatened Gustaffson's interests."

A cold worm of dread twisted around Yeager's heart and gave it a squeeze.

"I have a file," Mendoza said, "attached to an email, which mi compadres are to send in the event of my death... or if I fail to make a timely phone call... In this file are the details of our arrangement." Mendoza's eyes grew more soulless, something Yeager would not have believed possible. "It details how you plan to kill Gustaffson. The file includes your names and addresses and known details. It has the names and locations of your wife and your friend's fiancée, as well as that of the pilot who now resides in a Mexican prison. Gustaffson will not hesitate to unleash Borges to... neutralize the threat."

"You bastard," Yeager hissed. Blood thumped in his temples, and his hands squeezed his coffee mug so hard, the ceramic creaked with the strain. Victor's face had turned three shades of purple, and his shirt stretched tighter over his swollen biceps.

Mendoza took a step back, pulling a fat legal-sized manila enve-lope from his briefcase, and dropped it on the table. On top of that, he added two photos. One was of Alexandra Lopez, Victor's fiancée. The other was a long-range shot of Charlie standing on the porch of their home in Texas, holding John Riley. Mendoza tapped the enve-lope. "Inside is everything you need to know." He touched his finger to his forehead in salute. "I will be in touch. Good day, gentlemen."

Yeager watched him go.

After three minutes of silence, Victor blew out his breath and sank back into his chair, stuck his straw in his mouth, and sucked up the watery residue at the bottom of his glass. He looked at Yeager. "Hardball didn't work for shit. Now what?"

Blanca Trevejo sat through Hunter Davidson's briefing feeling like a victim of a Novocain overdose. Her nervous leg mercifully quiet, her brain fogged by a sense of unreality, she listened to the CIA's Guatemalan station chief drone on about threat levels, intel chatter, and her colleagues' reports of contacts made and intelligence gathered. It all sounded as if hearing a TV broadcasting in a different room.

"We have some flash traffic out of Syria," Dean Larssen said. Davidson's second-in-command, Larssen was an office cave dweller who made it his job to read through all the message traffic, "distilling it for any relevant material." Blanca had learned that meant "any material relevant to Dean Larssen." The mousy, Yale-educated Larssen had a pale complexion and flaxen hair and was about as unsuited to clandestine work in a Latin country as a gopher was to digging a gold mine.

"Go on," Davidson prompted, as Larssen seemed to be pausing for effect.

"A group of jihadis departed Latakia," Larssen said, referring to the main seaport of Syria, "on a freighter bound for Santo Tomás de Castilla, here in Guatemala. The ship was the MSC Leala. But the big news is..." Larssen swept the table with his eyes. "One of them is reported as Khayyat Halabi."

"Halabi?" Davidson perked up. "Why do I know that name?"

"He's a bad dude." Larssen connected his laptop to the room's projector and flashed up a picture of a bearded, dark-eyed Arab with a prominent nose and a cluster of moles on his right cheek. "Identified as a lead planner behind the Cole bombing, the Kafir Towers massacre last year, and numerous jihadist attacks against our troops in Iraq. He's responsible for the deaths of over sixty American servicemen. And"—Larssen held up a finger—"we think he had a hand in the Khost... incident."

"And he's headed here?" Davidson sat back and scrubbed his face with a palm.

"He's already here. The ship docked yesterday."

"Jesus Christ. Great timing." After a long moment of silence, Davidson looked up. "But that's all we know? Twelve terrorists, including Halabi, were on a ship from Syria to Guatemala? And that ship docked yesterday?"

Larssen confirmed with a nod. Pink crept up Davidson's neck, a sure sign of an impending temper tantrum. Blanca roused herself enough to focus on the moment.

"No timetable?" Davidson continued, his voice rising. "No other identification? No threat assessment? What kind of bullshit excuse for intelligence is that? How are we supposed to prepare for a possible incursion of Mus—Isla—Syrian terrorists!—with intel like that?" Even in his anger, Davidson was careful with his language. In the modern CIA, referring to a terrorist as a believer in the Prophet Muhammad could result in a black mark on an officer's permanent record. The modern CIA was nothing if not politically correct. Blanca tuned out the remaining back-and-forth between the station chief and his assistant.

As the junior officer present, her turn came last. When Blanca reported the conversation with Marisol, Davidson practically creamed his tan Dockers.

"The Scorpion!" he cried. "You mean Herman Gustaffson? That Scorpion?"

Blanca had taken time to run the alias through the database. She had gotten four hits on bad guys with the nickname El Escorpión: a mid-level sicario from Baja, since deceased; a Zeta lieutenant, whereabouts unknown; a Peruvian money launderer, currently in jail; and Herman Gustaffson, a major criminal figure with fingers in every tamale pie from Argentina to Canada, based right here in Guatemala.

"Yes, sir," she replied. "I believe that to be the one."

"Wow. Big anti-corruption guy like Modena, hopping in bed with Gustaffson." The CIA station chief jumped up and paced around the conference table. Davidson was feeling some heat from Washington to get some leverage on the firebrand, Modena. A relationship with Gustaffson would be a big lever. "Man. It would be great to prove that, wouldn't it? That guy is a big fish here. If we could get inside his organization..."

Blanca kept her mouth shut. It was hard for her to share in Davidson's excitement. The third day after the assault—*no, say it right: the day after I killed a man who was trying to rape me*—Blanca felt as brittle as bone china and as dull-witted as a stuffed doll. Getting worked up over yet another criminal oligarch corrupting a Central American government hardly compared to the sickening memory of hot blood spilling over her hands.

"All right," Davidson said. "Let's see who's going to this inauguration thing. Maybe we can get you in under your cover ID, Blanca. We need to confirm Gustaffson is connected to Modena somehow. I think you should go to the reception and see what you can see. If you can penetrate Gustaffson's inner circle, maybe get... you know, close to somebody there."

Blanca raised an eyebrow, and Davidson's cheeks turned pink. He would never order her to sleep with a target to gain their trust, but if she did so on her own initiative, well, he couldn't very well stop her, could he?

"Ah," Davidson continued after an awkward pause. "You haven't been in-country long enough to show up on anyone's radar yet, so you should be good to go. Find out... find out whatever you can. But be careful."

Privately, Blanca doubted the Guatemalan intelligence services were so inept, they had completely missed seeing her enter or exit the embassy grounds, but by that point in the meeting, she did not care. All she had wanted to do was get to her room, run the air conditioner down to freezing, and bundle up under the covers with her laptop dialed in to Netflix.

The meeting adjourned soon after, with Davidson issuing further instructions to Larssen about following up on the Syrian terrorists and their potential arrival in Guatemala. Blanca ignored that, brightening only at the thought she would need a party dress if she was going to a ball.

CHAPTER NINE

In Sanborns's restaurant, an undersized man carried an oversized cup of coffee from a nearby table and slid into the seat between Yeager and Victor, the one recently vacated by Captain Mendoza. He hung his weathered straw Stetson on the back of his chair and sipped from his coffee before placing it on the table. Built of leather and piano wire, Rudy Aguilar appeared to be exactly what he was—a vaquero from the tips of his dusty, steel-toed cowboy boots to the hat ring impressed in his oiled black hair. Aguilar had copper skin two shades lighter from the eyebrows up and carried with him the faint whiff of cattle no matter how often he bathed.

"Your guys marked him?" Yeager asked.

Aguilar nodded. A single dip of his head, no more.

"And they know not to get too close, right? We only want to confirm his identity."

One lifted eyebrow told Yeager his question was stupid and he should teach his grandmother to suck eggs. Aguilar pinched the tip of a smartphone from the top of his shirt pocket, showing Yeager the top of the device. "Pictures too," the vaquero said. "We will track this man. See he is who he says he is."

Victor was fiddling with his own phone and flicked a glance at Aguilar's device. "Mine's bigger."

"Thank you," Yeager said. "And thank the Don again for me. Please."

"You did a service for Don de la Cueva," Aguilar said. "And a greater one for Mexico. It has not been forgotten. Everything that can be done is being done."

Yeager and Victor had approached Don Raphael de la Cueva before continuing on to Mexico City and their meeting with Mendoza. De la Cueva had been instrumental in providing both the supplies and the logistics for the relief mission undertaken to the orphanage at San Felipe a few years back. The relief effort had evolved into a hot fight against superior firepower, and the result had been the loss of many good men, including, they believed, their pilot friend, Milton "Cujo" Quattlebaum. The "service" to Mexico had been the virtual eradication of an upstart drug smuggling cartel, which the wealthy landowner considered to be the single greatest plague on his country, producing nothing but heartache and misery and death.

Don de la Cueva had promised his full support when Yeager asked him for help. Along with looking into freeing Cujo by legal means, the Don sent a small cadre of men led by his foreman, Aguilar, to Mexico City in order to "take the measure of this man, Mendoza."

"Perhaps our interests are aligned," de la Cueva had said. "In the sense that Mendoza wishes the continent to be rid of the pestilence of men like Gustaffson. Even so, I cannot approve of his methods. Coercing men of good character to undertake an execution on behalf of our national interests... it is not right."

Yeager grimaced. *And more wrong now, given his coercion involves my family.*

"Mendoza has upped the ante," Yeager said to Aguilar after the waiter had cleaned away their plates and left the bill. Aguilar sat stone-faced over his coffee as Yeager updated him on Mendoza's threats against Victor's fiancée and Yeager's family.

"I have heard of this Macerio Borges," Aguilar said. "He is a *muy malo.*"

Victor looked up from his phone. "That's Mexican for stay the fuck away from that guy."

Mendoza's package of instructions included directions to a house located on the outskirts of a village called Valle de Café, at the southern tip of the Parque Natural Montes Azules, about a mile from the Guatemalan border, in the Mexican state of Chiapas. There, they were to meet the asset who would supply their gear and guide them to safe passage across the border. The instructions did not specify what form that safe passage might take, and Yeager dreaded finding out. "Safe passage better not mean hiking a zillion miles through a mountainous Central American jungle," he said to Por Que.

His friend had reached over, patted him on the belly, and said, "A little walking be good for you, homie. Too much easy living made you soft."

The drive from Mexico City to the asset's house ate up eighteen hours. Yeager and Victor switched off stretches of driving and trying to sleep in the cramped backseat of their economy rental. Dusk turned the sky pink and painted the rugged hills with a soft light. Yeager fought to stay awake behind the wheel as he lead-footed along Mexico's Highway 307, a two-lane blacktop that ran parallel with the border. The highway twisted and turned along ridges and through cuts of rock. His ears popped with the elevation change as the road dropped into a valley. Coffee trees grew lush and thick in the fields, and greenery crowded the verge of the highway, which had no shoulder and less room for error.

In his fatigue, Yeager nearly drove past the sign for the cutoff to Valle de Café. He stabbed the brakes and slewed the rental into a right turn, ignoring the undignified squawk from the backseat. Gravel pinged and popped off the car's undercoating, and the rearview window fogged with white dust kicked up from the wheels.

"I need to take a leak," Victor called from the back seat.

"Hold it," Yeager said. "We're almost there."

"Aw, Daddd, c'monnnnn!"

Entering Valle de Café felt like time-warping back to Afghanistan. Not so much the architecture but the evident poverty and Third World homeliness of the place echoed that of the Hindu Kush. The buildings were a hodgepodge collection of concrete boxes and heavy brick structures. Tin-roofed for the most part and festooned with ribbons of laundry, the dwellings crouched amid small yards of packed earth and tough grass.

The village was bigger than Yeager expected, with multiple blocks in a rough grid shape following the contour of the hills. Though poor, the residents of Valle de Café kept their streets relatively clean, and the people he saw were dressed modestly but well. A pair of women walking beside the road in dusty sandals, long skirts, brightly printed blouses, and head scarves glanced up as he passed, following him with curious stares. They carried gunnysacks over their shoulders. Despite the colorful attire, they reminded Yeager of burka-clad women of the Middle East.

There were no street signs, so Victor navigated from a crudely drawn map. "Turn left... here, I think."

"You think?"

"It's not like Google Maps, okay?"

Yeager rolled the rental car down a narrow road. Murals decorated some of the houses in this neighborhood, recalling the Mayan heritage of the population. One low-slung building indicated its heritage was more modern, having been painted with a Corona beer logo. Men seated around a table on the bar's patio locked on to their rental with flat, suspicious eyes, tracking them like attack radar.

"The natives don't look too friendly, huh?" Por Que leaned forward through the gap between the front seats, squinting from the map in front of him to the windows outside. "It looks like we go right at the third intersection."

Yeager slowed to allow a dog to climb up from his wallow in the middle of the road. The old hound unlimbered his bones and limped away, casting a hurt look over his shoulder. Yeager made the right as directed and followed Victor's directions to a plain building of dusty brick, much like any other in the village. Dry and tired yucca plants flanked two support posts struggling to hold up a tin awning over the front door, and a rickety fence enclosed the side yard.

"Green door," Victor said. "This must be the place."

"Green?" Yeager grunted a sound of disbelief. "Looks more bare wood than green."

The partially green door opened, and a man stepped out carrying a half-eaten tortilla. He wore stained jeans and a short-sleeved shirt, unbuttoned to reveal a hairy, sagging chest and a hairy, round belly. More black hair obscured his face, leaving only enough uncovered to make out a pair of dark eyes, a nose that resembled a barnacle-crusted diving bell, and the biggest lips Yeager had ever seen on a man.

"Madre de Dios," Victor muttered in awe. "Mick Jagger's ever in an accident, this guy could be a lip donor. He should buy stock in ChapStick."

"Come on." Yeager unbuckled his seatbelt and popped the door. "Let's go meet Mr. Lippy."

"Don't say nothing about the Botox accident. He might be sensitive, y'know?"

It was cooler than Yeager expected for August, somewhere in the mid-seventies, though humid. Heavy clouds towered to the south, dark purple in the late twilight, and the scent of rain flavored the air.

Lippy stuffed his tortilla into one cheek and extended an oily, damp palm to shake hands with Yeager. "Arturo," he said through the wad of dough.

Yeager resisted the urge to wipe his hand on his pants. He introduced himself and Victor. "You the guide?"

A nod.

"Where can a man take a leak?" Victor asked. "*A mear.*"

"Around back."

Victor muttered something uncomplimentary about outhouses and strode off around the corner. Yeager stretched his back and rotated his torso. His spine crackled and popped. He used the motion to survey the surrounding neighborhood. Squat brick houses set along an exhausted street meandered up into the hills to the south. To the north, the road led down toward the main thoroughfare. More structures radiated away from the main drag as if grown from weeds. Two men sat on lawn chairs in front of a house down the street. Both had AK-style rifles propped next to them. Another man slouched his way up the hillside road, a similar weapon strapped to his back.

Yeager hitched his chin at the armed men. "Who're those guys?"

"Zapatistas."

"Who?"

"*Comunistas,*" Arturo said, the sneer evident in his voice. He spat to one side. "*Rebelde pendejos.* Want to... ah... *tomar el control?*"

"Take over?"

"Sí. Take over the village. Claim it as a MAREZ territory."

Yeager had no idea what made MAREZ territory any different than other territory. "Take over from who? The government."

A shrug. "*¿Los narcotraficantes? ¿El gobierno? ¿A quién le importa?* Is all the same." With that fatalistic remark, Arturo waved a lazy hand, dismissing the Zapatistas as if clearing away a bad smell.

"What's the plan here?" Yeager asked. "You're supposed to guide us across the border, right? How's that gonna work?"

"Eat, now. Sleep. Leave early." Arturo walked his fingers across his palm. "Long way."

"Shit," Yeager muttered. "I knew there would be hiking." Hitching a thumb at the rental car, he asked, "What about the car?"

"Mi compadre will return it." Arturo turned to reenter his house. "*Venga.*"

With a last glance at the Zapatista watchers, Yeager followed the chubby man inside.

B lanca parked her CIA-issued van, disguised in UPS colors and decals, in a clearing on a ridge across the valley from Gustaffson's compound in the hills west of Guatemala City. Packages filled the back of the van, each affixed with labels for delivery in the surrounding vicinity. All of these packages would pass casual, or even an in-depth, inspection if she was stopped and questioned. Except for one very special container. To be safe, Blanca decided to venture no closer than her current position for fear of triggering the attention of the crime lord's counter-surveillance teams. She was under no illusion that a man like Gustaffson would have anything less than state-of-the-art video surveillance, super-sensitive intrusion detection devices, and highly trained human spotters ringing the property in concentric layers. It had required five and half hours of sweaty-handed driving along unpaved roads, defying death from oncoming traffic or sudden rollover due to unexpected twists and turns to reach this point, two-point-six miles due north of the target compound.

She got out and stretched, allowing the noon sun to warm her bones and the cool Pacific breeze from the west to dry the sweat soaking the back of her blouse. Traffic along this section of no-name road consisted of a dragonfly bobbing on the air current. A lizard basked on a nearby rock. Insects sang in the brush.

After a long pause to reassure herself that she was unobserved, Blanca opened the rear doors of the cargo van. Inside, nested in a foam-lined brown box, an AeroVironment RQ-11B Raven unmanned aerial surveillance vehicle waited, fully assembled and prepped for flight. The thing was hardly bigger than the RC airplanes her brothers used to build and fly around in the dry LA drainage canals near their home. Emilio and Stefan had always gotten mad and thrown her out of their room when they built their planes, telling her to go play with her dolls, that RC models were for boys.

The brats would die of jealousy if they could see me now.

The Raven was a hand-launched UASV, designed with a rear-facing pusher propeller, and this particular model had a thirty-megapixel fisheye camera as well as a small secure data link radio transceiver to allow for beyond line-of-sight communication. The CIA's model had been up-powered by the techs at AeroVironment for an enhanced ceiling of eight hundred feet above ground level and a forward-looking infrared camera that could capture the image of a cat's whisker in a cornfield, day or night. Painted with a matte-blue underbelly and with a super-quiet electric motor, it was nearly undetectable from the ground.

After a last look around to confirm she was alone, Blanca powered on and launched the Raven the way she would have thrown a paper airplane. The little aircraft whispered away, climbing for altitude as Blanca tweaked the thumb-sized joystick on the Xbox-type controller. Greenery jittered across the controller's three-inch screen as the UASV bounced in the wind currents. Blanca sat on the van's rear deck and dialed up the throttle to get the drone over the ridge.

She estimated a flight time of fifteen minutes, giving her about half an hour on target, which would be sufficient for her purposes. The exercise today was less about surveillance and more about developing intelligence on Gustaffson's operations. The few available satellite photos provided less-than-satisfying images, and sat time was precious, as the DEA tended to hog time on the Central American birds. Prying a satellite away from the drug boys was like taking a toy away from a two-year-old—not worth the screaming temper tantrum.

A pair of vultures wheeled high overhead, black specks against a cloud-spotted blue sky. Blanca was grateful for the breeze, though it made controlling the drone a bit of a chore. The scent of her peach-infused bodywash fought her sweat-infused body odor for dominance.

While she waited, she retrieved a sack lunch from the passenger seat and set it next to her at the rear of the cargo compartment.

Gustaffson's home crawled into view on the screen, on time and exactly where she expected to see it. *Hah! Who's the best RC pilot now? Boys aren't the only ones who can play with model airplanes! Yay gurl power!*

The Google Earth view she had checked earlier didn't do the place justice. The sprawling mansion of orange tiles and white stucco was as big as a city block. To the north, an enclosed area contained an elaborate pool with several levels connected by waterfalls and wet paved pathways. Umbrella-covered tables dotted the area, looking like mushrooms from above. A driveway entered the property from the eastern side and opened out into a wide parking apron. The scene crawled across her monitor, which was being recorded to a storage device for later viewing.

During her research, Blanca had uncovered three major Guatemalan properties belonging to Gustaffson. This one in the Western Highlands was a Spanish-style hacienda. The one in the northern mountains near the Mexican border featured a modern, cubist structure. In the east, overlooking Amatique Bay, was a beach house. As the hacienda was the closest and easiest to reach from the city, Blanca had chosen it as her initial surveillance target.

That's odd. Blanca's eyebrows contracted. A white van—a small bus, really, an airport shuttle—occupied a spot near the house. The vehicle was as incongruous with the flamboyant richness of the property as a wart on a supermodel's nose. *Transport for the staff?*

A second van pulled in then parked next to the first. The screen jiggled and blurred as wind buffeted the Raven. Blanca teased the controls to circle the craft in a holding pattern while attempting to crop the fisheye image to zoom in on the parking lot. She cursed the touchy joystick, which transmitted the slightest tremor into a disproportionate action by the UASV. There was a way to program the device to set a holding pattern so the operator could work the camera independently, but it had been a while since she'd sat through the training class, so she couldn't remember how to do it. By the time the image settled, the doors to the second van had been opened and a half-dozen men gathered around the vehicle. One individual caught duffel bags as they were tossed from inside and set them on the ground. Blanca fought to hold the image steady.

The men stretched and walked stiff-legged in small circles. Some held hands to their lower backs. She gathered the impression the men had been cooped up for a long ride. All were swarthy, bearded, and dressed in the nondescript clothing of workers from a Third World country.

"A construction crew?" Blanca wondered aloud. "Driven in from the city to do some work on the big house?"

The men gathered their bags, and the leader, or maybe the driver, led them all toward the garage entrance, where they filed inside and disappeared from view. Blanca circled the area with the Raven for another ten minutes, maintaining watch for more activity. She was about to pull off and continue mapping the property when two men exited the garage. Each hopped into the driver's seat of a van, and seconds later, the vehicles circled the driveway and motored away. Blanca zoomed in on the license plates, recording the numbers for later analysis.

She widened her holding pattern, noting the extensive grounds east of the ridge, which included a wide variety of trees and brush. Occasionally, she glimpsed a roving foot patrol, armed with military-style weapons and dressed in black tac gear. Switching to infrared, she spotted even more guards lurking under the concealment of heavy vegetation. She didn't bother counting the guards; once she could download the storage, Blanca would get a tech to run an analysis of the security measures, including a count of the guard force.

With thirty percent battery remaining, Blanca keyed the command that would return the Raven to its launch point. All she had to do now was wait and wonder. What common ground would a snake like Gustaffson and a firebrand do-gooder like Modena have? By all reports, Modena adhered to the Marxist-with-a-Capital-M school of communism, and though his proposed economic policies carried the same empty promises made by politicians everywhere, he was at least, by all accounts, uncorrupted by outside money. Was this the first crack in the shiny revolutionary armor encasing Modena?

The sound of an engine grinding its way along the road reverberated off the hillside. Blanca quickly stuffed the controller into the cardboard case, slapped the flaps closed, and shoved the whole thing deeper into the van. She dug into her lunch sack and spilled the contents on the van's deck next to her. A sandwich, an apple, and a bag of chips tumbled out. Her water bottle rolled off the deck and hit the ground, forcing Blanca to race after it.

She had just gotten settled back in place when a black Range Rover popped into view. The vehicle slowed as it approached her van. Two hard-eyed men pinned her with suspicious looks. The Rover stopped, and the driver's window buzzed down.

"Do you need help, señorita?" the driver asked in Spanish. With short hair and the lean look of a wolf, the clean-shaven man exuded a professional soldier's vibe: cold, deadly, and prepared for violence. The men were dressed the same as the guards patrolling Gustaffson's estate. *What the hell are they doing this far out?*

"No, thank you. I'm fine." Blanca held up her sandwich. She fixed a bright smile on her face. *I'm Juanita Alvares, UPS delivery gal, not a CIA spy. I wouldn't hurt a fly... or step on a scorpion.* "I only stopped for lunch."

The Rover idled while both men evaluated her. Their expressions remained neutral, as if the outcome of their analysis mattered little. They would leave her be or kill her and dump her body in the woods with equal lack of emotion. A trickle of sweat trailed down her breastbone. Blanca wanted to nonchalantly take a bite of her ham-and-cheese sandwich, but she was afraid her throat was too dry and that she would choke on it. She kept an ear tuned to the sky. If the Raven picked that moment to come bumbling back over the ridge to land in her lap...

"This is a dangerous area," the driver said at last. "You should not linger."

"No," Blanca said. "I will get going in a moment."

"Bueno." The driver held up his cell phone and snapped her picture. "Be very careful, señorita."

With that, the Rover's window buzzed up, and the black SUV rolled away. Dust billowed up and stung Blanca's eyes. She dropped her sandwich in her lap and swigged from her water bottle. The cap rattled when she tried screwing it back on.

CHAPTER TEN

The border crossing had been uneventful, marked by no geographic feature Yeager could discern. They had followed a trail from the village through a grove of coffee trees and into a canopied rain forest, serenaded by buzzing insects, twittering colorful birds, and the howling of unseen creatures. They carried backpacks filled with trail mix bars, water, and extra clothing. At one point, a big-ass lizard the size of a Chihuahua and the color of a piñata scampered out from underfoot, startling Yeager. He half turned to point it out to Charlie, only to remember she wasn't there—which pissed him off for no good reason at all.

"No weapons," Arturo had told them in Spanish before setting out. "Weapons will be provided at the end, when we reach our destination. We will not likely meet any border guards, but if we do, and we are carrying guns..." Arturo's expression left no doubt it would be a bad day in the jungle if that were to happen.

The trail topped out on a saddleback clearing on the crest of a mountain in the highlands of northern Guatemala. At least, Yeager called it a mountain. To his Texas eyes, anything higher than a speed bump qualified as a mountain, though he was aware that opinions differed. Victor, who had flown helicopters throughout the Hindu Kush, argued that these were merely tall hills. That he expressed that opinion while huffing for breath did nothing to dilute his steadfast defense of his position. Yeager was sucking wind as well and would until his lungs gave up struggling for oxygen and got used to doing without.

"Hold up," Yeager said between heavy breaths. "I need a blow." He settled his butt on a rock outcropping. The altitude taxed his lungs and had fired up a headache that clamped his forehead in a vise. The cool humidity left him sweating buckets, and he fanned his shirt to unstick it from his body.

Victor plopped beside him and rested with his hands on his knees. "Pretty up here."

"Hmpfh." Yeager was grumpy, generally unhappy, and irritated enough to hit something but had nothing hittable in sight. So he clamped his mouth into a grim line and vowed to ignore the scenery. He rinsed his mouth with a swig of water and spat. "We should've gone to that jail, busted Cujo out the old-fashioned way. This here is bullshit."

Arturo wandered off a ways and settled at the base of a tree. He fired up a thin cigarillo, and soon clouds of white smoke swirled away from his face. During their trek into Guatemala, Arturo had spoken little, offering nothing beyond basic directions and a vague "not far" every time they had asked about their estimated arrival time. By Yeager's watch, they had been on the move for four hours, so "not far" obviously meant something different in Spanish than it did in English.

Yeager savored the cool breeze ruffling his shirt. It felt good on his overheated skin. "Hey." He nudged Por Que. "Who are the Zapatistas? Arturo called them Communists."

"Eh. Kind of." Victor shrugged a shoulder. "Not Communists like Russians or Chinese. Or like, you know, Hollywood actors." He pulled a frown and gazed across the green valley. "Remember, Mexico is more feudal than capitalist. Lords and serfs, like. There is no such thing as 'work hard and get ahead.' There's work hard and stay a peasant or be born rich and keep the boot down on the help. The Zapatistas are, like, fighting back against the oppression of the central government, who wants to keep the fat cats rich and the peasants poor. Sure, they're all about redistributing the wealth and all the Communist shit, but for people who've been crushed under the bootheel for centuries, they don't see that as a bad thing. So the Zapatistas are fighting back. And winning. They've done some good things. Built schools. Hospitals. They run a pretty good piece of Chiapas at the moment and will probably take more territory as the people get sick of being oppressed. Communism, democracy, capitalism are like labels here, right? Like a jockey's colors, y'know? They make it easy for the US and Russia and what-all to place their bets and follow their horses around the track. The jockeys, they don't care about the colors. All they want to do is win the race. But then, on the other hand, the Zapatistas may turn out to be like all the other Communists in the world, where everybody is equal except those in charge, and they get to be in charge."

Yeager signified he understood with a noise in the back of his throat. The politics of Latin America had always seemed to him to be a constant mashup of villainous rebels and evil overlords, their roles changing depending on the tidal shifts of power. Today's freedom fighter was tomorrow's oppressor, with the most righteous being the one with the most guns and the keys to the treasury. All of it was complicated by the cancerous festering sore of the cartels and their self-absorbed paranoia and relentless greed. He admitted to himself that his was a schoolboy's view of a complex and culturally driven mixture of issues, akin to the snake pit of the Middle East in the depth of its tribal and historical identity mixed with oppression, genocide, and competition for resources. Both regions of the world mystified Yeager and left him depressed at the future viability of the human race.

"You look like a bear with a mouthful of shit, don't know where to spit it out," Victor said. "What's up? You worried Charlie won't let you back in the house?"

"Man, I don't know if I even ought to try."

"What? What kinda shit you talkin', homeboy?"

Yeager waved off a bloated, buzzing fly. "She said something, before I left, kind of hit me, you know? She said trouble follows me, and when it catches up, it splashes all over her at the same time. Somewhat true, when you think about it. Hell, she first met me, she had to pull a gun on a guy who wanted to kill me. Then when that guy comes back around, he damn near gets her and the boy in the crossfire. Bad luck has been chasing us ever since... Hell, what kind of... I mean, what good does having me around do for her, except bring trouble to her door? Might be best if I stay away."

"Aw, man, don't say that." Victor's eyes crinkled with concern. "I been around you a long time, pendejo. I got to say, hooking on to that girl the best thing you ever did."

"Yeah." Yeager bobbed his head in resigned agreement. "But what if me being around gets her killed?"

Victor offered no comment, so Yeager swatted at ear-whining bugs and stewed on the thought of calling it quits with Charlie. His impression when leaving the house for this little Mexican adventure was that Charlie might not be opposed to the idea of leaving him. The thought of a future without her left Yeager feeling like he'd been rolled over by a giant boulder and left out in the sun too long.

Arturo stubbed out his cigarillo and made motions like he was getting ready to resume the trek.

Yeager hitched his chin in their guide's direction and spoke to Victor in a low voice. "Why the hell are we doing this? Are we really gonna cap some asshole we've never seen, like some James Bond assassin bullshit? I can shoot, but I ain't no sniper, and neither are you, which means we gotta get close to blow this sucker's lights out. Cold-blooded murder, man. I've done a lot of bad shit, but that's not a line I've ever crossed. And then we expect Mendoza to hold up his end of the deal?"

"Preach it, bro. Is boolsheet," Victor said in his banger accent. "Chu gotta devise a brilliant plan to get us outta this shit. You the tactical genius, man. I jus' drive the choppers."

"Genius?" Yeager snorted and spat. "Shee-it. If you're counting on my brains, we're in trouble for damn sure, amigo."

Arturo had finished getting to his feet. He brushed his butt off and said, "*Vamanos.*"

Yeager shook his head, his expression of disgust mirrored by his friend's. "Come on, chopper boy. Let's *vamanos*. Maybe I'll stumble on a brilliant plan by falling off this mountain."

"Hill, you mean."

"Whatever."

The rain did not fall. It slammed, pounded, slashed, and hammered. It did not build to its crescendo from a rumble of thunder to a drizzle to a shower to a deluge like a normal storm. Instead, the air went from cool and humid to underwater in the space of a few heartbeats. Victor, Arturo, and Yeager slipped and slopped along a trail so obscured by rainfall, they might as well have been trying to navigate a mudslide on foot while being sprayed by fire hoses. Schlitterbahn of Guatemala. Water gushed around their feet and threatened to wash all of them downhill with one wrongly placed foot.

"Let's get under cover!" Yeager shouted.

"What cover?" Victor yelled back.

And he had a point. The valley floor was more than a mile away. The path wound down the flank of a mountain, with the bulk of the rise somewhere off to their left. They might be fifty yards from shelter, or five thousand—there was no way to know since visibility was near zero. The profusion of broad-leaf trees offered no protection from the downpour. Their branches acted more like flails as they whipped around in gusty winds. Taking a chance on finding a cave or overhang would require them to leave the trail and cut their way through the hip-high vegetation crowding the path toward the hillside, with no guarantee of success and a good chance of getting lost.

Their guide had forged ahead, recklessly ignorant of the treacherous footing or actively wishing to die by waterslide. Arturo's potato shape wobbled along ten yards farther down the trail. With the start of the rain, Mendoza's man had begun a litany of curses in three languages, varying in volume, inventiveness, and combination of ways in which one could copulate with farm animals. His voice trailed behind him, reaching Yeager's ears in fits and snatches of vivid description.

Yeager spotted the side trail by virtue of slipping and falling on his ass. Invisible in the bent-over grass from above, the narrow path through the foliage revealed itself when Yeager butt-planted with a splash right next to it.

"Hey! Arturo!" he yelled. "Back here!"

Victor clamped Yeager under the arm to haul him upright. "What is it?"

"A trail toward the mountain." Yeager pointed. "See? May lead to something. We should check it out!"

"*¿Por que no?* Nothing else, we need to quit slip-sliding away."

Arturo appeared reluctant when he made it back uphill and Yeager showed him the trail. Water dripped off their guide's barnacled nose, and his wide lips pinched into an expression of distaste.

"We should keep going," Arturo said in Spanish. "There is no time to go exploring."

"We keep going down this trail," Yeager argued, "one of us is going to break an ankle. We need to hole up till this rain stops." He didn't trust his border Spanish, so to Victor, he said, "Tell him so he gets it."

"We. Get. Off. Fucking. Trail," Victor said in loud, emphatic English.

Arturo remained skeptical but must have sensed the argument was lost. With a shrug, the round man led the way. A crack of nearby lightning lit the mountainside, and thunder banged like a cannon shot. The rain fell harder, as heavy as bullets, striking with almost painful force.

Yeager kept his head down and forged ahead. The dark bulk of the mountain reared up from the gloom, rising past the treetops, shrouded in misty sheets of rain. Goo sucked at his feet, though on level ground, the footing was more solid. For a time, they walked single file behind Arturo. The man's round body and bandy legs belied his ability to hump a trail faster than either Marine veteran, which was beginning to chap Yeager's ass. The combination of altitude and unaccustomed exercise was eating his lunch. Behind him, the muscular Victor Ruiz seemed equally bushed. The pilot flashed Yeager a tired grin when he checked over his shoulder.

Victor scrambled up and yelled in Yeager's ear, "I'm not sure which is worse: here or Buttfuckistan."

"Oh, definitely the Stan. At least here, no one's shooting at us."

The staccato burst of an automatic weapon rippled out of the darkness. Yeager's head jerked up in time to see Arturo fall backward, his arms windmilling. Another stutter of fire flared through the rain. Bullets whip-cracked as they flew past. Yeager spun off the trail, snagging a fist in Victor's shirt on the way past. Both men tumbled into the bracken and sought oneness with the earth. Mud splashed in Yeager's face, and the familiar taste of dirt overrode the coppery electric alarm that flooded his mouth.

The firing stopped. A man's voice called out. Another answered. Yeager lay in the scrub and strained his hearing over the sound of pummeling rain. He met Victor's eyes. His friend's expression very clearly said, *You had to open your mouth and jinx it.* Yeager shrugged with his face. *It's not my fault.*

A single shot cracked out. Yeager placed the sound as coming from the sheer side of the cliff ahead of them, about the place where Arturo had gone down. *A coup de grâce? Or a probing shot?*

Yeager mentally shrugged. It didn't matter. Evasion was their only option, as they had no weapons and no intel about the opposing force.

Men called back and forth. At least two voices, for sure. Yeager caught Victor's eye and motioned with a twitch of his head. *Let's get out of here.*

Victor nodded. He started crawling, veering off to his right in a wide circle. Yeager stayed on Victor's heels, belly in the muck. They snaked through prickly, saw-toothed scrub that offered little concealment, relying on the heavy shroud of rainfall to remain hidden.

After six full minutes of hard crawling, Yeager tapped Victor's foot to get his attention. He pointed to the thick cover of a low-growing bush, its dinner-plate leaves drooping from the rain. The plant sprawled over an area as wide as a king-sized bed. Victor nodded and slithered through the mud to reach the concealment offered by the massive bush. Silently, Yeager prayed no other Guatemalan beasts sheltered beneath the plant, as it looked to be a great place to hide a tub of snakes, a basket of poisonous spiders, and a face-eating monster or two. He eased his way under the concealing leaves, poised to squirrel away at the first sign of something wriggling in his direction. Yeager would face men with guns any day, but wrestling a rattlesnake did not appeal.

Yeager settled next to Victor, close enough to feel his body heat and smell the damp odor of wet exertion radiating off his friend. From under the dripping leaves, they had a clear view of the side trail they had followed to get away from the main downhill path. It remained empty. As yet, none of the gunmen had backtracked along the path to determine if Arturo had been alone, which Yeager considered poor operational security.

The rain tapered off moments later, as though someone had finished wringing out the clouds. A few last drops pelted the ground, then it stopped.

"What the fuck just happened?" Victor asked, his voice at a gnat's whisper.

Yeager shrugged and tamped his hand in a "hold still" gesture. A minute later, the expected security element appeared. A Latin male in his early twenties swaggered into view, wearing a straw cowboy hat and a green poncho over civilian clothes. He carried a stubby HK UMP submachine gun propped on his hip. The man paused and surveyed the area casually, as if he owned the hillside and everything on it. Another man appeared behind the first, older and more weathered looking, though just as arrogant. This one wore a serape and held a dun-colored FN SCAR in a loose crossbody carry, his finger inside the trigger guard. Yeager winced at the lack of trigger discipline. The two gunmen acted like village idiots out for a stroll with lethal weapons.

Maybe we'll get lucky and they'll both slip, shoot themselves in the head.

The fetid, damp earth filled Yeager's nose with a weedy, organic smell. The bray of a donkey pealed out in the near distance. Water dripped off the leaves, pattering onto Yeager's neck and squiggling across every exposed nerve from ear to collarbone. He held still and watched as the two men lollygagged around in an uninspired patrol of the surrounding area. They appeared in no hurry to leave, while at the same time remaining oblivious to any other intruders. Yeager felt good about his concealment. All they had to do was stay quiet and—

A prick of burning pain stabbed Yeager's chest, followed by another on his ribcage, then two more down near his belly. Yeager bit his lip to stifle the surprised hiss of pain. The tickling sensation of things crawling under his shirt frizzled across his skin. Cautiously, slowly, gritting his teeth against a sensation like hot coals burning his body, Yeager lifted himself on an elbow. In the impression left by his body in the moist soil roiled a supernova of disturbed ants. Victor looked over and recoiled in silent dismay. He inched backward from the expanding colony of angry devil ants, while Yeager, repeatedly stung by those trapped under his shirt, could only grit his teeth and endure. Any sudden movement would reveal their position to the gunmen. He could only watch as the ants expanded outward in an angry mass of incandescent fury, crawling ever closer to the Yeager-sized threat looming above them.

The serape-wearing man with the SCAR ambled closer and paused, one foot touching the outermost leaves of the bush under which Yeager and Victor hid. The sour smell of the man's unwashed body drifted down to where Yeager lay awkwardly propped on his elbow. Two more ants dug their poisonous fangs into Yeager's flesh, one under the arm and one up by his collarbone. The damn things were all over him, and they were righteously pissed. Each bite felt like a lit cigarette crushed into skin. Yeager held himself rigid and clenched his eyes shut against the assault. Every muscle was locked solid, and breathing was out of the question. His left elbow ached with the effort of holding himself upright, out of the mass of ants spreading from their nest.

It's just bug bites, he told himself. *They won't kill you. The guy with the gun will kill you.*

He watched the man's boot and waited.

Blanca Trevejo entered the National Palace of Guatemala on the arm of Thad Breem, the US Embassy's Deputy Assistant Undersecretary for Agriculture. Or something like that. Blanca had a hard time keeping the various diplomats' titles straight, let alone how they were situated in the embassy food chain. Mr. Breem had been underwhelmed when directed by his superiors to squire a junior clerk from the commerce department to the new administration's inaugural ball. The embassy people had pretty good radar concerning who was CIA and who was not, and like many on the regular embassy staff, Thad avoided spooks like they had leprosy. He was obviously not thrilled at having to provide cover for a spy, as he had not spoken six words since they climbed into the embassy limo. Every time casual action brought them close, he squirmed away from touching her, as if some secret spy dust would rub off on him.

On top of his spook aversion, Blanca was pretty sure Thad batted for the other team. She wasn't the most stunning of women, by her own admission, but if Thad was heterosexual, he should have at least once checked out her cleavage, modest though it was.

Which is a good thing, Blanca decided. *The last thing I need is to fend off a horny preppie while trying to be a super spy.*

She wore a bare-backed dress snug around the hips, with a V-front that showed enough of her skin to be eye-catching without being scandalous. Its butterfly sleeves were long enough to hide the four-day-old road rash scrapes on her right shoulder. It also concealed the bruises on her ribs and the raked-finger marks on her hips where Waldo's nails had scratched her. The memory of the attack floated near the surface of her conscious mind, twenty-four seven, ready to pounce lest she fail to remain vigilant.

Blanca glanced at her own lacquered nails, something she had started doing every few minutes since scrubbing her hands of Waldo's blood, sure that somehow she had missed a speck that would be spotted by some sharp-eyed cop and send her right to jail. She recognized the nervous tic for what it was.

Stop it. Your hands are clean. Washed that damn spot right out.

As she and Thad circulated through the ballroom of glittering people, Blanca played the part of his arm candy, the bright but vapid Juanita Alvares. Thad was an embassy-issue weenie, Grade Two, minted from the factory at Yale that mass produced State Department functionaries. Tall and toothpaste-ad handsome, the Deputy Assistant Underthingy made a perfect cover, as his job was exactly what it said on his business card. A bright, overeducated young man, Thad wanted only to help the poor coffee farmers of Guatemala learn how to grow sustainable and organic beans and market them in the United States. He would never be mistaken for a spook by the Guatemalan surveillance teams. Perfect camouflage. As his date, using her Juanita Alvares cover, she was free to hunt the jungle of the inaugural ball for possible assets without standing out like a jaguar in a black slinky dress.

The only person she wanted to avoid was Marisol. If spotted, Blanca would have to invoke a cover story about meeting Thad during a visit to her bosses at the coffee export company where she presumably worked. She would have to spin a tale where the definitely *not gay* man had successfully fallen for her charms and asked her to be his "plus one" at Modena's inaugural ball. *"Isn't it all soooo exciting! Yes, such a small world, isn't it?"*

Ugh. It would strain even Marisol's credulity.

But the hint about El Escorpión meeting with Modena had been too tempting to pass up. Blanca had to follow up that lead, even if it meant potentially arousing her asset's suspicion.

Now, standing next to Thad as he tried out his prep school Spanish on some agri-business contact of his, Blanca shivered as the reality of what she was attempting sank home. She had to assume the PNC national police or the D-2, Guatemalan military intelligence, had photographed her entering and exiting the embassy, forever connecting her with the US government, should someone care enough to connect the dots. Someone of Gustaffson's power would no doubt have hooks into both those organizations. Come to think of it, if the guys in the Range Rover belonged to Gustaffson, which seemed likely, there was good money on his security chief already having a file with her face on it. One raised eyebrow inside Gustaffson's organization, and Blanca might as well cut her own throat.

Relying on not tickling the paranoia of one of the top criminal warlords in the hemisphere had struck her as sane a plan as walking down the dark alleys of Zone 3 without a gun.

Someone laughed, a giggly, high-pitched hyena cackle that shook Blanca out of her thoughts. She blinked her focus onto the here and now. *Get on with the mission. Ignore the fuzzy worms of doubt crawling up your spine, girl.*

Finely dressed people did the diplomatic disco in knots and whirls of color across the red-and-gold tiled floor of the Palacio Nacional de la Cultura's ballroom, reminding Blanca of bees dancing on a honeycomb. Golden light filled the domed room from a massive center chandelier, aided by rings of sconces mounted on Corinthian columns around the perimeter. Flickers of laughter sparkled through the sound of chattering people.

The agri-baron turned from Thad and spoke to her directly for the first time. "And you, miss? What do you think of your young man's suggestion to use beneficial insects instead of pesticides on our coffee crops?"

Blanca plastered on the vapid look of a mental lightweight. "Bugs? Ew, I don't like bugs."

"Me neither!" The man favored her with a patronizing laugh and tried sneaking a glance down her dress.

Thad's smile seemed a little forced. He snagged two champagne flutes from a passing waiter and handed her one. She allowed a drop to touch her lips and surveyed the crowd like a bored nitwit.

There.

A tingle zipped through Blanca's nerve endings. Not thirty feet away, flanked by a pair of security goons and encircled by fawning supplicants, stood Herman Gustaffson, immaculate, urbane, and obviously wealthy. In a room full of black suits, El Escorpión carried off his cream tuxedo and dark-red bowtie with grace that a lesser man would find hard to emulate. Gustaffson's attitude proclaimed he had no patience for following convention, and he would wear what he damn well pleased. His bearing radiated gravitas. Dignity. Demand for respect. He was the black hole around which lighter, lesser bodies orbited.

His money man, Milosh Jovanovic, hovered nearby with a glass of sparkling water. From the thin file, Blanca had gleaned little about Jovanovic, other than he was a Serbian ex-pat who'd cut his teeth laundering money for Slobodan Milošević's regime before being forced to flee the country after his former boss fell from grace. Rumored to be a non-drinker, a non-smoker, and asexual, the man's myopic focus appeared to be solely on the flow of currency in its various incarnations and derivatives. Blanca speculated that he probably masturbated over a spreadsheet with a perfect pivot table. Jovanovic never strayed far from Gustaffson's side.

Hanging on Gustaffson's arm—much the way Blanca was pretending to hang on Thad's—lounged the Scorpion's trophy fuck. Supermodel-thin, with vaguely Russian features, the eye candy wore a red silk dinner napkin held up by her gravity-defying breasts. Of all the possible approaches Blanca could make, Ms. Boobsalot might be the best choice, assuming the woman left the arm of her sugar daddy long enough for Blanca to engage her in conversation.

Blanca had a lot of blanks to fill in about Gustaffson's operation. She needed to get onto his property in the hills in order to start coloring in the empty spots, yet security was tight, as she had observed firsthand. She needed to know who hired the staff, who ran security, who did the catering, who supplied the hookers... the list was long.

Her boss, Hunter, appeared unwilling to fight the internal battle and expend personal capital by sticking out his lily-white neck to demand the kind of agency resources it would take to employ long-range surveillance tools. He'd left it up to her to somehow get close enough to the mansion to plant some key listening devices or suborn someone on the oligarch's staff to inform on his boss's relationship with Modena.

Mission, meet Impossible.

As if on cue, the tall Russian woman leaned over and whispered something in Gustaffson's ear. The Scorpion made a dismissive gesture, his focus remaining on the over-decorated general standing in front of him. The rich man's trophy swayed off toward the arched doorway leading to the toilets. Every male eye within a twenty-foot radius followed her rolling hips as though magnetized.

Blanca squeezed Thad's arm to get his attention. "Excuse me, but I'll be right back."

He flashed her a tight smile, seemingly happy to be rid of her, and returned to his riveting conversation about this month's rainfall predictions for the highlands and what it would mean for the young green coffee cherries destined for winter harvest.

Blanca stalked after her prey, a sleek jaguar in a jungle full of danger.

My name is Bond. Jane Bond.

CHAPTER ELEVEN

Serape Man hawked and spat. He seemed in no hurry to move. Yeager held himself rigid, not daring to breathe or flinch, even when an ant found a new and tender spot to bite the shit out of him. Truly, he was seriously considering launching out of the bush and making a play for the guy with the gun, going so far as to rehearse the series of moves in his head. Jump up, tear through the vegetation, reach Serape Man and punch his lights out faster than the man could pivot and fire.

At least it would be over quick. Not stung to death by an army of angry ants.

If he attacked, Victor would take it as a cue to do the same, and with the likelihood of success being lower than worm crap, the risk was too great. Any move he made would get them both killed. Yeager gritted his teeth, clenched his eyes shut, and dreamed of sitting by his pond with a fishing pole.

Men called out, and more donkeys brayed. Yeager risked a look through slitted eyes. Serape Man moved away, heading toward a pack train of six donkeys and at least three other men. Each of the donkeys carried a canvas-wrapped pack the size of a steamer trunk. The young Latin with the UMP walked point, while a withered grandpa led the animals, followed by a middle-aged man in a broad-brimmed hat. Serape Man fell in as the last donkey passed, taking up the rear security position.

Yeager held his pose until Serape Man disappeared from sight. He allowed in a lungful of air and let it out, fighting the urge to move. *Take it easy. Count to one hundred.*

Victor mimed crawling out, and Yeager shook him off with a tiny movement of his head. *No. Stay put.* Sweat tickled his ribs.

Twelve... thirteen... fourteen...

Bird calls trilled. Wet trees showered the ground as a breeze shook water from their leaves. Yeager listened to his heartbeat and counted the seconds off in his head. The ant bites on his torso burned, and more of the angry little bugs hunted fresh patches of skin. One ant had burrowed into his waistband and was biting the *hell* out of his hip.

Twenty-six... twenty-seven... twenty-eight-nine-thirty... fuck it.

Yeager squirmed away from the enraged nest of ants, wiggling backward to a minimum safe distance before pausing to rake his palms over the itchy spots tormenting him. He eased onto his back and scraped his skin with clumps of wet, wadded shirt to crush anything moving on his chest and sides.

Victor worked his way over and pitched his voice to carry low and quiet. "Damn, ese. You need help?"

Yeager shook him off and gestured downhill. *Follow me.*

Low-crawling through the brush, Yeager put another fifty yards between him and the pack train of mules and their guards. Only then did he sit upright and shrug out of his shirt.

"Holy bug bite, Batman," Victor groaned with a sympathetic wince. "That must hurt like hell."

"It ain't rainbows and unicorns. Check my back, would ya?"

Sound traveled in the mountains, so they kept their voices pitched barely above a whisper. Yeager counted sixteen angry, puffy welts on his torso, along with countless crushed ant parts smeared in streaks across his skin. He also found three surviving ants, which he terminated with extreme prejudice.

"Your back's clear, homeboy," Victor said. "Don't ask me to check nothing down south. Your hairy white ass is the last thing I want to see right now."

With the last of the ants dispatched, Yeager leaned over, elbows on knees, and tried to collect himself. The echo of creepy-crawly things roaming his body remained with him, forcing him to check every tickle with care.

"You know," Victor said, "I heard of drug mules before, but I thought that was, like, a metaphor or something. I didn't think they used mules for real."

"Donkeys," Yeager corrected.

"Don't be an ass." Victor paused and cocked a lopsided grin. "I bet nobody is as *ant-eye*-drug as you are right now."

Yeager groaned.

"Too soon?"

"We better go check on Arturo," Yeager said.

"I'm pretty sure he's dead, bro. He walked right up on a bunch of druggies and took a full-auto facial."

"You better hope not. He was the only one who knew where we were going."

For Milton "Cujo" Quattlebaum, the day started out as just another day in a Mexican prison. Wake up in a four-person cell surrounded by seven other inmates. Take a leak in the semi-functional single toilet. Follow the smell of grilling tortillas and boiling refritos to the cell block dining hall. Wander into the yard for a game of cards or a walk around the perimeter. Some of the guys played cutthroat soccer, which was meant to be gringo free. Cujo had tried to join in once and needed medical treatment after ten minutes.

There was not a lot of structure inside the prison. The whole thing felt more like living in the projects of Chicago, except with a big fence around it. Anything could be had, for the right price. Booze, dope, women, stereos, TVs, good food—nothing was off limits. Everybody, of course, was cliqued up for protection, as the guard presence was minimal and investigations of assault laughable. One of the cell blocks was run by MS-13 guys, who lorded around like they owned the place. It would not surprise Cujo one bit if that was actually true. Prison life certainly seemed to bring them no hardship.

So far, all the bangers had left him pretty much alone, and Cujo figured Mendoza still had the fix in with whoever ran the inmates in this asylum. That meant Victor and Yeager were still in play. Cujo thanked God, Yahweh, Buddha, Muhammad, and Britney Spears every day for the loyalty of those two particular Marines. They made a good trio, Cujo and those guys. Like the Three Musketeers, but with automatic weapons.

The day took a turn when one of the runners—young men who hung out near the central admin complex and picked up tips for running errands—found Cujo at his favorite picnic table.

"Hey, man," the kid announced. "They want you over at the main gate."

"A visitor?" Cujo's heart jumped. It had been some time since Victor had visited, bringing with him hope and the chance to dream of a life with something better than tortillas and beans for breakfast.

"How the fuck do I know, puta gringo? Go see Sergeant Gutierrez at the main gate. That's it, end of message." The kid sneered and held out his hand.

"They already paid you to deliver the message," Cujo said.

"I know, but I could have done it tomorrow."

Cujo blinked at the twisted tenses of that sentence, dug a crumpled dollar bill—one of his last—from his pocket, and handed it over. "Live long and prosper, amigo."

"Go fuck yourself."

In the main gate building, Sergeant Gutierrez had another surprise, one that shocked Cujo to his toes.

"You are to be released today."

Cujo goggled. "Say what?"

"You are leaving, pendejo," the sergeant said. The man stood all of five-five in boots and was wrapped tighter than packing tape. He ruled his roost from behind a chipped and stained linoleum-topped desk. The only decoration on the desk was a pair of small crossed flags, one of Mexico and the other of the state of Baja.

"I'm leaving?"

"Sí."

"Just like that? What about a trial and shit?"

The sergeant steepled his fingers and growled, "Get your things and get back here, muy pronto, or I might forget who you are."

Cujo lifted his arms to indicate his prison jumpsuit. "This is pretty much all I got. The medicos cut away my clothes, and you issued me this when you checked me into this fine hotel."

Gutierrez twisted his lips as if he had swallowed a hard-shelled bug. After a pause, he dropped a clipboard onto the counter. "Fine. Sign here. And here, and here, and here."

The rest of the process passed quickly, as in, there was no more process. Cujo signed where indicated then guards opened the cage doors and pointed where to go. Footsteps leaden with dread that it was all a big joke, Cujo walked where he was directed to walk, stopped when directed to stop, and somehow moved from the inside of the prison through a series of locked partitions to a room of green-painted ugliness. A line of visitors filed past on his left, signing in and receiving their visitor chits. The final gate stood open, sunshine lighting the entrance like a beacon of hope. Cujo hesitated, waiting for the shoe to drop and the guards to grab him by the scruff and drag him back inside. His instinctive and well-nurtured paranoia kicked into overdrive.

This is where they shoot me "trying to escape."

Cujo twisted in place, checking his six. The guards stared back at him with blank expressions of pure boredom. The one standing by the gate rolled his hand and cursed him in Spanish to get moving. The visitors shuffling past ignored him.

None of the guards carried firearms, though Cujo discounted that as a smokescreen. *It'll be somebody on the wall.* In the prison movies, there was always a guy on the wall with a scoped rifle. The dumbass prisoner walks out, full of sunshine and hope, tasting freedom for the first time in years. Ominous music swells. Cut scene to a uniformed thug with a nasty expression and a .308 zooming in through the reticle. *Boom.* Dead convict.

"Move, pendejo," the guard by the gate said.

Cujo swiped his forehead with a sleeve, wicking off about a gallon of sweat. With the stiff-legged walk of a man kneed in the nuts, Cujo moved through the final gate and into the sunlight. He shielded his eyes with a crooked arm and spotted a dried cactus of a man standing by a dusty Ford pickup parked by the curb. The man wore a stained straw cowboy hat, a plaid shirt, jeans so old they were white, and down-at-the-heel boots. His craggy, weathered face could have been carved from a block of oak by a chainsaw.

"You Cujo?" the man called out.

A severe panic was building in Cujo's heart. He tried looking in every direction at once. The guard towers at the corners held particular interest. *Is the shot coming from there? Or is this cowboy the guy who's gonna kill me? How's he know my name? Why would they send a vaquero?*

"You fren send me," the man by the truck said with a heavy Spanish accent. "Por Que. Por Que and Señor Yeager."

More people flowed past Cujo as he stood rooted just outside the prison gate—wives, mothers, and families with children. Some glanced at him in passing, though most ignored him, not wanting to be potential witnesses. Learning to look the other way was a life skill in Mexico these days.

Cujo eyeballed the guy by the truck. "And who are you?"

"Rudy Aguilar," the skinny guy said. He stepped forward and offered his hand. "*Trabajo para* Don de la Cueva."

The name meant nothing to Cujo. He shrugged.

"The Don, he is the one arranged for your release." Aguilar rubbed his fingers and thumb in the age-old gesture for money. "And Señor Yeager, he say if we got you out, to tell you, 'Semper fi, you Army puke.'"

A wave of relief washed through Cujo so powerfully that it almost buckled his knees. He smiled for the first time since Christmas. Yeager had said that very thing the last time Cujo saw him. It was right after delivering Victor and Yeager to an airstrip in Texas after having pulled their asses out of a firefight near Monterrey.

"Semper fi, you Army puke," Yeager had told him. "You ever need anything, man, I'll come. All you gotta do is call."

Cujo's grin threatened to split the skin of his dry lips. "Well, hell, Rudy. You should've led with that." He stayed near the prison wall, though, hesitating before saying, "Can you pull your truck any closer? I don't want to give the guards in the tower a good shot."

CHAPTER TWELVE

Arturo stared at the ground as if mesmerized by the composition of the soil. Flies droned in lazy holding patterns around his body, waiting for clearance to land. The stink of blood and bowels weighed heavy on the air. Both substances leaked from holes, natural and unnatural, in their guide's body.

"Think he's dead?" Victor asked. "He looks dead."

A defeated sigh escaped Yeager. "Help me with this." He tugged the straps of Arturo's backpack off one shoulder, then the other as Victor rolled the body to assist. A search of the dead man's pockets turned up a small wad of mixed currency—mostly US dollars—a pocketknife, a box of matches, and a blood-soaked pack of Marlboro Reds. From the backpack, Yeager recovered a simple flip phone. He powered it up. No signal. A single number had been preprogrammed into the contact list. No name given, simply the initial *M*.

"Huh," Yeager grunted. "What's the country code for Mexico?"

"Fifty-two."

Yeager handed the phone to Victor. "Mendoza, you think?"

"Or, you know, the head of MI-6."

Yeager looked blank.

"James Bond?" Victor asked. "Got all them initial people... M, Q... Like that? No? Man, you gotta watch some movies now and again."

"No signal," Yeager said. "We need to get out of these hills. Find civilization."

"Forward or backward?" Victor asked, meaning should they continue the mission and try to reach Mendoza's contacts in Guatemala without their guide or return to Mexico and call it done. Victor tucked the phone into a pocket of his jeans.

The sky had turned brilliant blue, with only a few puffy clouds drifting overhead. Despite the mild temperature, the sun baked the hillside and humidity soaked the air. They moved away from Arturo and found a patch of bare, damp rock to sit on. Yeager rooted through Arturo's backpack for bottles of water. He kept one and handed the other to Victor.

"If we give up…" Yeager tested the idea as he formed the words. "If we head back to Mexico… what's the downside? We can try to convince Mendoza it can't be done. See if he'll back off his threat to feed our families to Gustaffson and his sicarios." He left it there, knowing Victor would pick up the trail.

"Mendoza," Victor said. "He don't seem the reasoning type."

"Then let's say he goes through with his threat and tattles on us. Gives us up as these half-assed assassins, out to kill Gustaffson…"

"And the Scorpion sends his real, no-shit assassins after Alexandra. Or Charlie and the boys."

"Which means we have to be on guard, twenty-four seven. Waiting for an attack." Yeager added no weight to the statement, not good and not bad. It just was what it was.

"Hard to do," Victor said, equally flat. "And Cujo's still in jail."

"Unless de la Cueva can do something."

"True."

"But protecting our people, that's on us."

Victor sniffed, tipped back his water for a long swallow. "What if… You think we could reach this Gustaffson? Reason with him? Tell him it's all bullshit?"

Yeager poured water over his chest, momentarily cooling the bug bites. The welts had started to lose some of their fire, but he was far from comfortable. The sun beat down on his bare shoulders. Yeager pulled his shirt on, hearing Charlie's voice in his head warning him about skin cancer. He left it open in front to avoid contact with the angry spots on his chest and belly.

"We would have to reach Gustaffson before we tell Mendoza the deal's off," Yeager said.

"Before Mendoza sends his little packet of joy."

"We still have to worry about Cujo."

"That is true," Victor admitted. He scratched his chin and stared off into the distance. "That prison's pretty loose. We could smuggle him in a nail file. 'Cept, knowing Cujo, he'd probably use it on his nails."

"And have the prettiest hands in prison."

"If I only had a helicopter..."

"We're not trying a jailbreak," Yeager growled.

"Man, when did you get to be such an adult?"

"Come on." Yeager got to his feet, brushing off the seat of his pants. "Let's get out of these hills. I need some calamine lotion and a beer, or just a beer. We can think about how to approach Gustaffson while we walk."

"Really?" Victor's eyebrows shot up. "You can do two things at once now?"

The whipcrack of a bullet snapped the air next to Yeager's head. He dove and tackled Victor, rolling both of them deeper into the brush. More bullets zipped in, cutting leaves and slapping the dirt.

Victor howled as the thin burn of a near-miss scorched his bicep. He scrambled after Yeager, who was belly-crawling away like a scalded badger.

"The druggies!" Yeager yelled over his shoulder. "They must have doubled back."

"What the fuck? Man, that ain't fair!"

"Move it, Marine." Yeager paused to push Victor ahead of him. "Keep low and keep moving."

"Roger-fucking-that."

A staccato burst of fire raked the brush to their left. Another probed right. One more burst would send a lead enema right up his ass. Yeager slithered between two rocks, dragging his bare belly through the muck, scraping his flesh like sandpaper. Firing paused for a moment, and the sound of two men calling out rolled across the hillside. They were coordinating their approach.

Damn, but what I wouldn't give to have a firearm in my hands right this minute. Anything from a .22 Woodsman to a .50-cal Barrett would be fine. Something more lethal than his command of foul language and a swinging cock.

Yeager clawed at the earth for momentum and thought about becoming a mole.

The men with the rifles came closer.

Khayyat Halabi did not like this place. He found sleep hard to come by this night. Halabi stared at the darkened ceiling and recited a *rakat* in his head, though he had completed the full *salat al-'isha* only an hour before.

Glorified be you, all praise is yours, perfect is your name, most high is your majesty and greatness. None has the right to be worshiped but you, the only one God.

He and his brethren were quartered in a wing of their host's enormous house in the hills of Guatemala, waiting for the transportation that would see them over the border into Mexico then on to their final destination in the United States.

As guests of the infidel, Halabi held his tongue and tried to keep the contempt from his face. But the obscene luxury of the infidel's mansion offended him. Soft beds with cotton sheets so fine, they caressed the skin. Fine art on the walls. Food served on delicate plates and tea poured from silver carafes into crystal glasses. A television screen that was bigger than a tribal chieftain's carpet hung from the room's focal point.

There were porcelain toilets with running water and rolls of paper for wiping. The third time their guide and keeper, a soul-shriven infidel called Fidel, had been forced to lecture them on the use of this paper and the flushing mechanism, the hothead Mahfouz had taken offense and nearly killed the man. Only swift intervention by Halabi had prevented an incident that might have jeopardized the mission long before they reached the Great Satan.

Though they were packed in four to a room, the accommodations were so far beyond anything the freedom fighters had known, it made them uncomfortable and edgy. Months of training in Western ways had done little to prepare Halabi for the reality of such abominations, things the people of this fortified enclave took for granted.

Halabi held his temper in check with prayer. *I seek Allah's shelter from Satan, the condemned. Allah grant me the serenity to continue in Your service and allow me the strength to ignore these seductions of Satan.*

To reinforce his commitment, Halabi slept on the floor. He used the toilet but wiped as a proper man should. He ate the food provided and watched the depravity on the big-screen television, all the while encasing himself in the armor of Allah's will through constant prayer.

They at least had proper *sajjāda*. Their host had provided the prayer rugs for the short time the fighters would be quartered at the mansion, a gesture much appreciated by Halabi and his brethren. Thank Allah, their time here would not be much longer. According to Fidel, they would be moved to a city in the middle of the country, where they would await the next stage. The timing of their journey depended upon entering a migrant caravan for the trek through Mexico.

As Fidel explained it, twelve brown faces in a sea of brown faces would not stand out, despite the obvious differences in bone structure and facial characteristics between Arabs and Hispanics. Halabi didn't bother trying to point out that only four of the group were Arab. Five were Persian, one was a Turk, and one Pakistani. He, himself, was a Pashtun from Afghanistan. He agreed with Fidel in principle, having seen the ignorance of the Americans firsthand while fighting in the Helmand Province. The average infidel soldier couldn't tell a Turk from a dog tick, let alone distinguish a true Persian from a lowly Mexican.

Soon they will know my face.

Halabi allowed himself a smile of grim satisfaction. Soon his face, and the faces of his brothers, would be as famous as Atta, the al-Shehri brothers, and al-Omari. They would be on Al Jazeera, CNN, and BBC.

The missions had been carefully selected. Weapons and explosives procured. Truckloads of ammonium nitrate and fuel oil gathered with meticulous patience and great cunning. Once across the border, Halabi and his eleven fellow warriors of Allah would melt into the underbelly of the Great Satan, aided by willing hands in various cities. Each target was unique. Each fighter had been briefed on his mission and none other, so if one were caught, the remaining eleven would continue without fear of apprehension. Halabi was destined to achieve martyrdom in the city of Arlington, Texas, on a Christian day of worship, on a specific Sunday. He would drive a gleaming bus filled with explosives into the main entrance of an iconic sporting stadium. One hundred thousand people would be in attendance, paying homage to American football. With Allah's blessing, the deaths of infidels would number as the stars in the sky.

At last, Halabi drifted into sleep, a faint smile etching his face.

The miles rolled by, and Cujo relaxed as much as he was capable of relaxing. He harbored a few lingering doubts about his rescuer, Rudy Aguilar, though the man's invocation of Yeager's specific language had gone a long way to turning down the heat on his raging suspicion. The pickup truck was as much work truck as transportation; tools and bits of gear rattled in the bed, and there was no air conditioning. They rode with the windows down. A hot, dry wind buffeted the interior, which Cujo didn't mind at all. The stink of jail clung to him like a fever sweat, and the air rushing through the windows scoured it from his skin.

It felt good to be free.

Was he free, though? The sudden reversal of fortune struck Cujo as too good to be true. Yeager's code word or not, he didn't know this guy Rudy Aguilar from Adam's left nut. He could be a mass murderer, a part of the cartel Cujo helped blow up a few months back. Could be, the cartel boys had sprung him from jail so they could torture him in private.

Cujo cleared his throat. "Um, where're we headed?"

"To *la hacienda* of Don de la Cueva." Aguilar drove with one hand draped over the wheel. Somehow his straw hat stayed firmly affixed to his head, despite the heavy wind buffeting the inside of the cab.

"And, uh, what happens there?"

Aguilar shrugged as if the matter held little interest and less concern. "We will try to reach Yeager and Ruiz. Call them off."

"What about my legal situation?" Cujo asked.

"The only charges were for entering the country illegally. The Don's attorneys made the deal with the prosecutors." Aguilar shrugged again. "You are free to go."

"Entering the country illegally..." Now Cujo knew the guy was lying. "What about blowing up a bunch of thugs with air-to-ground missiles? What about flying a homemade warplane into Mexican air-space?"

Aguilar slanted a look at him. "No witnesses."

"Say what?"

"All were Grupo Verdugo. *Muy malo hombres*. Or the villagers, who no want to... ah, *testificar*?"

"Testify?"

"Sí."

"So there's no case?"

"Sí. I mean, no."

"So what about all that bullshit Mendoza said to my buddy, Victor?"

Aguilar's nut-brown face hardened, and he cut a grim look that sent a shiver down Cujo's spine. "Don de la Cueva has, ah, *muchas conexiones en el gobierno. El Presidente. Generales de la Armada. Oficiales del gobierno.* All have looked."

"And?" Cujo prompted.

"There is no Capitán Mendoza in the CFE."

Yeager had never felt the compulsion shared by some of his friends to carry a firearm every day of the week. Right at that moment, he was seriously reconsidering that position. *What did they call déjà vu? Same shit, different day.*

How many times would he have to run through the damn jungle, dodging bullets without a way to fight back, before he learned his lesson? Given his experience of the past few months, from Hawaii to Guatemala, he would be damned if he ever left home without a weapon again. From now on he was going to be like, *Why carry a pistol? Because an AR won't fit down my pants.*

A deadly chunk of lead zip-cracked so close to his cheek, its heat scorched his whiskers. Yeager belly-flopped into a gully carved into the hillside by years of runoff. Leafy vegetation covered the cut like a canopy. It was dim and dank under the leaves, heavy with moisture and buzzing with hungry mosquitoes. He splashed into the muck; it splattered his face, and he tasted mud. Yeager wiggled deeper into the water-filled cleft, slipping and sliding downstream like a lost salmon.

He had split off from Victor several minutes earlier, deliberately crashing through the brush and making enough noise to sound like a herd of buffalo. The plan had been a success. The drug runners were hot on his trail, running him down with excited shouts and near-misses.

They're following me! Yay, I win.

The cleft joined a deeper cut, and the trickle of water merged with a heavier flow. Yeager kept his butt down and eeled into the new stream, allowing the water to carry him downhill. Confused shouts echoed around the hillside, though they were quickly lost in the rushing water filling his ears. Another tributary joined the first, and Yeager washed downstream like a log flume ride at an amusement park. He realized he was in trouble about two seconds too late. The current pitched him headlong into a rushing torrent of water. His head went under, and he choked. He whirled and tumbled, banging into unseen rocks with jarring force. Swimming was out of the question. The stream deepened, and his feet no longer scraped bottom. The world became a kaleidoscope of flashing colors—green trees, blue sky, brown water, and white foam. Yeager went under again, and water filled his nostrils. He popped up into the air for a too-brief moment, coughing and spitting.

Then he was floating, suspended in midair, with that sick, sinking sensation of having nothing under his feet but sky. His brain recorded the image of a deep chasm and a spray of water vaulting into the air before cascading in white sheets to a green pool filled with jutting rocks below him.

Gravity found him. Yeager fell with alarming velocity. He had time for one "Aw, fuck" before he smacked the surface with the force of a brick dropped from outer space. He hit the water and somehow avoided bashing his brains out on a rock, but that was small consolation, as hitting the water felt like hitting concrete. The air blew out of his lungs. Deep green embraced him and pulled him down with greedy force. His vision stuttered. Consciousness short-circuited. Yeager's world lost focus and drifted away.

CHAPTER THIRTEEN

Victor followed a literal goat path through a high-canopy forest. He came upon a trio of aggressive scruffy-chinned beasts holding firm in the middle of the trail, refusing to yield the right of way. He "yeehawed," threatened to swat them, and stomped his feet until they reluctantly scattered into the trees. Victor emerged from the cathedral of green into a village of shacks built of raw wood and roofed by sheets of corrugated tin. The dirt path morphed into a street paved with raw stone that sloped down in a moderately straight line. Women carried baskets on their heads, and many wore bright skirts with colorful blouses. The men of the village wore straw hats that shaded their nut-brown faces and reminded Victor of characters from old coffee commercials on TV. Everyone eyeballed him, offering shy smiles before looking away.

A gaggle of dogs converged and barked in a tail-wagging pack. They seemed more excited than upset, and Victor got a face full of tongue when he crouched down to greet the pack. A shadow fell over the group as one of the villagers approached.

Victor pushed the hounds away and found himself facing a work-worn man in jeans and a sweat-stained denim shirt. He sported a red bandana, faded to pink, tied around his neck, and his hat was old when Billy was a kid.

"Are you lost, señor?"

"Sí, mi amigo," Victor admitted. He winced and stretched, trying to work out the kinks in his aching back. "*Lost* is a good word for it. Mi compadre and I, we were separated, back up on the mountain." He hesitated a moment, assessing where this man's allegiances might be tied. He took a chance and added, "We spooked some narcos, and they chased us very hard. No offense was intended, but sometimes the narcos..." Victor shrugged and put on a sheepish expression.

The man cracked a smile. "Sometimes they do not listen before shooting, hey?"

Victor nodded, smiling ruefully.

"And your amigo?"

"I don't know." Victor's smile faded. "I think he tried to lure them away. I heard more shooting, but it came from farther and farther away. I waited awhile, then went back and looked, but I found nothing."

They stood together in silence, both looking into the forest. After a moment, the villager said, "Perhaps your friend has taken a different path. There are many ways off the mountain. We will spread the word to be vigilant for such a man. What does he look like?"

"A *norteamericano*. Double-tough. Built like a bull." Victor grinned. "Same kind of balls as a bull. Same kind of brains."

"I am Hector Colón. Come with me, to my house. You can eat. Rest. Perhaps your friend will come later."

"*Muy gracias*, Hector. That is very kind. I am Victor Ruiz."

"It is nothing, Señor Ruiz," Hector said with a sly smile. "It is a case of self-defense. My wife will not fuss at me so much if we have company."

Victor laughed and clapped the older man on his shoulder. "Bueno! Lead on." As they walked, he two-fingered Arturo's phone from his pocket. "You have cell service here," he said with surprise.

"*Un poquito*." Hector shrugged. "It comes and goes."

"*Perdóname un momentito*," Victor said. "I have to make a call."

Mendoza answered on the fifth ring. "Yes?"

"It's me, Victor. Listen, we have a problem..." Victor relayed the situation in a few terse sentences. Silence from the phone dragged on for a full minute.

"Where are you?"

"Where am I?" Victor called out to Hector, who had drifted a few paces away.

"Abrevadero, señor. Twenty kilometers east of Bulej."

"Did you get that?"

"Yes," Mendoza said. "Stay there. I will have people meet you there in... twenty-four hours or less."

"Have them bring gear and guns. If Yeager hasn't shown by then, I need to go back in the woods and drag his sorry ass out."

Mendoza hesitated. "Fine," he said at last. "Just wait there for my people. Don't move."

"Believe me," Victor said while massaging his aching lower back. "Moving is not an option at the moment."

Trying to draw a breath underwater brought Yeager out of his blackout with a convulsion. Water filled his nostrils and flooded his throat. The only thing that prevented it from filling his lungs was that he'd landed on his back and had the wind knocked out of him. His lungs were offline for the next couple of seconds. The thought of drowning sent Yeager into a panic. He thrashed the water in a frenzy, fighting it. His throat spasmed. There was no air to choke out the water clogging his airway, and he had to fight his panicky, instinctive attempt to breathe.

Daylight beckoned from above. Yeager stroked hard. Once. Twice. His face broke the surface, and he lost the battle with his instincts and tried to breathe. Big mistake. Liquid pain stabbed his chest. He choked. Went under again. Thrashed upward. Coughed out a spray of water. Breathed enough to cough some more. Bobbed like a cork, alternating between fighting to stay afloat and barking out the water in his lungs.

He must have drifted close to the bank, as his feet touched bottom about the time Yeager thought he might just possibly not drown. He stroked hard and got his feet under him long enough to reach the bank. On his hands and knees, Yeager dragged himself through the mud, rocks, and weeds lining the small pool at the base of the waterfall. He collapsed with his feet in the water and his cheek in the mud, coughing like a baby with the croup.

The thought of the unknown gunman trailing behind him forced Yeager to move much sooner than he wanted. Given his choice, he would have lain there until Pluto made a complete orbit around the sun. He didn't know how long that was in human years, but his boy, David, had told him it was a long time.

C'mon, Marine. Move your ass.

Yeager groaned and pushed off the ground. He staggered into the trees, out of the warm sun. Soaking wet clothes cooled instantly in the shade, and Yeager shivered. He stumbled along a meandering path until it broke into the open again. A talus slope opened out in front of him, spreading downhill, sparsely covered with scrubby trees until the forest grew heavy again, much lower in the valley. Opposite Yeager's position, another hillside reared up to a ridge crest, about half as high as the one at his back.

He was far enough away from the waterfall and out of sight of anyone trailing him. Yeager plopped his butt down on a rock and took stock of his situation.

In simple words: it sucked.

He had left his backpack behind after the first bullet nearly parted his hair, and along with it, all his spare clothes, water, trail rations, compass, paracord, first aid kit, wire saw, and fire starter. All he had left were the clothes on his back, a pocketknife, his cell phone, and his wallet containing a few soggy bills in pesos and dollars.

His shirt lay across his shoulders in Doc Savage rags. Mud slathered him from the roots of his hair to the soles of his boots.

Scrapes, welts, scratches, and incipient bruises marked every square inch of exposed skin as well as a good bit of the part covered by soaking-wet clothing. Both knees poked out of rips in his jeans, which had started out the day whole and now looked like something teenagers wore to the mall. He was exhausted. Every muscle ached. His joints creaked, and pain stabbed his ribs when he tried to breathe.

Silver lining? At least the ant bites had stopped burning.

He retrieved his cell phone from his hip pocket. The screen was shattered, and water drizzled out of the broken case. *Great. Just great. FUBAR'd.* He tossed the phone and watched it spin away. He planted his elbows on his knees, scrubbed his fingers through his hair, snorted, and spat between his feet.

Yeager slumped and let his hands dangle. "I left my wife for *this*?"

CHAPTER FOURTEEN

Two days after the inaugural ball, Blanca rose early, washed, then ate breakfast. She left her apartment as the sun pinked the streets of Guatemala City. Her street-level apartment came with its own garage, from which Blanca pushed her powder-blue 2008 Vespa scooter.

She had acquired both the apartment and the scooter in the days following her meeting with the station chief about the Modena-Gustaffson link. The apartment, rented under the name Juanita Alvares, was to add a layer of protection from any inquiries made by the Guatemalan intelligence services or Gustaffson's security people. Too little, too late, in Blanca's opinion, but who was she to contradict the wisdom of legendary super spy Hunter Davidson.

She had to assume the pair in the Land Rover belonged to Gustaffson's crew, and thus the UPS van was burned for further use. The scooter, however, was clean. She had bought it with her own money, for cash. No ID exchanged. As a bonus, the helmet, with its darkened face shield, defeated any identification of her features. For the moment, she was nothing but an anonymous scooter rider among thousands on the streets of the city.

Blanca's efforts at the ball had yielded little. Herman Gustaffson's well-endowed companion—named Tatiana, of course—spoke pidgin Spanish with a heavy Russian accent, and her English was worse. Communicating with her was like trying to order a dish she couldn't describe from a foreign waiter at a crowded restaurant.

Spies quickly learned the art of schmoozing a target, assuming they weren't born with the gift already. One of the common early tradecraft assignments in training was to enter a bar, approach a stranger, and within an hour, garner their name, place of birth, occupation, and as much personal data as possible. In the advanced stages, trainees were required to come back with some specific piece of personal intel, such as a credit card number or mother's maiden name. Blanca excelled at this, but the skill required her to be able to communicate with the mark. Grunts and hand gestures wouldn't get it done, so she had given up on Tatiana early in the conversation.

The single bit of information she had gleaned was the name of the hiring authority for household staff at Gustaffson's estate in the hills northwest of Guatemala City, the place she had seen from the air. Without conferring with Hunter, Blanca had decided to conduct a drive-by reconnaissance, maybe scout out access points where she might reach the hired help or play it by ear and see if she could get hired on. It would take a lucky shot to identify, let alone approach, a potential asset, but Blanca firmly believed opportunities seized by the bold became fortunes rendered in gold.

Her surveillance detection route took her under the arched span of the Torre del Reformador, a seventy-meter-tall approximation of the Eiffel Tower erected in memory of Justo Rufino Barrios, a former president of Guatemala. She turned left then left again onto Avenida La Reforma, watching her side mirrors for any trailing vehicles. Nothing.

Blanca zipped north, zooming her little scooter around the traffic circle at the Jardín Botánico garden, then continuing north toward the stadium. Traffic was light at this hour, and she spotted no followers, but to be sure, Blanca whipped a U-turn at the Monumento Olimpico circle and headed back south. After a few more twists and turns, she declared herself clean of ticks and powered her Vespa eastward, toward the outskirts of town.

She was slowing for the right turn on 21A Calle when a panel van swept up from behind and slammed into the back of the Vespa.

The hit jolted the bike scooter so hard, it skipped ahead a dozen feet. Blanca flipped over the tail and somersaulted onto her belly, smacking the pavement hard. Dazed and disoriented, she barely felt the hands of the men who hauled her upright and dragged her to the van's open door. They threw her into the darkened interior and piled in after her. Dizzy and disoriented, she tried fighting the tangle of bodies, but her muscles refused to cooperate. She gave up entirely when a huge man sat on her back, effectively pinning her to the floor. Her crushed lungs fought for air. Her vision tunneled out. Cold sweat broke out under the confines of her helmet. If she didn't breathe soon, she was going to... pass... out...

Two black GMC Yukons rolled into the village of Abrevadero as the sun topped the eastern horizon. Victor sat on the shadowed porch of Hector Colón's slat-board shanty and watched them come. Each vehicle carried four men, which seemed an awful lot of troops to be part of Mendoza's network in Guatemala. Victor was expecting one guy, not a full squad.

He sipped the grainy dregs of a very excellent cup of homemade coffee provided by Señora Colón. The lady of the house was a large, brassy, outspoken woman of middle years who ruled her kitchen with a ladle and the temper of a drill sergeant. The coffee beans came from their own small crop of "hard beans," hand-washed and roasted in the Colóns' adobe-brick oven over cedarwood fires. The result was perhaps the best coffee Victor had ever enjoyed. His tongue was having orgasms.

The smell of corn tortillas frying on a cast iron griddle drifted through the open door of the house where Victor had spent the night. The Colón family numbered in the thousands, it seemed, with grandparents, kids, grandkids, and neighbors' kids sharing the same three-room shack. After a simple dinner of goat meat, onions, and frijoles eaten fajita-style, Victor had been given a pallet in a room filled with children of all ages. He'd spent a restless night surrounded by snores, farts, and squirming. That was not what had kept him awake, though. He had kept one ear cocked for the sound of barking dogs, half-expecting—hoping, really—that Yeager would wander into the village, sore, cranky, and bug bitten, but otherwise healthy and whole.

He had spent the night tossing in restless agitation. He could do nothing good for his friend by bumbling around in the dark looking for him. It was a much wiser course to get some food and rest then start out fresh in the morning with some local people to help in the search. If only it didn't *feel* so much like betrayal.

And now this. Mendoza's Guatemalan contingent must have either been close by or gotten up very early in the morning to be here at this hour.

The pair of SUVs scrunched to a stop in the middle of the village street, sending a gaggle of chickens squawking for cover. Eight identical doors opened, and eight identical men got out, each wearing black tac gear and sporting military-style rifles. Eight pairs of sunglasses scanned the area. Each man covered a sector. None of the newcomers spoke, stretched, scratched, or yawned. Alert. Vigilant. Professional.

Victor grimaced. *These* were the men tasked to support him and Yeager as they whacked Gustaffson? If the evidence in front of him were to be believed, somehow Mendoza, a special forces captain from Mexico, had recruited a paramilitary force of at least eight men to infiltrate Guatemala for the sole purpose of helping two *norteamericanos* assassinate a foreign citizen. Murder for hire was frowned upon, even in Guatemala, and yet, here was a small rifle squad of trained soldiers ready to lend aid and assistance in such a conspiracy.

Why not just do it themselves? These guys seemed at least as capable—well, almost as capable—as Victor Ruiz and Abel Yeager.

As these thoughts crossed Victor's mind, the shotgun-seat passenger from the lead vehicle pulled out a cell phone and touched the screen. Seconds later, the annoying chirp of a ringtone sounded from Victor's pocket. Arturo's phone.

Two pairs of eyes and two muzzles swiveled in his direction. The remaining men kept watch on their sector and did not follow the distraction. On one hand, Victor admired the professionalism. On the other hand, he would rather have been in Toledo.

The man with the phone took two steps in his direction and called out in hesitant English, "Victor Ruiz? We to, ah, *escoltarte...* to be the safe."

Escort me to safety? Or arrest me? The men had "government issue" stamped on their foreheads, which was the last thing Victor expected. It made him wonder if the plot to kill Gustaffson was a conspiracy between Mendoza—on behalf of the Mexican government—and elements within the Guatemalan power structure. Or were they both rogue factions of the two countries' militaries with plans buried deep behind smokescreens involving a handsome and charming Latino pilot and his boneheaded best friend? Victor had less than a single breath to contemplate those questions as the guy with the phone twitched his hand in a quick motion. Two of the troops trotted forward and assumed mildly threatening positions to either side of Hector's porch, flanking Victor with their automatic rifles held at port arms. He recognized the invitation: "Come with us or come to Jesus."

"Yeah, yeah, do not get crazy," Victor said in Spanish. To Señora Colón, he said, "You wouldn't happen to have a to-go cup for this coffee? Hey? No, I guess not."

"*¿Dónde está tu amigo?*" the leader asked.

"My friend?" Victor shrugged and hitched a thumb at the hills to the north. "Somewhere out there. Probably shot to shit by some donkey-fucking drug smugglers. We need to get on the move and start the search."

The leader snapped off a brusque head shake. "No. I will detail some men to wait here for your friend. My orders are to get you back to... safety as soon as possible."

Victor scowled and considered his options. One of him against all of them. No guns versus lots of guns. The natural fighting spirit of a US Marine weighed against eight boys with their dangerous toys. One, maybe two, he felt pretty good about his odds. But eight? He sighed and glanced up at the northern skyline.

Sorry, buddy. You're on your own. For now.

"Hokay, amigo," Victor said. "Let's go."

Yeager spent a shivery cold night burrowed into the dirt like half-buried roadkill. The thin rags of his shirt provided little cover and less warmth, and he lay in a ball, huddled into a trench he'd carved into the loose soil. He estimated the temperature at a solid fifty degrees, with a wind chill of minus one hundred two.

He crawled upright as soon as false dawn lent enough light to see where to put his feet and started downhill while the last of the stars faded from the sky. His pace resembled a prisoner's shuffle. Aches racked his body, and his joints felt coated with sandpaper. At least the movement helped him warm up or at least to not notice the cold as much. He hadn't felt this tired since his days humping eighty pounds of gear through the mountains of Afghanistan.

After three hours of hiking, Yeager found a bare knob with a good view of the terrain ahead. The hill fell away below him for another thousand yards or more before flattening out to a floor cut between ridges on either side. He came to a jelly-legged stop and scanned the valley snaking away to the south. His gaze wavered and refused to focus on the evidence in front of him until he palmed his eyes and shook away the mud in his brain.

A village lay in the valley below. The white haze he had initially mistaken for fog was actually smoke from several early-morning cook fires. A collection of rickety structures lined both sides of a main road, which twisted downhill on a more or less southerly course. A few people went about their business, their forms made tiny by distance. He would have said they looked like ants, but ants were out of his vocabulary for the foreseeable future.

Was this the village Arturo was taking us to? Does that even matter? He was tired, sore, hungry, bug bit, and in need of new clothes, directions, and a bathtub full of calamine lotion. Any civilization would do at this point.

As Yeager plotted a route off the mountain and into the crease of the valley, the distant vibration of car engines caught his ear. Two black SUVs spearheaded a dust cloud along the road to the village, coming from the south end of the valley. The vehicles pulled into town and rolled to a stop about a third of the way along the main street. Doors opened, and men piled out. Yeager cursed his lack of binoculars. By their stance and body language, he got the impression the men carried rifles, but it was hard to see through the distance and the dust. Two men detached from the group and disappeared under a porch awning. A few minutes later, they reappeared, with a distinctly shorter man walking between them. Even from a thousand yards away, Yeager recognized the muscular strut of Victor "Por Que" Ruiz.

Victor climbed into the rear passenger seat, and the four unknown men piled into the same SUV. The second group boarded their vehicle. The sound of car doors thudding shut carried to Yeager's position several seconds later. The car containing Victor wheeled in a big circle, scattering chickens and nearly clipping the support post of a rickety shack, and accelerated back the way it had come. The second SUV backed into a gap between two shacks and did not come out. Yeager waited and watched, but the car did not reappear.

"Almost like they're waiting for somebody," he muttered to himself.

Were these Mendoza's guys? How could Mendoza have the infrastructure to dispatch a brace of black SUVs and eight operators on foreign soil, on a covert mission to pick up his special assassins? Given Arturo's... lack of sophistication... Mendoza's operation did not strike Yeager as tremendously well-financed.

"Ipso-facto-el-logico," Yeager muttered. "These guys ain't with Mendoza."

Yeager plotted a path down the mountain that would take him around the west side of the village, the same side where the newcomers had parked their shiny SUV. His best guess put the hike at an hour, maybe two if he had to belly-crawl to avoid locals. After that, he would need time to gather intel. He figured another hour for that. Every minute put Victor farther away and longer in the hands of people who did not have his best interests at heart. Yeager could not afford the luxury of a long interrogation or utilizing a subtle means of learning what he needed to know. His extraction of information would therefore need to be fast, brutal, and effective.

Yeager set his jaw into a grim line. Torture was not a step he wanted to take. Extraction of information derived from pain required skill and an iron stomach. There was also a knack for knowing the difference between truth and lies given under duress, and skilled interrogators had ways of validating a subject's answers to gauge their veracity. Despite what the idiots on TV shows claimed, torture could be a highly effective means of gathering intelligence—if you had the training and impartiality to inflict the correct dose of pain in the prescribed manner and could validate the information extracted. All Yeager had was a burning need to know the answers to some basic questions and the willpower to do whatever it would take to squeeze those answers from the foot soldiers left behind.

So be it. One way or another, he would get what he needed. And if he had to hurt four goons in the process, well... he would just have to add it to the scorecard he turned in at the entrance to the pearly gates.

Call it a four-stroke penalty.

CHAPTER FIFTEEN

The pain in Blanca's wrists pulled her out of the depths of unconsciousness. Her gummy eyes cracked open to reveal a concrete-walled room bare of any fixtures or furniture and lit by a single bank of fluorescent tubes suspended from the ceiling. The pain radiated from her wrists as she hung suspended from a pair of cuffs bolted to a single wooden plank, similar in size to a dining room table, which was somehow affixed so that it stood upright in the middle of the room. Blanca's feet sagged against the floor, and now that she was conscious, she realized she could stand on her own, relieving the pressure on her cuffed wrists. Her hands had gone numb and felt like packaged meat affixed to the stumps of her wrists.

Her hair felt gritty, and an itch tickled her scalp. She scrubbed her head against the rough wood of the plank. An ache sprang up in her shoulder joints, and a random selection of pains phoned in their complaints from her hips, knees, and back. Cold sweat broke out across her brow, chilled further by the frigid temperature of the room. Someone had cranked down the thermostat on an overactive air conditioning system to somewhere between meat locker chill and arctic expedition deep freeze. She shivered repeatedly, unable to huddle against the chill.

It's not just the cold making me shake.

Someone had taken her in broad daylight and chained her up in a basement. Nothing about that sounded conducive to long life and good health. Visions of every torture scene in every bad spy flick she'd ever watched played on a loop in her head.

What the hell is happening?

As if summoned, a door creaked open behind her, and two sets of footsteps entered the room. An icicle of fear staked her heart. She experienced an irrational desire for the unknown captors to leave her alone in the room by herself, even if it meant hanging from a block of wood in a freezing room for the rest of her life. At least that way she wouldn't have to face whatever horror came with the newcomers.

The footsteps halted directly behind her, out of sight. "Greetings and welcome, young lady," a man said. "I apologize for the discomfort. We will alleviate your situation upon a pleasant conclusion to our business."

"Who are you?" Blanca's voice quavered. She told herself it was how a frightened Juanita Alvares would sound, though she refused to admit how little she was acting. "What do you want?"

Shoe leather squeaked, followed by the click of hard heels. The man who circled to stand in front of Blanca reminded her of Dr. Ryburn, her freshman English Lit professor, all the way down to the corduroy sports jacket with leather-patched elbows and round glasses perched on his nose. A slight potbelly stretched the button-down shirt he wore above his polyester Sansabelt slacks. The fringe of brown hair around his bald head was going gray. A younger man trailed after him like a grad student attentive to the needs of his mentor.

"The first answer is simple," the older man said. "I am Macerio Borges. This is my associate, Dominic Martinez. The second answer is somewhat simple as well. We need to know, in any particular order, who you are, who you work for, and what you have seen. A corollary to the latter answer may well be: who did you tell?"

Jesus, he even lectures like Dry-Burn. Blanca suppressed an inappropriate giggle bubbling up from her diaphragm.

"I-I-I work for Martín Durante Coffee Company!" Blanca choked out. "My name is Juanita Alvares! I'm a secretary—"

Borges raised a finger to stop her speaking. The younger man handed him a phone, which Borges held in front of her. On it was a picture—of her, sitting on the tailgate of a UPS truck, waiting for her UASV to return from its scouting mission. A sinking ball of lead pushed down from her stomach and deep into her guts.

He sighed like a disappointed father. "I must also tell you—Tatiana reported your clumsy attempt at contact at the inaugural ball. The young lady's skill is not in her intelligence, but she does have a strongly developed sense of self-preservation, so when a strange woman approaches her in the ladies' room of the presidential palace and strikes up a conversation, Tatiana knows to report it to Señor Gustaffson immediately."

The cuffs jangled as Blanca shifted. The pulse thundered in her neck, and her shivering spasmed to a full-body shudder. Blown. She hadn't even gotten to first base with the Scorpion, and already she was utterly and totally blown. Caught spying by the most dangerous man in Central America, and at the mercy of this unassuming little toad who had the dead eyes of an iced shark in a Chinese market. She clenched her butt cheeks to keep from embarrassing herself.

"How did you find me?"

"You are not the only one with drones, little miss."

Figures.

"In the days ahead," Borges continued in his lecturing monotone, "you will tell us what we want to know. I confess, I find no honor in torture, and I despise the brutality of it. I have employed some young men from a local gang to assist me with the more unsavory acts. The things neither my associate nor I have the stomach for."

Blanca tried to swallow, but her throat had dried to a husk. Her thoughts raced in circles, as though nothing made sense. Yet everything was perfectly clear.

The younger man, Dominic, walked away at a gesture, his footsteps heading for the door. Borges began pacing as he spoke. "What are you most afraid of, señorita? Rape? Of course you will be raped. Bones broken? Yes, we will break your bones. Flesh burned with heated metal? Already being warmed as we speak." Borges waved a hand as Dominic rolled in a cart, as if bringing room service in Hotel Hell. On the cart rested several gleaming instruments, including a soldering iron propped in a wire holder. Dominic proceeded to roll out an extension cord from under the cart. He carried the plug to a wall socket and stuck it in.

"Fingernails pulled," Borges continued as though reading from a grocery list. "Toes cut off with shears. Nipples eaten by rats. Glass rods inserted in your rectum and broken off..."

Blanca's attention slid away on a tide of horror as the disgusting little man continued the litany of violations he planned to inflict upon her. Three days of SERE class had been a cakewalk compared to the reality of her situation.

Survival? Not a chance. Escape, evasion, resistance? What a crock of shit.

She was going to die horribly and suffer brutally in the process. The only question was how long she would suffer before giving up every secret she had ever known in exchange for the relief of death. She hardly noticed the pain in her wrists when she sagged against the pull of the handcuffs.

Herman Gustaffson never ambled, strolled, or meandered when he walked. He strode with purpose, an up-tempo quick march that often left his companions struggling to keep up. Trying to speak with El Escorpión while he was cantering about on his long legs required good aerobic capacity and an ability to quite literally think on one's feet. Reporting to his boss while Gustaffson tore along the hallways of his hacienda always felt to Macerio Borges as if he were trying to keep up with a train passing by a station platform.

He was lucky this time, as he caught up to El Escorpión at a rare moment of stillness, in the parking lot of the Quetzaltenango warehouse. The warehouse had been converted into a shelter for Gustaffson's less-wealthy clients. The structure was laid out with camp cots, basic toilet facilities, and a communal kitchen. Unlike the charitably oriented Casa Del Migrante in Guatemala City or the juvenile facility in Quetzaltenango called Casa Nuestras Raíces, everything in Gustaffson's shelter cost money—food, blankets, soap, everything. The temporary residents of these facilities, mostly criminals and fugitives, could not withstand the scrutiny of the more traditional migrant shelters. So they paid through the nose for the privilege of sleeping on a stinking mattress with one eye open to avoid waking up with their throat slit. There they waited until Gustaffson's coyotes moved them across the Mexican border and on to equally uncongenial shelters in that country before they made the final leg of their journey into the United States. At the moment, only the Arabs and the two prisoners occupied the building.

That El Escorpión had come to speak with him in person did not surprise him. Phone conversations had too great a chance to be intercepted by the various US governmental agencies' high-tech listening devices. A two-hundred-kilometer drive was nothing to Gustaffson if it maintained security. Borges appreciated the paranoia.

Gustaffson paused impatiently at the door to his limousine, waiting for Borges to arrive.

"You asked to see me?"

"Our guests have outstayed their welcome," Gustaffson said without preamble. "We need to move them along. Move them to north house."

The "north house" was Gustaffson's personal property near the Mexican border in the Santa Barbara region.

Borges raised his eyebrows a calculated degree, keeping his face bland but attentive. His expression said, "Why inform me? I am your killer, not your transportation manager. But I respect your authority and will do as you say." At least, he hoped that was what his expression conveyed.

"Turizo will arrange for the transportation," Gustaffson said, thus answering part of Borges's silent question. "Something is off about this situation with these so-called assassins reported by Modena. He wishes to have our cooperation and good feelings as he assumes office. It bothers me."

"You think Modena set up the assassination attempt as a... throwaway to gain your favor?"

Gustaffson compressed his lips into a frown. "Possibly. But regardless, we don't know what the CIA woman saw and reported with her drone flight."

Borges nodded with respect. "You called me away before we began to question the spy. She may have seen nothing of our visitors."

"It does not matter. It was a mistake to bring them here." Gustaffson ducked into the backseat and added, "And besides, these Arab assholes are trying my patience. I want them gone by the time I get back from the city. Attend me," Gustaffson said from the back seat. "While Jovanovic is doing business in Europe, I am going alone to meet the president-elect and his henchman, Bustamante, at the Santa Barbara hacienda—"

Borges blinked in surprise. "You want them there when we bring the Arabs?"

"Yes. I have a reason. Bustamante is the snake in the grass, if there is one. While I have them occupied, I would like you to snoop around Bustamante's house and office. Find out what you can."

The car door slammed shut before Borges could even nod his acquiescence. The limousine purred away, followed by the trail car with Gustaffson's security detail.

Borges was not offended by his boss's abrupt manner. He had worked for El Escorpión for many, many years and was well acquainted with the man's driving urgency to always be on the move. Only when focused on charming a politician, a business partner, or a future sexual conquest did the oligarch slow his normal high-speed momentum. At those times, he adopted the patience of a jaguar suspended over a trail and waiting for his moment to strike.

Very little upset Borges. He took pride in the serenity of his emotional state. Whether eating a meal or executing a family, Borges never hurried, never wasted motion, and never allowed emotions to intrude. He always strove for pure, analytical precision, and nothing about El Escorpión's orders disturbed his equanimity beyond a mild vexation. He would have the CIA woman taken to the same Santa Barbara property as well. If she didn't give him the information he desired, he would hand her to the Arabs for their pleasure. Maybe that would loosen her tongue.

Besides, Gustaffson was right for the wrong reasons. Given the CIA woman's possible observation of their guests, it was wise to keep them on the move. They had departed the western property the moment Gustaffson learned they might have been observed by the woman's drone. Had she reported to her superiors? Someone up the chain of command at Langley might be smart enough to realize the implications of twelve Middle Eastern men visiting the home of a known trafficker, one who specialized in the movement of humans through the porous borders of Mexico and into the United States.

Borges glanced up to the afternoon sky, half-expecting to see a bevy of black helicopters darting over the skyline or catch a telltale glint of a high-flying drone armed with Hellfire missiles. How much warning would they have before a Special Operations team struck the warehouse? Would they even see the flight of the Hellfire as it bore down on them? Borges controlled a shudder. Blown to bits like some cheap terrorists? Unthinkable. American assassins had no honor.

"Gustaffson is correct," he said under his breath. "We should move our guests to a safer location."

About halfway down the hillside, Yeager crossed from wild forest to a bare strip of earth. Beyond that grew rows of thick, chest-high coffee bushes planted in rows perpendicular to his direction of travel. Terraces of these plants stair-stepped down the hillside for another quarter mile before flattening out into the valley floor. Wild trees poked up from the cultivated rows, giving the field a weedy, unkempt look. The first buildings of the nameless village began a short walk beyond the last row of bushes.

Yeager crouched and entered the field, keeping his head below the bushes, each of which carried thick clusters of green, unripened coffee cherries. For some reason, he had expected a field of coffee plants to smell like coffee and was vaguely disappointed when he found it did not. The field smelled much like any field of growing things: raw earth and grass intermixed with the occasional pungent whiff of nature's finest fertilizer, manure.

He traveled laterally along the row until he reached a relatively straight path cut through the rows. The hard-packed earth of this path spoke of the tramp of many feet up and down the hillside as generations of peasants tended their crops. Yeager scuffed his way down the hill, digging his heels in, his aching legs protesting the long morning of descending into the valley. His eyes burned, and his vision swam with a combination of the heat, exertion, and residue of whatever toxin the devil ants had pumped into him. Add to that list a fair measure of hunger and thirst. Yeager dry-swallowed and eyed a nearby cluster of coffee cherries, which brought up an interesting question. Were raw coffee cherries edible? He paused long enough to decide that experimentation in his current situation would be a bad idea. Yeager moved on.

A few yards before the end of the trail, the slope flattened out. Beyond that, the village appeared to have rolled up for a siesta. Smoke from cook fires had trailed off to a few wisps. The air was damp and still. No dogs barked, for which he was grateful. Even the chickens seemed to be napping.

A single tree marked the last stop before the field ended and the village began. Under it, Yeager found a stack of tools propped against its trunk. At first, he thought they were rakes, but revised his assumption after closer inspection. Each pole was topped by a metal attachment that looked like two spread hands joined at the thumbs. A vague memory surfaced of seeing coffee pickers using these devices to either rattle the branches of coffee bushes to dislodge the cherries, or to rake them off directly using the tines. He couldn't remember what the damned thing was called... a derri-something-in-Spanish. But whatever. The name didn't matter. What brought a grim smile to Yeager's lips were the "fingertips" of the tool. They were long, pointy, and potentially dangerous. A spear with many points. He hefted one and swished it through the air.

Helluva thing. Going to war with a farm tool instead of a gun.

A light breeze rolled in from the south, carrying with it the tang of woodsmoke. From the village came a man's voice, raised in query, followed by a woman's rapid-fire, irritated response. Yeager smirked, glad that some other hapless husband was catching hell.

That made him think of Charlie, and a hot gust of emotion swelled in his chest, powered by self-recrimination and a heap of anger. Like a dragon's breath, it blew the ash from the coals that powered the warrior inside him. Yeager knelt, holding the rake as if praying to it. He dug his free hand into the soft loam at his feet and brought a handful of raw earth to his nose. He breathed deeply of the aromatic earth, connecting himself to the land from which came all life and to which everything returned at death. He fed from the soil as if drawing strength from the minerals within it, then he let the soil crumble and drizzle from his grip.

He'd tried burying the warrior many times. After Afghanistan, he had come home and tried to live a decent life. Then came Humberto's crew and the Sinaloa cartel. They'd awoken the nightmare creature living inside him, and he'd paid the price of his fall into hell willingly, to protect Charlie and David. He had just managed to bury the killer once again, only to have it reignited by Verdugo's persecution of the mission at San Felipe. Then like déjà vu, he had been forced to kill again, in Hawaii, to save Charlie and the other tourists. The fighting never seemed to end.

And now look at me. I've fucked over my marriage, and for what? To kill again.

No matter how hard he tried, the warrior refused to stay buried. Was it fate? Or was that all he was, deep at heart? Did he really want nothing more than an excuse to turn into an animal? If he lived through this, would he find himself so far over the line there would be no coming back? Charlie had tried to save him. Had saved him, for a time. In return, he'd brought her nothing but pain and misery. The dragon breathed again, demanding sacrifices, demanding to be fed. Yeager would have to become the thing he dreaded, yet welcomed. Hated, yet yearned for. It was time to unleash hell.

Yeager gathered himself and stood. He stalked toward the village, his improvised lance swinging at his side. It was time to kill. Again.

So be it.

The rattle of a key in the lock woke Blanca.

Right after Macerio Borges described all the fun he planned to have with her, he and his pal were called away by a hyperventilating guard, who had obviously run some distance to bring his message. Soon afterward, more guards had filed into the room. They had unlocked Blanca from the table and secured her ankle with a cuff on a three-foot length of chain, which in turn was welded onto a ring set into the concrete wall. They had left within reach a plastic pail filled with mold-scented water, along with an empty pail that reeked of stale urine, then they'd trooped out, all without a word. They left behind all the torture instruments, including the hot soldering iron. A thin wisp of smoke curled from its tip, as if to say, "Ready when you are."

Nice touch, that.

Were Borges and his pal coming back to start the interrogation? Icy fear clutched her heart. By her body's internal clock, she had been zonked out for at least a couple of hours, and she desperately needed to use the stinky pail for its obvious purpose. If they started on her, she would pee herself at the first touch of pain unless her bladder was already empty. That little bit of indignity seemed one straw too many.

Blanca kept her eyes closed and played possum, listening to the shuffle and stamp of many feet at the door to the concrete room.

The door clanked open, and a man said in Spanish, "Who do I call to complain? This room stinks. Is there room service even?"

"*¡Cállate!*"

There came a thud of a punch to the body, followed by a grunt. Then in a wheezing voice, the man said, "Aw, man, that tickles. Hey, I didn't ask for double occupancy. Who is the señorita? Hola, señorita!"

Blanca ignored the voice and held still. The clink and jingle of a chain, then the rasp of a cuff indicated the man was being secured to the wall. The new prisoner continued his stream of nonsense chatter, despite further commands to shut up, which were punctuated by sharp blows.

"Do you treat all tourists to your country—*uhh*—like this? Travelocity did not say anything about a—*hummf*—torture room in the reviews. I plan to write a strongly—*hup*—worded—*uuh*—Yelp review."

Footsteps receded, the door creaked, slammed shut, leaving the room in silence. For all of eight seconds.

"Hey!... Yo!... You awake?" Then he muttered, as if to himself, "How could she sleep through all that? Or maybe she's dead and just don't stink yet."

"I'm alive." Giving up her ruse, Blanca rolled upright. She tossed her hair back and got her first look at her new companion—a short Latin male with a buzz cut and a cheerful, open face. His biceps bulged like grapefruit from his overstretched T-shirt. A swollen red bruise over his cheek marked the beginning stages of a black eye. "Although the part about not stinking, I'm not so sure."

"What are you in for, chica? You an innocent tourist, like me? What is your name?"

"Juanita Alvarez," Blanca said. She had no intention of opening up to this stranger. For all she knew, he was a plant working for Gustaffson, inserted into her cell undercover to ferret out her secrets the easy way. "And you?"

"I am, ah, Juan."

"Okay, Ah-Juan," she said with a smirk.

The man ducked his head. "Sorry, that was stupid. They already know my name, so why am I pretending?" He grinned and added, "Victor Ruiz, at your service."

Ruiz shifted his attention to the rest of the room. He stood with a wince and a muffled curse, holding his ribs, and shuffled to the end of his chain to study the cart with the tools of torture, and the wooden slab where she had recently been held. His leash terminated a dozen feet short of the cart, so there was no way to reach it. "Dios! They really laid out the silverware, didn't they? This for you or for me?"

"Both, I expect."

"Well... okay then."

From her seat on the cold floor, Blanca watched Ruiz explore the room, clinking in a semicircle from the eyebolt holding his chain. Concrete walls. No windows. About the size of a family room. Only the plank on which she had been chained seemed to be a permanent fixture, as two support arms were bolted to thick beams that ran parallel to the slab. The arms pivoted on hinge-like connectors, allowing the table to be lifted from the horizontal to the vertical.

"They didn't get this at IKEA," Ruiz said, eying the device.

"Special order from Torture Rooms to Go," Blanca said. "And please note the convenient drain in the middle of the floor, making the room easy to clean."

Ruiz grunted. He sat down, planted both feet against the wall on either side of the eyebolt, and wrapped a length of chain around both fists. With a grunt, Ruiz hauled backward. The chain snapped taut. Straining, eyes squeezed shut, Ruiz pitted his strength against the iron and concrete holding him captive. His arms bulged, the big veins standing out like cables under his skin. He held the pull for longer than Blanca thought humanly possible. That he was trying, she had no doubt. The chain quivered under the strain, and his hands turned white from effort.

"Dammit," Ruiz gasped and let go. He gulped several large breaths before adding, "I knew I should have eaten my spinach this morning."

The lock rattled again, seizing Blanca's heart with another spasm of fear. This time, her terror was not misplaced, for in walked Macerio Borges and his... lieutenant? Protégé? Dominic-something. The younger man closed the door and stood behind Borges's left shoulder.

The professorial Borges spoke to the newcomer first. "Señor Ruiz. A welcome addition to our hacienda. We already know much about your mission here. You and Señor Yeager. All that remains is for you to tell us where your friend is hiding, and the rest of your life will pass much easier. Should we start with you?" He turned to face Blanca but continued speaking to Ruiz. "Or perhaps you would care to wait and watch the show we have planned for our mystery guest. We believe she works for the CIA, and we are still unsure what she may have observed during the course of her spying activity. We will be extracting that information shortly."

"What are you," Ruiz asked, "the Guatemalan Gestapo? You look like Mr. Rogers, if Mr. Rogers had been sexually abused as a child and grew up to be a sick, twisted fuck."

"Dominic," Borges said as if ordering from a menu. "I believe we will start with Señor Ruiz. It will be instructive for the young lady to get a look at her future. Maybe that will encourage her to be more forthcoming."

Ruiz caught her eye. "Hey, chica. If I scream, promise not to tell anyone, okay? It will ruin my manly image."

CHAPTER SIXTEEN

A light breeze filtered through the trees, causing the crow to shift and cock its wings for balance. Many winters had passed since the crow first cracked his shell and emerged into the world. He had lived long near humans and learned much of their behavior. He knew the signs when food might be available, either as crumbs or scraps thrown away, or when an animal was to be butchered and offal tossed to the pigs and the dogs. He recalled vividly how well he had feasted when humans attacked one another and left their dead to rot in the deep forests and rocky hillsides. He had learned of the humans' killing tools and the noise they made and learned to follow the sound to the dead bodies.

The crow remained silent now, roosting in a tall tree through the heat of the day, but aware of the comings and goings in the village below him. His tree was on the outskirts of the village, on the sunset side, and commanded a view of the backs of several human dwellings. This was a good vantage, as the humans often threw tasty bits into the burn pits behind their houses. Very little happened at the moment, so the crow drowsed and waited.

Activity caught his eye, and he shuffled on his perch, sharpening his gaze. A single human, in black like the crow, had ventured into the woods and approached the crow's roosting tree. The man paused to urinate against the trunk. The crow tilted his head as he spied another human slipping through the brush on near-silent feet. The crow recognized the second human's stealthy approach and appreciated the silence of the hunter.

As the stalker closed on his victim, the crow cocked his wings and prepared to leap into the air should the attack cause him danger. The strike, when it came, was so fast and well-executed, the crow barely stirred. The hunter sprang from concealment and speared his prey with a *derricadeiras*. The tool struck the victim in the neck with a meaty thud. Blood sprayed, rich and tangy to the crow's senses, and the man fell with barely a squawk. The hunter finished his kill by driving down with his tool, forcing the tines deep into the black-dressed man's throat. More blood spilled, and the crow shifted impatiently, the scent of it triggering his hunger.

Rather than eat his kill as a normal beast would, the victor paused only long enough to remove several objects from the dead man's clothing, including the human tools that barked and killed from a distance. The hunter stalked away, toward the village. The crow fluttered to a lower branch, but waited before acting on his impulse, which was to drop to the ground and sample the dead flesh below him. He had grown wise from experience, and wisdom curbed impatience.

Sure enough, the rapping of human weapons cracked the stillness of the day. Two pops, followed by voices raised in anger... and the day went quiet again. The crow shifted nervously, but nothing happened for a long, long time. He was about to allow his hunger to drive him downward when the screaming began. A human voice, raised in howling agony, sent a quiver of fear through the crow's breast. He cawed his displeasure, upset only that he needed to wait for his meal. He settled again, content with the knowledge that after such a war among the humans, many would die. The bodies would be plentiful. He would feast well upon their corpses.

Yeager gathered the dead men's weapons. He removed the magazines and cleared the chambers, then he laid the rifles in a row along the cargo compartment of their black SUV. The pistols followed, as did all the spare magazines he had collected. When he was finished, Yeager surveyed his haul. He considered himself lucky that each man carried the same type of weapon: an FN-57 pistol and a Taurus T4 battle rifle. The latter was a clone of the US-made M4, standard-issue rifle of the US military and a descendant of the infamous M16. Yeager needed no familiarization with either weapon.

Extracting information from the foot soldiers had not proven as difficult as he'd feared, though more so than he wished. After the last man had gasped out his pleas for mercy and taken a bullet to the head, the bile and acid left Yeager's stomach in a rush. Bent over and weak-kneed, he had wiped his chin with a shaking hand and allowed himself a moment of self-loathing. *Was it only yesterday I said I was not a murderer?*

Two minutes later, Yeager shoved his disgust into a little box, forced the lid closed, and got on with what was required. He went about the task of collecting gear from the dead—wallets, cell phones, and car keys—with the emotionless distance of operating a machine on remote control from a long way away.

At the first gunshots, the entire village had fled for the forest and had yet to return. Yeager was grateful for the solitude. The SUV, a GMC Yukon, sat next to a large house on the outskirts of the village, nose pointed toward the road. Under the home's shaded porch, food had been laid out for the armed men. Yeager helped himself to a platter of *pupusas* and a warm bottle of beer. The alcohol made his head a little swimmy and added a welcome layer of cotton to his senses. He laid a damp twenty-dollar bill on the table and weighted it down with the empty bottle. A grim smile twitched his lips.

I may be a killer, but I'm not a thief.

A diamond-bright blue sky hung overhead, patched with crisp white clouds. The silence, almost physical in its intensity, blanketed him. Every thump and clatter of his actions reverberated in the stillness. The raucous caw of a crow echoed from the forest, but all other animals seemed to have taken a vow of silence.

Yeager slumped in the driver's seat of the Yukon, cranked the engine to life, and pointed all the air conditioner vents to blow on his face and chest. His shirt was a wreck, more hole than fabric. It revealed patches of bare skin covered in the red bumps of fading ant bites, scrapes, bruises, and chest hair matted by sweat. One of the dead guys was his size, and sooner or later, Yeager would need to gut it up and take the man's shirt. The idea revolted him.

The crew, he had learned, worked for Herman Gustaffson, and they had been ordered to pretend to be Mendoza's men. Their objective was to capture Yeager and Ruiz once Arturo called in their location. His... subject—*No, let's be blunt. The man I tortured*—said Arturo was a friendly and not to be harmed.

Yeager propped his head on the Yukon's leather headrest, closed his eyes, and tried to connect the dots. Option one: Mendoza's operation had been compromised and—no, that wouldn't play. They would not have treated Arturo as a friendly. They would have captured or killed Arturo, the same as him and Victor.

Which means what?

That meant Mendoza had possibly conspired with Gustaffson from the beginning. Arturo's phone and the number they were supposed to call for pickup went straight to Gustaffson's foot soldiers. The man Yeager had questioned said their orders had come directly from Gustaffson's top killer, the guy named Borges, who'd told them to answer the line when it rang, go to the location specified by the caller, and capture Victor Ruiz and Abel Yeager, leaving Arturo alone. If they resisted, they were to be killed.

But what possible motive could Mendoza and Gustaffson have for coercing two American citizens to presumably assassinate Gustaffson, only to snatch up the dupes in Guatemala? Was it to embarrass the United States? Yeager snorted in self-mockery. Hardly likely. Two worn-out Marines being picked up for conspiracy to murder a Guatemalan criminal kingpin would barely rate a blip on the daily news cycle. A lot of trouble for very little profit.

Yeager closed his eyes and let his thoughts wander...

And snapped out of a doze when his head dipped. He jerked upright and scrubbed his face. It would not be long before the villagers filtered back from the surrounding forest, and he needed to be miles down the road before that happened. The folks around here might or might not have access to a telephone, and if they did have phones, they might or might not call the local law. It was best not to trust to luck. Distance was his friend.

It was time to get moving.

The vehicle had an in-dash GPS unit. Yeager poked at it for a bit, searching the menu until he found a link to HOME. He selected it, and a map popped up with a helpful green route snaking across it. A voice in Spanish told him to turn right and proceed eight kilometers to the next turn. The display told him it was over three hundred kilometers to his destination and estimated the time of trip at five hours and thirty-six minutes.

He scanned the area around the center console then the steering column. Then he did the same thing again. *Where the hell's the shift lever? Wait. Are you kidding me? Push buttons?*

Yeager touched the right button on the dash, putting the vehicle into gear, and drove away.

The stench of burning flesh clogged Blanca's throat. She wanted to gag.

Chained spread-eagled on the table, the man named Ruiz did not scream so much as he discharged a long, guttural exhalation through gritted teeth, like a kettle with a broken vent. Every muscle of his well-defined upper body swelled as he strained the cuffs around his wrists.

Macerio Borges supervised from the side, watching with clinical interest as his protégé applied the tip of the hot soldering iron to the chained man's torso. Thin tendrils of smoke curled up around Dominic's head and feathered away. A fried beef smell permeated the room.

"The male or female nipple," Borges lectured his student, "is one of the most sensitive places on the human body. If you apply the iron to the tip—yes, just there—I think you will find you get much more response than from doodling on the pectoral."

The iron hissed when it touched flesh, and Ruiz's body arced. The tendons under his skin snapped as taut as bowstrings. He did scream then, a howl of male rage, pain, and anger that reminded Blanca of a lion caught in a steel trap. That scream promised, "If I get loose, I'm going to kill something."

Blanca found herself unable to look away, silently enduring her fellow captive's misery and praying for it to end. Except... a tiny, craven, unworthy, shriveled little worm lived deep in her subconscious. The worm knew once Borges was finished with Ruiz, she would be the next guest on his table. The worm did not want them to finish, for as long as Ruiz was under their care, she remained unharmed. Blanca shivered at the thought of the blazing-hot iron touching her nipple, sizzling and sinking into the soft flesh beneath it, searing the sensitive nerves with white heat.

She squeezed her legs together to control the sudden urge to empty her bladder. *I won't last five minutes. Maybe three.*

"Tell us," Borges said once the iron had been removed and Ruiz lay panting and shivering on the table. "Tell us where your friend is. We know his name. We know your name. We know your mission here was to kill Señor Gustaffson. We have you, and we will soon have him. Tell us where to find him. Tell us who sent you."

"You are not..." Ruiz gasped out in short bursts, "asking... the right... question."

Borges cocked an eyebrow. "And what question should I be asking?"

Rivulets of sweat trickled off the prisoner's brow and soaked his hair. He had fever-bright eyes, glittering with a crazed, killer-clown madness. "Tell us," he bit out. "How many ways... can you go fuck yourselves? That's the question... you should be asking."

Borges nodded to his helper. "Do the other nipple."

The younger man circled the table, lifting the soldering iron high so the power cord cleared the prisoner's feet. His back was to Blanca, mercifully blocking her view. He bent over, and Blanca tensed for the hiss of hot iron burning into flesh.

A quick rapping at the door startled her. A guard stepped into the room, dressed in black battle dress and carrying a weapon slung over one shoulder. He headed straight for Borges, sparing only a passing glance at the man on the table, and practically snapped to attention as he rattled out a report to the head torturer. He pitched his voice too low for Blanca to hear well. After a few moments of back and forth between the two, Borges dismissed the guard and turned to Ruiz.

"Well, my friend, looks like you get a reprieve for a bit. Our transportation has arrived. Dominic, with me."

Dominic carried his tool back to the cart and slotted it carefully into its stand, then he followed his boss to the door, which the guard had so thoughtfully held open.

"Hey, Holmes, wait up," Ruiz called out, straining his head upside down to watch them leave. "You dudes ain't done playing with my titties, are you?"

Borges smiled and left. The door swayed open, revealing a section of hallway. A particularly frustrating bit of theater, that. The open door beckoned while their chains held them in place.

More mental torture.

"Did you hear what the guard said?" Blanca asked.

Ruiz shifted and winced. "Ah... something about their Muslim guests throwing a fit because they found pork in their *pupusas*. The other guy said something like 'I can't wait for these assholes to go north,' and the first guy said, 'One is too many, but we have twelve of the *pendejos*.' Then something about Turizo. A name maybe?"

"Muslim guests..." Blanca whispered. Mental gears whirred and clicked. On her drone over-flight, she had observed a vanload of at least six dark-haired, bearded guys disembarking at Gustaffson's villa—and there was a second van already parked there. Borges wanted to know what she had seen and to whom she had reported her observations, implying they believed she had information on something secret. *Was that it? Seeing the guys in the van? Why would Gustaffson have twelve Muslim guests, and why would he care who knew about it?*

Gustaffson had his fingers in many shit-pies, including a widespread network of human traffickers who guided people to the land of their dreams, *Estados Unidos*.

Ah, wait! Another puzzle piece clicked into place. In the briefing she had attended, Assistant Station Chief Larssen had mentioned rumors of a group of jihadis traveling into Guatemala from Latakia, purpose and destination unknown, but... was that the connection?

"Oh, man," she moaned. "How could I have been so dumb!"

"I learned when women ask that, it's a trick question." Victor Ruiz spoke to the ceiling. "I'm not supposed to answer, right?"

Borges's footsteps echoed along the converted warehouse corridor. Grungy windows high along the perimeter let in soupy daylight, enough to see the warehouse interior had been built out with drywall and two-by-four studs. The interior walls stood at a height of three meters and were internally divided into twelve open-ceiling dormitories, each large enough to hold twenty cots with stinking mattresses and threadbare blankets.

Spotted with mold and moist from roof leaks, the gypsum board sagged and threatened to separate from the studs. The only decent room in the facility was the cinderblock cell—once an office—built into the corner that they used for such guests as the CIA woman and the so-called assassin.

The facility could house and feed two hundred forty immigrants until transportation north could be arranged. Now it was empty but for the Arabs and the two captives, and sounds were strangely muted. The place stank of unwashed bodies and truck-stop toilets.

Borges walked the single hall between the dorms to an open space in the front-right corner laid out with plastic tables and chairs. An industrial kitchen filled the length of the space up against the front wall, complete with a serving line, like a school—or jail—cafeteria. A smattering of Arabs occupied seats, sipping tea and gabbling in their foreign tongue, and fell silent as he passed. Their hooded and sullen eyes followed him.

The leader of Gustaffson's security force waited near the main entry doors. Fit, hawk-faced, and approaching forty, Patricio Turizo had the build of a gorilla, with long arms and platter-sized hands. Gustaffson had once joked Turizo could tear through the concrete walls of an orphanage with his bare hands, strangle all the children inside, then eat breakfast among their twisted bodies, all without twitching an eyelid. By his thunderous expression, Borges guessed the security chief was not bringing good news.

"What is it, Patricio?"

"We have lost contact with our team in the north." Turizo's voice carried none of the diffidence men typically displayed when addressing Borges. The head of the security detail was roughly Borges's equal in Gustaffson's hierarchy, though Turizo tended to defer to Borges in matters of policy and higher-level decisions. Turizo was a weapon. A powerful weapon, of course, but even the most destructive guided missile needed someone to program and aim it. "All the men's cell phones go straight to voicemail."

"How long since last contact?"

"Seven hours and twenty minutes," Turizo said without consulting his watch.

"Any chance they are..." Borges chose his words with care. "Larking about?"

In Borges's experience, it was not unknown for armed squads of men in remote villages to let their baser impulses get the better of them. There had been an incident many years ago involving a group of men sent to escort a small caravan of clients to the border. Alcohol, boredom, and the presence of several young women among the travelers had led to an unfortunate incident. Turizo had executed those men. However, that lesson might have worn off.

"Not these men," Turizo replied through gritted teeth. He did not appear willing to explain his confidence in their discipline. "No. There is something wrong."

Borges accepted this at face value. It was always best to prepare for attack and be pleasantly surprised when nothing more happened than be caught flatfooted.

"I am informing you as you may want to speed up your... work... on the *pendejo* in the basement. Find out more about this partner of his."

Borges scratched his chin. Learning more about the man identified to them as Abel Yeager would no doubt be helpful. If this man had eliminated the team left behind to apprehend him, it spoke highly of his ability. The bare facts provided by President-elect Mendoza included little more than names and general descriptions of the men sent to eliminate Gustaffson and mentioned both had served in the armed forces of the US military, though branch and rank were unknown. It was possible they were ex-special forces, mercenaries employing their skills for the highest bidder after mustering out. If so, that meant the man in the cell had some training in resistance to interrogation. Breaking him would take time—time he did not have if these men were somehow connected to a US covert intelligence operation. Though doubtful, Gustaffson's suspicion about Modena seemed a more likely answer. The two assassins were probably dupes, sent on a fool's errand for no greater purpose than to allow Modena to betray them and thereby gain Gustaffson's gratitude and support.

If so, there was nothing much they could reveal. If they were part of a US-led covert op, then torture would take many hours to bear fruit. During those hours, more US forces, led by this man Yeager, would be approaching with bloody vengeance on their minds.

"We need to get the Arabs moving," Borges said at last. "Señor Gustaffson wants them staged at his Santa Barbara hacienda for their trip north."

"First-class accommodations," Turizo said with faint surprise.

Borges pursed his lips. He recalled Gustaffson saying he was meeting with Modena and Bustamante at his house in the high hills in the northern corner of the country, and now he wanted this gaggle of stinking would-be martyrs to join them. Why would he bring together the terrorists and the future president of Guatemala? The answer was obvious. Blackmail. Stage a photo op with El Presidente and the jihadists, thus guaranteeing Modena's cooperation by threatening him with exposure, implicating Modena in the scheme to help the Arabs slip into the United States.

Rather than explain everything to the security chief, he simply said, "I think El Escorpión has a dual purpose for this request, but yes, first-class for the Arab pigs. Load them up and send them north. I do not have a good feeling about this, so I recommend you do it quickly."

"And the other two?"

Borges sniffed and looked at his shoes. Holding on to the CIA woman and Victor Ruiz risked having them recovered by US Special Forces, which meant exposure to Gustaffson's organization. They might not know much, but they could point the finger at the Scorpion. The CIA did not need the same degree of proof as a criminal trial; they would not hesitate to exact revenge if they learned Gustaffson had sent terrorists to their land.

On the other hand, eliminating the captives meant losing whatever information they possessed, and Borges hated losing that intel, as it could clarify so much about who was pulling the strings and how much the United States might already be aware of Gustaffson's involvement with terrorists.

Borges let out the sigh of a tired old professor grading a very poor essay. He straightened and looked Turizo in the eyes. "Take them with you. Kill them and dump their bodies in the jungle."

CHAPTER SEVENTEEN

Once Yeager left the kidney-pounding back roads, he was able to pick up speed, and the ride smoothed out. The highways of northern Guatemala varied from passable to fair, with a mix of asphalt, concrete, and, in some cases, hexagonal tiles laid like cobblestones. He drove through villages and towns, passing tin-roofed houses that were either painted in bright, eye-watering colors or were four walls of scrap material, tinged with neglect and rotting from poverty. Shining white churches adorned the bigger municipalities, standing alongside blue-walled stores featuring Pepsi logos. The road snaked around and up and down ridges, valleys, and mountaintops. What bits of scenery he was able to catch while keeping the car out of the ditches was amazing, as was the abysmal destitution of the many villages dotting the hillsides. Squalor and beauty mixed together, like warts on a movie star. Mayan ruins and modern ruins coexisted in the mist-shrouded mountains. Thoughts kept popping up, all following the same theme: *Charlie would love to see this place.*

After hiking through the rough country for two days, driving the luxury SUV felt like paradise. Air conditioning, leather seats, and a multi-speaker stereo system. Yeager fiddled with the radio until he settled on a Guatemalan top-forty station blasting out peppy tunes played by manic DJs. He cranked up the radio and turned down the temperature on the AC in an effort to stay awake on the rare stretch of straight pavement.

At the halfway point of his journey, Yeager entered the city of Huehuetenango. It knotted his Texas tongue trying to pronounce the name of the town, so he ended up thinking of it as Way-Way-

Tango. He stopped at a bank and exchanged a few dollars for quetzals then found a modern supermarket, where he stocked up on bottled water, packaged bread, peanut butter—Smucker's, of all things—and a jar of *gelatina de fresa*, or strawberry jelly. He added toiletries to the cart, then he stopped by the clothing section and found a new chambray shirt, a pair of jeans, socks, and underwear. He added a backpack to replace the one he'd lost in the hills.

He moved through the shoppers in his own cone of silence, a head taller than most of them. A stranger in a strange land. The people seemed friendly enough, although they kept their distance, and he noticed more than one sidelong look of curiosity. Yeager guessed the folks in Way-Way-Tango didn't get many mean-looking, grim-faced gringos wearing a dead man's shirt and pushing a shopping cart through the aisles of their *supermercado*.

At a gas station, Yeager filled the SUV's tank with what he thought was damned cheap petrol—until he realized the price was per liter and not per gallon.

His last stop was a phone store, where he bought a prepaid cell phone with a thousand minutes, a car charger, and an international calling card. He had the clerk activate the phone and show him how to use the international card.

A decent stretch of two-lane blacktop led the way south out of Huehuetenango. Yeager settled into the drive with a pair of PB&Js and a cup of gas station coffee. He drove on autopilot, his mind returning to the questions that had nagged him since leaving four dead bodies in a nameless village. The guy he interrogated had filled in a lot of blanks, but some things remained a mystery.

"Why take us captive?" Yeager had asked the man. "Why not just kill us?"

"I do not know," the man had mumbled through bloody lips. "I am just following orders."

Yeager could not develop a single bulletproof theory of why Mendoza and Gustaffson would cook up such a goofy scheme. They get together over drinks, and Mendoza says, *Hey, I know. Let's recruit two numbskulls, send them across the border, and have your guys pick them up on the other side.* Gustaffson would be like, *Yeah, sure. That sounds like fun!*

No. That was insane. *What if somebody on Mendoza's team talked?*

"Hmm." Yeager sipped his coffee and steered with one hand.

What if Mendoza put together an operation, but a flunky sells out the Mexican captain and brings the info to Gustaffson? The traitor could be anybody in Mendoza's chain of command—maybe even the Guatemalan contact that Arturo was supposed to call to arrange pickup. The contact approaches Gustaffson and says, *I know some guys who are coming to kill you. For a pile of quetzals, I'll tell you all about it.*

That made more sense. If the traitor gave up only the two numbskulls and said, "Don't kill my pal Arturo," then Gustaffson might not know who sent said numbskulls or why. Or maybe it was Arturo himself who'd set it all up, betraying his two new pals but not giving up his boss's name. Just Arturo's bad luck to catch a face full of automatic weapon fire before collecting his blood money.

The construction of his scenario had a couple of missing supports. The whole thing hung slightly askew, but Yeager was damned if he could cypher out the rest of the story, not with the sparse set of clues he had to work with. Yeager considered himself a knuckle-dragging Marine, a fire-and-forget engine of destruction that took orders and got the job done. See target, vaporize target, go have a beer. He was no Sherlock Holmes or James Bond and was as likely to piece together a mosaic of criminal conspiracy as he was to dance *Swan Lake* in a pink tutu.

All his rumination brought him was the scant comfort that Gustaffson wanted information first, and dead bodies second. That gave him time. Tough on Por Que, who was no doubt getting the shit beaten out of him, but ultimately better than the alternative. It also made his mission one of rescue, not revenge, which relieved him of having to tell Dr. Alexandra Lopez that he'd gotten her fiancé killed. He would rather take a bullet to the testicles than have that conversation—the outcome of which would have the same result as the bullet.

Yeager glanced at the GPS. One hundred kilometers to go. His foot settled more heavily on the accelerator, and the Yukon ate up ground.

Capitán Cristiano Laureano woke to light streaming through the dingy window of the one-room apartment on Calle Mina, due south of Cerro de la Campana. His first action after sitting up and grinding the sleep from his eyes with the palms of his hands was to reach for the half-empty pack of cigarettes on the nightstand. He tamped one out and lit it with a cheap plastic lighter. He shook the pack to feel how many cigarettes remained.

Am I a pessimist or an optimist? Is my cigarette pack half empty or half full?

As a veteran of the Ejército Mexicano's Fuerza Especial de Reacción—he still thought of the Army's Special Reaction Force by its older name: Fuerza Especial del Alto Mando, High Command Special Reaction Force—his outlook tended toward the darkest of bleak cynicism. Nineteen years of fighting the cartels that infested his country had burned the bright young man he had once been into a charred cinder of bitterness. Like a tank hit by an armor-piercing incendiary round, burned and blackened from within, all his humanity had been cooked to a husk within the hard outer shell.

The first hit of scratchy smoke soothed the itch in Laureano's chest and energized him enough to find his boxers and pull them on. He meandered over to the table that he called his kitchen, trailing smoke. Laureano turned on the hotplate and set about preparing a pot of coffee. Coffee and cigarettes. Breakfast of champions, he had once heard it called by a US Green Beret sergeant he had trained with. He recalled laughing at the man, thinking it a joke. Now, not so funny.

His body ached.

Training today, too. His enthusiasm for training had burned away along with all his other enthusiasms. The two missions of the Special Reaction Force seemed to be training and waiting. Waiting for the call. Waiting for the mission. Capture a cartel leader or interdict a major shipment of narcotics, neither of which did a single thing to stop the flow of drugs heading north, nor the flood of money filling the pockets of the evil bastards who crushed his fellows under their heels. True peace and prosperity were a pipe dream. The cartels would never die, whereas men like Laureano and his colleagues would pass from the earth, unnoticed and unremarked. No family, no friends—who could risk emotional attachments?—and no legacy other than duty and service to a country that was ambivalent, at best.

Laureano finished dressing as his coffee boiled. Training fatigues, of course. Lace-up boots. And mask. Must not forget the mask. The training facility in the Sonoran Desert was supposed to be secret, but secrets did not last long in Mexico, and revealing one's face to cartel spies was the first step to having one's head separated from one's body. Laureano tucked his balaclava into his trouser pocket.

A quiet rap at the door sent a charge of adrenaline through his nervous system. Laureano tugged his holstered H&K P7M13 free and held it down by his thigh before approaching the door. He was not expecting company. Unexpected knocks at the door did not come to men like him without good reason.

Without bad reason, I should say.

"Who is it?" he called after sidling up to the wall next to the knob side of the door.

"Capitán Laureano? I am Rudy Aguilar, foreman for Don Raphael Martinez y Beltran de la Cueva. I would like a moment of your time."

"That's a lot of names, señor." Laureano's heart kicked up a notch. He paid in cash for this apartment, using an alias with the landlord, and used surveillance detection routines coming and going. Nothing at all should have traced Capitán Laureano to this address. "What does such an august person want with me?"

"That is simple. We would like to understand why you posed as Capitán Mendoza and enticed two gentlemen from the United States to undertake an assassination in Guatemala. I have with me Señor Quattlebaum. He, too, would like to know the answer to this question."

Laureano sagged against the wall.

CHAPTER EIGHTEEN

Yeager pushed the Yukon hard. The greenery rushed past as the day wore on. Cocooned in the luxury SUV, Yeager racked his brain to remember the phone number given by Rudy Aguilar, which he had blithely plugged into his cell phone as a contact then promptly forgotten. Back in the Stone Age, also known as the days prior to smartphones, he could memorize a double-handful of phone numbers and kept an address book with dozens more. Today, the only number he could recall was the one he specifically did not *want* to call. Reaching out to his wife would rip the scab off a very tender wound, and the follow-up explanation would rub salt and lemon into it.

"Hi, honey. I lost Victor. And my cell phone. And got bitten by habañero devil ants. Then I killed a guy with a pitchfork, stole his rifle, and killed two more. I tortured the last guy for information then put a bullet through his head. How was your day?"

Ugh. No. He didn't need to add her tight-jawed, silent condemnation—or was it castration—to his stress. One thing made him feel better: since either Mendoza had betrayed them, or someone in his organization had been compromised, it meant all deals were off. The mission had changed from killing Gustaffson to retrieving Victor and vacating Guatemala faster than a rocket on roller skates. Not having to assassinate a man lifted Yeager's spirits—right up until the moment he remembered Mendoza's threat to unleash Gustaffson's horrific killer on Charlotte and the boys. *Has he done it already? Was that part of the betrayal?*

Yeager fought the urge to spin the Yukon around and head back north. The GPS showed him to be fifty kilometers from his destination. Less than an hour, and he could have eyes on the place where Por Que had been taken. With luck, he would find his friend and the target of the original operation, Herman Gustaffson. El Escorpión would tell him whether or not he had sent Borges to harm his family, and if so, Yeager would put a gun to the man's nuts and order him to call off the hit.

And then?

Then I'll pull the damned trigger.

Alfonso Bustamante's cell phone rang at a very inopportune moment. The effects of his medication had just kicked in, and Marisol's ministrations on the softness of his member had begun to have an effect. His secretary lifted her head from between his legs and pouted at the interruption.

Bustamante plucked the phone from his desk, glanced at the caller ID, and sighed.

"Sorry, my dear, but I must take this," Bustamante said, then thumbed the answer icon. "Hola, mi amigo El Presidente."

"We did it," Guillermo Modena said. "Our friend from the hills has asked for a meeting."

"Our friend from the hills" translated as Gustaffson. One of the bricks weighing on Bustamante's back lifted. If Gustaffson was requesting a meeting, he was maybe beginning to believe that Modena and Bustamante could be trusted. The two gringos must have been caught, verifying the intel he and the president-elect had passed on during their meeting in the mountains. All the two gringos could reveal was that a Mexican special forces captain had ordered

Gustaffson's death, leading El Escorpión to believe Modena had perhaps saved his life.

Cementing Gustaffson's allegiance would allow Modena a wider base of power and ensure the cooperation of many key players, both inside and outside of Guatemala.

"That is good news, my friend." Bustamante's eyelids fluttered as Marisol resumed her efforts. "Have you set the meeting?"

"Sí. The bastard wants us in his place up north again. Eight p.m."

Bustamante glanced at his desk clock. He had an hour before they had to get on the road. Plenty of time for his secretary to finish satisfying him before he had to dress for the meeting. "That is fine. I will let my cousin know his efforts bore fruit."

"Yes, thank him for me. He supplied the perfect, ah…"

"Resources."

"…resources for our needs. I feel bad for them, though."

"I do, as well," Bustamante said without conviction. Truly, his attention was beginning to drift as Marisol seemed rather determined to bring him to completion. His office chair squeaked with the bob of her head. "But that is the way of pawns. They get sacrificed."

"Politics. It is a nasty business."

"Politics, yes…" Bustamante sighed and tipped his head back. "I will see you in an hour, Guillermo. Right now, I have a rather… urgent situation developing."

Guillermo laughed. "Give Marisol my best."

"I am about to give her my best."

They shared a schoolboy laugh before ending the call.

Blanca asked, "Are you okay?" then winced. *Stupid question. The man just had his nipple burned off with a soldering iron.*

"*Estoy bien*," Ruiz said in a detached voice. He stared at the ceiling, breathing evenly, and appeared to be meditating. The injured side of his body was opposite of where she sat on the floor, so she could see nothing of the wound. Asking about it felt cruel, so Blanca racked her brain for something to say. She felt a compelling need to talk, if only to hear her voice and to take her mind off her situation.

She blurted the first thing that came to mind. "Were you a SEAL?"

"Do I look like I balance balls on my nose for a living?" His response held such true contempt that it took her aback. Then he added, "I was one of Uncle Sam's Misguided Children, ma'am. Semper Fi."

"I see."

Scuffing footsteps from the hall drew her attention to the door. A shaggy-haired, swarthy man strutted into the room. Though dressed in Western jeans and a worn denim work shirt, there was no mistaking the man's hawk-nosed features, complete with a cluster of moles on his cheek. Blanca fought to keep her poker face blank when recognition struck.

Khayyat Halabi. Oh shit, oh shit, oh shit.

Halabi loomed over her, his hip near the head of the torture table, and spoke in thickly accented English: "I came to see for myself this CIA spy. You are CIA?" He sniffed and spat a glob of mucus on her shoe. "You are a whore. The Americans use whores to fight their battles. Allahu Akbar! He gives each of us the strength of ten. We will push you all into a sea of fire and crush you from the face of the earth."

"Hola, *cabrón*," Ruiz piped up. "You smell like the strength of ten unwashed assholes from where I sit. Find the room with the indoor plumbing and take a bath."

Halabi seemed to take notice of Ruiz for the first time. He sneered at the man on the table. "I heard you say about being a Marine. I have killed many US Marines. Many. They all die screaming like dogs, crying for their mothers."

"At least they had mothers with two legs instead of four."

Halabi's eyes narrowed under furrowed brows. It must have taken him a moment to work out the meaning behind the Marine's insult. Blanca read the moment the light bulb came on by the bloodred rage that flowed into Halabi's face. The terrorist circled the table to loom over Ruiz.

"That wound. Is pain, yes?" Halabi jabbed a thumb into Ruiz's chest. The Marine grunted and his restraints rattled as he bowed up in an arc. Halabi ground his thumb into the burn like a child crushing an ant. "You like that, US Marine?"

"Feels like... your sister's... tongue," Ruiz ground out through clenched teeth. "Lick the other one... and I'll know for sure."

Halabi jabbed his thumb down like a man calling an elevator, grinning with glee as Ruiz bucked and twisted. He let up after one final, big twist.

"I must leave now," the terrorist said. "My brothers and I are going to your putrid homeland. As you came to us, bringing blood and death, we will do the same to you."

"Bye, now," Ruiz said through pants. "Don't forget to write."

Blanca watched Halabi leave the room, scuffing on his heels in the Arab way of walking. The terrorist did not look back.

"There goes bad news," Blanca said. "We have to get out of here. Warn our people."

"Really? I think with some curtains, we could really make this place homey."

Borges spotted Dominic in the warehouse's kitchen, downing a bottle of sparkling water. Borges also liked that about Dominic: he rarely drank and never did so while there was business to be done.

"Dominic," Borges said while retrieving his own chilled bottle of Perrier from a refrigerator big enough to hold an entire horse, tail and all. "The Arabs are departing in a moment. Please go and prepare our subjects in the basement for their final journey. They will go with the Arabs to the Santa Barbara house." Borges shrugged off his ill temper at having to lose the opportunity for information. "Never dwell on the past, Dominic. Learn from it and move on."

"It shall be done as you say. Where should I join you?"

"I have to go see to a matter for Mr. Gustaffson. We... have suspicions about our new friends in the Guacamole Castle. Once they have been loaded on the van, leave them to Turizo and go to the villa. Get some rest. I imagine we will be quite busy in the days to come, assuming Modena and Bustamante have played us for fools."

"Sí."

Borges clamped his subordinate on the shoulder. The boy was really shaping up to be a first-class assistant. "Good man. Take care, and I will see you soon."

Yeager entered Quetzaltenango from the north. Thick, ropey knots of tension tightened the bunched muscles between his shoulder blades after two hours following the twisty two-lane route from Huehuetenango. The Pan-American Highway wound along high ridges and switchbacks so sharp, it could cause whiplash if taken too fast—though the danger of speeding was much curtailed by the pokey traffic clotting the narrow road as it bisected villages and farmland.

Clusters of multicolored buildings grew denser, signaling the entry into the outskirts of Quetzaltenango. Pinks and yellows predominated, though a few blue and red structures competed for their place on the color chart. Half the businesses seemed to be auto repair shops, though he passed more than one multistory hotel. In the middle of a traffic circle, he passed the reddish-toned statue of a backpack-wearing man with his hand raised to the north. The title on the base proclaimed it to be *Homenaje al Emigrante Salcajense.*

Monument to the Salcaja Immigrant?

Yeager shrugged and followed the traffic around to the first exit off the circle. He continued, following the GPS. It led him to a maze of streets lined with two-story buildings jammed together like Lego blocks. He eased the Yukon into a narrow lane crowded with parked cars along each curb. The road ahead appeared to terminate at a T-junction.

"In one hundred meters, you will reach your destination," the GPS said in Spanish.

"Sure I will," Yeager muttered. The neighborhood seemed rather crowded to hide the lair of a criminal overlord, though truth be told, Yeager had too little experience with criminal overlord hideouts to know what one should look like. He shut off the GPS and scouted for anything resembling a criminal overlord's parking lot for his Yukon.

He stopped at the crossroad, realizing his impression of a T-junction was wrong, as directly ahead ran a stubby dead-end street. Parked cars nosed into slotted spaces along each side, filling about half the available spots. A pair of shuttle buses—Yeager thought of them as church buses, or more like airport shuttles—filled most of the space, and a group of men clustered around them, waiting their turn to board.

The road behind him remained clear, so rather than drive into the parking lot and draw a lot of attention from the men in the lot,

Yeager backed the SUV into a space against the right-hand curb. He tucked the Yukon in behind an 80s model Caprice Brougham four spaces from the intersection. The Caprice left him plenty of room to see over the car's curling and scabrous vinyl top while offering a slice of concealment.

Though it didn't seem to matter—none of the gathered men so much as glanced his way. Yeager switched off the engine to conserve fuel. Winding mountain roads, combined with stop-and-go traffic through Podunk villages, had burned fuel faster than a fire at a refinery.

Yeager had barely settled back into his seat when one of the buses, apparently full, shut its folding door. Yeager squinted, counting passengers, and thought he could make out eight heads, although the tinted windows made it hard to be sure. The second bus was still loading. Three men stood at the door, carrying small packs. They were dressed in work clothing—checkered shirts worn over plain T-shirts, and pants of blue or brown denim. Ribbed boots.

"Hairy bastards, aren't you?" Yeager muttered.

Each man sported a thick black beard and shaggy hair. The last man to board paused long enough to scan the parking lot with coal-dark eyes. A chill washed over Yeager when the man's stare swept over him, as if his gaze projected a stream of negative energy that turned the air to ice.

This guy is as creepy as a horror movie puppet coming to life and leering at you.

Yeager pretended to be a statue as the man completed his survey and boarded the bus. Two steps, and he was gone. Yeager relaxed the tension in his shoulders with an effort.

Out of the warehouse came a new player. A young dude, mid-twenties, dressed in a polo and slacks, a jacket thrown over his shoulder. Slick and superior, the dude wore purpose and haughty disdain like a good cologne. At his waist, he sported a semi-auto pistol in a high-rise holster.

"Ah," Yeager told himself as the next person passed through the warehouse door. "I guess I came to the right place."

Handcuffed and shirtless, Victor Ruiz was pushed from behind by a gorilla from the planet GrowEmBig. Bullet head, heavy features carved in the shape of an angry Mayan god, and arms long enough he could damn near touch his knees without bending, the big man tugged another captive by her manacled wrists.

The Yukon's wheel creaked in Yeager's grip when he noticed the raw red ruin of Por Que's left pectoral. Muscular and razor-cut from hours in the gym, his friend's torso appeared to have been decorated by a kid with a crimson Crayola, centering on the left nipple and wandering outward. Yeager's nostrils flared, and he shook the wheel as if trying to tear it free of the steering column.

Breathe in. Hold it. Breathe out.

Going nuts would not help. He had to focus on a plan. The dude and the gorilla loaded their prisoners into the van before Yeager could even try to make a play. He paused with one hand on the door handle, a half-formed plan of jumping out of the Yukon, scrambling for the loaded rifle tucked into the backseat footwell, then blindly charging face-first across a good forty yards of open street to... what? Kill the driver first, obviously. Ram open the bus door? Climb aboard and hose down the interior? The guys inside would most definitely sit quietly while he did all that, right?

"Dammit!" Yeager hammered the padded leather center console armrest with a closed fist. So close! The insanity of this jaunt into Guatemala continued to twist into convoluted tangles of ever-deepening difficulty. If he could only recover Por Que, Yeager vowed to get the hell out of this country, go home, and try to make peace with his wife. Damn Gustaffson, damn his hired killers, and double-damn the slimeball Mendoza. He would do the thing he should have done to start with, which was to hire the best damn attorney in Mexico to bribe whoever needed bribing to get Cujo out of prison.

"I'm so fucking stupid," he growled. "So, so *fucking* stupid."

The two buses cranked up and started moving. The bus with Por Que took the lead, flasher blinking a right turn, and pulled into the main street. The second bus followed a moment later.

"Okay, then," he said after scrubbing his face with his palms, "let's get back on the road. Just another drive in the country." Yeager fired up the Yukon, punched the gear lever into Drive, and headed out. "One more run, like you've done a million times before."

CHAPTER NINETEEN

ell, this sucks. This sucks like the giant vacuum of space.

W Victor Ruiz laid his head down on his hands, which were cuffed through a plastic grip loop atop the seat directly in front of him. He was pretty sure he could tear the loop loose from the seat without much effort. *But then what? Use it like a club? Who brings a plastic club to a gunfight?*

The shuttle bucked and bounced over rugged streets, and Victor winced at the stabs of pain reminding him of his burned chest. *Forget it. Block it out. Things to do, places to go, people to kill.*

The shuttle had six rows of seats. The ugly man with the ape arms had shoved him into the second seat on the driver's side of the bus. While the junior torturer held a pistol on him, Giganto had fixed his cuffs to the grip. Then they had taken the skinny chica—fake name Juanita Alvarez—to the back row, cuffed her and taken up the next-to-last row. Four fuzzy scuzzballs hailing from desert countries rich in oil, sand, and jihadi martyrs were scattered in between.

One of those very special specimens, the head murder boy called Halabi, kept looking to the back of the bus, where Juanita was cuffed. He scratched his thick beard—searching for lice, Victor suspected—and allowed evil thoughts to beam forth from his deep-sunken eye pits. Victor clocked the positions of the other terrorists.

First, Mr. Halabi, I beat you to death with my plastic club. Then I plastic-whip you, and you, and you. And you two guys in back. I'm gonna plasticate you until yo' own mamacita won't recognize you. Ground beef au bad guy, seasoned with my bootheel compost.

Victor checked out the window. The terrain gradually morphed from urban Third World poverty to farmland Third World poverty. By the sun glaring into his eyes from the top of the bus window, he judged it to be around three o'clock in the afternoon. The ride smoothed as they reached a two-lane highway, and the shuttle sped up.

Junior Torturer had said they were heading for an embarkation point near the Guatemala-Mexico border. There, he and Juanita would each earn a bullet to the head and a shallow grave. The time to make a move was dwindling, and damn him if he was going to just walk quietly to his own execution. No. He needed to make something happen. What exactly that was, he had no idea, but it needed to be soon, because...

He side-eyed Halabi, who continued radiating repressed lust along with his gut-clenching personal odor. Halabi was obviously working himself up to host a rape party, with Juanita as the victim of honor. If Victor couldn't create an opportunity to break free and somehow get control of a weapon with more firepower than a plastic stick, then not only would Juanita suffer before her death, but Victor would be unable to face God with a clear conscience, knowing he had allowed it to happen.

And I ain't talking to God like I'm some punk-ass bitch. No way, José.

Victor tensed his hands, and the grip squeaked in protest.

The sun drooped toward the western mountains, and Yeager followed the convoy northwest with Huehuetenango fading in his rearview mirror. This was new territory. Earlier in the day, he'd followed his GPS into that city from the northeast before striking due south. Now he was on the other branch of the Y-junction, motoring along Highway 7W as it snaked toward Mexico's southern border. Having seen Way-Way-Tango twice in one day did not improve his mood.

Different highway, same twists and turns. The road offered up every curve in the Highway Engineers Manual of Challenging Construction—hairpins, salients, re-entrants, and corner bents. If not for the signs in Spanish, he might as well have been driving through rural Arkansas or Tennessee. Shacks, shanties, stores, and sheds. Chicken houses, empty houses, farmhouses, and warehouses. Blind curves and no-passing zones lined with grubby weeds and roadkill. Trees, hills, and barbed-wire fences.

Sweat stains bloomed under the armpits of his new shirt, and his unwashed body soaked the air-conditioned interior with a vinegary smell. Yeager barely noticed it. The gut-clenching terror of fighting in the Afghanistan mountains, followed by eye-burning hours driving a rig, had all but inoculated him to his own sweat stink. Only when Charlie wrinkled her nose and pointed to the shower did Yeager snap to and recognize he was wilting flowers on their stems. The fun part was when she joined him in the shower to help him come clean.

Yeager quirked a crooked grin. *Hah! Pun intended.*

He held steady at about a quarter mile behind the pair of shuttles. Sometimes there would be intervening traffic, sometimes not. He stayed close enough that he would see the vans turn off in time to follow if they took a side road. But not so close as to be an obvious tail. Or so he hoped. The only spy craft he knew came from James Bond films and the audiobook thrillers he listened to on the long-haul routes as a trucker.

But he had a problem, and it added to the perspiration soaking his pits. The fuel gauge was like a ruler, with full on the left and empty to the right. Every time his eyes flicked to the gauge, the bar appeared to have dropped bit closer to the *E*. And the gas stations were getting farther apart the deeper they traveled into the hinterlands.

The dreaded indicator light of a dry gas tank lurked in the very near future.

Should he chance a pit stop and maybe miss seeing where the shuttles left the highway or stick with the buses and hope they stopped before he ran out of gas? He had skipped his chance in Huehuetenango, reasoning that he could easily lose his quarry if they vanished into the city instead of continuing onward. That turned out to be a mistake. The two-bus convoy jogged left at the split south of the city, heading northwest, and barreled around the edge of Huehuetenango before venturing deeper into the highlands. He passed gas station after gas station, thinking, "Just one more."

Signs of habitation thinned. Gas stations stopped appearing. No people, little traffic. He needed something to happen and happen fast.

An idea bubbled up and took root.

Yeager's eyes narrowed. "Time for Plan C."

The cops had a word for it. *Pitting* or *porting* or *potting*—something with a *P* that Yeager couldn't recall. The technique would deliberately cause a pursued vehicle to lose control and spin out. It involved striking the rear quarter panel of the target car with enough directional force to pivot the vehicle into an uncontrolled spin. Cops used the maneuver sparingly, as inducing the target vehicle into an uncontrolled spin invited unforeseen consequences—like attorneys crawling out of hell to scramble after ambulances carrying injured or dead civilians. Yeager had seen the principle put into accidental practice in the free-for-all of the American Interstate highway system, where a full quarter of the population drove with either complete absorption in their phones or with the wild abandon of meth-addled lemmings trying to find their own cliff to jump from. High in the cab of his rig, he had a front-row seat to more than one amateur hammering the rear quarter panel of another driver and sending the struck vehicle sideways.

Going sideways at high speed was frowned upon in every driver's manual ever printed. The results at high speed were unpredictable, the carnage unimaginable. Those producers of TV and film found the need for drama outweighed the facts. In the shows, one car inevitably motored up side-by-side with the other, and both proceeded to bash into each other as if in a demolition derby. High drama, sure. Effective, no.

From the rear quarter panel forward, the leverage shifted to the pursued versus the pursuer in a parallel chase. At that point, it was anybody's game. If the pursuing driver wanted to play Hollywood, he gave up his advantage. The lead driver could wait until the chase car passed the balance point—about the driver's-door position—then lean hard into the chase car to move it sideways, assuming similar weight and size of the two cars.

On a twisty mountain road, with the last rays of the dying day shooting light beams through the gaps in the trees and his fuel gauge needle merging with the empty mark, Yeager studied on the best way to intersect his SUV with the ass-end of a bloated shuttle such that it would knock the larger vehicle for a loop while leaving the Suburban undamaged enough to continue the mission... for however long his fuel held out.

There are people in the van.

Who were they? Innocent immigrants headed north to violate the borders of two sovereign nations to reach the promised land of free schooling, health care, and McDonald's Happy Meals? The shuttles seemed to be first-class travel accommodations, not something enjoyed by the average migrant seeking exploitation by the Great Sugardaddy to the north. No, this was more of a...

What was the word? Boutique experience?

"Rich immigrants?" he wondered aloud. "Or at least with money enough for a nice bus ride?"

How about drug smugglers? Yeager pinched his lips in rejection. Smugglers didn't convoy their product north in airport shuttles.

Do they?

Yeager rubbed his forehead. A needle of tension stitched tight the muscles between his shoulder blades.

No way around it. If he jacked up the trailing bus in order to cause a disruption and bring the lead bus to a stop, he risked sending eight or more people to a Guatemalan morgue. The roads here meandered along bluffs overlooking steep drops when they weren't splitting through flat sections of country. Port or pit or pot the shuttle at the wrong time, and it might crash over the guardrail and plummet hundreds of feet down the side of a mountain, killing everyone inside.

What did a few more dead bodies matter? He was already a murderer.

I had to kill those guys to rescue Por Que.

He sneered at his own excuse. *Keep telling yourself that. Besides, you seen the body count you've left behind? Charlie was right. Death and destruction follow you everywhere. What's one more busload? Nothing but a statistical blip on your balance sheet.*

Yeager followed the curves, leaning the big SUV into the turns with greater and greater speed. Tires protested as he gunned the Yukon through hairpins, salients, re-entrants, and corner bents, slaloming the vehicle as if entered in the Guatemalan Grand Prix. He punched the accelerator on the straightaways, eyes fixed on the road ahead, vision tunneling to match his skill to the narrow ribbon of concrete spooling under his wheels.

Yeager powered the SUV toward his target. He had a bus to catch.

Khayyat Halabi could not keep his thoughts away from the Western whore in the tight jeans that revealed the entire length and shape of her legs and outlined the slight curve of her boyish hips. He found himself repulsed by her. She wore no face covering, offering up a whore's lips, and her blouse accented petite breasts.

Just like a whore to inflame a man's lust and distract him from his purity of purpose. His eyes returned to her as if drawn by magnets, no matter how often he forced himself to look away. Something should be done about her, or his brothers might begin to doubt Halabi's manhood. He knew he should feel lust, but all he really felt was fear that his men would lose respect if he didn't lead as a man should.

She should be punished, whispered the voice in his head. Halabi had come to believe this was the voice of Allah, prodding him to action, all praise be to Allah. Filling the woman with their Muslim seed was a holy duty. After all, the Koran did state that infidel women were good for one thing only—the pleasure of Muslim men. Such women were the spoils of war, to be used and discarded by the true believers of jihad. That this woman was an agent of the Great Satan made her an even greater prize for the sexual release of him and his men.

And yet he hesitated. Why?

I know why, whispered the devil's voice in his head.

The slick Guatemalan man-boy, Dominic, and the ugly gorilla, Turizo, would have to cede control of their prisoner, and they might balk, causing friction between Halabi and the people he considered his hosts. If he demanded the woman for his use, that might insult the Guatemalans and jeopardize his mission. That must be the reason he hesitated. That and nothing more.

But they intended to kill the woman, after all, so what would it hurt?

Halabi ground his teeth. Taking her now, on a crowded bus, would be awkward. It meant performing for an audience too. His brothers would gather around, cheering him on as he took the leader's position as first in line. Following his lead, they would all want their turn and would watch him as he fucked the infidel bitch. He did not perform well with an audience, or at least he worried that he might not, as the opportunity for such performance had yet to present itself.

The whore is a female...

His success with women had always been... lacking. The only time he had managed erection, let alone penetration, had been when he closed his eyes and remembered *bacha bazi*—boy play—in his small Pashtun village. The beardless boys would dress in women's attire and dance for the men, exciting Halabi with the sway of their hips, the enticement of their slender arms, and the flash of dark eyes. The dancing of the *bacha bareesh* culminated in sexual congress performed under hot blankets, skin to skin, with the heady aroma of incense and woodsmoke, frying meat and sweaty bodies.

Halabi shivered and licked his lips. Those memories stirred him like no other.

That is why you hesitate, the devil whispered. *You prefer sex with—*

No! I do not!

And yet if he tried and failed in front of his men, he would be an object of ridicule at best, a pariah at worst. Would they attribute his softness to a lack of piety? Would they sense his reluctance was due to a perversion within his soul, a dark secret that he dare not speak, even to himself?

I am not a homosexual!

His times with the *bacha bareesh* had merely left him... confused. Many Muslim men availed themselves of the beardless boys. They went on to marry and spawn many offspring. The boy play was nothing but a way for a man to relieve his tension without dishonoring the daughters of his friends within the village. Such trifling amounted to nothing more than wrestling with a younger man, no? Copulation in such circumstances did not cause perversion, no more than it did among some of his acquaintances who labored long in hills and sometimes found release among the animals they tended. It was a biological necessity, after all.

The shuttle rumbled over a rough patch of highway, vibrating and rattling through a small cluster of homes. Halabi looked across the aisle and found the male prisoner watching him through hooded eyes. A killer. Halabi recognized the type, not least from looking in a mirror. An American Mexican, they said. Short. Dark hair. Heavy brows. Thick, well-defined muscles. He appeared as though he wanted to strangle Halabi with his bare hands.

Halabi sneered and looked back to the woman. Quite boyish, she was, and as slim as a reed. Maybe if he turned her facedown and used her the way he would a boy... He pictured peeling those jeans down over her butt, pushing her face into the seat... His prick stirred to life.

The woman was a prize of war. It was his duty to Allah to use her as he saw fit.

I am not a homosexual.

Halabi had climbed out of his seat before he realized he was moving. The two escorts, Dominic and Turizo, looked up as he approached along the central aisle. His five Muslim brothers regarded him with speculation and the beginnings of grins tightening their lips. They knew what was coming, and they relished it.

"The woman." He spoke to Dominic, the lead host on this journey. "I will have her, as will my men."

CHAPTER TWENTY

The shuttle bus loomed in his windshield. Fifty yards and closing. Huge and becoming huger. Like an elephant on wheels, with a bloated rear compartment that filled the lane from side to side, it cut over the center stripe on the inside curves and hung over the gravel shoulder when the road bent the other direction. Was the Yukon big enough to nudge the bus into a spin?

An idiot message on the dashboard flared to life. The low fuel indicator had made itself known.

"That tears it," Yeager hissed under his breath.

He grimaced and floored the accelerator. The monster engine roared, happy with the big gulp of fuel dumped into its cylinders. Power, luxury, towing capacity—the SUV featured all the above in spades, though it lacked something in rabbit acceleration. But gain speed, it did, and once gained, it seemed happy to gain more. The needle climbed through seventy, and was affirmed by the digital readout in the center screen: 72... 74... 76...

The rear of the shuttle bus expanded in his windshield. A red caution indicator flared on the dash, and his seat vibrated. Yeager had grown used to the vibrations when he got too close to someone or drifted over the lane marker. The vehicle's safety warning system chided him for such behavior.

A curve bent to the right, with no visibility beyond. Yeager edged into the oncoming lane, craning for a better view. Buzzing from his seat nagged him. But it would be a hell of an ending to such a pleasant drive in the country should he connect head-on with a station wagon before he could crash into the big-ass bus, now, wouldn't it?

He held to his speed, allowing the gap to close to a few feet between the nose of his SUV and the shuttle's rear bumper. The high center of his ride pulled at the roof, and the lack of traction whispered up through the frame to his butt, sending a message of imminent rollover if he didn't slow the fuck down on the curves. The danger-close warning light flared—oncoming traffic.

Figures. No one for miles, and just when I want to have a wreck, here comes someone.

Yeager eased off and slid back to his lane. The blur of a passing car flashed by on his left. Yeager flexed his hands on the wheel and squared up for another run. Odd how hard it was to deliberately cause a wreck, as years of avoiding collisions had plowed grooves in his muscle memory such that he found himself missing chances to swing out and take the plunge, only to regret his reluctance when the road shifted and the opportunity passed. And the Yukon seemed aggravated that he kept ignoring its warnings—or was that his imagination?

The shuttle driver had to be aware of the jackass crowding his tail, jockeying around behind him as if he wanted to pass. He was probably eyeballing his side mirror and grumbling curses as Yeager dithered around at bumper-tasting distance. Even so, the driver did not offer an easy pass by leaning his shuttle onto the shoulder and opening up half a lane, as would a more courteous driver.

They topped a rise, and the highway straightened out for a quarter-mile stretch of pavement, high hills on the left, and a slope down to the right. Not a cliff, but a rough pitch of scrub trees and jutting boulders interrupted by the odd farm building chamfered into the hillside. A snap view ahead showed no approaching traffic. Yeager got a brief glimpse of the lead vehicle before the road leveled and it disappeared behind the bulk of the trailing shuttle.

Now or never.

Yeager clamped the wheel and tromped on the accelerator.

"The woman. I will have her, as will my men."

Well, that fucking tears it. Victor eased his feet against the seat in front of him and gathered his muscles. The chain of the cuffs ran through a molded plastic grip atop the seat. Victor fisted his hands together. He breathed in then let it out on a three-count. Rinsed and repeated as he oxygenated his cells and steadied his heartrate to a sniper's level of Zen.

The lead terrorist jackass dead-man-stalking stood in the center aisle, holding a support pole to brace himself against the swaying of the bus. Four inches taller than Victor's five-five-and-three-quarters, the man called Halabi weighed maybe a buck and a half, with an average build. He carried himself with an Arab stoop to his shoulders. Altogether, he was not very imposing, though Victor reckoned the man had done some killing, so no sense letting appearances make him overconfident. Best to take Halabi down hard, fast, and with maximum prejudice. Besides, he would have only seconds before a scrum of jihadis would drop all over him and play football with his head.

"What? Now?" Torture Boy Dominic asked. He sounded annoyed, like a parent whose kid wanted Dad to stop the car so he could go pee.

"Yes, now." Halabi stood one row back from Victor, who focused forward and tracked the action with his other senses while he Zenned out and built up steam for the trigger that would set his body into motion. "The woman is a whore-spy of the enemy. She belongs to us to use as we wish."

Victor closed his eyes and tried to tune out the stupid wafting through the van's interior. *Jiminy Crickets, can't you at least be original?* He mimicked Halabi's cadence in his head. *She whore-spy! To use as we wish! Me dick very big! See!*

Breath in. Let it out. Plastic creaked as he tensed. *Snap through the grip with one clean jerk. Leap into the aisle. Go all freaky kung fu, badass Mexican mofo on the stinky little prick. Use his dead body as a shield… Then what?*

Then the Mexican Action Hero dies heroically from a hail of bullets.

"We'll reach our destination in… fifteen minutes," Dominic was saying. "It will be much more, ah, convenient there." To Victor's ears, the younger man's tone had turned from annoyed to appeasing. This Halabi guy had to be a big cheese, and Dominic didn't want to cause any friction. "For one thing, you will have much more room to, ah, spread out. Real beds."

Halabi hesitated, and Victor relaxed a bit. Maybe the refugee from a bad action movie would see sense and let it go until they reached journey's end. Though journey's end meant journey's-fucking-end for Victor Ruiz.

What would Yeager do?

Yeager would move now, of course. Waiting for the end of the road was just not his style.

Victor tensed and drew back, as if trying to row a boat with its oars stuck in ice. Plastic creaked. His muscles bulged. The seatback grip bowed inward at the point where his cuffs pulled at the middle.

"See," Dominic said at the edge of Victor's hearing. "We're pulling off now. We'll be there in minutes."

Victor slipped a glance over his shoulder. Halabi blocked the view of two men with guns—they would be out of action until they cleared the obstacle. They couldn't see him and vice versa. By the sound of it, Torture Boy had no problem giving the woman up for sport but was not thrilled with the inconvenience of it on the bus.

Keep talking, fuzz face. One more pull, and I'm all over you.

Though not as good as Yeager at the hand-to-hand stuff, Victor Ruiz was a US Marine and thus felt himself capable of dropping a metric ton of whoop ass on any enemy, foreign or domestic.

Victor sucked in a new breath, braced himself, and pulled…

The terrorist turned to regain his seat. There was no blocking the firing lane from the men with guns. Victor relaxed his pull an instant before the terrorist turned and sat. He breathed out slowly. Frustration leaked out through his nostrils.

The van's signal indicator blinked on and off as the shuttle slowed for a turn. Victor could only watch as the highway turned onto the shoulder and approached a gate with a guardhouse.

Yeager zoomed up on the rear of the shuttle. Oncoming lane: clear. Shoulder: flat and level. The trio of vehicles zoomed through tunnels of dwellings lining the shoulders—homes, businesses, farms, and auto shops, abandoned and occupied—all crowding the pavement in long rows, broken by stretches of raw land. Kids played on the verge of the highway, kicking balls, riding bikes, or simply squatting over some game. They were inches from disaster, should one stray a little too far from the impossibly narrow shoulders. More people lived along the side of the highway than Yeager would have imagined, and all of them seemed determined to die on the grill of his stolen car.

The straightaways were double rows of dwellings. The blind curves invited death to anyone leaving their lane. He had the horsepower to overtake the slow-moving shuttle, but the road kept throwing curves or presenting him with innocent bystanders, forcing him to hold off the gas.

Clear stretches of straight road, when they appeared—

Like this one...

Now or never.

Yeager tipped the SUV left and tromped the accelerator, kicking the automatic transmission down a gear and punching him in the back with a burst of speed.

The highway straightened out. Bumpers came level. Warnings flared on the dash.

Goose the gas, and he would be on target.

Another curve pitched him left. Yeager gripped the wheel hard, holding into the curve with gritted teeth, praying for a break in the traffic. An oncoming collision at this speed would kill him, airbag or no airbag. The shuttle cruised on, as if unaware of the idiot trying to pass on a narrow two-lane road with limited visibility. He was close enough to taste the shuttle's paint.

The Yukon's nose crept forward.

His target: get the bumper of the SUV level with the shuttle's rear wheel. Then a hard right into the big body would push its rear to the side, inducing a spin.

The fuel gauge? Don't look at the fuel gauge.

A glance ahead. Still clear. A blind curve to the right coming up. Bad angle for an impact. Centrifugal force would be against him. He would be pushing the shuttle against its natural momentum if he tried forcing the left-rear quarter panel to move right.

Okay then.

Move now.

Now, now, now!

Yeager slugged the accelerator with the weight of his entire leg.

The Suburban coughed. Shuddered. Coughed again.

It dropped back, despite his foot clamped down hard enough to drive the pedal into the firewall.

"No, no, no, no, no," Yeager pleaded. "Please, God, don't do this to me."

God wasn't listening.

Or God's sympathy with the likes of him had long since vanished. No spare drop of fuel materialized. The Yukon's engine died. Lights sprinkled the dashboard. The power steering went out. Power brakes went out. Yeager fought the big car to the shoulder, pumping hard to get some action from the brakes. He tapped the emergency brake button to bring the car to a halt. Dust billowed around him.

Ahead of him, the pair of shuttles cruised on as if nothing had happened. Ten seconds later, they disappeared around the curve. And Yeager watched them go.

CHAPTER TWENTY-ONE

The wind from a passing semi buffeted the Yukon, rocking Yeager. Inside the big SUV, it was quiet enough to hear his sweat drip. Quiet enough to hear his hopes die.

So close.

Just that morning, he had killed three men. Tortured another, then killed him. So that made four.

He'd driven four hours to find Victor, only to watch him be herded onto a bus. Followed that bus another three hours. Been inches from knocking one shuttle off the road, maybe killing a bunch of immigrants.

And then.

Running.

Out.

Of.

Gas.

At the last second.

Yeager clapped his hands over his face and dragged them down, as if trying to pull his skin off. Raspy whiskers crackled under his fingers.

Now what?

Long shadows reached out from the western hills as the sun burned the skyline, inches from disappearing over the horizon. Every few minutes, a vehicle zoomed by, headlights on more often than not. A valley dropped away a few feet beyond the passenger side. Thick and scrubby trees overhung the Yukon's hood. All around in any direction, in the distance, rose soft mountains. Old mountains. Raw edges eroded away and covered in greenery.

Fifty feet ahead, a low-slung building with a rusted tin roof sat among the dust and high weeds. Painted signs of a white hand, with the thumb raised, against a red background advertised support for the LIDER, which Yeager recognized as a political affiliation, though he had no clue what flavor was packed into that box: conservative, communist, or devil worshipers.

"Time to move," he said into the stillness of the cabin.

The alert chimed as Yeager shoved open the door.

"Shut up, car. I've had enough of you." He found a flashlight in the Yukon's glove box and flicked it on. A D-celled hardware store special, the flash threw out a decent yellow glow. Not great, but it would do. He dragged his rifle from the back seat, slipped on a load-bearing vest, then hip-checked the door closed. He slung the rifle over one shoulder and found a pocket on the vest to carry the flashlight, rearranging a few magazines to make room. The load out was heavy, but not horribly so.

Be like a picnic in Fallujah.

Heat and dust rose from the hard-packed soil under his feet. The strong smell of manure wrinkled his nose. A cock crowed from somewhere far away, completely out of phase with the time of day.

The road curved away. No telling how far the shuttles would drive before stopping. No telling where they might turn off.

That didn't matter.

Of all the idiot things he had done to this point, only one choice remained: find Victor Ruiz. Shoot anybody who tried to stop him. Get out of Guatemala. Go home and try to fix his marriage. And never, ever, leave home again.

Yeager started walking.

Victor's interest perked up when the shuttle approached a gated entrance flanked by a guard shack. He clocked a pair of guards in black tac gear holding military rifles, one inside the guardhouse and one flanking it.

The guard inside the shack waved the shuttle through a wrought-iron gate that swung open on motor-driven hinges. The property beyond the gate appeared to be a botanical garden, chock-full of blooming plants crowding the space between thick-rooted trees whose broad canopies overhung the lane.

"Are those alpacas or llamas?" Victor asked the back of the driver's head. "I can never tell the difference."

The driver gave no answer.

"Well, never mind." Victor shrugged, rattling the chain of his cuffs. "The real question is: are they good on a tortilla?"

Again, no answer.

"Glad we had this talk." Victor sniffed and hunched down for a better view through the windshield at the structure rising just beyond the end of the lane. "Wow. Did you guys have some extra Lego blocks left over, or what?"

White cubes with big windows appeared to have been stacked together to build a house of rectangles. Interior lights shone out from the broad windows, pushing back the gathering shadows of dusky twilight. Brilliant-white exterior spots filled in the blanks, giving the scene enough light to be seen from space.

The shuttles followed the concrete path to a parking apron abutted against the far side of the cube monster. The open bay doors of a multicar garage invited them into a space as big as an aircraft hangar, where the shuttles parked side by side.

Victor side-eyed his fellow passengers. Halabi and his pals shared grins and leers. This would be their payoff for waiting—a chance to get the woman in a room all to themselves, where they could take turns using her for their pleasure. Turizo and Torture Boy seemed relieved, stretching, yawning, and exuding that air of a job well done. He caught Juanita's eye for a brief moment and read acceptance in her dull gaze. Defeat.

Not if I can help it, sister. He broadcast a look of hope in her direction, trying to communicate telepathically. *This might be our chance. While they're all relaxed and happy. Keep your eyes open and be ready.*

She flicked her head. No. Message not received.

There came a general scrum of people disembarking and mingling in the garage. One of Halabi's boys led Juanita off the bus as Turizo held a gun and watched while Torture Boy unlocked Victor's cuffs.

Victor jerked loose from the man's grip when the cuff came off. "You really gonna just let them have her? What kind of asshole does that?"

Turizo waggled the pistol in his fist. "Shut up! I'd kill you here, but I don't want to get blood on the seats. Twitch wrong, and I'll forget all about that."

Torture Boy twisted Victor's hands behind his back while kneeing him in the shoulder. Turizo shifted to keep his line of sight clear, never giving Victor a moment where he might have taken Torture Boy by surprise and used him as a human shield. The cuffs ratcheted tightly around his wrists.

"Move," Turizo ordered.

"You should really work on the whole guest experience, *hijo de puta.*"

Alfonso Bustamante kept an office in a modest two-story building at the crossroads of 9A Calle and 7A Avenida, blocks away from the Plaza de la Constitución, as befitted the closest political adviser of the country's newly elected president. If Bustamante had been given a title other than presidential crony, Macerio Borges had yet to learn of it. Politics did not interest him all that much. There was no honor in politics.

Ten doorways opened off the second-floor hallway, and a few of the offices remained staffed. The muffled sounds of people on telephones, humming printers, and the occasional cough broke the quiet of the well-lit tiled hallway. The air circulating carried an "old building" smell with it, slightly ripe though not unpleasant. Bustamante's office was the third door from the elevator bank, on the left-hand side, overlooking 9A Calle.

Breaking into Bustamante's office proved to be much easier than it should have been. There was no security to speak of, merely an alarm system older than Cortés and a lockset whose main security feature was rust. Borges bypassed both easily: the alarm via a magnetic strip door shim and the lock by a dose of WD-40 and a pick gun.

Inside, Borges found a modest space devoted to a receptionist and a single interior door of laminated wood. It had been left ajar, so Borges pocketed his pick gun and entered Bustamante's inner sanctum without effort.

The inner office was a shrine to Alfonso Bustamante. Thick chair-rail molding separated a red-painted lower wall from a cream-colored upper half. This upper half held clusters of photographs, plaques, and framed certificates and diplomas—all attesting to the brilliance and importance of the great man who held the reins of the next president of Guatemala. So many items decorated the walls, Borges was half afraid the structural integrity had been compromised and an inadvertent sneeze might bring down the entire wall.

A battleship of a desk dominated the far end of the room, backed by floor-to-ceiling bookcases. Two windows, their heavy drapes pulled back, allowed in enough of the fading daylight to navigate the furniture without tripping. Borges targeted the desk first, finding it unlocked.

"Tsk. Stupid man," he muttered. "If you are to be the brains behind the leadership of our country, I am not confident of our future."

He was head down in the first drawer and somehow missed hearing the outer door open. The woman's shocked voice came as an unpleasant surprise.

"Who are you, and what are you doing here?"

Borges straightened and projected a stern look of disapproval. "I am a chief inspector for the National Police. And who are you?"

"M-Marisol," the woman said, suddenly unsure of herself. Mention of the National Police tended to dash cold water over anyone on the receiving end. "Marisol Pareda. I am Señor Bustamante's personal assistant."

Borges smiled. A much faster way of obtaining the information had just landed in his lap. Borges produced a pistol from his jacket pocket. "Please, Señorita Pareda. Come in and have a seat. We have much to discuss."

D*éjà vu,* Bustamante thought.

"You drive as if you're tempting God," he said to Modena. Accompanied by dramatic gestures and a passionate voice, he added, "'Send us off the cliff!' you're saying to God. 'Have a peasant boy step into the road so we may flip this car while trying to avoid him and end up wadded like chewing gum. Have this fine Mercedes throw a tie rod at two hundred kilometers an hour so we end up in a fireball big enough to roast all the coffee in the fields. I'm so full of hubris as the Presidente of Guatemala, I cannot die so mundane a death.'"

"I'm not doing two hundred kilometers per hour. You're an old woman."

Modena powered the heavy sedan along the same path they had traveled on their previous visit to the lair of El Escorpión. The twisty two-lane with dirt shoulders—where there were any shoulders at all—and blind curves offered myriad possibilities for instant destruction.

They flashed by a man walking along the shoulder.

"Did you see that?" Modena demanded with the early flickers of righteous anger heating his tone.

"I am seeing nothing," Bustamante said. "I am keeping my eyes closed to review my life as it passes behind my eyelids."

"That man was carrying a military rifle! Out in the open, walking along the highway! Carrying a rifle."

"A hunter?"

"No, a military rifle. All black, with a big magazine sticking out."

"A mercenary, maybe? With the cartel?"

Modena slapped the wheel. "And he looked like a gringo!"

"This is worse?"

"It is worse!" Modena shouted. "We don't need gringo mercenaries to come down here, kill our people!"

"Damned right!" Bustamante shouted right back. "We must only allow our people to kill our people. It is only fair! And just! No gringo killers."

Modena rolled his eyes. "Don't be an asshole. You know what I mean."

"I really don't." Bustamante sighed and settled into his seat. He tugged his seatbelt for the hundredth time, ensuring it remained tight across his chest. "But I concede that you know what you mean, and that's enough. How much farther?"

"Two kilometers or thereabouts."

Bustamante gazed up at the ceiling. "Please, God in heaven, do not kill me before we get there."

The smell of fresh blood saturated the small office. Borges always found the particular scent of hot blood, newly let from the human body, to be the most intoxicating of aromas. Often described by others as having a metallic tinge such as copper or iron, the liquid essence of human life carried a bouquet indescribable in its complexity. Earthy, salty, metallic... all that and much more. The scent turned bad quickly, meaning only the freshest of opened veins could supply the purest experience.

"Ah, Marisol," Borges lamented. "It is the blood of the young that is the most piquant of all."

Marisol said nothing, her eyes already having dimmed as her life flowed from her abused body and dripped to the floor in splatters as thick as paint. Borges wiped his hands on her wadded blouse and delicately picked out keys on his phone.

"Yes," Gustaffson said when the line connected.

Borges chose his words carefully, as he would with any type of communication over the airwaves. "You will be interested to know your suspicions were correct. The man you mentioned extorted two ex-soldiers to come and... pay you a visit. It was arranged to gain your trust and support."

"I see. Very well. Please come north, and we'll discuss your findings in more detail."

Borges thumbed off the connection and dropped his phone back into his pocket.

With one last deep inhalation, he soaked up the intoxicating scent of Marisol Pareda before leaving the office. A final droplet fell from the dead woman's fingertip and soaked into the carpet.

A Mercedes sedan whipped past, buffeting Yeager with the wind of its passage. Dust and grit peppered him. Taillights shrank, grew distant, and disappeared.

Yeager had found his rhythm and fallen into perfect parade-ground marching cadence. He could hold this pace all day and never tire, schlepping forty pounds of gear, a rifle, and an aggressive attitude with thirty-inch steps, through hot jungle, sandy desert, high mountains, or the dusty shoulder of a narrow highway in Guatemala. Give him a marching pace, and he could outwalk a camel across the bare dunes of an Arabian desert. Walk, yes. Run, no. Running was for faucets. Fuck running and double-fuck jogging. He wasn't built for either activity. But walking. Oorah. He could do some walking.

Not that there was much point. Who was he fooling? The shuttle buses were traveling at fifty-plus miles per hour, gaining nearly one mile per every minute he traveled. The shuttle buses would have gained seventeen football fields for every one of his. Unless they stopped for a siesta, like the hare did for the tortoise, he would not catch them. And presumably, they would turn off somewhere along this road, onto a paved path that would leave no tracks, disappearing as effectively as if they had levitated into the air and been taken away by giant Sikorsky helicopters.

That didn't matter. Moving forward was all that mattered.

The last of the sunlight disappeared behind the mountains. With the onset of darkness, the temperature cooled, and the breeze dried the sweat on Yeager's forehead. A goat bleated its annoyance at the passing stranger disturbing his evening graze. The first stars twinkled to life along the horizon. Yeager marched on.

L ots of activity was happening in the garage. Two of Turizo's minions took charge of Victor. Both carried their rifles—Taurus T4s, if he guessed correctly—at the ready, while Turizo directed traffic. Torture Boy disappeared through an interior door that Victor deduced led into the house.

"Torturing all done?" Victor called after him. "Time for a *cerveza, pendejo?*"

"Go take a piss," Turizo told the shuttle drivers. "Get a coffee. Get out of here. Back to Huehuetenango."

The two drivers nodded and shuffled away toward a different interior door.

Halabi gripped Juanita by the bicep and held her against his side. The terrorist's eyes had gone twerky, as if overloaded on meth and caffeine. His eleven amigos drifted around the interior space, carrying their slung backpacks and either admiring the vintage Austin-Healey parked under the lights at the far side of the garage or twisting their necks and stretching out the kinks of the journey.

"Take our guests," Turizo said to another of his minions, "to the east wing rooms. The woman goes with them." To the men watching Victor, he said, "Take him down the trail. You know where."

"Ooh, scary. You read that line in *Villain's Monthly*? 'Ten Ways to Terrorize a Victim'?" Victor eyed his executioners. One was no more than a boy, still with spots and a sparse mustache, and the other was a veteran killer, with dead eyes and a pocked nose. Those dead eyes called his stare and raised it to a gloat.

"Start walking," the younger one said. He tried shoving, but Victor set his feet and refused to budge. "Move!" Another shove. Victor swayed but kept his feet planted. The instant before the pimply-faced minion reared back to buttstroke him, Victor executed a sharp right face and stepped off toward the open overhead, leaving the minions stumbling to recover.

CHAPTER TWENTY-TWO

With the onset of evening, the temperature began to drop almost immediately, making Yeager regret not buying a jacket when he stopped for clothes and food a million years ago that morning. The sweat under his load-bearing vest chilled his body every time the wind ruffled through the highlands.

Not smart. Though if I'd been smart, I would have gassed up the Yukon when I had a chance. Wouldn't be none of this bullshit hiking. Be riding instead.

Yeager shrugged and put it out of his mind. *Drive on.*

The ground to his right had leveled out. No longer a drop into a valley, as it had been for quite some distance, the terrain flattened, and trees grew thick along the shoulder of the highway. Seeing more than a few feet beyond the tree line was impossible. Only when a passing car lit up the scene with its headlights could Yeager see more than a dark, hulking mass that hissed and cackled with the sighing wind.

Then forest gave way to something else. He sensed it more than saw it. Yeager angled closer and found himself faced with a stone wall, eight feet high and paralleling the road as far as he could make out. He ran his fingertips across the stone. Granite, not sandstone. The wall suggested a degree of craftsmanship beyond that of the average construction he had passed in his journey north. This was a rich man's wall. Only the stupidly wealthy could afford a hand-built wall of jig-sawed rocks mortared together for such a distance.

Yeager shifted his line of march out of the weeds and back onto the hard-packed shoulder.

A glow appeared ahead, from behind the wall, then resolved into headlights spearing outward, about fifty yards ahead of Yeager's position. An electric gate powered up. Its chain rattled. The brightening glow revealed a guardhouse set next to a pair of opening wrought-iron batwing gates that swung outward. The first vehicle that drove through and turned toward him caused Yeager to dive into the weeds.

He went to ground and stared in shock as first one shuttle bus powered by, headed back south, followed closely by the second shuttle. By the dim illumination of their interior lights, it was obvious both vehicles were empty. Having stared at these shuttles all afternoon, there was no doubt in his mind they were the same vehicles he had followed from Way-Way-Tango.

All he could do was shake his head in wonder.

Luck. Pure, dumb luck.

Yeager held still while the gate rattled closed. He stifled the impulse to rush forward in an attempt to get through before it closed.

Hurry slowly. One of the laws he lived by.

And it saved him from a messy and premature death. The guard inside the shelter lit a cigarette a moment later, revealing a security guard standing close by—and like cockroaches, if there were two sentries, there were bound to be more. Getting past the perimeter would take some study. But get past it, he must. The shuttle carrying Por Que had left this property empty, which led to the logical conclusion that his tough little friend was on the other side of this wall.

Another car passed, bathing his clump of weeds in white light. Yeager kept his face down and held his breath until the vehicle had motored past. Once darkness returned, he scrambled up and reversed direction.

Por Que didn't have—couldn't have—much time left. It was a mystery to him why Gustaffson's people were bothering to drag him around from place to place. First from the mountains to the warehouse in Huehuetenango, then from the warehouse to this seclud-ed property in the mountains near the Mexican border. It made no sense. Why not simply shoot him and be done with it? There had to be a reason, and yet for the life of him, Yeager couldn't figure it out.

But whatever the reason, the sand was running out of Victor's hourglass. Yeager could feel it. They had to know by now that the men left behind at the mountain village had been taken out and that the operation to take Yeager had failed. There was no reason to keep his friend alive at this point. Was there?

Yeager found the corner of the wall and turned left, into the for-est, where the visibility went from pitch to black. He slowed as the footing became treacherous. Roots, rocks, and tree stumps tripped him up every few steps. Yeager fished out his cheap flashlight and fol-lowed its yellow cone of light. He picked up his pace.

A path had been cleared between the forest growth and the wall, creating a dead zone where no limbs overhung the perimeter. Yea-ger traveled down a channel with a ceiling of stars above, trees to his right and wall to his left. Insects buzzed in their cadence of love. Somewhere in the darkness, a large animal crashed through the veg-etation, startling Yeager into a full-body heart attack.

He had walk-jogged about two hundred yards by his estimation when a sense of space seemed to open ahead of him. Yeager slowed further and was glad for it when he came to the edge of a drop-off. He cast about until he found a deadfall limb about as big as a base-ball bat, then he tossed it into the open space. He stared wide-eyed into the darkness and counted.

"One Mississippi, two Mississippi, three Mississippi, four—" The muted crash of the branch striking something solid stopped his count. "Huh. Speed of sound times number of seconds equals... a long fucking way to fall. So let's not go that way."

To his left, the wall turned away, running parallel to the drop. He pointed the flashlight beam to the base of the wall and cursed under his breath. The construction people had run their wall right up to the lip of the drop, leaving about eight to twelve inches of a ledge. A suicidally obsessed high-wire circus athlete could plaster himself against the brick and scooch himself along on his heels. Maybe. And for how long?

More careful probing by the flashlight showed him the wall continued on indefinitely.

Walking was one thing. Walking was easy. Nothing to it. However, scooching along on the balls of his feet, face pressed to the wall, translated to Mama Yeager's boy becoming airborne without a chute. He would then deploy vertically into the Guatemalan hillside at terminal velocity. And who knew how far the wall stretched? Maybe it covered the entire back of the property, so scooching along its length would accomplish nothing.

He swept the beam of the flashlight higher and froze. His balls tightened when he realized the implications of what he was looking at. A hint of an idea bounced up and took hold, refusing to let him walk away and try to think up another way over the wall.

"Oh, hell no," he muttered. "No, no, no, no, no. Ruiz, you ain't worth it. Hell no."

Every part of his body said no... but his mind whispered yes.

Blanca Trevejo knew in her heart she would be dead before dawn. She hung limp in Halabi's grasp, wrung out, as if she'd run a marathon. So tired. A radioactive bowling ball had settled in her colon and hung there, saturating her insides with poisonous fear. First would come the gang rape. Twelve or more sweaty, bearded misanthropes would pump their fat pricks into her and spray their noxious semen there. Her imagination fed her a steady diet of the upcoming horror show she was bound to endure. Then would come the bullet to the brain, which would at least bring an end to her torture.

Can we fast forward, please? Please, God? Let's cut to the chase and let me die now.

Heat burned her eyes, and she clenched her teeth to keep from crying. Halabi tugged at her arm, and she stumbled. The crew of terrorists filed through a doorway at the back of the garage. Halabi trailed the pack with her in tow. The Hispanic man, Victor Ruiz, was being marched to his death. He cast a look over his shoulder at her and hitched his chin in a gesture of solidarity.

A black Mercedes swooped into the garage, and Ruiz danced out of the way to avoid getting clipped by the car's fender. Tires squeaked when the driver hit the brakes, apparently surprised by the crowd in the garage. High beams forced her to squint.

"Hey!" Ruiz barked. "Watch out, ese. You tryin' to kill me before I die?"

Halabi yelled something as well, a curse in a language she didn't recognize, but thought might be Pashtun. He jerked at her arm again, and she fell to one knee.

Two men emerged from the car—one as round as a beach ball with lank, oily hair slicked down, the other slender and handsome. Blanca blinked and sucked in a surprised breath.

Guillermo Modena and Alfonso Bustamante.

What the hell? Wouldn't her station chief be excited about this? The newly elected leader of the nation of Guatemala, here in the presence of twelve jihadists intent on attacking American targets. What did it mean? Was Modena involved in the plot? Both men acted as if they weren't sure they had come to the right place, casting nervous looks at the men clustered around their shiny new car.

An interior door opened, and Herman Gustaffson entered the garage. In his mid-sixties, with gray hair and an aristocratic bearing, he was the kind of man who believed he could piss fine wine and shit gold nuggets.

Blanca forgot about rape and death for a moment, her mind whirling with questions.

Gustaffson beamed a grill of bright white teeth and called out with gusto, "Guillermo! Alfonso! Your timing is impeccable. You should meet our guest of honor." He motioned to the men escorting Ruiz. "Bring him over here."

"Also, I would like you to meet this gentleman," Gustaffson said, and this time, he motioned to Halabi. "Come. Shake hands with the next president of Guatemala."

Halabi's lip curled in an expression that said he would rather stuff a live scorpion down his pants than shake hands with anyone.

"Who are these men?" El Presidente's expression had frozen in a sickly mask of polite horror, a politician caught with his fly open in a crowd of reporters.

Gustaffson wasn't taking no for an answer. He arranged for Halabi and the man named Guillermo to stand together and shake hands in a tableau resembling a chamber of commerce lunch.

"Turizo, take a picture." The oligarch snapped his fingers at his gorilla-sized security man. "Put the CIA woman at Halabi's feet, like she has been conquered by the warrior."

Turizo grabbed her by the hair and dragged her into position, then he backed away to snap photos with his phone.

"Good, good, good," Gustaffson said. "Halabi, you may go. Please. Enjoy your spoils of war." He motioned to Turizo. "Bring the Mexican. I would like to introduce him to the man who arranged his visit to our country."

Instead of leaving, Halabi stayed put, obviously as interested in the play being acted out on the impromptu stage of Gustaffson's garage. This suited Blanca, not only because it delayed her becoming the "spoils of war" but because it also fed her instinctive drive to learn great secrets and shine a light on the cockroaches in the corners that might threaten her country. *Once a spy...*

The two guards pushed Ruiz to stand in front of the three men, Gustaffson, Modena, and Bustamante. Modena's complexion resembled a sweaty ghost—pale and clammy skin shone under the fluorescent overheads, and his politician's smile seemed pasted on his face with Elmer's glue. The president-elect's right-hand man, Bustamante, held his composure better; only the dampness of his forehead hinted at the man's nervousness.

Ruiz raised an eyebrow at Modena. "Yo, wassup? I'd shake your hand, but..." He shrugged so as to indicate his cuffed hands. "These dudes, they ascared of me and won' let me loose."

"Who is this man?" Modena's voice had regrown some bark. He visibly took hold of himself and straightened, adopting the mask of a tolerant general overseeing the inspection of a slovenly soldier. "Why is he cuffed?"

Gustaffson curled his lips in a vampiric smile. "This man? You mean you don't know? This man is one of two whom you extorted into attempting my assassination. Then you used the certain knowledge of their effort to gain my trust."

"Wait, wait, wait," Modena cried, his tone colored with dismay. "The assassins I warned you about? Are you saying I arranged this? No. You are mistaken. Or you are trying to gain some influence by pretending this is so."

"It's true, I'm afraid." Gustaffson directed his thin smile toward Bustamante. "Your man's secretary revealed everything."

Modena whirled to look at his friend. A dozen emotions raced across his expression until he settled on one of wounded disbelief.

"Alfonso." Wounded betrayal dripped from his words. "Alfonso, how could you deceive me so? I trusted you."

His performance was so good, Blanca almost believed him.

Bustamante gaped. His mouth worked, but no sound emerged.

Ruiz laughed. "Dude, you should see your face right now. Bet you didn't see that one coming."

CHAPTER TWENTY-THREE

Huddled near the corner of the wall, on his haunches, Yeager studied the problem. The space between the base of the wall and the cliff edge averaged about eight to twelve inches—enough to scuff sideways, back pinned to the wall and toes hanging over the drop. That part, he could do.

The next part scared the piss out of him. Every time he thought about the required acrobatics, the space between his nut sack and his asshole prickled.

A single branch of a big tree hung over the wall from the inside. Every part of the wall he had examined up to this point had been meticulously maintained to create an air gap between the trees and the stone barrier. Good security practice. The cliff side of the property had not been maintained as well. Who in their right mind would inch out onto a narrow ledge in order to lean out far enough to grab an overhanging limb, somehow snagging it before plummeting to their death, haul themselves up onto the branch, and monkey their way over the wall?

Nobody was that stupid. *Right?*

Yeager felt the pressure of time bleeding through his fingers. The more ticks of the clock, the closer Victor was to a bullet behind the ear. He had no time to retrace his steps and look for another way in. A frontal assault against the gate would be certain death if more than one or two guards were on duty. He had no armor to crash through the gate. No ladder. No grappling hook connected to a sturdy rope. No demo gear or C4.

Do the math. I got me. I got a rifle. Sixteen magazines of dot-two-two-three. He sighed. *And I got a tree limb.*

Yeager narrowed his eyes and examined the overhanging limb. It looked doable. He would have to commit everything on one try, though. That was the problem. If he tilted out far enough to grab the limb, he would not be able to recover and pull himself back to the wall. If he missed...

He grunted. "Splat."

And if he did grab the branch, then he would have to chin himself up by main strength and awkwardness. If he slipped...

"Splat."

He estimated the limb at a three-inch diameter at the point where it crossed over the wall. It *looked* solid enough. Leaves indicated the tree was living and was therefore not brittle with rot. Wouldn't that be shitty? Get up on the branch and *snap!* Surprise!

"Splat."

Yeager shook his head like a prizefighter shaking off a sharp punch to the face.

"Fuck it. Drive on. Por Que, you better not be dead, you son of a bitch. I do this and find you dead, there will be hell to pay."

Yeager took off his load-bearing vest full of magazines and threw it over the wall. Every bit of equipment he carried would only drag him outward, and if he fell, it was useless anyway. The vest vanished over the wall and crashed through the brush, quieter than he expected. With a prayer to the gods of firearms, he tried easing the rifle over the top by extending it up butt first as high as he could reach and giving it a shove with his fingertips. He winced at the rattle of its fall.

Yeager tried stuffing the flashlight into various pockets, but nothing seemed secure enough for the acrobatics required, so that followed the rest of his equipment. He retained the pistol in its high-rise hip holster and his prepaid cell phone. The phone had a flashlight feature, which left him with at least one light source, and the pistol rode snugly, leaving him with a functioning weapon in case he had buggered up his T4 rifle by tossing it over the wall.

The night breeze ruffled some leaves and made the branches sway, including the one he had targeted. Not much, but enough to make him wonder if a stray breeze might move it at the exact moment he reached for it. A small miscalculation, a small error due to a moving target, and...

"Yeah, I know. Splat."

A night bird trilled. It sounded a bit like a screech owl, though not like the type he knew. It sounded like laughter. Insects sang harmony.

Yeager inhaled and let it out. He eased onto the ledge, heels first. *One small step for man, and all that. Keep going.* He palmed the wall, and his fingers sought any rough patch they could find, hoping to spider-grip the imperfections. He kept his head and shoulders back. He slid his left foot out. His right followed. Six inches of progress. Once more. Grit and sand cracked underfoot. The breeze ruffled his hair, chilling the sweat on his forehead.

In front of him, all Yeager could see was the dark bulk of mountain ridges outlined against the lighter black of the sky. Low clouds prevented any starlight from seeping through, though silver moonglow permeated the cloud cover to the east, giving enough contrast to make out a few details. A sense of yawning openness pulled at him from the area directly in front of him. In the dark, he had no way of knowing if the cliff dropped hundreds of feet or merely dozens, though his earlier test with the broken limb argued for the former. He could feel its tug, as though somebody had turned up the gravity dial.

Another glow became evident as he inched along. Farther down the wall, the artificial illumination of man-made light seeped outward. Shape and texture materialized as his eyes adjusted to the dark.

A long way away, it seemed. Too far to ledge-walk over to it without a guarantee of an entrance.

Windows? Or security lights? Headlights?

Could be all of the above... or something else.

The ledge widened a bit, giving his feet a more stable platform. Yeager paused and practiced breathing until his heartrate slowed. *Left foot slide. Right foot glide. Call it the six-inch shuffle. Halfway there.*

His heel scuffed sideways, disturbing small rocks that trickled off into the abyss. The ledge thinned, and Yeager's toes poked over the edge. He slid his left foot out another six inches and started bringing his right foot alongside. Something cracked, and the rock supporting his left foot crumbled away.

The man called Bustamante floundered like a drowning man sinking fast. Victor could almost picture air bubbles floating up from his open mouth.

"Don't look now," Victor told him, "but you gotta thing, you know? Sticking out of your back? I think they call it a knife."

The other guy, Modena, opened up with a full-on ass-kiss to the old guy, Gustaffson. "Señor, you must believe me when I say I had no idea of this duplicity. I can assure you I will get to the bottom of it."

He would have continued, but Gustaffson chased the words back down his throat with a gesture. "Shut up, Modena. You are embarrassing yourself and destroying friends at a time when you will need all you can get." He waved a delicate hand at Halabi. "I have photographic evidence of you shaking hands with a known terrorist. Once this man commits his acts of atrocity in America, the CIA and FBI will back-trace his route into their country. If they come for me, I will merely say I acted at the request of my dear friend, Guillermo

Modena. And now that we have put you with a soon-to-be-missing CIA agent…" He paused to let that sink in. "And as to this little drama with the assassination attempt… Well, you sought to gain my assistance with your anti-corruption effort. Rest assured, you will never see the reconstitution of the CICIG in your lifetime. Historians will instead ascribe to your term as president the most corruption in Guatemala's history—which is saying something, I admit."

Modena looked like a man who wanted to throw up but couldn't find a toilet. To his left, Bustamante had deflated and appeared to be melting into a puddle.

Victor chuckled. "You still want me to kill him?"

"Shut up," Bustamante retorted without heat.

"Tell me, American," Gustaffson said to Victor. "What did they promise you in exchange for this little trip to my beautiful country?"

"A new Xbox. But now, I'd do it for a Nintendo. You know, one of those little ones with the tiny knobs on the side?"

Gustaffson held the question with a raised eyebrow for a moment then shrugged. "No matter. You are a pawn, but a pawn who knows too much." He waved a languid hand. "Take him through the gate."

"Sí, jefe." The older guard tugged Victor's handcuffs. "Come."

"Now, then." Gustaffson turned to Modena again. "Shall we go inside and discuss the fine points of our new relationship?" Victor looked over his shoulder when Gustaffson added in English, "Halabi? Will you be, ah, disposing of the young lady? Good, good, good. We will speak later. Turizo will get you anything you need."

Victor tried catching Juanita's eyes again to… *Do what? Send a message of hope? Tell her to stay strong?* It didn't matter, because she didn't look up as Halabi dragged her away behind Turizo.

"Don't give up," was all he could think to say.

The dead-eyed guard laughed.

Yeager's foot went out from under him, and for a half-second, he teetered on the brink. His fingers dug at the wall behind him, and he swayed in place as he dragged his foot back to solid ground. Or what he hoped like hell was solid ground.

When he felt stable enough, he tried breathing again.

"That's not good for the blood pressure," he said to himself.

Peeking down, he found the chunk of missing rock extended only a few inches—a few inches he would need to cross by lifting his feet over one at a time. Was the bit of ledge on the far side solid enough to hold?

Does a cow need a dictionary?

Yeager lifted his foot and with all deliberate caution, stepped left. Tensed. Held the pose. Shifted his weight. Shifted more of his weight. Found the footing firm.

"So far, so good. Now for the second shoe to drop."

He leaned and brought his other heel over the gap. Set it down. Shifted a little to get a better base under him. Remembered to breathe again. Went back to the shuffle step.

With ten more shuffles, he arrived under the branch. Of course it looked much farther out than when he'd eyeballed the thing earlier. The limb extended a full twelve feet out from the wall, and the main branch hung down at a forty-five-degree angle, almost touching the wall on its way over. It was not a single, clean chin-up-bar kind of limb, though. Secondary branches split off and poked out in various directions. One of those smaller branches fell within Yeager's reach, assuming he committed to reaching out for it, past his center of gravity.

His plan remained simple: Pull the smaller branch in so he could snag a hold on the larger branch. Lift his big ass up like a kid on a playground. Crawl along the big branch until he reached the top of the wall. Drop with maximum Marine stealth down the other side. Fetch weapons. Rescue Por Que. Kill people as necessary. Get the fuck out of Guatemala.

Simple.

All it required was a commitment to hanging his life by a tree limb.

"Victor Ruiz," he muttered again, "you better not be dead. I meet you in hell, I'm gonna kick your sorry butt."

Yeager reached out. The drop pulled at him. He extended outward, beyond the point of no return. His reaching hands circled the lowest, smaller limb. He scrabbled for a grip, feeling gravity tug at his middle. His legs trembled. Leaves rattled and fell.

He hung, suspended over the cliffside, bowed out belly first.

CHAPTER TWENTY-FOUR

"What's this gate, huh?" Victor toggled his head to pop his neck, then he rolled his shoulders like a boxer. He wanted to be loose when his chance came, slim though it might be. He tested the handcuffs for the dozenth time in the past five minutes, achieving the same results as all the previous times: nothing.

"Shut up," Dead Eyes said. "Keep moving."

The younger guard led the way across the parking apron to a narrow gap at the edge of the lighted space. They came to a path through the trees, kept open by garden tools rather than animals, as evidenced by the neatly trimmed brush flanking the trail. Darkness swallowed them as they crossed from the concrete drive to the forest trail. The lead guard flicked on the flashlight mounted to the fore grip of his rifle. The older guy did the same moments later, lighting up the trail at Victor's feet.

He couldn't see six feet into the jungle on either side of the trail, leaving him to speculate about cutting and running sideways. Maybe he could lose his captors in the bush and squeeze his hands through the cuffs so at least he could use them to do some damage.

Dead Eyes must have read his mind. "Don't try it. You will only die tired. There is a three-meter wall around the property. The only gap is El Jefe's big picture window in the entertainment room. Two gates. One with guards in front, one at the back. You will use the back gate soon."

The lead guard grinned over his shoulder. "We will escort you through that gate. You may step right out. Only a three-hundred-meter first step." He looked away, cackling to himself.

"What do you say when they find the body?" Victor asked. "Oops. He fell."

"No one will find your body," the man said from behind. "No one has been found yet."

"Well, that's not ominous at all," Victor grumbled.

Okay, no going back now.

Yeager tested his grip on the small limb, dug in with his toes, and heaved downward, pulling the mass of branches toward himself. Holding tightly with his left hand, he snaked his right onto the thickest limb until he had a good anchor. Then he let go with his left and groped upward until he had both hands on the main limb.

No going back now, he repeated to himself.

An explosive grunt blew from his midsection when Yeager jackknifed himself upward. His toes left the ledge, and he swung his lower body out over the abyss. Yeager hauled himself up, first wrapping one arm, then the other, around the main branch. Leaves shuddered and fell like rain. His feet groped upward, seeking purchase. Small branches and minor limbs tried to push him away, seemingly with malice. Yeager panted and strained, fighting to wrap himself onto the tree. Sweat burned his eyes.

He fought one ankle over the limb, relieving some of the strain, and with one ankle secure, the other followed. Yeager paused for a moment, heaving oxygen into his system, hanging like a hammock suspended over a bottomless pit.

Slowly, cheek pressed to hard bark, Yeager chinned himself upward. The tree shivered. More leaves pattered down.

He fought the tree, inch by inch, until he could lever himself over the top of the hanging limb.

When he could stretch out atop the limb and gravity no longer threatened to drag him to his death, Yeager rested his aching muscles and wiped the sweat from his eyes with his sleeve.

And to think I used to like climbing trees.

Yeager caught his breath and edged forward, catching his shirt on twigs, dragging his belt over rough bark. He cracked a knee hard enough to see stars, and bark scraped his skin raw as he pulled himself up and along the drooping branch.

He sensed more than saw the moment he crawled over the wall. The quality of darkness below his perch changed to a thick black soup. An echo of hard earth and a short drop chased off the sense of openness. The smell of soil and plants grew stronger. Yeager risked fishing the cell phone from his pocket and lighting the scene below him to make sure he wasn't about to make a fatal error in judgment. The light revealed he was well past the wall and the drop was no more than ten feet.

Yeager slid off the branch feetfirst, dangled from both hands, and let go. He absorbed the drop on battered knees, falling to a squat with a grimace of pain. His breathing came in giant bellows, passing through his open mouth to reduce noise. Sweat soaked his shirt, chilled by the night breeze, and countless aches and pains signaled distress from every segment of his body.

Curl up and take a nap, his body said.

Then came the sound of a voice he knew well, hollow and attenuated by trees: "Hey, are we there yet? This Bataan Death March is taking forever."

Por Que.

Yeager grinned in the darkness. Some days, it was better to be lucky than good.

"Uhh!"

At first, Victor thought the thud and the grunt from behind him was the result of the dead-eyed guard tripping over a stone in the path. Then a large body crashed past him and slammed into the lead guard with the force of an avalanche. The man had started to turn when the new arrival full-body tackled him and drove the guard into the turf. A big fist pistoned up and down, producing a sound like smacking meat and cutting off the younger guard's startled cry.

The shape moved, and Victor's jaw fell open.

"Yeager! Cabrón! What the fuck? How did you find me?"

His friend faced him and shrugged. "I went out on a limb."

Relief washed through Victor so hard, his legs jellied, and he swayed in place. "Dios mío," he muttered. "Never have I been so happy to see your ugly jarhead face."

Yeager clapped him on the shoulder. "Likewise."

They stood together for a moment, energy flowing back and forth through the contact of Yeager's hand on Victor's shoulder.

Finally, Victor said, "If you're not gonna kiss me, at least find the key to these cuffs."

Yeager grinned and set to work. He found the cuff key and released the restraints from Victor's wrists. Together, they stripped the guards of their weapons and gear. The dead-eyed guard dripped blood from a knot as big as a mouse over his left ear. He appeared to be deep in dreamland, whereas the younger guard groaned, and his eyelids fluttered.

"Where were these guys taking you?" Yeager asked.

"There's a gate somewhere down this trail. It opens out to a cliff or something. They were going to pitch me off. Can you believe it?"

"Knowing you? Easily."

Victor squatted over the younger guard. The kid's scraggly mustache caterpillared across his upper lip. Victor sighed. "Doesn't seem right, doing unto them as they wanted to do unto me."

"Let's cuff 'em to the gate. Then we need to get the hell out of here. I'm fucking sick of this country and want to go home."

"Sorry, ese, no can do. We got some business to do, back at the big house."

"Business? What business?"

"Got a house full of jihadi motherfuckers fixin' to go across the border into the homeland, blow shit up. Also got a CIA lady left in their tender care. She won't last the night, we don't get in there and do something."

"Jihadis? How the hell did you find jihadis in Guatemala?"

Victor shrugged. "Lucky?"

Yeager spat off to the side and shook his head. "You fucking amaze me, Por Que. You really do."

"I know, right?" He gestured to the burn on his pectoral. "See? I'm a one-tit wonder."

Yeager's jaw dropped. "Ow. That must've hurt."

"Something else I owe the guys back at the house."

"Jesus, Mary, and Joseph." Yeager sighed his trademark all-patience-exhausted exhalation. "Let's get these punks secured. I've got some ammo back off in the bush. We'll go find it, and you can fill me in on the story as we go."

"Oorah, Marine."

"Oo-fucking-rah."

Turizo led Halabi and his captive through a door off the expansive garage. Beyond the door, steps led downward to a corridor that stretched two dozen meters before making a left-hand turn. Halabi counted eight doors along the hall, each marked with a number in Western numerals.

"Here is dormitory," Turizo said in poor English, the only language he and Halabi shared. "For guest of Señor Gustaffson." He opened the first door on the right, gesturing for Halabi to enter the small room beyond. It was a simply furnished space: a bed, a dresser, a nightstand, and a lamp. "Toilet is there. Three doors down. Three." He held up three fingers. "Use toilet. Not floor."

Halabi flared, but his attention was caught by the woman, who pulled back at that moment. Her eyes were fixed on the bed, and she balked at the doorway. She jerked away, and he almost lost his grip.

"No," he shouted at her, and followed it up with a cuff to the face, dazing the woman. She sagged to her knees. Halabi picked her up by the arms and threw her onto the bed. By the time he turned back to deal with Turizo, the security man had moved on, showing Halabi's men to their rooms.

"Never fear, brothers," Halabi shouted in Pashto. "All of you will have your turn with the infidel bitch!"

Shouts of approval greeted his pronouncement. Fists were raised in the air, and wolfish grins were cast in his direction. Halabi grinned back and closed the door, shutting off the noise from outside and bringing blessed peace—except for the whimpering woman on the bed, who cowered and retracted herself into a corner against the wall.

A small thrill tingled Halabi's groin, bringing a mixture of anticipation along with a small measure of relief. Maybe his fear of failure had been misplaced and his concerns about performance had been nothing but jitters brought on by worries about having an audience. Perhaps alone, with the woman under his control and her terror whetting his appetite, he could sate his lust upon her as a true man should. If not, he could still use her as if she were a boy, all the while pretending he was back in the tribal elder's home and the body under him was that of his favorite plaything.

No one would know if he failed to be excited by a female. The object of his lust did not matter; the completion of the act would be proof of his manhood.

"Clothes," he ordered the woman. "Take off clothes."

With trembling fingers, the infidel bitch reached for the buttons of her blouse.

CHAPTER TWENTY-FIVE

Alfonso Bustamante's insides shifted like a sack of broken crockery. He had once taken a speeding football to the groin that had hurt less than Guillermo Modena's betrayal. He followed his once-friend into Herman Gustaffson's living room as if he were a deflated beach ball, tethered to his habitual position behind the man he had helped make president. *Why am I even still here? What is left for me?*

"Please, gentlemen, have a seat." Gustaffson gestured at the white leather furniture arranged before the grand picture window. Bustamante recalled they'd used the same furniture only recently, when he and Guillermo had broached the subject of assassins on their way to end Gustaffson's life. The scheme had now been revealed for the ruse it was: an attempt to garner favor with the criminal oligarch who held so many throats under his heel. A scheme Guillermo had completely embraced.

Bustamante hung back until Guillermo found a seat in a chair near the window before taking his place not at the president-elect's side, but on a couch closer to the middle of the conversation pit, leaving several open spaces between himself and the man who had just attempted to betray him. Glass surrounded the conversation area on three sides. Every way he turned, Bustamante could see himself—sweaty, rumpled, and pathetic.

Guillermo studied his hands and refused to make eye contact.

Their host seemed amused by the scene. Smiling like a man who had just won a year's supply of sexual favors from the women's national football team, Gustaffson took his place across from Guillermo, settling into a broad leather armchair. An ashtray and a cocktail glass of tan liquor with a single ice cube had already been placed on the armrests. He sipped from the drink before speaking.

"Let us discuss this new dynamic, shall we?"

"Why?" Bustamante scoffed. "You own us, correct? If, as you say, the wild man in the garage is a known terrorist, soon to be martyred in the United States, then we are fucked. One leaked photograph turns... turns Señor Faithful here into a war criminal." Bustamante accompanied his comments with a dismissive wave at the cowering politician he'd once thought of as his closest friend. "The US will kick him in the balls so hard, his screams will echo all throughout the Big Guacamole."

His stomach churned, and Bustamante tasted vomit in the back of his throat. How could he have been so stupid? So naïve? For twenty-six years, since their days in college, he and Guillermo had dreamed of reaching the pinnacle of Guatemalan politics, bringing honesty to the government for the first time in decades, and launching a new era of prosperity for all the tiny towns and villages throughout the nation who were held hostage to the wealthy and corrupt.

"And now this," he said aloud, muttering to his freshly polished shoes.

"And now this," Gustaffson repeated. His voice slid over Bustamante's skin like a razor parting flesh. "Facing reality is harsh, Alfonso. Politics at this level is a killer's game. You are no killer. That little scheme you hatched to curry favor? A child's game. Transparent."

No killer?

Little Maria weighted his coat pocket as if it had grown from a tiny pistol to a giant machine gun.

They dog-trotted to the corner of the garden, where Yeager had tossed his equipment. Now that he had a new rifle with a mounted flashlight, the only thing he really wanted was the extra magazines from the vest. With numbers anywhere close to what Victor said they faced, two magazines would not last long.

Yeager spoke as he dodged tree trunks. "How do we know these guys are terrorists?"

"The CIA woman told me the guy was a known jihadi. Plus, the guy, he bragged on how he was gonna fuck us up. Blood and death, mass destruction, blah, blah, blah."

"Do the jihadi-types have weapons?"

"Not that I saw. They had backpacks, and I'm thinking they're on the move, not geared up."

"You're thinking maybe ten in the security force."

"That's all I saw. Plus Turizo and Torture Boy."

"So twelve, then."

"I didn't know you could do math."

"Then we have to deal with Gustaffson and the fucking president of Guatemala. You sure it was the president? Like of the country?"

"Could have been president of the Rotary Club, man." Victor's tone came back a touch warm. "Shit, how should I know? I got my tit burned up, could've affected my brain and shit."

Directly ahead, Yeager found the southern stretch of wall. He turned left and reached the corner in another minute.

"Should be around here." Yeager swept his light in short arcs, focused on the ground in front of him.

"Got it!" Victor sang out a moment later, holding up the ammo-laden vest. "We got ammo and attitude. Now all we need is a plan."

"The plan is the same plan as always."

"We go in hot, shoot everything that ain't us or the woman. Snag a car and make tracks."

"That's the plan."

"That's a stupid plan." Victor stuffed a magazine into each back pocket and handed the vest to Yeager. "But I like it."

Blanca Trevejo had a plan. And it was working.

"Clothes," Halabi said. "Take off clothes."

Blanca made a production of fumbling with the buttons of her blouse.

Halabi leered over her with the expression of a vulture crouched over fresh roadkill. His hands worked his belt buckle as if undoing it for the first time—fumbling and slipping at the brown leather and black metal. His breathing was that of a teenager climbing into the backseat with his high school sweetheart. He was a man preoccupied with visions of her weeping and whimpering as he forced his penis into her unwilling body.

They had made a mistake by shutting her into a room alone with Halabi. On the bus, with six guys, Turizo and Dominic? No way in hell was she getting out of that group unmolested. *Unraped? Is that a word?*

One on one, she had a chance.

Too bad I don't have my knife. Like that guy in the alley? With the Waldo shirt? That guy learned what happens to dicks who want a piece of Blanca Trevejo without her permission.

Blanca pictured herself kicking the goo out of Halabi's testicles with a hard-as-fuck heel strike, then beating him senseless with the desk lamp sitting on the side table. She rehearsed the series of moves in her head as she put on her victim act.

To reach the goo-kicking stage required her to pretend she was thoroughly cowed, without a spine or the will to fight back. To play-act the persona of a terrified woman, completely at the mercy of her male abuser, she had to tremble just so. She kept her eyes downcast, wet with tears. She would sniff and choke out meaningless protests. All of it was an act to lull Halabi into complacency so he kept his guard down. If he saw one speck of resistance in her eyes, he would beat her senseless, and there would go all of her slim hope of getting out of this situation alive.

Blanca didn't bother to picture what would happen after Halabi lay bleeding at her feet, his testicles smashed into pudding and his head lumpy with bits of lamp embedded in it. Her dad's voice said in her head, *One problem at a time.*

Keeping her eyes down, she slipped her blouse off her shoulders but edged a look under shaded brows to calculate the distance to her target. Immediately, she regretted it when she got an eyeful of Halabi's turgid, semi-erect penis poking out from a black bush of curly hair. He was uncircumcised.

Well, duh.

"All of clothes," he ordered.

His pants, she noted, pooled around his ankles.

Even better. He would be clumsy, tangled up and slow to react.

Blanca lay back on the bed and fiddled with her buckle. "Please," she whimpered, her real fear adding sauce to the meal she was offering. "You don't have to do this."

Halabi stroked himself and growled at her. "Turn over. Take off pants." He seemed more angry than excited. His arm pumped like a man plunging a toilet, but not much seemed to be happening with his erection. "Turn over!"

Blanca's heartrate leveled out. It was go-time. Time to rear back and kick like a bee-stung mule.

Pop-pop-pop!

The unmistakable sound of small arms rattled from somewhere nearby. Halabi dropped his member and grabbed his pants faster than a man given a reprieve from a death sentence. His attention swiveled to the door, leaving Blanca a wide-open shot at his junk. She didn't take it, though, because Halabi was out the door before she could draw her legs back for the kick.

He left her with an open blouse and a bemused expression. Vaguely dissatisfied.

Khayyat Halabi rushed into a mass of confused men clogging the basement hallway. His fellow fighters spilled from their rooms, shouting and spitting curses, demanding answers.

"What is going on?"

"Who is shooting?"

"We are under attack!"

Turizo appeared at the far end of the hall, at a door Halabi guessed led to the main house.

"Quiet!" Turizo shouted.

Halabi pressed into the crowd of fighters, determined to reach Turizo and demand answers.

"Quiet," Turizo repeated. "Our men are—stop her!"

Halabi whirled to find the woman racing away, the tails of her shirt flying behind her. She ran for the garage stairs. Her hair streamed out in a black ribbon.

The closest man—a Persian named Reza—ran after her, followed by two others. They tackled her at the base of the stairs, knocking her hard to the concrete floor. The infidel bitch screamed and kicked, twisting like a snake. She struck Reza with an elbow to the chin and was rewarded with a punch to her midsection that doubled her over. One of the other men clubbed her over the eye with a clenched fist, bouncing the woman's head off the stairs. She went loose and wobbly after that.

Reza left the woman and jogged up the stairs. He stuck his head through the open door, only to jerk it back when bullets whacked the frame. He had the presence of mind to slam the door shut and engage the thumb lock.

"That lock is no good!" Halabi yelled at Turizo. "Not good to hold long. Weapons. Give weapons. We fight."

The apelike security man furrowed his thick eyebrows into a single hedge of black fur. He appeared on the point of saying no, but then touched the earpiece he wore and posed in the stance of a man receiving communication via radio.

"Copy that," he said. "Mobile force, fall back toward the house. Post One, hard lock the gates. No one gets in or out." Turizo looked at Halabi and offered him an ugly smile. "Follow me."

CHAPTER TWENTY-SIX

The light from the open bay doors of the garage cast a white glow on the parking apron. Above the doors, security floodlights added to the brightness of the scene. The light guided Yeager to the end of the path, where he paused and dropped to a knee. Victor slid in beside him.

"Blocks stacked on blocks," Yeager commented.

"Criminals. No taste," Victor muttered back.

The rectangular garage, as big as a warehouse, invited them to stroll right in. No guards, no terrorists—nothing bigger than the moths fluttering and bumping into the security lights. Some of those were big enough to be a threat to an unarmed man, though.

"Where is everybody?" Yeager hissed.

"Watching *Survivor: Guatemala*. Come on, let's go."

Movement from the far side of the parking apron flickered in Yeager's peripheral vision. A man in a black uniform stepped into the light, rifle held low. He spotted Victor at the same moment Yeager marked him.

"Down!"

Victor dropped.

Yeager twisted at the hips, T4 already at his shoulder, cheek pressed to the stock. Muzzle flashes sparked from the guard's rifle. He stood left of center at thirty yards. Yeager triggered a fast return-to-sender. Three shots, tight group. The security man spun away with a squeal of pain. Yeager ate dirt before reacquiring his sight picture.

The guard stumbled for cover, disappearing into the darkness at the far side of the parking apron. More flashes of fire spattered from where he vanished, meaning the man was still a threat.

Victor cut loose, hosing Yeager with spent brass. He ignored the burning metal bouncing off his collar, wincing at the percussive noise of Victor's rifle. Yeager added a few pops of his own to the cascade of fire. The rifleman across the way stopped firing, dead, injured, or shifting position out of the hot zone. Impossible to tell which.

He yelled at Victor to be heard over the ringing in his ears. "We need to take the house. Find the boss!"

Dodging bullets and bad guys in the dark was a losing proposition. They would never defeat a trained enemy force in a running firefight on their territory. No, first goal was to recover the woman held captive. The second goal was a little fuzzy. Do something about the terrorists. The primary mission objective was Yeager's First Law: come home at the end of the day. His vague plan for accomplishing all three was to reach the big man, Gustaffson, and put a gun to his head. See what happened from there.

"Leverage."

Victor nodded. They were operating on the same wavelength, and Victor grasped the concept immediately. "Good plan."

Running into the lighted garage seemed a bad idea, though. The space was bare but for some benches and shelves lining the back wall, a black Mercedes, and a vintage two-seat sports car in emerald green. Two doors, both closed, were set into the far wall—one at the corner and one in the middle. Forty or fifty yards of open concrete separated them from either door.

"We need another way in," Yeager started to say, but at that moment, movement in the interior doorway arrested his attention. A face appeared in the frame. Dark, bearded, angry. Yeager had the angle, so he leveled his rifle and sent the face back where it'd come from by an application of lead paint.

Victor rose onto one knee, and a bullet zipped overhead, driving him back down. "Fuck! That one parted my hair."

Yeager banged out suppressive fire in the direction of the muzzle flash, which came from a position thirty degrees off from where the first man had disappeared. More muzzle flashes joined the first group as the guard force reacted to the threat. The zip and zing of incoming rounds tuned up to a symphony of angry hornets.

Coordinating by radio.

A bullet impacted the dirt in front of him, spraying his face with grit. The copper-jacketed round spit back out of the earth, ricocheting up past his face close enough that the heat of it warmed his cheek.

"Fall back," Yeager ordered, half-blinded by dirt and half-deaf from rifle fire.

"Falling, hell," Victor grunted from somewhere close. "Running. Running back."

Yeager belly-crawled backward until he was deep enough into the trees to wriggle around and face the opposite direction. He followed Victor's muffled curses to a position behind a pair of trees with a shared root system and a tangle of growth at their base. He scrambled over to fall next to his friend, who was changing a magazine.

"This is fun, huh?" Yeager asked. "Just like old times."

"Old times, yeah. You funny." Victor blew out a deep breath. "I hated old times."

"Come on." Yeager levered himself into a crouch. "Let's swing wide and see what's behind the garage."

In the grand room with the enormous picture windows, Bustamante watched the scene via the reflection rather than as a participant in the drama. The window might as well have been a big-screen

TV, albeit with muted colors and watered-down contrast. The scene: three men in suits, in a room of modern elegance, seated in a triangle. Bustamante saw himself, sitting in the middle. Modena was on the right, his posture slumped, beaten. A child who had just been told his dog had died. Gustaffson, on the left, was serene and cold. Happy as a snake eyeing a rodent dropped into its cage.

And me? What does my posture say about me?

Bustamante watched himself sit upright. He loosened his tie so that it resembled a noose around his neck. Suits had never fit him well, and ties were a torture. *Is this how Julius Caesar looked after the knives were driven into his back? Pale? Sweaty? Watery eyed?*

Angry?

Yes, now that his shock was starting to recede, Bustamante discovered beneath it a hard rock of anger emerging. Gustaffson had beaten them, yes. Their plan, which they'd believed to be so brilliant, had turned to shit. Stupid in hindsight. Play games with a scorpion, and eventually, they would feel the sting of its revenge. Then the ultimate betrayal. His loyal friend, Guillermo Modena, had turned on him with a desperate attempt to shift the blame and salvage his image, to maintain his shaky alliance with a monster.

The monster going on about who would be appointed to the new cabinet, how Modena would direct the military and police toward Gustaffson's enemies and away from his own operations, how Modena would facilitate migrant traffic through the country from all of Central America and points south...

"What did you do with Marisol?" Bustamante interrupted the litany of planned corruption. "You said my secretary had told everything. What happened to her? What did you do?"

Gustaffson raised an eyebrow, as if to an unruly child. "Frankly, dear sir, I don't give a fuck." He smirked. "Though if I know Macerio, I imagine whatever happened, it was not quick. Until the end."

A crackle of fireworks, distant but distinct, drew everyone's attention. All three men looked up and cocked their heads. Modena was the first to say it.

"Is that gunfire?" Modena, whose color had only now returned, blanched anew.

Bustamante sat up straight.

One of Gustaffson's people, a young man who could have been a college student attending a school function in polo shirt and sport coat, burst into the room and quick-marched over to the conversation area.

"Señor," he said to Gustaffson, "we have intruders inside the perimeter."

Bustamante's mind raced. Terrorists in the building. A captive CIA agent. Gunfire. "SEALs? Have the US come for their agent? Or to kill your guests? We are all truly fucked."

Gustaffson favored him with a sneer, though Bustamante read a thin line of self-doubt in the man's expression.

"Turizo is arming the sand monkeys," the college boy continued in a steady voice with only a tiny tremor. He further betrayed his nervousness by wicking the sweat from his forehead with an open palm. "Between our force and them, we have twenty fighters to defend the property."

"Against SEALs?" Bustamante coughed out a harsh laugh. "Are you insane?"

The boy flicked an irritated glance his way. "Reports so far indicate one, maybe two shooters."

"Curious," Gustaffson said.

"Shouldn't you—uh, would you like to retire to the bunker?"

Gustaffson waved a lazy hand. "Twenty against two? I will take those odds. I think we are safe for now, but monitor the situation and keep me posted."

Obviously dismissed, the college boy dipped his head, spun on a heel, and departed. Silence descended as everyone listened for the sound of more shots. When nothing happened for a time, Bustamante's thoughts returned to his growing anger. The name and nature of the attackers mattered little. Unless they burst in and killed or captured Gustaffson, nothing would change. The Scorpion would retain his leverage over Modena, and corruption would flow through Guatemala like pus from an open sore. Bustamante's dreams for a new, safe, and thriving land would die stillborn. And Modena would remain a backstabbing asshole.

Bustamante sat forward, elbows on knees, and stared at the carpet. His breathing came short and hard, and heat began to build upward from his neck into his face.

No. I won't stand for it.

Yeager and Victor snaked through the brush, at a crouch or belly down, depending upon how close the searchers approached as they quartered the brush, looking for the intruders. As they crept closer to the house, Yeager froze. Victor, following close behind, stopped and touched his shoulder to signal his position.

The sound that had arrested his movement was a man's voice murmuring a terse word, probably into his radio. A check-in.

Yeager plotted the sentinel's position as midway along the side of the garage, somewhere in the trees bordering the open space between the forest and the wall. They would need to run across about five seconds of cleared ground to reach the rear of the garage. Spotlights along the eaves lit up the strip of bare grass as bright as a football field. They would be spotted in an instant.

Yeager signaled for Victor to stay put. He eased to his left, oozing one foot at a time, displacing the ground cover rather than crushing it underfoot. His footsteps were not silent; true silence in a forest was a myth told by those who believed in superhuman powers. Rather, the sound he made blended with the natural noises of the forest—underbrush rustling in the breeze, animals rooting for food, and the clatter of tree limbs as they moved with the wind. It was Yeager's element. He became a predator in the dark, his senses opened up, and his skin tingled with the thrill of the hunt. This was what he was born for. A thought flowed underneath his calm, as if a shark cut through still waters, leaving behind disturbing ripples: *This is the creature I brought into Charlie's life. This is what damaged her. This is why I need to stay away.*

He smelled the man before seeing him. Stale sweat and cigarette smoke. A trace of flowery aftershave. The guard shifted, and Yeager saw him—an outline of black against the glow of the lighted gap behind him. As Yeager suspected, the sentinel stood right at the edge of the trees, trying to watch 360 degrees at once. At that exact second, he faced away from Yeager, watching the strip of open space between here and the parking area.

Close enough.

Yeager sprang from concealment. The guard's head started to whip around, only to meet the crunch of Yeager's buttstroke. The guard's legs noodled, and Yeager caught him then eased the man to the ground. He didn't bother feeling for a pulse. The hard vibration through the rifle told the story of a man either dead or so badly concussed, he was out of the fight for good.

Yeager felt no remorse. His predator nature would not permit it. The recognition of the hollowness inside came with a bitter realization.

No wonder she can't stand me. Hell, I can barely stand me.

Yeager turned and crept back along the forest periphery. He found Victor and motioned for him to fall in. With the solid presence of the smaller man at his back, Yeager prowled toward the rear corner of the garage. The clear, cold, dangerous spirit of the predator sealed off his emotions and drowned all thoughts of Charlie, David, and John Riley. He was not a part of them, at least in this state, nor did he want to be.

Family had no place inside the heart of a killer.

CHAPTER TWENTY-SEVEN

Foggy.

Gray.

Coming into focus.

Blanca Trevejo blinked, and the world slid back into place. An ax had split the back of her head open, or so it felt. Flashes of pain cycled from intense to brutal. She kept herself very still to avoid anything worse. Her observation point resolved into a floor-level view of a basement rec room. The painted concrete of the floor cooled her cheek.

Men's feet shuffled in and out of her view. A pool table eclipsed the center of the floor and blocked most of her view, but what she could see looked as utilitarian as a corporate breakroom, painted gray and outfitted with generic fixtures. A kitchenette filled one wall, complete with a standard refrigerator and basic dishwasher. A common room, she surmised, for the dormitories fitted into the basement.

Her perspective was from a position against the wall. Across the room, the security man, Turizo, stood in the doorway of an open closet and passed out battle rifles to willing hands. Halabi and his jihadi brethren chattered like hyperactive children on Christmas morning. She thought for a brief moment she might have been forgotten again, and a quick thought of running flickered across her consciousness.

"Reza," Halabi barked and spoke a phrase in Pashto while pointing at her. The man he addressed walked over and glared down at her. A scrawny piece of cat vomit, wearing tan jeans and an untucked work shirt, the man seemed very happy to be armed, cradling his rifle the way a woman would hold a child.

Blanca groaned and closed her eyes, muttering to herself, "Fuck you, buddy."

Noises waxed and waned as the men armed themselves and chattered at each other in excited voices. The clack and clatter of bolts being worked and chambers being charged made her cringe. No telling what kind of trigger discipline this group of turds brought to the party. She expected an accidental discharge to crack off any second. Blanca blocked out the danger to focus on her breathing and to control the aching inside her skull. Raised voices dragged her eyes back open.

"Stay here," Turizo was telling Halabi in emphatic tones. "Too much confuse"—he waved a hand in a circle overhead—"outside. My men. Your men." He mimed shooting a rifle. "Kill wrong men."

"We no die in hole!" Halabi shouted back. "We men. We fight."

Turizo's Neanderthal brow lowered, and his thick jaw clenched. Blanca guessed he was rethinking his decision to arm the Middle Easterners. The bearded young men had already begun to filter out of the room by ones and twos, ignoring Turizo's orders to stop. Halabi delivered his own orders, which Blanca guessed countermanded the security man's.

Despite the glowering cat-vomit guy standing over her, Blanca pushed herself into a sitting position and fingered her hair out of her eyes. Turizo, in his agitation, had drifted away from the storage closet with all the weapons. Racks of rifles, handguns, and other things that went bang awaited inside. Situated directly opposite her position, on the far side of the pool table, the open closet door beckoned.

Blanca licked her dry lips and looked away before Cat Vomit noticed the direction of her attention. As the men ventured out, the room drained of opposition, shifting the odds a little at a time in her favor. All she had to do was wait.

Yeager approached the rear of the house and found a twelve-foot gap between the back of the garage and a very familiar-looking stone wall. He circled around the back corner of the garage and discovered where the wall terminated. A deck extended along the rear of the house. The corner post for the wooden deck abutted a concrete anchor post for the stone wall. On the far end, the deck ended at a room of glass jutting from the back of the house like an ice cube.

The deck poked into space, as did the rear of the cube room. Putting two and two together, Yeager surmised this room to be the source of the glow he had seen while on the ledge outside the wall. Yeager sighed and shook his head.

Look at that. Another fifty yards of scooting along the ledge, and I could have stepped right onto the back deck.

But then he wouldn't have run into Por Que, who would have been escorted to whatever fate awaited him at the end of his walk.

Silver linings.

Bright lights streamed from inside, revealing a room of modern appointments and leather furniture, bright paintings, and glistening fixtures. Three men occupied a grouping of white sofas and chairs set in an intimate arrangement near the room's rear window.

"Gustaffson and two others," Yeager mouthed.

Victor sidled up next to Yeager, hunkered down by the edge of the deck, and peered through the rails.

"The thin guy, with his back to us? His name is Modena, and he's the president-elect," he said. "Of, like, Guatemala and whatnot."

"Whaaat?" Yeager mocked. "I thought you meant the US."

"Look, don't give me shit. My boob hurts."

"Who's the other guy?"

"I dunno. He came with the president. Probably a flunky."

A sliding glass door provided access from the deck to the room. From where he crouched, Yeager couldn't tell if the latch was locked or not.

"Okay, mini-Hulk," he said. "Time to smash. Your wounded breast up to it?"

"Hell, yeah! Let's get some."

They rose as one, lifting themselves over the deck rail and easing down the other side. The polished boards underfoot creaked a bit. Yeager and Victor crossed the open space, steering clear of the scattering of outdoor furniture dotting the deck. They were halfway across when Yeager hissed a warning, and they froze.

Inside, the tableau had changed. The round butterball of a man—the president's flunky—rose from his seat, a thunderous expression clouding his features. His face was brick red. He pulled a pistol from his pocket.

L ittle Maria. A pet name for a pocket pistol.

Bustamante had carried the weapon as a totem. A good-luck charm. He had never fired it in anger, nor really paid attention to his little icon of security in many years. It was pocket ballast, much like keys, a wallet, and coins. Something to celebrate and remind him of a moment when he had been brave, bold, and heroic.

When he had taken it from one of the thugs who had broken into his boyhood home, he'd found stamped on the top of the barrel the words "H&R Arms Co., Worcester, Mass." The top half of the pistol broke open and tilted forward when he pulled the lugs located near the hammer. Five cartridges nested in the cylinder, each marked ".32 S&W." At the time, he had no idea what any of those things meant. He learned many years later that H&R translated to Harrington & Richardson, and that it fired bullets of .32 caliber. The S&W

referred to a particular cartridge size, suited to the weapon, and to fire any other .32 cartridge was problematic.

"You blow your hand off," the old geezer at the gun store had advised.

He had replaced the original bullets after an afternoon plinking cans, one of three times he had fired the weapon. *How long ago was that? Ten years? Twelve? Would twelve-year-old cartridges still work?*

Modena hung his head, refusing to look Bustamante in the eye. The unexpected betrayal hurt, as if his entire body had been slapped. Guillermo had always been an opportunist; Bustamante knew this. It should have come as no surprise that he would try to salvage his position with Gustaffson by seizing on the one solution that might save him from their predicament.

Surprise! Bustamante laughed to himself without humor. *I am an idiot. Look at him. A whipped dog has more courage. This is the man I have followed since boyhood? Forty-plus years of being the butt of his jokes and the ugly, fat companion of the handsome and athletic Guillermo Modena. This is the man I have pushed on the people as the next savior of our country? Well, fuck him. And fuck all of this.*

The anger simmering under the pain boiled over. Years of slights, years of staying in the background while the dashing, handsome, and oh-so-articulate Modena stole all the glory, had built a powder keg in Bustamante's chest. This latest betrayal was the match that lit the fuse.

Bustamante powered up from his seat. His hand dipped into his coat and came out with Little Maria.

"You worthless piece of shit!" Bustamante screamed. He pointed his pistol at his lifelong friend then hesitated. Tears spilled free and watered his cheeks. He shifted his aim.

Little Maria spat. A round dot appeared in the space between Gustaffson's wide eyes.

"I didn't see that coming," Victor said.

"He just shot our leverage," Yeager said.

A thunderous torrent of fire ripped across the deck at their rear. A bullet burned Yeager's hip, and more whipcracked past him. New holes rippled across the glass wall, pocking it with spiderwebs. Victor squawked and fell, grabbing the back of his leg. Yeager spun.

At the edge of the deck, a bearded man held a smoking military rifle down by his hip, barrel pointed skyward from muzzle climb. Yeager punched out two rounds, and the man spiraled backward over the rail.

"How the hell did he miss?" Yeager wondered aloud.

"He didn't." Victor sat with his legs splayed, both hands clamped around his left thigh. "At least, not enough."

"You got shot?"

"Yes."

"Again?"

"Fuck you, Holmes. It's a lot easier than winning the lottery."

Yeager took a knee next to him. "Artery?"

"I don't think so," Victor gritted out.

"We need to move. Someone heard that idiot cranking off a full mag."

Yeager scanned ahead. The hail of bullets through the glass had driven the chubby guy and his skinnier pal to seek cover in the conversation pit. The men hunkered down like a pair of brown bears rooting for insects.

"Dammit," Yeager snapped. "The jihadis are armed. Let's get inside. See if we can find your woman and get the hell out of here."

"Don't say it like that."

"Like what?"

"Like she's *my woman*. Alex will hear you, even from a thousand miles away."

Yeager tried the sliding door. Unlocked, to his surprise. He slid it open and went back to help Por Que to his feet.

"Not my fault," he said while crouching to support the shorter man. "I'm not the one who hooked up with a sexy spy."

"Who said she was sexy?"

"Is she ugly?"

"Well... no. Not—uh!—the point." Victor grunted as he hopped along by Yeager's side. "My heart belongs to another."

"By heart you mean balls, right?"

"Them too."

"Hey, you!" Yeager called out to the two men in the seating area, who had just begun to lift their heads. "Drop the popgun and come out with your hands raised." He swung the muzzle of his T4 to emphasize his demand.

Yeager shuffled to his left, pulling Victor along with him. The expanse of glass and the open door at his back prickled his skin with anticipation of a bullet storm sleeting in from the darkness. Being inside the brightly lit fishbowl made them well-defined targets for any dipshit with a gun who might be creeping up their six.

A wet bar with a gleaming granite countertop divided the space down the middle, splitting it into two living areas. Gustaffson's surprised corpse and his two guests filled the sunken conversation pit near the windows, and another grouping of sofas and chairs were arranged in the room on the far side of the bar. Adjacent to the living area, beyond the bar, the room morphed into a dining area, complete with a long glass table—*What is it with all the glass?*—surrounded by fourteen high-backed chairs of chrome and white leather. Rectangular entryways suggested more rooms at the far side of the dining area and directly to his left, beyond the living room.

Yeager's shoulder blades relaxed a notch when he moved away from the windows and put a solid wall at his back. He allowed Victor to sag off his shoulder and slide down the wall to sit on the floor.

"You," he commanded the fat man. "If I don't see that pistol fly away from your hand in the next second, I'm punching your ticket."

The big man blinked owlishly. He looked at the small revolver in his hand as if it had grown there without his knowledge. He swallowed, nodded, and tossed the pistol underhand onto a narrow rug near the bar.

"Who are you?" asked the slim man—Modena, the one Victor claimed to be the president of Guatemala—crouched behind a chair.

Victor looked up from clenching his thigh. "We're the chumps you fucked into trying to kill that dude. The one your buddy just offed." He waggled a bloody finger in stern disapproval. "We're not very happy with you right now."

"Get us out of here." The so-called president's voice shook. Modena appeared to be on the verge of tears. "We can pay."

"Yes, you will," Yeager growled. "Get over here, away from the windows."

As if to validate his concern, a rattle of small arms fire sounded from outside. No rounds came close, but the staccato burst of fire drove the two politicians deeper into their conversation pit. Yeager shrugged mentally. He wasn't deeply invested in protecting the two men. If they wanted to hunker down rather than get out of the line of fire, it was no skin off his ass. Then another thought occurred.

"Can you really get Cujo out of prison? Or was that all bullshit?"

Modena looked to his companion, confusion written on his face. "Alfonso?"

The round man with the florid face peered up from his position at the foot of a long white sofa. "This is not bullshit. We can get your friend out."

"Get over to the bar," Yeager ordered. "Find a towel or something for my friend's leg."

Victor leaned forward. "And tell us where they took the woman."

"Woman?" Modena's brows contracted. "What woman?"

"The CIA woman, you self-centered prick," grumbled the round Alfonso. "The one from the garage? Remember?"

Modena blinked his owl eyes. No light bulb appeared over his head. He might as well have been a stuffed doll for all the intelligence he exhibited.

Another crackle of fire came from somewhere deep in the bowels of the house.

"Wouldn't it be good," Victor said, "if these guys shoot each other all up, leave us nothing but dead bodies to clean up?"

"From your lips to God's ears," Yeager muttered. To the pair of Guatemalans, he said, "If you're coming with us, you need to get your asses in gear."

CHAPTER TWENTY-EIGHT

Halabi did not like the strange environment in which he found himself. Trees. Thick trunks and a heavy, foreboding canopy closed around him like a carpet of thick wool. He could not see ten meters in front of his nose. The foresight of the weapon in his hand was all but invisible. He buried the rifle's buttstock into his hip as he quartered through the dense forest. Unseen vines and exposed roots snagged his feet and tried to trip him at every other step.

The scents were strange. The sounds were strange. All so vastly different than the mountains of his homeland, where vegetation grew sparse and tough among the rocks and sand, and where he knew the night animals and the sounds they made. Strange creatures—some kind of monkey, he suspected—chittered and bounded among the branches overhead, dislodging leaves and small twigs to patter around his shoulders, further confusing his senses as he probed the darkness for the intruders.

The guard force complicated matters. The men, dressed uniformly in black, ghosted through the trees on the same mission. Twice now, Halabi had nearly blown away one of the guards when the men loomed up from the darkness, unseen until the last moment. Almost, Halabi had come to regret his need for action. Had he acted rashly by demanding he and his men be armed and set loose on the grounds against an unknown force? They were all blundering about in the pitch black, in a bewildering labyrinth of trees, seeking contact with a mysterious group of attackers. Random shots belted out, here and there, impossible to place by sound alone. For all Halabi knew, the guards and his men were shooting at each other, doing the enemy's work for them.

This is stupid. Time to return to the house. The goal of any attack will obviously end up there, sooner or later.

Halabi pivoted in the direction he believed the house to be. A figure stumbled through the forest into his path, visible only as a vaguely lighter patch of clothing against the cave-like darkness of the forest. Halabi's skin went electric.

An enemy! Sneaking in for the kill!

Halabi ripped off a sustained burst. The unfamiliar rifle in his hands climbed upward, spitting a lance of fire from its muzzle. His rounds stitched a course up the intruder's torso from crotch to neck. Only after the last round from his magazine had left the barrel did Halabi recognize the man he'd shot. Bhaswar Bhatti. A Pakistani from Bahawalpur who had joined Halabi's team in Syria the day before they boarded the ship that would take them to Guatemala.

Blessed be to God, but he had done just what he was worried the other jihadis were doing. Shooting his own men. Halabi screamed in frustration.

Breathing as if his lungs were on fire, he checked the rifle and found the bolt locked back. He fumbled through a magazine change in the dark, his fingers clumsy with adrenaline and the unfamiliarity of the Western-made weapon. He charged the bolt before orienting on where he believed the infidel pig's mansion to be.

"I'm sorry, my brother," he whispered to Bhatti's corpse as he passed. "May you find Allah's grace."

Halabi stalked onward, itching to be out of this jungle and back to a place he understood.

His name was Reza, not Cat Vomit, though she much preferred the latter. Blanca had gathered that much from the cross-talk before Halabi had charged out of the room to do battle with whoever was shooting at Gustaffson's security team. She entertained a momentary fantasy that a CIA hit team had dropped from the sky to rescue her, that somehow her station chief, Hunter Davidson, and his 2IC, Larssen, had managed to track her kidnappers via SIGINT and collectively scraped together the single serving of balls they would need to authorize a wet team insertion to pull her ass out of the fire. This fantasy evaporated after an application of logic: only pure random chance would have allowed her superiors in the embassy to learn of her abduction, and secondly, if a black-ops squad was descending on Gustaffson's mansion, where the fuck were they? She should be hearing a steady progression of dead terrorists falling to lethal gunfire, and as yet nothing of the sort appeared to be happening. The CIA employed a class of special contractors for just this situation, guys that matriculated from Delta, Rangers, SEALs, and Marine Recon. Real meat eaters that would rip through a gaggle of fuzz-faced martyrs like hot shit through a blue goose.

C'mon, guys. There's only twelve of the bastards.

Reza divided his attention between her and the door, jerking every time a random shout or a rattle of gunfire filtered down the hall. The man's skin jumped as if sporadic bursts of electricity sparked from a downed power line.

Blanca sighed. It was time to quit waiting for the appearance of red-bearded, Skoal-dipping hunks in backward baseball caps and watermelon biceps to pop through the door and drill Reza the Terrorist a new forehead portal. If she was going to be saved, she needed to do some of the work herself.

She pressed her back against the wall, pulled her legs under her, and slid upright. The motion drew Reza's attention. He swung the muzzle of his weapon to point at her belly.

"What are you doing?" he screeched. "Sit down! No move!"

"Calm down," she said, palms out and spread wide. "My butt hurt, and I needed to get up." Blanca rested her hands on her knees, bent over like she could barely stand. The way the iron spike in her skull throbbed, that didn't require a lot of acting.

Reza continued to rail at her, shaking his rifle and stabbing it at her like it had a bayonet affixed to the muzzle.

Blanca kept her head down and waved him off. "Yeah, yeah, yeah. I hear you. Just give me a second." She pretended to fall forward, resting her forearms against the pool table. "Oooh, I'm feeling sick," she moaned while side-eying her guard through the waterfall of black hair covering her face.

A shout from the hallway drew Reza's attention.

A second was all she needed. The pool table provided a cluster of weapons.

Reza stood to her right, so she used her left hand to scoop up a pool ball. The eight ball as it turned out. It fit her palm, cool and heavy. She whipped it sidearm, a screaming fastball aimed at Reza's head. He ducked, and the ball skipped across his shoulder and clipped his ear. No real damage, but a ton of *what the fuck*.

Next up, a pool cue. A couple of pounds of lacquered wood. A staple of bar fights, both real and cinematic, for the past hundred years or more. Blanca slashed the stick across Reza's blocking arm, the one holding the rifle's pistol grip, earning a howl of pain from the shaggy little fuck. He dropped the rifle as the nerves in that arm went into shock.

Blanca wound up and spun a full circle, whipping the cue across Reza's unprotected ribs. The cue broke off, leaving her a stick the size of a butcher knife and nearly as sharp.

For the moment, she had the momentum. Reza was surprised. Reactive. Any second now, he would realize he wasn't that badly hurt, then he would turn the tables on her and bring his superior body mass to bear. Though not a big man, he had enough poundage on her to mop the floor with her in a fair fight.

There is no such thing as a fair fight. Words delivered by her unarmed combat instructor at Harvey Point. Five-eight and a buck-sixty, Damian Crow resembled a school principal more than a lethal weapon, except for his frosty-cold eyes. "You're in a fight, it means things have gone pear-shaped, and it's do or die. Use everything. Bring out your murder and put. The guy. Down."

Blanca drove the sharp end of her broken stick into Reza's belly. It felt like punching into the heavy bag in the gym, though a bit squishier. Thick, plastic resistance underlain by a mushy center. The tip of the cue pierced Reza's abdominal wall and drove in a full two inches. That was as far as she got before the strength of her punch lost momentum. Not enough to put the man down.

Reza bent forward, his mouth pulling into an O. He was more surprised than hurt, at least until the pain hit.

Blanca stepped back and kicked out with a heel strike to the chalk tip of the cue, driving it a full six inches deeper. That one hurt.

Reza dropped to his knees, his hands cupped around the bit of shaft sticking out of his stomach, a handspan down from the bottom of his ribcage.

Blanca toed the rifle away from him, sliding it under her feet. She snatched it up and stepped back. Stock to shoulder. Front sight. Rear sight aligned. Center mass in the frame.

She breathed in. This was the real deal. Waldo in the alley had been all terror, reaction, and instinct. Here, Reza was badly injured. She was ninety-eight percent sure the belly wound would be the end of him. Leaving him badly injured would give her conscience the distance it needed to separate herself from merely defending her life versus being a cold-blooded killer. He was not much of a threat, not with a gut full of slick pine sticking out of him. Shooting him now would serve no purpose but to ensure he would never be a threat to anyone again, eliminating the two percentage points of doubt remaining. But it would be crossing a line. By pulling the trigger, Blanca would be taking a step beyond self-defense and putting herself squarely in the camp of no turning back. She would be making the decision to kill him.

Can I live with that?

The gunshots slammed her eardrums hard, magnified by the enclosed space.

"I guess I'll find out," she said, barely hearing herself over the ringing in her ears.

"**W**hy did you give them weapons?" asked Dominic, the baby assassin, for the fourth or fifth time. A hacksaw on bone would be no less irritating.

Patricio Turizo tightened his grip on the little scrap of patience he possessed. It hadn't been large to begin with, but the man he tauntingly referred to as Borges's Butt Boy had stretched it to the limit. The little poser couldn't fool Turizo. For all his nice clothes and good looks, the assassin's apprentice had come from a little shit-stain of a village—poor, uneducated, and with the morals of a rat. As had Turizo himself.

Where Dominic had been handpicked by Borges to become his personal cocksucker, Turizo had fought his way up through the rank and file of Gustaffson's security force, joining as an illiterate teenager and learning the trade from the ground up. He'd surpassed his better-educated and better-spoken colleagues with a combination of ruthless violence and animal cunning. He knew his value to the Scorpion was not for his intelligence, but for his willingness to do any gruesome task efficiently and without remorse.

Arming the ragheads had been a mistake. He realized that now. They were running loose throughout the grounds, shooting at each other, at monkeys in the trees, the ground, the sky, the moon, and any of Turizo's men who were unlucky enough to cross their path.

"Fall back to the perimeter," he ordered into his radio mic. "Let the Arabs kill each other until they run out of ammunition." To Dominic, he said, "Come with me, back to the house. We have left Señor Gustaffson unguarded for too long."

"Yes, that was your second mistake."

Turizo ground his teeth, wishing he could wipe the superior sneer off the younger man's face with a buttstroke of his carbine. After the initial volley of fire, he and Dominic had met at the garage entrance. They'd watched as the Arabs dispersed into the night, wild-eyed and shouting about their god's greatness.

He and the kid had followed for a time, skirting the edge of the road as it cut through the jungle. The sounds of gunfire ripped staccato bursts from all points, and at first, Turizo had been convinced they were under a full-scale assault. Reports over the radio had been erratic, confused. Turizo had crouched a hundred meters from the house, taking a knee and pressing his fingers against his earbud.

Then came the first complaint from the baby-faced assassin. "You should not have given them guns."

And the shit-stinking prick was right.

Turizo jogged to the hacienda's front door and keyed his way inside, with Dominic on his heels. Turizo could feel the self-righteousness vibrating off the younger man like a tuning fork held to his ear. He crossed the main entry, the first living room space, and passed beyond the wet bar separating the great room in half. He entered the lounge with the picture window... and crashed to a halt.

His brain refused to accept the reality presented by his eyes.

"What have you done!" Dominic howled. He brushed past Turizo and dashed to the conversation pit. Dominic bent over the slumped form of Herman Gustaffson and tilted their employer's head to the side. A small, blue-ringed dot of red leaked a single trail of blood over Gustaffson's wide-open left eye. "Call a doctor!"

Turizo had seen death often enough. He'd caused death often enough. "There is no longer need for a doctor."

He ignored the look of hatred Borges's Butt Boy threw at him and instead focused on the details of the room. The shattered glass of the windows overlooking the deck. Furniture knocked askew. Bullet holes pocking various surfaces.

Where are the shit-sucking politicians?

Blood. A trail of blood drip-dropped from the south side of the room across the white tile leading to...

"The kitchen," he said. "They went toward the kitchen." He press-checked the chamber of his rifle and threw out a challenge to the younger man. "Follow me if you have the balls. We will kill these bastards who shot El Escorpión. We will have our revenge, if nothing else."

"What's your name?" Yeager asked as the heavyset man finished bandaging Victor's leg with a pair of knotted-together dish towels.

"Alfonso Bustamante." He flicked a glance at his near-catatonic companion before going back to struggling with the final knot. Blood welled under his fingertips. "That is Guillermo Modena. Believe it or not, he is to be sworn in as President of Guatemala next month. I was to be his Minister of... something. It was not decided."

The four of them huddled in the mansion's kitchen, a gleaming room of brushed-nickel appliances, black granite countertops and stainless-steel fixtures. A canopy of copper pots, pans, and utensils hung from hooks above the cooktop and built-in grill. Victor sat on the floor with his back against the center island as Bustamante labored to stop the bleeding with his makeshift bandages. Yeager crouched near him, dividing his attention between entrances at opposite ends of the kitchen. One led to the living area they had recently vacated. The other opened into a hallway of utilitarian gray with a staircase at the end. Modena slumped against a refrigerator the size of a small motor home.

Yeager spun at a sound from the back hallway. A figure all but stumbled down the corridor. Glassy-eyed, with a tumbled mass of black hair falling around her face, the woman moved like an overwound spring-driven toy, all jerky and quick. Amped on adrenaline was Yeager's guess. She wore jeans and a peach blouse, the latter unbuttoned down the front to reveal a lacy white brassiere. Yeager centered the front sight of his rifle on the narrow strip of fabric in the middle of her sternum.

"Hold it!" he ordered, causing the woman to shudder to a stop and fix him with hot, feverish eyes. "Easy now," he soothed. "We're on the same side, if you're who I think you are."

"Juanita!" Victor sang out from the floor. He craned sideways around Bustamante's bulk to get a better view. "We've been looking for you, chica!"

"You, I know." Pointing to Bustamante and Modena, she added, "Him and him, I know. You," she said to Yeager, "I don't know."

"Staff Sergeant Abel Yeager, US Marines, retired. And you are?"

The woman regarded him through narrow eyes for a long second. "Blanca Trevejo, Central Intelligence Agency."

"I knew it!" Victor crowed.

"Great," Yeager said. "The gang's all here. We can go now."

He reached for Victor's arm to help him up. A hail of bullets blew in from the living area, whanging off pots and blowing chunks out of the walls. Yeager dropped to one knee, huddled behind the central island, cursing life, Guatemala, and the day he was born.

"It's not all bad," Victor said. "At least you ain't shot."

"He's been shot?" Blanca squinted from where she hugged the floor. White ceramic dust frosted her hair. "How bad?"

"Bad enough," Yeager said. "I keep telling him the red stuff works better inside than out, but does he listen?"

Another rattle of incoming fire spattered the kitchen. All of it speared in from the doorway to the dining room, making Yeager wonder if they were being driven toward the jaws of a trap. He blind-fired over the center island, buying time. If enough guys bull-rushed the door, he would be hard-pressed to keep them out.

"Okay," he said under his breath. "Back door, it is."

CHAPTER TWENTY-NINE

Halabi reentered the garage and made his way through the interior door and down the stairs to the dormitory level. He kept his rifle snugged into his shoulder and followed the barrel, swinging it in wide arcs as he continued down the hall. He cleared each bedroom as he passed their open doors. He recognized the room where he had taken the woman, cringing at the memory of his fruitless attempt to achieve an erection. Despite the privacy of the moment, the look in the infidel bitch's eyes burned his cheeks with shame. Could she see it? His lack of desire? His... other needs? Of course she could.

I must kill her. She must not be allowed to spread rumors about me.

Halabi entered the recreation room with the pool table. It was empty.

"Reza? Where are you?"

A foot protruded from behind the pool table. Halabi rushed around the obstacle, only to find Reza tumbled to the floor in a pool of thick crimson. The bullets to the skull had distorted the shape of Reza's head. Shocked eyes bulged out from the misshapen orb.

Of the woman, there was no sign.

"She is a devil," Halabi muttered. "Shayatin."

No other way could such a small woman have overcome and killed the much larger Reza. No other explanation for how she had made him soft when he sought to use her. There was no question he was a man; the memories of boy-play were merely a distraction, something she threw up into his mind to make him doubt himself.

"She will die now," he vowed to Reza's corpse. "Find peace, my brother, knowing I will stop at nothing to send this devil back to hell."

Gripping his rifle, Halabi returned to the hall. From somewhere ahead of him, the sound of shots banging into something metallic echoed down the corridor. Halabi hurried onward.

Yeager ducked behind the central island as more rounds zipped through the entrance. A spice rack suffered a direct hit. Terracotta jars shattered, and a pungent dusting of condiments fogged the kitchen.

"Trevejo? What's back there?" Yeager shouted at the new arrival. "Where you came from?"

The woman huddled near the floor and blinked owlish eyes at him. Something clicked, and she seemed to snap to. "Hallway to a bunch of dorms. Beyond that, the garage."

"Garage. That's where we need to go." Herbs and seasonings drifted like snow, and Yeager's eyes watered. A sneeze built up pressure in his sinuses. He swiped an arm across his forehead, smearing an oregano-thyme-basil mix into a greenish paste before tapping Victor on the shoulder. "Can you hold the rear?"

Victor motioned to the grill built into the center island. "We can set a booby trap. Turn on the gas? Put something on the cooktop to catch fire? Cause a 'splosion?"

"A gas explosion?" Yeager snorted. "Let's not blow ourselves up, okay? Just get moving—"

A shape loomed in the rear hallway—a man with a weapon. He appeared in the same place the Trevejo woman had moments before. Half-blinded from watery eyes, Yeager fired from the hip. Though clear misses, his rounds drove the newcomer back the way he'd come.

"That was Halabi!" Blanca Trevejo panted like a wild animal in a corner of a small cage. "That little cockroach needs stomping. In the worst way."

"I'm on point. Trevejo, follow me," Yeager said. "See terrorist, shoot terrorist. Modena and Alfonso, get on the woman's hip and stay there. Victor, bring up the rear. Don't fuck around trying to play chef, okay? Just stick and move." He laid down two bursts of suppressive fire through the living room doorway. Return fire peppered the kitchen wall.

"Go on, chica." Victor pushed himself stiff-legged from the floor into an awkward crouch. "Get your killer face on and go shoot some bad guys."

Trevejo snarled a sharky smile. "Just like back in East LA."

"Without the lights and sirens." Yeager pointed at Modena and Alfonso. "And you two—cling to her ass like her favorite blue jeans. *Comprende?*"

Nods came back from the pair huddled by the stove. Victor popped his weapon above the grill top and ripped off a pair of controlled bursts. The percussive beat of hammering shots pounded Yeager's eardrums, over which he somehow heard the tinkle of spent brass bouncing off the floor tile. No return fire answered Victor's challenge.

"Okay, then." Yeager crabbed past the CIA woman, head down near his knees. "Let's go."

Turizo crouched behind a sofa. Made of wood and leather, the piece of furniture would no more stop a bullet than tissue paper, but when he popped his head up, it gave him a good view of the aperture from the dining area into the kitchen. He couldn't see much through the narrow opening: the center island, the stove top beyond it, the spice rack...

A rifle appeared over the center island, held aloft by a pair of brown-toned hands. Turizo dropped to the floor an instant before the rifle opened up, and unaimed rounds spat through the sofa's back, blowing out puffs of stuffing to drift in lazy currents. Another burst passed higher, chewing into the plaster of the far wall.

Turizo low-crawled to the left side of the sofa and peered around the base. He caught sight of Dominic, who had swung wide of the door. Dominic now crept along the dining room wall adjacent to the kitchen, approaching the doorway beyond which the shooters were concealed.

Or shooter. Turizo had a pretty good idea they faced only the Mexican American, the muscular little bodybuilder named Ruiz, and the man named Yeager. The two men he had sent to escort the prisoner off the cliff had dropped out of radio contact. The volume of fire from the kitchen indicated one, or maybe two shooters. He had also lost contact with the group left up north to detain the gringo partner of Ruiz. Grudgingly, Turizo had to admit that maybe that man had taken out his team and somehow joined up to free his partner, and that they had managed to fulfill their mission to assassinate Gustaffson.

Irony, Dominic would call that.

Bad fucking luck was what Turizo called it.

The rational, logical part of his brain suggested to Turizo he should cut bait. Pack his gear, grab what valuables he could lay his hands on, and fade into the hills. Gustaffson had no superiors who would exact vengeance on the security staff who failed to protect their principal. Only Jovanovic, the money man, could possibly care, though he held no real authority. There was no cartel to whom Gustaffson reported. A power vacuum would soon suck all of Gustaffson's subordinates into a vicious fight for control of El Escorpión's network of agents and assets. They would not be after Patricio Turizo's skin... rather they would probably pin a medal on him for allowing them the chance of advancement. If he walked away right now, no one would stop him. No one would care. Patricio Turizo could slip into the jungle and, chameleon-like, disappear from view, never to be seen again.

All of this he considered for the space of two heartbeats.

No.

Fuck no.

These men had killed his employer. Unlike the slimy prick Borges, Turizo cared not a whit for honor. The concept of honor held no meaning for a man who had done the things he had done in service to the Scorpion. No, the truth was, Patricio Turizo was angry. Embarrassed. Fucking pissed off.

These two American pussies had kicked him in the nuts. They had slaughtered his boss while Turizo's back was turned. He had been charged with protecting Gustaffson and had failed miserably.

Nothing but blood would wash away the sting of that insult.

He hissed to catch Dominic's attention. Once the younger man looked over, Turizo communicated via charades and hand signals that he hoped Dominic understood.

On three, I will lay down covering fire. You assault. Comprende?

Dominic nodded.

Okay, then... One. Two.

Three!

Blanca followed the man named Yeager into the narrow hall beyond the kitchen. Baker's racks of stored food lined the hall on both sides of the corridor—industrial-sized containers of beans, coffee, tomatoes, and canned vegetables filled the racks, along with sacks of flour, corn meal, and rice.

At the end of the hall, a set of stairs led to the basement, where the corridor continued along a path leading to the recreation room and the dormitories beyond. At the far end of this hall lay the stairs to the garage where she had first entered the hacienda.

Blanca felt disconnected from her body, as if she were a driver at the controls of a meat machine, navigating the steps of a dance without a tune. She was not an operator. Not a warrior. Her job was to convince, to coerce, or to entrap members of foreign governments into compromising their state's secrets. To suborn, pry, and seduce bits of information away from those desperate enough, greedy enough, or naïve enough to slide into alignment with her honeyed rationalizations for their betrayal. And yet, here she was, shoulder snugged into a rifle butt, hoping to find the swarthy, bearded face of a jihadist enemy of her country centered in her sights.

GI Jane.

The man in front of her paused at the top of a single flight of stairs leading to the basement level.

Yeager. Big and bold, with eyes made from chipped granite. Though not bearded, dipping Skoal, or tattooed, he checked every other one of her mental boxes for a special operator of the badass variety. Powerful, broad-chested. His weapon an extension grafted to his hands. Hard-used and looking lightly chewed on by the dogs of hell. Ready to bring the pain down on Halabi and his crew.

Blanca shivered and breathed deeply.

He twitched two fingers. *Move on.*

Blanca took the stairs by feel, careful to not let her muzzle stray. She kept her cheek to her weapon, eyes aligned down the barrel and tracking the front sight along the path ahead. Down, left, right, check. Step. Repeat. Gray walls painted with a glistening finish. Treads and handrails of metal. Industrial lighting overhead.

No Halabi. He remained somewhere ahead. But not for long.

Khayyat Halabi ducked an instant before the stranger's bullets tore through the air. In the split second before he dived for cover, he had seen the infidel whore, the Mexican man, and another Westerner. The strange man had struck like a viper, so fast, Halabi's heart still raced at his close call with death.

He backed down the stairs into the basement hallway. It ran a good twenty meters before making a sharp left turn. On the right was a pantry filled with more food than Halabi had seen gathered outside a marketplace. On the left was the room with the pool table, where Reza lay dead. Beyond the turn, the hallway stretched out another fifty meters and was lined with the sleeping rooms.

Halabi crouched at the base of the stairs, aiming up them in case the infidels decided to show themselves to his gunsights. Which way to go? What was the best tactical decision? Sneak back up the stairs and engage, or retreat and find a good ambush point? The woman and her companion were in a small space—the kitchen—with a narrow opening to the hall. He could easily edge back up and blind-fire into the room, with a good probability of wounding or killing the Westerners.

He could just as easily miss.

Halabi wiped the sweat from his forehead. Nothing moved at the top of the stairs. His feet felt like stone blocks. They did not want to mount the staircase. Halabi's heart thumped against his ribs. With a final glance up the stairs, Halabi retreated, scuffing down the corridor, seeking a good ambush point.

CHAPTER THIRTY

Yeager oozed down the steps, fully focused on the slice of hallway as it grew in his vision. The hairs on the back of his neck crawled as Trevejo—the unknown entity—carried a loaded weapon directly behind him. All it would take was one wrong step...

"Watch your footing," he growled over his shoulder.

"My footing is just fine," she snapped back. "Watch yours."

Yeager tracked Modena and Bustamante by the sound of their heavy footfalls clanging on the treads behind him. Every enemy in the building would hear them coming from a mile away. He twisted his lips to one side and hissed, "Can you keep those two quiet?"

By the pause, Yeager imagined he was on the receiving end of a very dirty look. Then came Trevejo's voice, directed upstairs, berating the politicians for being blundering buffoons and other things his Spanish was too rusty to make out.

At the base of the stairs, the hallway was as gray and utilitarian as a government storage room. Fifty or sixty feet then a right turn. Two doors, both closed.

"Dammit. Okay, Trevejo. Nice and easy. We have to clear every stinking room before we move on."

"Makes sense. I don't want to get shot in the back."

"I don't want to get shot anywhere." Yeager checked up the stairs. Still no Por Que. Where the fuck was he? He stifled the urge to yell upstairs and tell Victor to get a move on. If the bad guys were thinking about storming the kitchen, his call might just provoke the assault.

He ground his teeth and spat out a disgusted "Fuck."

"Want me to go check on him?" Trevejo asked.

"No," Yeager said through a tight jaw. "He'll be along. I have no doubt about that."

Blanca Trevejo side-eyed him but said nothing.

"Let's move," Yeager said.

As the two Guatemalans disappeared, Victor Ruiz started poking at the grill controls in the center island, a task hampered by keeping one eye on the doorway through which the attackers would charge. The idea of leaving behind a booby trap worried him.

Except...

"Son of a bitching-motherfucking appliance." The knobs had no markings visible from eyeball level. He only wanted to stick his head up a few inches, and even that was pushing it. He turned a knob. There came a snapping sound followed by a whoosh of flame.

"No, fuck, that's not what I want." Victor sighed through his nostrils. "Fuck it. I get you turned on full gas, you *hijo de puta*, then I gotta find something to set on stove so it catches afire." He grimaced. Or put a steel pot in the microwave? He'd seen that on TV once, but would it work in real life? And if it did, would it blow them all to hell, like Yeager said? "Fuck you, Abel Yeager. Always spoiling the party."

Victor dropped behind the island an instant before another round of shots zipped through the doorway. With more clangs and bangs, cookware danced on their hooks. More ceramic jars shattered. More herbs and spices peppered the air. Victor squeezed against the island and pinched his nostrils shut to avoid sneezing.

I'm gonna smell like a pizza after this.

Footsteps. Running footsteps, coming through the entry. Other side of the island, moving away from the door.

Victor went low and slid across the spice-slicked floor. Ceramic bits from the spice containers scraped against his bare arm as he slid partially out from behind the island.

A pair of trouser-clad legs came into view, followed by the rest of the attacker.

Hah! Torture Boy!

Victor snap-fired from the floor. A full three-round burst. The bullets ripped through the younger man's thighs from point-blank range. The impact knocked his legs out from under him, and the attacker lost his balance. His pistol flew wide. He stumbled forward. Torture Boy tried to stop his fall, palms out against the grill top.

A shriek tore the air, and Torture Boy toppled to the kitchen floor, eye-to-eye with Victor Ruiz, one burned hand held before his face.

Victor grinned. "How you like that shit, motherfucker? Payback's a hot bitch."

Halabi scouted the long hall of dormitory rooms, looking for a place to set up for an ambush. He discarded the idea of hiding in a room and waiting for the infidels to pass. The idea of trapping himself in a space without a back exit did not appeal to him, plus not knowing whom he was fighting and how they were armed left him with fewer choices. One hand grenade would end his life before he managed to achieve greater good in the name of Allah.

Who are these people?

The CIA woman and the Mexican American, he had seen before. The infidel with death in his eyes was an unknown, though Halabi had seen the type in battles back home. He regretted now not paying attention to the conversation among Gustaffson's men about the Mexican. A prisoner, obviously. Destined for execution the last time

Halabi had seen him. The Guatemalan's men had failed at that, just as they had failed at protecting the compound from outsiders.

He sniffed. *Idiots.*

It was quiet in the hallway. Sounds carried. The faint scrape and louder clang from behind him meant the Westerners were coming. He did not have much time. If worse came to worst, he could fire from the cover of a bedroom door then hold the escapees in the hall until Gustaffson's men got off their asses and did something.

What is their goal?

The instant after he asked himself that question, the answer came to him. *The garage. They will try to escape by stealing a vehicle.*

Halabi smiled and hurried up the stairs to the garage. To get out, the CIA woman and her accomplices would have to exit the landing at the top of the stairs through a single door. The garage afforded many ambush opportunities. Much cover.

Finally. My luck is turning.

When Torture Boy fell, he trapped the foregrip of Victor's rifle under him. The muzzle stuck out the other side of the man's body, depriving Victor of the option to trigger a burst and blow the bastard away. Lying on his side, right hand all but trapped by the pinned weapon, Victor had no leverage. His looping left-hand punch lacked power. He hit the man smack in the middle of his surprised face, doing little damage.

Torture Boy recovered fast. He blocked Victor's follow-up strike, and in seconds, he and Victor were twisted like snakes on the kitchen floor, clenching, scratching, and punching. The tiles soon became slick with blood, most from Gustaffson's man. They rolled and slipped in the mess. Blood slicked both of them within seconds.

New sport. Blood wrestling.

Victor found himself with his nose in the younger man's hair. He rooted for an ear. Found it. Bit it. It tasted of earwax at first, then the iron taste of blood filled his mouth.

Torture Boy howled, and Victor knew joy.

"Fuck up my tit, will you?" he said through a mouthful of ear. It came out more like *Fuddupmmtit, willya.*

A shape appeared at the edge of his vision. A closer look revealed Turizo standing over him with a rifle muzzle touching his cheekbone.

"Move. I don't want my bullet to kill this butt boy." He smiled through a picket fence of bad teeth. "Though it wouldn't hurt my feelings too much if I did, so maybe I shoot you now."

When Halabi entered the cavernous garage, he rejoiced. Two of his men, Moubarak and Hamad, sat on the trunk of the black Mercedes, weapons across their laps and cigarettes dangling from their lips. The car was parked in the middle of the great space, leaving room enough for a vehicle to park on each side. A little sports car huddled against the side wall farthest away from the stairwell landing.

Halabi whistled sharply. "Salaam! Where is everyone else?"

Moubarak shrugged one shoulder. He waved a lazy hand at the darkness outside the open bay door. "Out there, lost in the woods. There are no intruders, so we came back."

Halabi smirked. "There you are wrong. Hurry and get set. The *amrikaayi* guests are coming soon. *Allahu akbar!*"

CHAPTER THIRTY-ONE

Victor squinted one eye up at the man holding the rifle to his face. *Mierda.*

Turizo stood over him in khaki pants and a black polo—a chimpanzee dressed for a day at the range. Shooting range. Victor appraised the man's eyes and saw the same thing he had seen before—an utter lack of a soul, as if God or, more likely, the devil had built this man of mud and animated it with enough juice to pretend to be alive, but not enough to have emotions, pity, or empathy.

And Victor was in no position to do anything but die. Wrapped up with Torture Boy, one ear clamped in his teeth and both hands occupied with fistfuls of his opponent's shirt, left him with not a single move to make. The pain in his injured leg came back to life and stabbed him repeatedly in the thigh. Adrenaline fired his muscles, but already, he felt it ebbing out of him like a slow tide.

"Okay," he said and released the shard of bitten ear from between his teeth. It dangled by a thread.

Torture Boy bucked and threw him off. The younger man scrabbled through slick puddles, his face ghost white and twisted in pain.

Victor rolled once and came to a stop on his back, hands spread. His head rested on cool tiles, and it felt good. "I give up. Take me to your leader." He grinned with the rank taste of blood in his mouth. "Oh, right! You don't got one!"

"Bastardo!" Turizo trained the muzzle on Victor's forehead. "I have had enough of you."

Three sharp cracks split the air.

Turizo's head flew back, gore spraying the face of the microwave oven behind him. Two other red blooms appeared, centered where his heart should be.

Victor sneered. *If the pendejo cunt had a heart.*

Abel Yeager appeared over him.

"I wish you would quit fucking around and keep up."

"Trying to make friends, jefe."

Yeager huffed a humorless laugh. "Doing well, too." He flicked a look at Torture Boy. "This the guy that burned your manly chest?"

"I'm thinking of friending him on Facebook." Victor gathered himself and began the process of sitting up. His body ached and protested even that small movement. "Except I think he's bleeding out and won't be on the internet anytime soon."

Weak pulses of blood welled out through Torture Boy's loosening hands. More blood sheeted the side of his face. He watched Victor without saying anything, his expression one of profound terror.

A moment later, he gurgled and slumped. Staring at nothing and everything.

"Sad," Yeager said.

Victor cut him a sharp look. "Say the fuck what?"

"Guy knew how to use a soldering iron. Might have made a good electrician."

S*urreal.*

Blanca crept along a wide, bright air-conditioned hall. Following like baby ducks behind her came Modena and Bustamante. *The freaking President-elect of Guatemala. Nobody is ever going to believe this. Not in a million years...*

Modena's eyes were shiny, and his complexion had turned to parchment, overlaid by a sheen of sweat. Blanca could smell the panic trying to break out of his skin. He had not said two words since the kitchen.

Equally silent, Bustamante shuffled along like a man walking to the electric chair. Dull. Defeated. Infinitely sad.

I guess I'd be sad, too, if my best friend had thrown me under the uptown bus.

Bedrooms that lately housed terrorists lined both sides of the corridor ahead. Any or all rooms might contain a jack-in-the box shooter, ready to pounce out and kill her dead, like some kind of shoot house for training rookie cops. Shoot-or-don't-shoot scenarios, where a target popped up and you had to make a split-second decision to fire or not. Frowny face if you hit a civilian.

Well, fuck that.

Here there were no civilians. Everybody in this zip code wanted to either rape her or kill her. Maybe in that order. So screw it. Fire first, pray for forgiveness afterward.

She kicked open the first door then swung in, gun first. Empty.

Blanca exhaled long and hard, mopping her forehead with a sleeve.

Great. One room down. Only eleven more to go.

B lanca cleared six rooms by the expedient method of slamming the door open and jumping inside, acting like a TV hero, both bulletproof and brave. She felt wired tighter than an electric motor. She checked all the adrenaline-boosted boxes—heart hammering, palms sweaty, short of breath... and a tight sphincter.

Her gut unknotted a bit when she saw Yeager and Ruiz. The sight was almost comical, with Ruiz hopping along on one leg, his arm awkwardly thrown over the taller man's shoulder. Yeager had to bend halfway over to help his friend move along.

"You should just carry him," Blanca said.

"I tried," Yeager said. "But then he started nuzzling my neck."

"*Mi cariño,*" Ruiz crooned.

A giggle born of fear and overexcitement threatened to bubble free. Blanca caught it at the last moment and drew on a straight face. If they could play it cool, so could she.

"I'm clearing these rooms as I go," she reported. "Don't want to leave any surprises behind us."

"Good." Yeager allowed his friend to sag free and slump against the wall. "Por Que. Six."

"On it."

Yeager glanced at Modena and Bustamante, both of whom were doing their best to be unobtrusive.

At least, up until that moment.

"Please, señor." Modena reached out and seized Yeager's arm as he moved past. "Please. Help us to get out of here."

Yeager looked at the hand on his arm until Modena released him. He studied the new president for a long moment before replying, wearing an expression Blanca could not interpret.

"We need him," Blanca said.

Yeager turned his brooding eyes on her. She held his look, steeling herself to not flinch. His presence filled the hall, and his warrior soul radiated deadly intent. It required all her nerve to not back down from the silent challenge.

An eon later, his eyelids flickered with agreement.

"All right," he said.

Blanca nodded once. "All right."

To Modena, Yeager added, "Do what you're told."

"Of course," Modena said, sinking back from that stare. "Of course. Gracias. Thank you."

Yeager brushed past Blanca, so close that she felt the strength of him all the way down to her toes. His salty tang smelled of sweat, blood, and something feral she couldn't name. A tremble vibrated below her belt.

Jesus, Mary, and Joseph, Blanca, get a hold of yourself.

Overexcitement, that's all it was. Keyed up on adrenaline. Life-or-death situation. All of it was making her crazy.

"C'mon, Trevejo," Yeager barked. He stood in front of the next door, rifle raised. "Less gawking, more action."

She twitched, and her paralysis broke.

"Aye, aye, Sergeant."

Bustamante sagged against the wall and waited as the man called Yeager and the woman cleared the remaining rooms. Ruiz sat on the floor across from him, injured leg stretched straight out, the other gathered cocked up to provide a rest for the rifle he carried. He guarded the direction from which they'd come. Bustamante was relieved his focus was elsewhere.

That way, he did not have to make eye contact.

How fast things had gone to hell. This evening, he and Modena had been atop the world. They'd come to make a deal with the devil, of course, but a deal they could enter on equal terms. Instead, Gustaffson had turned the tables on them.

Well, now Gustaffson was dead. And Guillermo...

Bustamante wagged his head, infinite sadness making it feel as heavy as a block of cement. And a block of cement, it should be.

How did I not see this side of him? All fiery speeches, but no courage when the time for courage mattered most.

Bustamante touched his coat pocket. He had secretly retrieved Little Maria. The small pistol seemed to weigh more now, as if it had grown larger in the last few minutes.

But who should I use it on now? Guillermo, the traitor? Or me?

Was there even a difference?

Yeager gathered everyone in the vestibule atop the staircase. A ten-by-eight-foot rectangular room, the vestibule left plenty of room to stand without crowding, though Victor preferred to sit on the top step with his leg straight and his rifle trained back the way they'd come. A door in the corner of the long side led to the garage. It hung slightly ajar.

An open invitation to come get shot.

"They'll be waiting," Trevejo said, as if reading his thoughts.

"Everybody get back down the stairs. Take cover."

"Why?"

"Ricochets are not your friend. Bullets come flying into this concrete coffin, and we could be cut up into confetti."

Yeager waited until Modena, Bustamante, and Trevejo had vacated the landing and Por Que had scooted on his butt down the stairs. Yeager poked his rifle barrel into the gap and eased the door farther open, half-expecting a blast of hot copper-jacketed bullets to rip through the open space.

Nothing.

Yeager let out a breath. "Okay then..."

He slid up next to the open doorway and began "cutting the pie"—edging one step at a time in a semi-circle, aiming down his sights as more and more of the garage came into view.

Side wall. Sports car. Left side of open bay door. More bay door. Night sky beyond. Clear floor, polished as bright as kitchen tile. White ceiling with bright overhead lighting. Front bumper of black Mercedes...

A swarthy man with a black beard crouched behind the right front wheel of the sedan. He and Yeager saw each other in the same instant. Yeager snapped off a single round and ducked back.

Then the hail of gunfire came pouring in. Rounds sparked off the concrete walls and howled like scalded cats inside the enclosed space. The shooter tore off at least half a magazine before subsiding.

Over the ringing in his ears, a furious voice in a foreign language echoed from the garage. To Yeager, it sounded like scolding from an authority figure.

Yeager knew the sound of a pissed-off combat leader. By tone alone, he translated the ass-ripping to "You spoiled the ambush, dumbass."

"You okay up there?" Por Que called.

"Just fucking peachy. Get up here. We have a problem."

When the group had regathered, Yeager laid out the situation. "We go through that door, we get cut to pieces. Two guys, maybe more, armed with automatic weapons. They have cover, we don't."

"So what?" Trevejo demanded. "We sit and wait? Phone a friend? What?"

"None of the above." Yeager fixed her with a grim expression. "What I have in mind depends on you. You game?"

The fierce little Latina curled her lips in a wicked grin. "Lay it on me, big man."

"**M**oubarak!" Halabi snapped. "You have the brains of an ad- dled sheep! Are you an idiot? Have you never laid a trap?"

Moubarak, a young Arab with a birthmark the size of a grape on his cheek, sputtered in outrage. "He-he shot at me! See?"

"Idiot! Duck next time."

Halabi crouched by the trunk of the black car, gun braced and aimed across the driver's-side rear quarter panel. Moubarak had the right-front quarter panel, by the wheel well. Hamad had taken a position behind a red tool chest against the wall to Halabi's left. With the car parked at a slight angle, both Moubarak and Halabi had a good view of the door to the basement. Hamad had a good position, as well, though his cover lacked the bulk of the big sedan.

The Westerners were trapped. Playing cat and mouse with a superior force was not a game they could win. Carrying the burden of a useless woman and two politicians, the Mexican and the American needed to acquire transportation to break out of the box they were in. And Halabi controlled the access to the only transportation available.

Wait. That was all he had to do—wait, and they would come to him.

CHAPTER THIRTY-TWO

Blanca Trevejo retraced their route through the basement at a jog. Her captors had taken her wristwatch early on, so she counted Mississippis in her head. She had to be in position by three hundred Mississippis or risk blowing the kickoff, and she really, really did not want to see the result of that, thank you very much.

Her thoughts raced ahead of her. What if they pulled Modena's chestnuts out of the fire? What kind of gratitude might the next president of Guatemala feel if the CIA saved him from death by terrorist? Could she turn him into an asset? *Hey, Modena, guess what? Not only did we save your ass, we have all this incriminating evidence of you consorting with terrorists and criminal oligarchs.* Yeah. She could totally see it.

But that was not what drove her to run recklessly through the basement and up the stairs through the kitchen. She barely paused at the gore and cooling bodies of Turizo and Dominic Martinez.

Disappointing Yeager. That was the catalyst that sent her sprinting through the dining room and into the front living area. Damn, those sad brown eyes. And bristly jaw. And bulging he-man biceps.

Shit. What if he's married? That... would be unhappy-making in the extreme. *Fuck it. Problem for the future. If I have one.*

Blanca reached the front door and bolted outside, heedless of anyone who might be on the other side. Anyone getting in her way would get swatted aside like Reza.

She had a mission. Yeager was depending on her.

You better not be married. I have plans for you.

"**P**or Que," Yeager said. "Watch the door in case they get tired of waiting for us." He looked first to Modena then Bustamante. "You two. Here's the deal: when the balloon goes up, I'm going out that door. Now, hopefully, Trevejo has done her job and eliminated or distracted the blocking force, but there's a chance I might take a round. If I go down, your job is to get everyone into the car and get us out of here."

They huddled near the top of the stairs, the door eight feet away. Yeager eyed it, not thrilled with the idea of charging through it. But he didn't see any other way.

Bustamante raised his head. "What happens at the gate? It is closed, yes? A guard force is always there."

"That's a problem for ten minutes later," Yeager said.

"They should let us out," Modena said, half hopefully. "If you and the others hide, maybe in the trunk, the guards have no reason to hold us." Faint derision tinged his words. "We are guests, after all. Correct?"

Yeager thought about it. His head swam with fatigue. He had burned through so much adrenaline, he felt as hungover as the time he came back to Panzer Kaserne Marine Base after three days in Munich during Oktoberfest. Sweat and grime soured his skin, and his legs protested every time he shifted position.

He frowned. "Maybe. I'm not excited about being stuffed in a trunk, waiting on the good intentions of a bunch of agitated security goons."

Yeager glanced at his watch. "One minute. Por Que, watch the rear until I'm out the door, then come running—hopping—out behind me."

"Call me Bugs Bunny."

Yeager extended a hand and helped Victor stand. His buddy leaned against the wall, still favoring his leg. Victor was hurt and no doubt slowed by his injury, but Yeager knew Por Que would be on his ass from the jump.

"You two. Modena. Bustamante. Get back, into the corner."

Modena obeyed at once, though Bustamante lingered. He moved to stand in front of Yeager. "Señor, however this turns out, I am very sorry to have involved you. It has been... not my best moment."

Without warning or telegraphing his move, Bustamante shoved Yeager back. Off balance and unprepared, Yeager stumbled and would have fallen had not Victor grabbed him around the upper body. His friend grunted in pain and staggered, further tangling Yeager as they fought to stay upright.

Bustamante's hand dipped into his coat and came out with his tiny revolver. Moving faster than Yeager would have expected from a man so large, Bustamante strode for the door. And through it. Then gunfire kicked off in a burst of thunder.

Blanca slowed her rush as the garage appeared. Light spilled out onto the parking apron from the open bay door, so she had no problem navigating the landscaped grounds. Flowering bushes flanked the parking apron on the side closest to the mansion. She was able to catfoot into the brush without making a sound.

Two hundred and ninety Mississippi. Two hundred and—

Rifles cracked, as did the popping of a smaller weapon.

Fuck. I miscounted somehow.

Blanca crashed through the low brush. The thick foliage snagged her flapping blouse, which she had never had time to properly button. A hank of it tore loose with a long ripping sound, and she was through.

Bright overhead lights bathed the garage in white. She could not have asked for a better target range. To her left, a jihadi crouched by a toolbox. In the center, the very special prick Halabi knelt behind the Mercedes' trunk. Farther right, another terrorist. All were firing at—

Bustamante! What the actual fuck!

The big man paced forward, as deliberately as a man in a funeral procession. In his fist, a tiny popgun spat. Bullets sparked off the ground near his feet and peppered the walls behind him. At first, Blanca thought he was somehow miraculously walking through the barrage unscathed. Then he staggered. Blood spots bloomed on his shirt front. A grim look of determination remained fixed on his face. He kept coming forward, even after the little gun in his hand clicked empty.

Get in the fight, stupid, she cursed herself.

She wanted Halabi, but the closest shot was the guy by the toolbox. Her rifle rose, and the sights leveled.

Center mass. Squeeze. Done.

The jihadi crumpled to a puddle.

She shifted aim, but Halabi had moved. He was running around the side of the car to the right. Bustamante had fallen to his knees, pistol stuck out in front of him, clicking away. Blood soaked his shirt.

How is he even still alive?

As soon as the question crossed her mind, he toppled forward onto his face. The pistol stopped clicking.

Halabi remained crouched by the front fender, working on a magazine change. His pal was down.

Yeager sprinted from the basement door, going right to get an angle on Halabi.

Too late, Mr. Hunk. This one's mine.

Blanca sighted on Halabi's spine. "Hey, *kooni!*" she shouted.

Halabi froze, and his head spun around. His mouth opened in a comical look of surprise.

Breathe out...

Squeeeezzzze...

Done.

Yeager approached the downed terrorists with caution. One down by the toolbox. One next to the car, dead for sure. Birthmark on his cheek, tiny bullet hole by his left eye, right at the tear duct. Pressure had bloated the eye, and it bulged out like a sticky golf ball. Halabi lay on his back, legs twisted under him. He stared at the ceiling, his mouth working as he labored to breathe.

Trevejo approached in good tactical form, ready to engage the threat if needed.

Yeager hitched his chin in a silent nod of approval. Trevejo's hyper grin lit her face.

"What was that you called him?" he asked.

"*Kooni.* Butthole person."

"It got his attention."

Victor had hobbled out of the vestibule. "Hey, Yeager. You need to see this."

Yeager circled to the driver's side of the Mercedes. The left front tire sat flat on its rim. Another hole had been punched through the grill, and green radiator fluid bled out onto the floor in a spreading puddle.

"Okay," Victor asked the room at large. "Who shot the getaway car?"

Everyone looked at Bustamante's lifeless body.

Yeager shook his head. "For a guy with a little gun, you sure did a lot of damage. Gustaffson, a terrorist, and a Mercedes."

"Alfonso!" Modena rushed to the side of his fallen friend. "What have you done?"

Yeager's skin itched with danger warnings. "We need to get out of this garage. Gunfire will draw them in like magnets."

"How about that one?" Victor pointed to the Austin Healey.

Yeager jogged over to the vintage sportscar. It faced outward, ready to go. "The keys are in it. Victor, shotgun. Trevejo, pick up that asshole and get him in the back with you."

The CIA woman craned her neck to see inside the car. "Are you flipping kidding me? I have tampon boxes bigger than that back seat."

"You can stay here..."

"I'll make it work."

Yeager laid his weapon between the seats and helped Victor get settled. A sharp crack startled him so badly, he jerked and whacked Victor's bad leg into the door.

"Ow!"

He ignored Victor's squawk of protest.

Trevejo stood over Modena, and for an instant, Yeager thought she had shot the president-elect. Then he followed her aim and found a dead man at the garage entry. Not a security guy, but another jihadi.

She pursed her lips at him in a speculative frown. "You were right. They heard the gunfire." With that, she pulled Modena to his feet and push-dragged him toward the car.

"I will make it up to you, Alfonso," Modena swore as he stumbled away. "I swear."

Yeager finished seating a cursing and complaining Victor, then he ran for the driver's side and hopped in. He found the adjustment lever and pushed his seat back to get his knees out of his cheeks. It was a snug fit. Trevejo and Modena rocked the car as they settled in back.

"Get down, El Presidente," Trevejo ordered. "I'll sit on the back deck with my feet on the seat. You hold on to me, so I don't go flying."

"Let's see," Yeager muttered. "Keys in the ignition…"

"Car this old," Victor said, "gotta be a choke." He had his rifle held alongside the door, muzzle just over the front fender.

"What's a choke?" Trevejo asked.

Yeager growled, "I know there's a fucking choke. I have to find the fucking—Oh. There."

Yeager pulled a knob on the dash and closed the choke. He twisted the keys with a muttered prayer. "Come on, baby, start."

The Austin engine cranked to life with a throaty burble and clattered on at a rough idle. Yeager played with the choke, and the idle smoothed out. He kept the clutch down and levered the shifter into first but did not release the clutch.

"Let's go," Modena cried after a long moment.

"Need to let it warm up a sec." Yeager hunted for the headlight switch. Found it. Twin beams stabbed out.

Crack! Crack!

Two shots banged out, one from Victor and one from somewhere over his right shoulder. Another jihadi spun and toppled just inside the garage.

"As long as they keep blundering into the light," Victor said, "we can keep a-shooting them, hey? Like a bug zapper."

"What?" Yeager yelled over the deafness in his right ear. He stabbed Trevejo with a look. Her face twisted into a contrite look.

Sorry, she mouthed.

Yeager felt more than heard when the Austin's engine was ready for action. He opened the choke, slipped the clutch, and fed the gas. The roadster shot off the mark with a squall of tires. Yeager spun the wheel at the first curve and found the steering tighter than expected. Trevejo spewed frantic curses as she was whipsawed back and forth.

Yeager almost smiled. *Serves you right for blowing out my eardrum.*

A weapon clattered off from somewhere behind them. If any of the rounds came close, Yeager did not clock them.

The narrow drive twisted and turned through a dark tunnel defined by the Austin's headlights. Trevejo whooped, and Yeager glanced back to see her grinning from ear to ear, hair flying, shirttails whipping in the wind. In the rearview mirror, all he could see was the twin peaks of her white brassiere molded to her small breasts. It reminded him of Charlie.

Light brightened the trees ahead. A lot of light. Too much for one gatehouse. Yeager slowed.

"What now?" Trevejo asked.

"Let's find out." Yeager switched off the headlights and slowed the Austin to a walking pace. Victor leaned sideways and put his cheek to his rifle's stock.

Yeager killed the engine, and the car crept around the last curve before the gatehouse.

What the hell?

Two SUVs slanted in at the gate, which stood open. Headlights bathed a scene of armed men in Western wear and cowboy hats milling around a group of black-garbed security men, all of whom knelt on the ground with their hands cuffed behind their backs.

"Hey," Victor said after a full thirty seconds of astonishment. "Isn't that Cujo?"

"What? Where?" Yeager squinted and tried to process the various shapes into something that made sense. "Oh shit, it *is* Cujo."

"What's a Cujo?" Trevejo asked.

They gathered at the tailgate of one of the SUVs, where Victor was being tended by a curly-haired man with a first aid kit. The man claimed some basic field medical training, so Yeager left him to his task and spoke to Rudy Aguilar, foreman and troubleshooter for Don de la Cueva. The slim man looked as unflappable as ever, like Gary Cooper if Cooper had been dried to a husk and left in the sun too long.

Yeager said, "There are some jihadi assholes with automatic rifles running around the jungle. I don't know how many."

"Six," Trevejo interjected. "At least six."

"Six jihadi assholes," Yeager amended. "I don't think playing hide-and-seek with armed fanatics is a good idea."

Aguilar nodded.

"Leave them to my people." Modena held a cell phone to his ear. "I will have the army deal with this mess."

"We will close the gate," Aguilar promised. "And station some men here to keep them contained."

"Good." Yeager pulled Cujo by the back of the neck into a rough hug. "How the hell did you get out? And how did you find us?"

Cujo grinned through a mop of fuzzy black beard. When Blanca Trevejo had first seen him, she said, "He looks like Animal from the Muppets." Yeager could see what she meant.

"We had people all over Gustaffson's way points. His warehouses and whatnot. Trying to find you and get you to abort. The Don got me out. And we found Mendoza. Except his name isn't Mendoza, and he's the cousin of some guy down here named Bustamante." Cujo paused for breath, then continued. "So anyway, one of our guys spotted you in... Quetzel-something—"

"Quetzaltenango," Aguilar supplied.

"Yeah, there. But before he could make contact, you were off, following some buses. Except he lost you in Waywahtengo. We had a

Quick Reaction Force of de la Cueva's guys standing by, so once we got word, I flew everybody into the airport in... Waywa—"

"Huehuetenango," Aguilar interjected.

"Yeah, there. We had to make a guess that you were headed this way. We rented some cars and came on, fast as we could. We heard the shooting and knew it had to be you. And Don de la Cueva got me released, to answer your other question. I think he paid somebody off, but Rudy won't say."

The man rendering first aid stepped back and peeled off bloody gloves. He wore a happy, cheerful look as though it were a habit. "We need to get this man to a proper facility. The bleeding has stopped, but he needs fluids and proper surgery. Antibiotics."

Aguilar looked at Yeager. "You understood the Spanish?"

"Mostly. Do you have a place?"

"Yes." Rudy shrugged. "It is a long drive north."

"Then we best get started." Yeager found Blanca Trevejo watching him with an unsettling look. "What about you? Coming or staying?"

She arched an eyebrow. "What are you offering?"

"I... uh..."

Trevejo laughed. "No, I'd better stay." She shot a look at Modena, who remained glued to his phone. "I have a few things to work out with El Presidente here. Like the future shape of relations between the US and Guatemala."

"Well... Okay then."

Yeager hovered for a moment in silence before offering a tentative handshake. "Good luck, Trevejo. You're hell on wheels in a fight. You can have my back any day."

She slipped past his extended hand and wrapped him in a full-body hug. "You're not so bad yourself," she said to his chest before stepping back. "Tell me something?"

"Huh? Sure."

"Are you married?"

Yeager sighed and rubbed his forehead. "Uh... good question. I guess we'll see when I get home."

CHAPTER THIRTY-THREE

Yeager pulled his tired old Ford truck into his gravel drive an hour before dawn. The familiar sight of the two-story Victorian-style farmhouse he shared with Charlotte, David, and John Riley infused him with a love so profound, it was painful. To think he might have tossed it all away on what turned out to be a fool's errand torched his heart with dread. Charlie had been suffering from PTSD, he kept telling himself. Maybe she didn't mean what she'd said. Maybe she had reconsidered in the two weeks he had been away.

He killed the engine and listened to the quiet.

An early-rising bird twittered in the predawn cool. When the sun rose, the temps would climb into the nineties, but for now it felt quite pleasant. Wind blew through the trees and over the thick grass surrounding the house.

Needs mowing.

He wondered if the truck engine had woken Rascal, and if the fool dog was even now barking, waking the house. Yeager didn't hear anything, but that meant nothing. He was still half-deaf from having a rifle fired next to his ear.

Yeager opened the squealing door and eased out of the truck. He would say everything ached, but that disrespected the word *everything*. Luckily for him, he only had bruises, welts, bug bites, and sore muscles. It could have gone much worse.

He winced. Like when Por Que made it back to Mexico and Alexandra blew into the small clinic in Tuxtla Gutiérrez, Chiapas. That was one hurricane Yeager was extremely glad to escape. He had caught only a brush of her fury before evacuating the room in a near panic. For a small woman, she carried a temper big enough to blow down strong buildings. Yeager had traded stricken looks with Por Que before he scampered out of there like a scalded dog.

Now he had his own storm to deal with. Would it be an icy-cold blue northern that froze his heart, or a tornado that blew him all the way back to Guatemala?

Best get it over with.

Yeager mounted the porch steps and unlocked his front door. He yawned, and his eyes grated with fatigue after the long drive.

Coffee. Best get a pot started. It'll either be a long morning, or a very short one. Either way, I need coffee to get through it.

Though he tried to be quiet, Yeager's boots thumped on the hardwood floors. The familiar smells of old wood, lemon-scented polish, and lived-in house greeted him like an old friend.

Where's the dog?

Usually by the time he hit the porch, Rascal would have jumped him in a spasm of joyous greeting. But no Rascal. Had everyone left? Was he coming home to an empty house? The thought sent cold fingers of dread to clamp his heart and squeeze it.

He entered the kitchen and froze. "Who the fuck are you?"

An older man sat at the kitchen table. Dry, nondescript, hair going gray, and wearing glasses, the man could have been any-body—banker, lawyer, teacher...

Except he held a pistol trained on Yeager's belly.

"Sit down, Mr. Yeager," he said, indicating a chair pulled out from the kitchen table... the same table where they had gathered only two weeks ago with Por Que as he told his story about finding Cujo. Borges sat on the far side, with the kitchen behind him.

Rascal lay on the kitchen floor. Not moving. Yeager's chest swelled with anger.

"Don't worry about the dog," the stranger said. "A tranquilizer dart. He is merely asleep. As are your wife and children. For now. Please sit. Hands atop the table."

Yeager followed directions, seating himself across from the mild-mannered little man. The table was bare but for a medicine bottle and a glass of water. Everything else had been cleared away.

No potential weapons.

"Who are you? What do you want?"

"My name is Borges." He held the pistol steady. "I am—was—employed by Herman Gustaffson."

"Since you said 'was,' I'm assuming you know he's dead."

"Indeed. You have upset me very greatly by killing my employer."

"I didn't kill your employer."

"Please," Borges said with a withering look. "Don't insult me. I know the whole story."

"Then you know shit." Yeager checked his anger before it boiled over. Breaking things was not called for—yet... "If you wanted to kill me, you would have done it already. What's your game?"

"It is simple," Borges said. "I am offering you a choice. You have two options. You may take the honorable way and swallow the pills in this bottle. The medication acts within fifteen minutes. You will go to sleep peacefully and pass without pain."

"And the dishonorable way?"

"I shoot you dead here, then I go upstairs and kill your entire family."

"What's to say you won't do that anyway, if I take the pills?"

Borges frowned as if he'd gotten a lesson wrong. "Please, Mr. Yeager. I don't kill without cause. That would be dishonorable."

Yeager looked at the medicine bottle then looked back to Borges, appraising him. What he saw chilled his body and sent a tickle of fear up his back. No soul resided behind the bland eyes that regarded him from behind wire-frame glasses. What was the line from the movie? No pity, no remorse, and absolutely no stopping him.

The pistol was a Walther P99, he noted absently. Nine-millimeter, probably, though it also came chambered for the .40-caliber S&W cartridge. Ten rounds or more in the magazine.

Enough to do the job.

Yeager slumped a little. Besides the two options offered by Borges, he had one other, which was to attack, hard and fast. Throw the table in his face and plow forward. He might take a hit, maybe two, before he grappled with the smaller man. Physically, Borges was no match. Yeager could snap the man's neck and call it a job well done.

"I know what you're thinking," Borges said. "Maybe you can overpower me, yes? I have played this game many times, Mr. Yeager. Believe me when I say the moment your hands move anywhere except for the pill bottle, I will shoot you. My reaction time is excellent. Then I kill your family."

Yeager's thoughts collided and scattered like so many balls on a pool table—he would no sooner grasp at one than it would fall in a pocket. His brain felt dull, disengaged. Sleep beckoned. He would give anything for a shower and the cool sheets of the bed, snuggled against the warm body of his wife.

Going out without a fight was not in his nature. But what if...

If he gambled and lost, he had no doubt this man would do exactly as he promised. He remembered now where he'd heard the name Borges. This was the guy Mendoza had told them would come and murder his family if he and Victor refused the assassination of Gustaffson.

Yeager sagged. "I don't reckon..." He trailed off, sniffing the air.

"Don't reckon what, Mr. Yeager?" Borges gestured to the medicine bottle. "Please, you are wasting time. Are you an honorable man, or would you risk the life of the lovely Mrs. Yeager? And your children?"

Yeager smiled for the first time since he'd arrived home. He sat up straighter.

Apple blossoms.

"I reckon you don't know much about Texas women. For one, they rise early. And for two, they pack iron."

The clickety-click of a revolver's hammer cocking punctuated his sentence.

"That right there," Yeager said, "is a .41 Magnum revolver. My wife's daddy gave her that gun and taught her to shoot it. She has sent more than one bad man to hell with it. I suggest you set that Walther down on the table, real careful like, and scoot it over this way."

Charlie stepped out of the kitchen. She wore a sleep T-shirt, and her red hair had twisted into a serious case of bed head. To Yeager, she was the most beautiful sight he had ever seen.

"About time you got home," she said. "Who's your friend?"

Yeager dropped the tailgate of his truck and climbed in. He had parked at the lip of a rock quarry, fifteen miles from his home. Trees surrounded the dig and blocked all view from the road. A pond of green water filled the bottom of the quarry, and the tang of stale algae floated up from it.

Borges lay in the truck bed, tied with baling wire. Yeager snipped him free and hopped down, drawing the Walther P99 and holding it on the prone man.

"Sit up," he ordered.

When Borges was upright, Yeager produced the pills and a bottle of water and set it on the tailgate. Borges raised an eyebrow, and a tired smile creased his lips.

A rooster crowed, a tiny sound, far away. The sun peeked over the trees, and already the day had turned warmer and a bit muggy. Mosquitoes whined in Yeager's ear.

"You have a choice, Mr. Borges."

"Of course."

"You may take the pills. In about fifteen minutes, you will fall asleep and pass painlessly."

"And my other choice?"

"The new president of Guatemala owes me a favor. So does the CIA. I can tie your ass back up, make a call, and boom! You're off to a black hole somewhere for the rest of your miserable life. I don't even have to shoot you." He pondered a moment. "Of course, you could rush me, which means I shoot you until the mag runs dry. Your choice."

Borges lifted his face to the sun and breathed deeply with his eyes closed. Yeager let him have a count of thirty. At the end of the count, he opened his mouth to prompt Borges, but the man opened his eyes and said, "You are a man of honor, Mr. Yeager."

He reached for the pill bottle, shook the contents into his palm, and swallowed them with a big gulp of water.

"I think I would like to go for a walk in the woods now."

Yeager smiled grimly. "That's fine. I'll just mosey along behind you and make sure you don't stick a finger down your throat."

"Do as you will, Mr. Yeager, but I will honor the deal."

Borges climbed down from the truck bed with the deliberate caution of an old man. He stood upright, straightened his clothes, then pushed his glasses up. He peered around the quarry.

"Which way should I go?"

"Don't matter to me. Nowhere you can get in fifteen minutes that'll make a difference." Yeager shrugged, palms up. "Anywhere's good. Just knock yourself out."

"Is it over?" Charlie asked.

Yeager sat at the kitchen table, a cup of coffee steaming in front of him. Rascal's tail thumped on the floor, and he watched with sleepy eyes. The boys were still asleep, according to Charlie, who had checked on them before coming downstairs with her pistol to investigate the voices coming from her kitchen table.

"Yes," Yeager said. "It's over. All of it."

"Good."

He couldn't read much from her tone. Charlie had dressed in jeans and a work shirt. Her hair was brushed out and lay soft on her shoulders. Yeager's heart hammered harder than it had when he was hanging over the drop behind Gustaffson's house, trying to climb a tree.

Maybe that's the problem.

"Look, Charlie..."

"Are you home for good now?"

Yeager met her brilliant eyes, shimmering now with unshed tears.

"Do you want me to be?" His throat tightened, and it was all he could do to get air into his lungs.

Her smile trembled at the edges. "I married a warrior," she said in a husky voice. "Sometimes, I forget that. Sometimes, I want to be normal. And safe. But—no, shut up a minute." A raised finger stopped him from speaking. "But the world's not a safe place. It needs people like you. Dangerous men, and all that."

"And dangerous women," Yeager murmured.

Charlie's lips twitched. A tiny break in the clouds. "Yes, and dangerous women." She reached across the table and put her hand over his. "You're mine, Abel Yeager. And I'm yours. Don't ever forget that."

The sound of a diesel engine pulling into the drive woke Yeager from a nap. He glanced at the mantelpiece clock. Four-twenty in the afternoon.

After a shower and breakfast with the boys, he had made it as far as the sofa before sleep claimed him, and now he awoke, groggy and sore.

Charlie entered the living room, drying her hands on a dishtowel. She crossed to the window and looked out. "Who the hell is this? And what is this?"

Yeager joined her and leaned over to peer out.

A flatbed wrecker stopped behind his truck with a hiss of brakes, yellow lights along the top of the cab flashing in the afternoon sun. A tarp-covered object rested on the flatbed.

"What the hell?"

The driver hopped out, clipboard in hand. Yeager and Charlie met him on the porch. A round man, skin dark as coal, the driver wore overalls and a ballcap.

"You Abel Yeager?"

"Yup."

"Sign here." The driver extended a clipboard with a carbonless triplicate form attached.

"What am I signing for?"

"Uh... says here, a 1962 Austin Healey Sprite."

Charlie looked at Yeager with a bemused expression. "You bought a sports car?"

"No, but I think I know where it came from."

The driver went about the business of tilting the flat bed and rolling the car to the ground. Rascal barked and ran in circles while the driver and Yeager pulled off the cover, revealing the Austin Healey Yeager had last seen in the driveway of Gustaffson's hacienda.

"There's a note," Charlie said. "On the dashboard."

Yeager picked off the paper taped there.

Courtesy of a grateful Guatemala. Call me sometime.

~~Blanca

XOXO

"Hugs and kisses. From Blanca." Charlie's eyebrow climbed her forehead. "Abel Yeager, is there anything you would like to say in your defense before I find the pistol that I use to send bad men to hell?"

About the Author

Scott Bell has over 25 years of experience protecting the assets of retail companies. He holds a degree in Criminal Justice from North Texas State University.

With the kids grown and time on his hands, Scott turned back to his first love—writing. His short stories have been published in *The Western Online*, *Cast of Wonders*, and in the anthology, *Desolation*.

When he's not writing, Scott is on the eternal quest to answer the question: What would John Wayne do?

Read more at www.scottbellwriter.com.

About the Publisher

Dear Reader,

We hope you enjoyed this book. Please consider leaving a review on your favorite book site.

Visit https://RedAdeptPublishing.com to see our entire catalogue.

Check out our app for short stories, articles, and interviews. You'll also be notified of future releases and special sales.

www.ingramcontent.com/pod-product-compliance
Lightning Source LLC
Chambersburg PA
CBHW061519210726
48287CB00006B/1737